GALE HARBOUR

Revenge of the Space-Surfing Butt Monkeys

ISBN: 978-0-9947704-4-8

Published by Stories I Found in the Closet
www.cdgallantking.ca

Second Edition
Copyright © 2022, 2025 C.D. Gallant-King

Edited by Chrys Fey
http://chrysfey.com

"Stories I Found in the Closet" Logo by
Ann McDougall Design & Creative Services
www.facebook.com/AnnMcDougallDesign

For Mom and Dad.

GALE HARBOUR BOOK 2:
REVENGE OF THE SPACE-SURFING BUTT MONKEYS

C.D. Gallant-King

PROLOGUE

Cast Into the Shade
June 18, 1915
Limeville, Cape-de-Cape Peninsula,
Dominion of Newfoundland

Tommy Rickets coughed and wiped the limestone dust from his face. He doubted that the fine, white powder tasted like a lime, but he couldn't be sure because he had never actually eaten one. He wasn't sure if he had ever even seen one.

The great limestone quarry at Jack of Clubs Cove—sorry, *Limeville*—towered over him like a monstrous white wall, the cliff face sparkling in the morning sun. The quarry was located on the north side of the peninsula, on Cape-de-Cape Bay. Tommy liked to imagine it was the other side of the world from St. Stephen's Bay on the south side, even though the two bodies of water were but a few hundred yards apart at the isthmus of the peninsula near the Gravels. Sure, it was all the North Atlantic, but those two bays were the entire distance Tommy had travelled in his short life, so he had to make up adventures where he could.

Tommy kept calling the community by the old name. His mother and uncles refused to use the new one. They said it was a stupid name, and Tommy agreed. He could not imagine why the Dominion Iron and Steel Company renamed the town Limeville. They claimed they wanted the world to take their operation more seriously, but they picked *Limeville*? Who was going to take the place seriously with a name like that? Tommy always heard the adults talking about foreign places with fanciful, interesting names like Sarajevo, Vienna, and Alsace. He doubted if people in Europe would speak about Limeville the same way.

Not a chance. Not unless they had a war in Newfoundland, too.

Tommy had tried to sign up for the Royal Newfoundland Regiment last year when the call went out for volunteers. He'd been thirteen at the time, and small for his age, so the recruiter sent him home. His best friend, Edouard Bouchard, had been almost fifteen and six feet tall, so they took him. Edouard's family received a letter from England a few months later, before Edouard and the rest of the Blue Puttees shipped out for Egypt. They hadn't heard from him since.

Denied his chance to travel the world and fight the dirty Huns—he didn't know why they called Germans "Huns"—Tommy had no choice but to get a job at the lime quarry in Jack of Cl... *Limeville.* His father had died the winter before last, accidentally shot by his brother on a caribou hunt. They rushed him out of the bush and to a doctor, but he died a few days later from blood loss, leaving Tommy and his mother to take care of his seven younger brothers and sisters. The next oldest was ten, and the five youngest were still in diapers. The one in between, eight-year-old Maxim, was in charge of washing those diapers. Everyone had to do their part, and someone had to bring in money. If that meant Tommy had to leave school and crawl through cracks in limestone to plant dynamite charges, then so be it.

"Rickets!"

At the call from across the quarry, Tommy snapped out of his daydream and dropped his shovel. He ran across the worksite, nearly crashing into another worker and causing the gnarled old man to spill half the load from his wheelbarrow. Tommy apologized without even slowing. Aucoin would beat him senseless if kept waiting.

Emile Aucoin was the foreman, a burly, sweaty Frenchman with more chins than fingers. He was the largest man Tommy had ever seen, both in height and width. He was also the smelliest. Despite missing multiple fingers on each hand—supposedly the result of a fishing accident from years back—Aucoin could still swing a mean cane and used it freely against any of the workers who displeased him. Being the youngest and smallest on the worksite, Tommy felt the sting of that wooden stick across his back often. He still had a bruise on his shoulder from last Thursday, and Tommy didn't want to add another one.

"I'm here, sir!" Tommy slid to a stop in the mud in front of Aucoin, just outside of cane-swinging range. The distance was not an accident.

Aucoin looked particularly red in the face this morning. Either something was bothering him or he'd started drinking early. Tommy took another step back, just in case.

"Go grab yourself a stick o' nitro from Fitzsimmons and run a line behind da nort'side. Dere's a bloody big rock d'size of yer mudder's arse, and I wants it blasted before I goes 'ome fer supper."

Aucoin's bastard French accent caused the words to come out damn-near unintelligible. Tommy only recognized one word in four, but it was enough to get the gist. You learned to get the gist of the foreman's orders quickly at the Dominion quarry, or you went home with bruises, welts, or worse.

"Yes, sir!" Tommy was gone in a heartbeat, ducking around several other men to get far away from Aucoin as quickly as possible.

John Fitzsimmons was already waiting for Tommy at the bottom of the North Pit, with his blasting caps and wire laid out on a rough wooden table. His trembling hands fumbled with a stick of dynamite. Fitzsimmons had the shakiest hands of anyone Tommy knew. How in God's name had the man not blown himself up yet?

Fitzsimmons held out a familiar, paper-wrapped tube with quivering fingers. He held it carelessly, as one might pass a butter knife at the dinner table. Tommy took the tube quickly but carefully, preferring to take on the responsibility of it himself rather than leave his life in the hands of Flipper-Fingers Fitzsimmons.

"You knows that big boulder they've been digging around the last week?" Fitzsimmons gestured vaguely at the limestone wall above them, but Tommy did indeed know what he was talking about. "They found a deep crack what looks it goes right up behind it. You get a charge in there, I'll feed you the wire, and we'll blow the rotted thing wide open."

Simple enough. That was Tommy's primary job on the worksite, after all; getting dynamite charges into small places a full-grown man could not. He didn't mind it so much. He had been terrified the first couple of times, but he hadn't blown himself up yet. If Flipper-Fingers could do this for years and still be in one piece, surely it couldn't be *that* dangerous. Of course, he tried not to think about Albert LeBlanc, the boy who did this job before him. Tommy had never met him, but he occasionally passed the dark stain on the bottom of the South Pit.

The crack was a tight fit. Usually, a crevice this small was not deep. He'd reach in as far as he could and shove the dynamite stick in whatever gap he could. Hopefully there'd be enough light to attach the wire properly on the first try. Then he'd climb out of the hole and duck for cover with the men, praying that everything worked like it was supposed to while Fitzsimmons giggled like a monkey.

But there was something different about this crack. Tommy wiggled his way into the space, holding the dynamite carefully in front of him so as to not scrape it against the rocks or jostle it too hard. He crawled deeper and deeper, at least ten feet into the side of the cliff face, and then the crevice widened into a large, open area.

It was a cave, but Tommy couldn't tell how big it was. He braced his feet on the uneven ground and stood, with plenty of room to spare above his head. A thin strip of light came from outside, not enough for him to make out any features of the cavern, or judge its true size, but it was definitely larger than anything he'd been in before.

"How's she gettin' on, boy?" Fitzsimmons called from outside, his voice muffled by the thick granite and limestone between them.

"I'm in some kinda cave! Can you pass me a light so I can get a look?"

"Like hell. You got a stick of nitro in your hand. I knows you're not stunned!"

Fair enough. Lighting a match wouldn't be the best idea under the circumstances.

"Just plant the charge and get your arse out here. I ain't waiting 'round all day."

Tommy sighed. If there was something interesting in the cave, there wouldn't be anything left of it after Fitzsimmons blew the dynamite.

He ran his fingers across rocks, looking for a place to wedge the stick. What if there was old pirate treasure, or dinosaur bones, or...

Tommy's fingers stopped. The rock felt warm. He had never felt warm rocks in one of these crevices before. They were always cold, from never having seen the sun since God created Adam.

It moved.

Tommy screamed and fell. He dropped the dynamite. The rock was moving!

Fitzsimmons was calling to him, but Tommy couldn't form words. He couldn't get his mouth to describe the strange and terrifying things he was seeing in the hole. Something glowed like the burning halo of a torch. It grew brighter, and the rocks continued to shift and move like a man standing up, but it was too big to be a man.

Tommy screamed again. He wanted to run, but his legs wouldn't respond. He wanted his mother. If he died, he would never see her again. He hoped he would see his father, but he was afraid the devil, the thing in the cave with him, might drag him down to Hell for disturbing his sleep.

The lights grew brighter and expanded until Tommy could see the thing clearly by the glow of its fiery wings. The wings grew larger and larger until the tongues of flame touched the ground, right where Tommy's stick of dynamite lay at his feet.

And then the whole mountainside came down upon his head, and Tommy saw and heard no more.

CHAPTER ONE

Lovers in a Dangerous Time
Saturday, May 29, 1993, 7:29 pm
Gale Harbour, Province of Newfoundland

Niall O'Neil stood at the door, contemplating his destiny.

The night sky above him was clear and full of stars. Despite the chill in the evening air, sweat rolled down the back of his neck inside the collar of the black dress shirt his mom had bought for him at Woolco. They were on sale, two for fifteen dollars. The other shirt was orange; he was never going to wear it.

Another bead of perspiration rolled down his forehead, over the tip of his nose. Fingers trembling, he reached for the doorbell. He couldn't get his hand to do what his brain wanted. Maybe he had played too much *StarFox* on his Super Nintendo and had developed Carpal Tunnel Syndrome? His brother Nelson claimed he'd gotten Carpal Tunnel from playing *Excitebike* back in the day, but Niall was pretty sure he'd picked it up from... other activities.

Niall tried his other hand. Nope, that one didn't work, either.

What was wrong with him? He had fought a Psycho Hose Beast from beyond time and space. He had not only survived but also defeated it and banished it to the outer regions of God-only-knows-where. Maybe Madagascar. Or Labrador. So why was he so terrified? Was some unseen force manipulating his will?

If anyone asked, he would say it was a seventh-level *confusion* spell clouding his mind.

Summoning every drop of his courage and screwing up all his willpower, Niall thrust his hand forward and tried to mash the glowing doorbell. He missed it the first time and scraped his fingernail on the door frame. He tried again, and a familiar, electronic *ding-dong* trilled through the night. He didn't remember ever ringing this bell before; it sounded familiar because half the houses in Gale Harbour had the same doorbell chime. When most of the houses in town were built in the early eighties, it had been the only one available at White's Hardware store.

No turning back now. He supposed he could run away, but he would look like quite the jackass.

A moment later, the door opened, and there stood Samantha Jeddore. She was a vision in her pink nurse's scrubs and her hair in a tight bun. Niall had had a crush on his best friend's mom for years, but lately some of the glow had worn off because of who was living in her house now.

"Niall?" she asked, puzzled. "Why did you ring the bell? You know you can come in—"

"Is Harper home, Mrs. Jeddore?"

Understanding dawned on Samantha's face like a blossoming flower. She smiled, which brought a small piece of comfort to Niall's racing heart. "Oh, the two of you are going out tonight, is that it? On a date? How sweet."

She turned back into the house and called, "Harper, your date is here!"

Niall's cheeks burned. Why did she have to make this even more awkward?

In the porch behind Samantha, the small, bespectacled head of Niall's best friend, Pius, appeared from behind a corner. The long, black rat tail dangling down the back of his neck looked particularly whimsical today because of a new hair elastic with brightly-coloured baubles at the end. "Niall? You're going out with Harper?"

Niall groaned. He had hoped to keep this low-key. Why was everyone making a big deal about this? "We're just going to The Hangar for some milkshakes and fries."

Pius' eyes grew wide, and then he adjusted his glasses. "The Hangar? Niall, are you trying to get your ass kicked?"

Niall rolled his eyes. "Pius..."

Samantha's face took on a look of motherly concern. "What? What are you talking about?"

"Guys like us don't go to The Hangar," Pius explained. "Guys like us get beat up at The Hangar."

Niall resented being lumped into the same category as his diminutive, glasses-wearing, mathlete best friend. Niall had a date for crying out loud! Not to say Pius was wrong, though...

"It's the underage dance tonight," said Niall. "It's fine. We're going to play some arcade games and eat French fries."

"You know who else goes to the underage dances?" Pius counted them off on his fingers. "Bernie Budgell, Chris Tobin, Steve Cutler, and Keith Doucette. They all go to look for fights and for nerds to pick on!"

"Well, I'm not looking for a fight," said Niall. "And Keith is our buddy now."

"He would still kick your ass to look cool in front of his friends."

"Pius, stop saying 'ass'!" Samantha scolded.

"What are you all blabbering about?" Harper asked, materializing in the porch like an angel descending from Heaven.

Niall's breath caught. She had put her onyx-black hair back in a braid, and he detected a hint of make-up around her big, brown eyes. She wore her favourite green army surplus jacket, the one with the Sarah McLachlan and Suzanne Vega patches. She had even polished her Doc Martens. Harper Jeddore was a bit rough around the edges, but that didn't stop Niall from crushing on her, like how Pius obsessed over Power Girl. The awkward grittiness made Niall like her more. And at least Harper was real.

Harper scowled so hard that Pius took two steps backward. Even Samantha looked off-balance. Harper had the harshest glare of any thirteen-year-old girl Niall knew. "First of all," she said, "Pius, you're a fart-knocker, and it's none of your business where I go."

Pius waved his hands. "I'm not worried about you, Harper. I'm worried about Niall."

Realization crept onto Harper's face, softening her scowl. "Oh, right. Well, that's fair."

Samantha bobbed her head in agreement. "We're all worried about Niall."

Niall scoffed. "What? What are you talking about?"

"No offence, Niall, but you're a bit of a wuss," said Harper.

Pius and Samantha nodded.

Niall's heart sank. After everything they had been through, she was calling him a wuss? After he had given her months of space and she had turned him down several times, Harper was the one who had finally asked Niall out. So, why was she insulting him?

Niall's hands shook, and he wasn't sure if he was about to explode in anger or run away in tears. Before he could decide, Harper's scowl shifted to a mischievous smile, and she winked at him. "It's a good thing you're cute, Dork-pie."

Niall relaxed. From Harper, "Dork-pie" was a term of endearment. She was just messing with him.

"Seriously, though, Aunt Samantha," Harper continued, "we will be fine. I promise we'll stay away from bad guys, and if any trouble does come up, I'll watch out for Niall, okay?"

Samantha folded her arms. "Fine. You two, be careful, okay? You're right; we wouldn't want anything to happen to Niall's cute little face. Now, would we?" She pinched Niall's cheeks, immediately negating any warm, tingly feelings he might have developed from her comment about him being "cute."

Niall and Harper walked to The Hangar. Despite being cool out, it was a beautiful evening. Even with the notoriously fickle Newfoundland weather, Niall was warm enough in his dress shirt and an acid-wash jean jacket. It wasn't a long walk. Their route took them down the Jeddores' street and West Street to the club. They didn't talk much on the way. Despite everything they had been through together, Niall still had trouble finding things to say. He had looked forward to this night for weeks—it was their first official "date," after all—but all the topics of conversation he had dreamt up in his head vanished. It was usually Harper who started the conversation, but tonight she didn't seem to want to open up, and Niall didn't have a friggin' clue what to do.

Finally, when they were a few hundred metres from the club and could hear the music blasting in the distance, Niall got up the nerve to ask, "You seem distracted tonight. Everything okay?"

"It's all these stupid June bugs," she complained, gesturing to the cloud of large bugs buzzing around the nearest street lamp. "They gross me out."

Harper was afraid of June bugs? But Harper wasn't scared of anything. "We've passed millions of them on our way here," said Niall.

"And it has taken all my self-control not to turn around and run back home screaming."

Harper glanced at him and smirked, and for a moment, Niall didn't care about the awkwardness or if the night ended right there. A smile from Harper was worth John Merrick's remains and all the Kraft Dinner you could eat. "Sorry," she said. "I guess I have a lot on my mind. My mom called earlier today."

"Your mom?" Niall asked before he could stop himself. He hoped his face didn't look as shocked as he felt. Like almost everyone in Harper's grade, Niall had assumed for years that Harper's mom was dead. He recently learned that was not the case. Pius had known, of course, since Harper's mom was his aunt, but it was such a taboo topic, even among their own family, that he never mentioned it.

"She called to wish me a happy birthday."

"But your birthday was weeks ago," said Niall.

"Yeah, I know that, but *she* didn't." Harper wouldn't look at him, but Niall was pretty sure a glimmer of tears reflected in her eyes. "My mother doesn't remember my birthday."

"Was that..." Niall almost stopped himself but pressed on. It was so rare to get Harper to open up; he had to do it while he had the chance. "Was that the first time you spoke to her since your dad—"

"Yep," she said, mercifully cutting him off so Niall didn't have to finish the sentence with "was brutally torn apart by a Psycho Hose Beast from outer space."

Harper continued, "She said 'sorry about your dad,' and that was it."

"That's it? I was kinda worried she would ask you to come live with her."

Harper laughed bitterly. "Are you kidding? She didn't want me when I was born, so she sure doesn't want me now. She didn't even ask me how I was doing."

She froze at the edge of the parking lot. A dozen paces away, a group of teens were gathered outside the club smoking cigarettes. Under the streetlight's glow, they passed the time between drags by swatting June bugs that flew too close. Behind the smokers, a green neon sign spelled out "The Hangar" in letters so garishly bright they'd hurt your eyes if you stared too long. At the other end of the parking lot, the enticing smell of fried chicken wafted from KFC, the third-best fried chicken shop in a town that was way too small to have three fried chicken shops.

"Harper," said Niall, fumbling for words. "Your mom is—"

"A bitch? Yeah, I know. I don't need her, and I don't want her. I'd rather stay here with Uncle Ray, Aunt Samantha, and my friends."

Harper couldn't hate her mom completely, could she?

"But she called. The fact that she called at all is why you're upset?"

Harper nodded. The tears were flowing now. "Why would she do that? She didn't even ask how I was doing. If she didn't even remember my birthday, why would she call just to upset me and disturb my life? It's easier if I forget she exists. It would be easier if she were dead."

They were now moving deep into territory that Niall did not know how to deal with, certainly not on a first date. True, he and Harper had lots of history together, but he figured a first date would include getting to know each other's favourite bands and childhood pets's names and what their families did on summer vacation. Heck, Niall didn't even know

Harper's middle name, so he was not prepared to deal with her messed-up relationship with her estranged, drug-addicted mother.

Yet, at the same time, they had nearly died together. Niall was there when Harper's father was killed. They had destroyed the Psycho Hose Beast together. Their bond went way beyond awkward teenage dating, and Niall had been foolish to assume they would have anything even remotely resembling a normal relationship. If he wanted to date someone, he could have asked out any number of girls at St. Paul's High School. They would have said no, but that was beside the point. He wanted Harper and already had a relationship with her that he hoped to build into something more.

Throwing caution to the wind, Niall put his arms around Harper and hugged her. When she didn't punch him, he relaxed and leaned into it, and she hugged him back tighter than he'd ever been hugged before.

"We don't have to go out tonight," said Niall. "I can take you back home."

"No, it's okay," she replied, pulling away slightly and wiping her tears with the sleeve of her jacket. "I want to go out. I need to have fun and forget about things."

"That's cool, that's great," said Niall, revelling that his body was pressed against Harper, that she was actually in his arms, and she was not running away. He literally had fantasies that kept him awake at night that were less steamy than this.

"Besides," she added, "I really want to beat the crap out of someone."

Niall froze, and Harper slipped out of his arms and stomped toward the club, her Doc Martens pounding on the asphalt.

Pius was waiting for his dad when he came out of the bathroom. He had a dozen books on the table, several fresh notebooks and pencils, and a cup of coffee just as his dad liked it—three sugars and a splash of Carnation canned evaporated milk. Pius knew it would take some convincing to get his dad to go along with his plan, so he had also contemplated getting chocolate or candy to make the situation more palatable, but Pius honestly didn't know what kind of sweets his dad liked. In fact, despite the amount of sugar he put in his coffee, Pius wasn't sure if his dad even liked candy. Perhaps he simply didn't like coffee.

Raymond Jeddore came out of the bathroom, a Newfoundland Herald magazine tucked under his arm and headed for the living room. He gave Pius a nod, not acknowledging the avalanche of books on the kitchen table. Pius was always studying up on something, so his dad obviously didn't think much of it.

"Dad?" Pius asked. "Do you have a minute?"

Raymond stopped, clearly shocked because Pius rarely said a word to him when he had his nose stuck in a book. "Is everything okay?"

"Yeah, it's fine. Since Mom's working and Harper is out, I wondered if we could hang out a bit?"

Ray, still confused, sat next to him at the table. "Uh, sure. As long as we're not playing one of those weird dungeon games with the dice and stuff."

"I don't play those games anymore," Pius lied.

"Son, I know that's what you tell your mother, and I don't care, but I found your books under the couch in the basement. I would rather if they had been Playboys or something, but it's fine. We all hide stuff from our parents."

Pius felt his cheeks start to burn. His dad was trying to be nice, but it still put Pius in a difficult position to negotiate. Ray Jeddore looked almost exactly like his brother, Harper's father—big brown eyes, broad nose, easy smile—with a few more wrinkles and gray hairs. Ray was also blunt and brutally honest like his brother, which was tricky to navigate for a kid who was afraid of his own shadow. "Dad, *Dungeons & Dragons* isn't satanic..."

Ray put up his hand. "I told you, kid, I don't care, and I don't want to know about it. Just like I told your mom, I don't go to her church and pray to a man who turns wine into blood in my mouth. I don't give a crap if you draw pentagrams and chant the names of demons or whatever. Just don't sacrifice any cats in my house."

"Dad, seriously, *D&D* isn't like that." Pius did not, however, go into detail about how he had lived through events that *were* very much like that. He hadn't told his parents about everything that happened with the Psycho Hose Beast monster last year. As far as he knew, neither had Niall or any of the other kids involved. With how religious his mom was, Pius was pretty sure it would not go over well if he told them. "And besides, that's not what I wanted to talk to you about."

Raymond finally looked closely at the books laid out in front of them. His dark brow furrowed. "*Introduction to Electrical Theory? Study Guide for Apprenticeship Exam?* Pius, you're a little young to be thinking about a trade, aren't you?"

Pius took a deep breath. This was the moment. He had been planning this since last year when he discovered that his dad, the man he looked up to and was supposed to be his shining role model, didn't have a university degree. He hadn't even gone to community college.

"The books are for you, Dad."

"Me? Why do I need to go back to school? I have a job."

"Yeah, but you could have a better job. And are you even qualified for the job you have now?"

Raymond made a face Pius couldn't quite place. Was it... hurt? "Pius, I'm good at what I do."

"I'm sure you are, Dad, but I looked at the requirements for Light & Power. When you started working there fifteen years ago, a college diploma wasn't necessary. It is now. In fact, most people have a university degree. But you've been grandfathered in, so you don't have to pass the education requirements."

"Pius, that's a good thing! That means I didn't have to waste years sitting in a classroom!"

"Waste? Dad, you've always told me going to school and studying hard was the most important thing in the world."

Raymond sighed. "I did. I'm sorry. It is important, and I want you to have all the opportunities and options I didn't have. I got a decent job, but I got lucky. Like you said, it doesn't work that way anymore. You have to have a degree."

"Don't you feel guilty? That you didn't do the work that other people have to do?"

"You want me to feel guilty?"

"That lady you work with... Jenny. She went to school for four years and finished top of her class. She makes half of what you do, and you guys seem to give her a hard time because she has a degree."

Raymond sputtered. "I don't... we don't... we just rib her a bit because she's new..."

"I want to be proud of you, Dad, but if you had a better education, you could move up and get a better job! You could be a supervisor, or a trainer, or..."

"What's wrong with being a line repairman?"

"Nothing. Except that you could fall off a crane truck and die."

Pius was vibrating with anger. The fear lurking beneath his career counselling came out in a torrent.

"Pius..."

He couldn't hold it back now. "You know I don't like you working up there on those wires, ten metres above the ground with thousands of volts of electricity flowing past your head. What if something happened to you?"

Raymond put a hand on his shoulder. He had such big hands. It made Pius feel tiny, but he shook him off. "Pius, you have nothing to worry about."

"I bet Uncle Dick told Harper the same thing."

The room fell deathly quiet. It had been bothering Pius ever since last year. Of course, the death of Harper's father made Pius worry about his own father's mortality. It didn't help that he looked so much like Uncle Dick, either.

Pius, afraid of the silence even more than he was of the words, cleared his throat. "I know it's not the same thing. I know what happened to Uncle Dick isn't going to happen to you, but you do work in a dangerous job. What happens if you get hurt or worse? What would happen to me and mom? To Harper? If you could get a job in the office, you wouldn't need to be up on those wires all the time."

Raymond sighed, releasing the breath he'd been holding. He stared at Pius a moment, and Pius' heart felt like it was going to pound out of his chest cavity, spraying their study material with gore. Mrs. Aucoin, the librarian, would be very upset if he returned these books covered in blood.

Finally, Raymond said: "This is really important to you." It wasn't a question.

His father's concession released some of the tension that clutched Pius' chest. His terror and rage faded but were quickly replaced with excitement. "I can help you study. I find all this stuff interesting. Did you know that they have two-hundred-and-twenty-volt outlets in Europe?"

"Pius, for you, I will do this. I'll try. I don't know if I'm up to going back to school at this age, but because it means so much to you, I will at least give it a shot. It would be pretty nice to be the boss and give the other guys a hard time. Oh, and I love you, but there is no way in hell I'm going to have my thirteen-year-old kid teach me how to do my job."

Pius leapt up and threw his arms around his father. "Okay, we can figure something out. Thanks, Dad. I want to be proud of you. And I want you to be safe."

They embraced, but before Raymond could respond to Pius' comment, they were interrupted by a knock at the door. Raymond glanced at the clock on the microwave and grumbled under his breath about people showing up at this hour. He got up and crossed the kitchen to open the door.

Two men with buzz cuts and dressed in black suits stood outside. One of them flashed an ID card that Pius couldn't see. "Mr. Jeddore? Raymond Jeddore?" He had what sounded like an exaggerated American accent. "We would like to talk to you about your son."

CHAPTER THREE

All That She Wants
May 29, 8:10pm

The Hangar was part of a small strip mall on the west side of town, near the bridge into Keeping and next door to a furniture store. Over the years, it had been many things before it became a teen club—most recently, an adult bar and club. Before that, it had been a paint and decor store.

The current owners realized that Gale Harbour had more than enough bars for adults, a dozen more than was necessary for a town of ten thousand people, but kids needed something to keep them off the streets, too. They opened The Hangar to cater to the younger crowd and give them entertainment options besides vandalizing park benches and drag racing on the old airstrip. They didn't serve alcohol most nights, played music that anyone over the age of nineteen hated, like Nirvana and Cypress Hill, and had a small collection of pinball machines and arcade games in a dimly lit corner. Niall and Pius would have spent more time at The Hangar for the video games, except half of them were out of order, and there was always the looming threat of getting the snot beat out of you by the older teens.

Niall and Harper walked through the choking cloud of cigarette smoke at the front door and into the club. "Two Princes" by the Spin Doctors blared over the PA speakers while crowds of teens in plaid, overpriced sneakers and too much denim danced awkwardly. The lingering, acrid smell from the fog machine hung in the air. Harper grabbed Niall by the hand and dragged him straight to the middle of the dance floor. Niall was so shocked by the physical contact that he momentarily forgot the terrifying look that Harper had on her face a moment ago. He did not, however, forget that he did not know how to dance.

Niall had to yell over the music. "You promised we wouldn't dance."

Harper settled on a spot dead centre in the middle of the floor, surrounded by other teens in baggy sweatshirts and jeans. "I changed my mind." She wasn't even looking at him but scanning the room and searching for someone or something else.

Niall felt incredibly self-conscious. He had the rhythm of a thirteen-year-old boy; that is to say, he had sweet-frig-all in terms of dance moves. Every movement felt weird to him. His body wasn't built to shake and jive. The most moving he ever did was with his fingers on a Super Nintendo controller. Dancing was not a skill he had ever needed to practice.

Fortunately, no one paid him much attention. In the flashing, coloured lights of the parquet dance floor, all the teenage boys looked uncoordinated, ready to take out someone's eye or trip their date at any moment. Everyone except for Steve Goosney. That scrawny little twig could dance circles around anyone in town and could probably be a backup dancer in a Michael Jackson video. A pale, pimply-faced backup dancer missing three teeth from a hockey fight last winter. The dude was tearing up the floor like Jim Carrey on crack with a bumblebee in his pants. The Spin Doctors song ended, and "Whoot, There It Is!" started, which further powered Steve's spastic ecstasy.

Once Niall was confident that no one was watching him, he stared at Harper. He couldn't believe he was here, dancing with her. She was so pretty, funny, smart, and interesting. In short, she was way too good for him. Sure, he pretended to be well-read and interesting himself, but he had read way more *X-Men* than Lord Byron. While he legitimately liked Depeche Mode and The Cure, his claim of enjoying Tori Amos was somewhat exaggerated for Harper's benefit.

Of course, Harper's good qualities were overshadowed the moment she hauled off and slapped another girl across the face.

"You bitch, what was that for?" The girl holding her cheek was Sally Alexander, a mean brunette from Niall's grade with a withering, poison-laced tongue. She wore high-waisted jeans and a matching denim vest over a white blouse. Niall had asked her out once, and her response had left him crying for a week and made him consider becoming a priest.

"You hit me first, butthole!" Harper barked back.

The girls were already drawing an audience.

Sally did not back down. She was up in Harper's face immediately. "If I did, it was an accident, you stupid skank. What the hell do you think you're doing?"

Harper had faced down an unkillable monster from another world. There was no way under creation she would back down from Sally Alexander. She stepped back up to Sally despite the other girl being half a head taller. "Wasting my time with a trash-smelling skeeze."

For a second, Niall thought Harper was talking to him, but the way she was up in Sally's face left little doubt about the target of her insult. What was Harper doing? Niall had never seen her act like this before. She was purposefully antagonizing this girl, and Sally Alexander was not someone you wanted to piss off. She loved to fight and was like a female version of Chris Tobin or Keith Doucette. A weekend didn't go by that she didn't end up with a black eye or send another girl home or to the hospital with worse.

Which was precisely why Harper was picking a fight with her.

Niall's guts turned to water. Holy crap, Harper had been serious when she said she was looking for a fight.

"Oh, you wanna go?" Sally hissed.

"You wanna take this outside?"

"Nope." Sally smiled and sucker-punched Harper square in the face.

A dozen kids around them moaned or gasped as Harper went down to one knee.

The music still didn't stop.

Niall didn't even have time to react before Harper came back up and grabbed Sally. Her fingers caught in the taller girl's sweater so she couldn't get her in position for a solid punch, but she was too close for Sally to swing back, too. They pulled and shoved for a moment, and the crowd around them started to chant, "FIGHT! FIGHT!" Harper smashed Sally in the nose with a vicious headbutt that staggered her backward.

Finally, the music stopped.

"Hey," someone shouted from off the dancefloor, probably the DJ or club manager. "Break it up!"

Niall, seeing an opening, moved to yank Harper away. Scrawny Steve Goosney, of all people, tried to grab Sally Alexander, but she flung him away, like how Pius threw his controller whenever Niall beat him at *Street Fighter II*.

The back of Steve's head hit the parquet floor with an audible crack.

Niall got his arms around Harper and pulled her back several steps, but it was like wrestling a rabid weasel. She struggled and kicked and nearly yanked Niall off his feet. Blood covered the bottom half of her face from Sally's punch to her nose. She looked like a crazed vampire going back for another meal. There was no way he could hold her for long.

The room quieted as most of the gazes turned toward the still form of Steve Goosney on the floor. All except Harper and Sally, of course. Sally rushed at Harper again, and Niall knew he would be caught between them, so he lifted one arm up to hold Harper back and reached out with his other hand toward Sally. "No!" He braced for the impact of being crushed between two teenage girls, which would not be as much fun as he had always fantasized.

The impact never came. Instead, Niall's vision started to swim, and the world swayed around him. Everything slowed. His throat and sinuses burned from the fog machine smoke. Blood rushed in his ears. He felt Harper's heartbeat through her jacket and shirt. A sudden tingling took over his body like an electric shock, and an instant later, he felt tired, so incredibly tired. His limbs turned into stupid, heavy dumbbells. Like the ones his brother Nelson claimed to work out with but really were gathering dust in the corner of the basement.

A scream snapped Niall back to reality. What just happened? He was on his hands and knees, but he didn't remember falling. The crowded dance floor had parted, and five metres away, Sally Alexander lay crumpled against the wall; the drywall above her was cracked and splintered as if struck by a great force.

Harper pulled on his arm. "We have to go." Her anger and pain from earlier had completely washed away. Her voice was tense, her eyes darted around the room nervously.

Niall didn't argue or fight. He let Harper help him to his feet and lead him toward the exit. His legs were as stiff and heavy as anchors.

Several people eyed him as they hurried out, but he didn't know why. Was it because Harper's face was bloody? Was it because Sally may have killed Steve Goosney or because she had fallen and nearly killed herself? What the hell was going on?

Niall noticed two older teens staring at him intently as they passed through the door. He didn't recognize them. They were nineteen or twenty and dressed in weird clothes you never saw people around town wear. The girl had on a tight black corset that pushed her full cleavage up to her chin. The guy wore a long black coat and a matching top hat. Both were pale as sheets and wearing black lipstick.

Despite their crazy outfits, the weirdest thing about them was that they were the only people looking at him and *smiling*.

When the cool night air and cigarette smoke hit Niall in the face, he came to his senses and realized Harper was staring at him. She looked more worried than he had ever seen her.

"What?" His voice sounded weak to his own ears. "What's wrong? Are you okay?"

In the streetlight of the parking lot across from KFC, Harper raised his hand in front of his own face so he could see it. It was covered with blood. Was he hurt? Besides feeling dizzy for a moment, he didn't remember getting injured.

Niall looked at Harper, with blood on her nose, lips and chin, and then it hit him. It wasn't *his* blood on his hand. It was Harper's.

"What is this about?" asked Raymond Jeddore as he sat across from the two men in black suits at the kitchen table. "And who are you again?"

Pius hung up the phone and watched from the kitchen. The two men were emotionless, like Arnold Schwarzenegger from *The Terminator* movies. Honestly, with everything they had been through last year, murder cyborgs from the future were not out of the realm of possibility.

"We are part of a government service that tracks potentially dangerous threats to national security." The man speaking had slightly darker hair but otherwise looked nearly identical to the other one, who hadn't said a word yet. "We would like to talk about what happened to your son when he disappeared last year."

Raymond looked concerned momentarily, but then it dropped, and his face returned to a state of caution and distrust. "When my son got lost in the woods and was kidnapped by a crazy old woman? We know all about that."

The two men turned and looked directly at Pius. He jumped and let out a small, embarrassing sound like the noise his hamster made when he stepped on it and killed it by accident. Pius hadn't realized the men knew he was watching. He wondered if they really were machines with enhanced omnidirectional sensors. Still, he refused to run. He had faced worse.

"That's not exactly what happened, is it, Pius?" asked the speaking robot.

"Pius, what is he talking about?" asked his dad, the concern returning.

Pius shook his head. "Mrs. Kane held us in a bunker and tried to kill us." He reiterated the story he and his friends had been retelling for months. Technically, she had not tried to kill them directly, more like she had tried to *get* them killed, but it was close enough that he didn't feel bad lying about it.

"What did you find in the tunnels, Pius?" asked the Talking Robot.

Was he talking about the monster? Did they know about the Psycho Hose Beast?

Pius felt like he was being torn apart. Part of him wanted to run to his room and hide, and another part wanted to come out with everything and get it off his chest. But Sergeant Tanguay and the RCMP had been so insistent that they not reveal the truth. They said terrible things would happen to them, their families, and the town if word got out about what happened last summer.

Wait. If the RCMP wanted to keep it a secret, then who were these guys?

"Pius?" his dad asked. "Is there something you want to tell me?"

"You said you work for the government," said Pius, his voice trembling. He was not used to talking back to authority figures. Niall, and especially Harper, were much better at this sort of thing. "Which department, exactly?"

The men said nothing.

Raymond looked confused. Why hadn't he thought to ask?

"Which nation is it you're trying to protect?" Pius asked.

The men stared at him with icy, inhuman gazes. And Pius knew because he had actually faced down an inhuman gaze before. His stomach churned, and he wanted to run away again. What was he thinking? He was afraid of his teacher whenever she spoke firmly to him if he didn't raise his hand in class. Now he was talking back to these giant, emotionless androids in black business suits?

Fortunately, he didn't find out if they planned to kill him or merely torture him because a moment later, a fierce pounding sounded on the door.

"Who is that?" demanded the Talking Robot, as if Pius' dad had magical door-reading abilities.

His dad sighed as he stood from the table. "I don't know. We seem to be popular tonight."

For a moment, it looked like the cyborgs might make a move to stop him. They glanced at each other and half-stood before changing their minds and sitting back down. It was as if they had silently decided that whoever was at the door couldn't possibly be a concern or threat.

They were wrong.

Royal Canadian Mounted Police Sergeant Marie-Ann Tanguay burst into the kitchen, dressed in her black and tan patrol uniform and a bulletproof vest. She was not a tall woman but made up for any height deficiencies with enough brazenness and force of will to increase her size tenfold. She was like a female Wolverine with a sharp jawline and a ponytail. Being on the small side himself, Pius looked up to Sergeant Tanguay, both literally and figuratively.

She strode straight to the table without hesitation. "So, who the hell are you boys?" she demanded in her strong, French Quebecois accent.

"Excuse me?" The Talking Robot asked. Still seated at the table, he had to look up at the RCMP officer, putting him slightly off balance.

"Who are you to barge into the home of private citizens in the middle of the night and interrogate them?" She held out her hand. "Identification, please."

Instinctively, the Talking Robot reached into his suit pocket and withdrew a plastic ID card. He hesitated at the last second, but the sergeant snatched the card anyway.

"Robert Stone? Central Intelligence Agency? Elevator Inspection Division?"

Pius squirmed. The CIA? What the heck were the American Secret Service doing here?

Sergeant Tanguay was not impressed. "Is this a joke?"

Finally, the cyborgs found their courage and stood. The Talking Robot adjusted his narrow black tie. "I assure you, Sergeant, we are official agents of the United States government."

"Well, last time I checked, Newfoundland wasn't part of the United States. You have no jurisdiction here, and if you don't get your arses out the door this instant, I'm going to haul you in for forced entry and malicious threats of bodily harm."

The Talking Robot smiled. It was a reasonable facsimile of human emotion, but even Pius could tell it was fake. "We were just asking the Jeddores a few questions."

Tanguay scoffed. "If you want to ask private Canadian citizens questions, you can have your boss ask the State Department to contact the American Embassy in Ottawa. They'll call the RCMP, and my boss will ask me to arrange something for you."

"That's not how we do things, Sergeant Tanguay."

"That's how you do things in my town and my goddamn country. Now, if you would be so kind as to vacate the premises, I would hate to have an international incident on our hands."

"Yes," said the Talking Robot, giving another fake smile. "We wouldn't want that. Pleasure meeting you, Mr. Jeddore, Pius. Sergeant, we will meet again."

"*Je m'en sacre*, I hope not," Tanguay grumbled.

They turned to leave, and on their way out the door, the one who had never spoken muttered something to the other, though Pius didn't quite catch what he said. The door banged closed, and their car drove away a moment later.

"Sergeant Tanguay, thank you... I think," said Pius' dad.

"You shouldn't talk to those men. Not without a lawyer and a government representative with you. They have no right to barge in here asking you questions."

"They were asking about Pius' time with Ms. Kane last year when the kids were lost in the tunnels." Raymond looked at Pius. "Pius, was there something else that happened that you didn't tell us about?"

Pius glanced at Sergeant Tanguay, who did not react at all. She had been there and knew everything, but her poker face was perfect. "No, Dad, I have no idea why they wanted to talk to me."

Technically, that was not a direct answer to his question, but fortunately, Pius's dad was so rattled that he did not follow up.

"They may have been looking into Ms. Kane," said Tanguay. "She was missing for a long time, and we suspect she might have been in the States. It's possible she was wanted for crimes there as well."

All of that was a lie, too, but it sounded plausible.

Pius' dad nodded. "Shouldn't they be asking you about that? Not us?"

"Yes, they should, but you know how Americans are. They're full of themselves and think they can march anywhere in the world and act like they run the place. I'll make a few calls and find out what they're doing here. If they come back, don't let them in. Call the detachment and tell them to page me right away."

Raymond had a puzzled look on his face. "How is it that you happened to show up tonight?"

Tanguay smiled. Pius loved it when she smiled. She was usually so harsh that the contrast was stunning. She looked so warm, like a mom. Not Pius' mom, though, but definitely someone's mom. "Pius called me. Fortunately, I was close by."

Raymond looked at Pius, surprised.

"That's a good kid you have there, Raymond. Smart and quick thinking. He's going to do well someday."

"He's already doing pretty well. I think he talked me into going back to school earlier tonight."

"Good for you. Education is important. Right, Pius?"

"The most important," Pius agreed, glad that Tanguay had steered them away from the topic of last year and the tunnels. She was pretty smart, too.

After the sergeant left and Pius excused himself to go to his room, something still bothered him. It wasn't that there would be further questions from his parents tomorrow. It wasn't that he would have to find a tutor for his dad to get him to study for his electrician exam. No, his mind kept returning to the two men and what Sergeant Tanguay had read on the ID badge.

"*Elevator Inspection Division*?" Why would the CIA even have an Elevator Inspection Division? And what the heck would Elevator Inspectors want with him?

A realization struck Pius. The muttering he heard on the way out the door—it wasn't English. He couldn't be sure, but he thought it sounded... Russian?

<u>CHAPTER FIVE</u>

Black No. 1
May 29, 9:05 pm

"What the hell do we do?" Niall asked for the fiftieth time. "I just killed Sally Alexander."

He was hiding by the dumpster behind KFC with Harper. It reeked of grease and rotting coleslaw, but Niall barely smelled it. Okay, he *could* smell it, but it was the least of his concerns, considering he had just committed eldritch manslaughter.

"*We* killed Sally," Harper reminded him, pointing at her bloody nose. "I mean, maybe. But we did it together."

That was true. The magic, however it worked, only functioned when he touched Harper's blood. He had done it once before when he banished the Psycho Hose Beast last year. And since then, he hadn't had anyone to ask about it. The one person who could explain magic, Theolina Kane, died in the tunnels beneath the town. His Nana Josephine, who had been possessed by the spirit of Theolina's dead sister Ethelinda, had completely forgotten everything she knew about magic after the dead woman's soul was put to rest. So, here he was, walking around with a potential bomb in his fingers, and he had no idea how to turn it on or off. Well, besides punching Harper in the nose.

"Yeah, we did, but no one will know that. They saw *me* shove her." Niall got up and paced through the greasy discarded boxes and half-chewed bones.

"No one who knows you will think you could throw Sally Alexander across the room. I mean, no offence, but you're not exactly that tough, you know?"

"Thanks? I guess?"

Harper grabbed Niall and held him still. She looked into his eyes. "Seriously, Niall, stop pacing. You're freaking me out."

Niall froze, and his gaze locked with Harper's. This was supposed to be one of the best nights of his life. He was out with the girl of his dreams, dancing close to her, chatting and laughing. At least she was touching and looking at him now, even if there was blood on her face and a dead girl in the building next door.

He took a deep breath. "You're freaking out? I'm the one who killed her!"

"*Maybe* killed her. Honestly, I'm jealous," admitted Harper. "I wish I had slapped the taste out of Sally Alexander's mouth myself."

"That's something else," said Niall, remembering what had gotten them into this mess in the first place. "Why the hell did you go in there looking for a fight?"

Harper let him go and averted her gaze. Immediately, he regretted speaking harshly but wanted to know what was happening.

"I was angry," she said. "Angry at my mom. God, I'm angry all the time these days, but that phone call from her... it set me off. I couldn't punch her, so I wanted to punch somebody."

That should have frightened him, but instead, it bewildered him. Harper had so many unresolved feelings bottled up, not only about her mom but about her dad's death, too. He didn't have the slightest clue how to talk to her about any of it. Would it be inappropriate to get her the business card for a therapist or psychiatrist or something?

"Please, talk to me the next time you feel that way. Or hit me if it helps."

Harper chuckled. "Oh, please. If I had hit you, you would have ended up worse than Sally."

"Sally, crap." Caught up in his concern for Harper, he had forgotten. "I killed Sally Alexander." He started to pace again.

"Maybe," Harper reminded him. "*Maybe.*"

A moment later, they were blinded by a car's headlights.

"It's the cops!" Niall hissed and started to run, but Harper caught him by the hand.

"Where the hell are you going to go?" she whispered. "Who do you think you're going to outrun? Pius is faster than you."

This was true. His best friend had been working out, hoping to be ready the next time an otherworldly monster chased him. He wasn't going to make the cross-country team or anything, but he could outrun Niall in a foot race. And everyone knew it wasn't about outrunning the monster—all that mattered was that you outran the other guy.

Two car doors opened, and a figure emerged from each side of the car. With the headlights in their eyes, Niall couldn't make out who they were, but he imagined burly RCMP constables with their guns drawn.

"Hey, are you Niall O'Neil and Harper Jeddore?" one of the figures asked. It was a deep voice.

"Maybe?" Niall replied. He tried to sound cool, but his voice picked that exact moment to change and crack.

"I'm Bart Simpson, who the hell are you?" Harper demanded.

"Oh, sorry, the lights," the figure said, reaching inside the car to turn off the ignition.

When the spots cleared from his vision, Niall made out that it was not a couple of police officers standing beside the ugly, rusted green Chevy station wagon but the weird Goths they had passed on their way out of the club.

"I'm Anna," said the busty girl, who was nearly spilling out of her low-cut, lace-and-leather top. Under different circumstances, she would have been a focus of fervent fascination from Niall. She gestured to the guy in the top hat on the car's driver's side. "That's my boyfriend, Keenan. You should come with us if you want to live."

The girl was pale as a ghost and had an intense look in her grey eyes, like Pius when he got excited talking about the *Batman* cartoon series. She would be downright terrifying if it weren't for her weird Townie accent. She must have been from St. John's on the East Coast.

Niall and Harper glanced at each other.

"What the frig are you talking about?" Harper snapped.

Anna's gaze darted back and forth as if reconsidering what she'd said. Then she smirked. "Sorry, not really. I just always wanted to say that. Although, I mean, your life might be in danger. Kinda? Sorry, this all sounded way cooler in my head."

"We are not getting in that car with you," said Niall. He held Harper's hand and felt strangely comforted by it. It wasn't even the one with blood on it, which he could have used to blast these two weirdos into smithereens.

"Look, we know you knew Theolina Kane," said Keenan.

Niall didn't think he'd ever met a man, grown or otherwise, who wore lipstick when it wasn't Halloween. Not that there was anything wrong with that, and in fact, he found it pretty cool, but he was painfully aware of how odd it seemed at the moment.

"You probably also know her real name was Theolina Benoit. We want to ask you a few questions about her. And we might be able to answer some of yours."

This was freakishly coincidental and unnervingly convenient. On the same night, in the exact spot where Niall accidentally wasted a girl with magic, a couple of weirdo goths show up, claiming to know about the one other person who knew how to do magic?

After a moment, when they didn't answer, Anna shrugged and added, "Or you guys can wait here and explain it to the cops. No skin off our asses."

"Fine," said Harper, pulling Niall forward.

"You sure this is a good idea?" he whispered.

"You wanted to know what's going on, didn't you?" she whispered. "These two yahoos seem the type to know about witches and black magic, right?"

Niall wanted to remind Harper that they knew plenty about witches and black magic. They had read David Eddings and RA Salvatore and played *Dungeons & Dragons*. He couldn't imagine that Anna and Keenan knew much more than what TSR, the publisher of *D&D*, had taught them. Except they claimed to know something about Theolina, which was not something you could look up in the *Player's Handbook*.

A moment later, they were in the backseat of a decidedly un-goth-like station wagon. The plaid polyester seats were worn and patched with duct tape, and the floor was littered with McDonald's wrappers and empty drink cups. Niall had to shove a pile of The Cure and Siouxsie and the Banshees cassette tapes aside to sit down.

"Sorry about the mess," said Anna. "We've been on the road awhile." She reached into the back seat and grabbed a large, black studded purse from the floor by Harper's feet, spilling half its contents in the process. She rummaged through the bag and held out tissues.

"How did you know our names?" Harper took the tissues and wiped at the blood around her nose.

"Saw them on the news a few months ago. You were the kids that Theolina kidnapped, right?"

Keenan backed the car up and turned around in the parking lot. They were pulling out right as a police cruiser rolled up in front of The Hangar. Niall unconsciously slid down in his seat, away from the car's window. Harper grabbed his jacket and pulled him back up. "Stop looking so guilty. Yeah, that was us, so what?"

"We've been studying Theolina Benoit for a while," said Keenan as he drove down West Street toward "downtown" Gale Harbour. "We know she was a witch, and we know she was trying to keep a monster from coming into our world."

"That's crazy," said Niall at the exact moment that Harper said, "How do you know?"

Niall sighed.

Harper was never big on following the official story that they were supposed to tell people.

"Go ahead, show them," said Keenan.

Anna returned to her bag and pulled out a small, old leather-bound book. Her painted lips spread in an expectant smile, and she reverently passed it to Niall. He took it and opened it carefully.

Harper leaned in to get a closer look.

The pages inside were yellow with age and filled with neatly penned writing he didn't understand. Was it Middle Eastern? There were also diagrams and a few sketches of horrific-looking monsters that wouldn't be out of place in the Monster Manual.

"Most of it is Arabic, mixed with some Greek and Latin," explained Anna. "We're still working on translating it, but we know it belonged to Theolina. And we know it's full of spells."

"Spells?" Niall asked, trying to keep his face neutral, but he probably looked terrified.

"What kind of spells?" asked Harper.

"Mostly stuff for summoning, binding, and banishing demons," Anna explained. "Plus, there's at least one love spell in there and one that appears to be for making a dog's tail grow longer. Some of them are even weirder than that. I've tried but can't get any of them to work. Keenan won't let me use blood sacrifices anymore."

Keenan glared at her. He pulled off Main Street into the Tim Hortons drive-through. "And yet, you cast a spell in that club tonight without much trouble."

Niall didn't know what to say. These two, whoever they were, knew about Theolina and magic, but he couldn't admit to them that he had done it himself, could he? He had denied it for nearly a year, but a part of him needed to talk about it.

"Welcome to Tim Horton's. Can I take your order?" asked the distorted voice from the speaker beside Keenan's open window. It struck Niall as incredibly odd to be ordering coffee at a time like this, and the goths must've sensed his unease.

"I told you, we've been driving for days, and Keenan hasn't slept for like twenty-four hours," said Anna.

"Gimme two large double-doubles." Keenan turned to the backseat. "What do you kids want? Do you drink coffee?"

"Sure," said Harper.

Niall felt weird asking for chocolate milk when everyone else ordered coffee, so he nodded.

"Make that four large double-doubles," he corrected. "And a box of twenty Timbits."

Keenan paid and received his order, and Anna passed two steaming paper cups to the backseat. Niall took one and held it in his hands, feeling the warmth seep into his fingers. His mind spun.

Harper sipped her cup. She was the only thirteen-year-old Niall knew who drank coffee. "Awfully convenient that you guys showed up here tonight at The Hangar the same time we did."

Keenan drove the car around and parked in the Tim Hortons parking lot.

"That was luck," replied Anna. "We thought you guys might've been the last people who saw Theolina alive, so we wanted to know what she might have said to you. We didn't know where any of you lived, so when we got to town, we went by the youth club to ask around to see if anyone knew you. It was a fluke that you guys showed up at the same time."

"And used magic," added Keenan, turning back to look at them. "Which was super cool, by the way."

"I'm so jealous," Anna agreed. "Do you have to sacrifice animals to do the magic? How much blood do you need? Can you use your own blood?"

Niall was uncomfortable, and not because Anna looked at him like he was an ice cream sundae she was about to devour. No, he was uneasy because two different people had said they were jealous of him brutally murdering an innocent girl.

"So, who are you, Niall O'Neil?" asked Keenan. "And where the hell did you learn to do that? Did Theolina teach you?"

"I just... I don't..." Niall was having trouble forming words. Something didn't feel right. A part of him wanted to talk about this, but another part of him...

"Don't mind him. He's usually way more eloquent," said Harper. "You can't get him to shut up most of the time. I think he's still worried he killed Sally Alexander."

"The girl on the dance floor?" asked Anna. "Don't worry. She's alive. We heard her talking after you guys took off."

Sally Alexander was alive? He hadn't killed her after all. A huge weight lifted off his chest, and he took the first deep breath he'd managed in over an hour. The overwhelming relief was so draining that he had no energy to find any words.

Harper found some for him. "Why now, though? Theolina died last summer. Why did you wait until now to look us up?"

Anna blushed with embarrassment. "Well, we weren't sure how to approach you. We weren't sure if a couple of random strangers showing up to talk to some kids might freak somebody out."

"Fair," replied Harper. "And judging by Niall's reaction, you did just that."

Anna grimaced. "We're sorry. Look, we came now because... well, this is going to sound crazy."

"Try us," said Niall softly. "You'd be surprised how familiar we are with crazy."

Anna sighed as if to say, "Well, you asked for it." Then she said, "Next Friday is a total lunar eclipse. It's also the peak of the Arietid meteor storm."

"I know you are, but what am I?" asked Harper.

"No, I've heard of this." Niall sat forward. "Pius and Skidmark were getting all excited about it last week. It's a meteor shower that happens every year around this time, right? And sometimes you can even see the falling stars during the daytime?"

"Correct!" Anna clapped her hands and tittered. "The last time there was a total lunar eclipse during the Arietid meteor storm was June 25, 1964, the same day that Theolina escaped from the Waterford Mental Hospital. We think she knew something was happening that night. We don't know exactly what. Her journal stops short the day before, but she wrote a lot in the weeks leading up to it about an important celestial phenomenon about to happen and how she had to be free to either deal with or witness it."

Keenan sipped his coffee. There was a growing stain of black lipstick around the rim of his cup. "We've been studying her notes, and some of the things she observed back in 1964 have started again. Something happened back then, something so important dont that Theolina had to break out of The Mental to deal with it, and then had to go into hiding for the rest of her life. And it looks like it might happen again next week."

Harper scrunched up her face in consternation, the look that, under normal circumstances, Niall found irresistibly cute. "So, what you're saying is that you are using the journal of a mental case, words that she wrote while locked up in an asylum, to predict... what, exactly? Is the sun going to blow up? Zombies climb up from their graves? Are monkeys going to fly out of my butt?"

"Theolina wasn't mental." Anna looked insulted. Judging by her blood obsession, she was probably a bit unhinged herself. "We think there's going to be an alien invasion."

Niall expected something preposterous, but hearing it out loud still sounded unbelievable. "And what if you're right? If she was right? What do you want us to do?"

"We told you, we hoped she had told you something before she died. A warning about what was to come. Maybe a hint or clue for how to deal with it."

"She was preoccupied at the time," said Harper.

"She didn't tell us anything," said Niall, mostly the truth. There were bits and pieces about her background, Nana Josephine, and a little about the Psycho Hose Beast. But nothing about meteor showers, lunar eclipses, or *alien invasions*.

"There must be something?" Anna asked, hopefully.

"Nothing," Niall insisted.

"But she taught you how to use magic."

"No, she didn't." That was also mostly true. The stuff that Theolina had told him didn't work. What he had done to the monster, what he had done tonight to Sally Alexander, he had done instinctively, without understanding or controlling it. He was afraid of it, and despite what he had believed a few hours ago, he was not ready to talk about it. Certainly not with these strangers who were little more than Theolina superfans. "I'm sorry you wasted your time. We can't help you. Come on, Harper."

Niall was afraid for a moment that Harper might disagree and want to stay. She was far more fearless than him and may want to go with these two to see what kind of adventure it might bring. Hell, she might end up leading their coven, for all he knew. After Harper went picking fights tonight, he didn't know what to expect from her anymore.

She shrugged, said, "Smell ya later," and followed Niall out of the car.

Keenan leaned out the driver's side window. "Look, we'll be here all week if you change your mind or if you think of anything she might have said that could be important. We don't have a number or an address in town or anything, but we'll come back here every night around this time. If you want to talk to us, come look for us here, okay?"

Harper held up her paper cup. "Hey, if you're buying, I might come by every night."

Niall didn't say anything. He turned and walked away.

Harper fell in step next to him. "That was weird," she said.

"I hope I'm doing the right thing."

"Of course you are." Harper grinned. "Those guys are total buttheads. They'll probably do messed-up things to you and then dress your body like a clown and bury you under a gas station."

Niall recoiled and gaped at her.

"What? I saw it on *Unsolved Mysteries.*"

June the fourth. Less than a week from tonight. What the hell could be happening next Friday? It couldn't be aliens. Those guys were off their rockers.

Of course, last August, he had fought a millennia-old, other-dimensional being possessing the water-logged corpse of a witch who'd been lying on the floor of the Atlantic for sixty years. But that was a once-in-a-lifetime sort of thing, right? Freaky stuff like that didn't happen regularly in a boring town like Gale Harbour.

Without thinking, Niall put his Tim Horton's cup to his lips and took his first sip. It tasted like drinking hot, milky water from the bottom of an ashtray. He gagged and spat it out.

"This is disgusting." He turned to Harper, who was looking down at her coffee-splattered jeans, too stunned to form words. "Oh my god, Harper, I'm so sorry!"

"Oh, Niall." She sighed. "You Dork-pie. That was a terrible end to an awful first date."

<u>CHAPTER SIX</u>

Fields of Gold
Saturday, May 31, 9:50 pm

Greg Blanchard sat beside his small fire, warming his hands. The burly man was dressed in a light coat, and it would get cold tonight.

Dark trees loomed over his head, their skeletal branches lit only by the small, flickering tongues of flame. He could hear the croak of toads and the buzz of crickets in the brush, a calming, welcome sound. He hated the modern world's noise, the radios, phones, and cars. Blanchard was happy out in the middle of nowhere, thank you very much, and hid out here at every opportunity.

No wife to annoy him, no bratty kids to piss him off, just his quad ATV, his trusty 12-gauge, and a bottle of Crown Royal in the bottom of his packsack.

His hunting buddy, John Lyver, used to tell him a 12-gauge shotgun was excessive for grouse and a poor shot would leave you with little but a mess of feathers. A 20-gauge was better, John said. Blanchard told him to learn to shoot straighter and never asked John to come hunting with him again. John talked too much for Blanchard's taste anyway. He came out here for peace and quiet.

The shotgun was resting on the log to his left. The Crown Royal was in his right hand, and the butt of a cigarette hung from his dry, chapped lips. Every few minutes, he would take the cigarette with his left hand and pull a swig of whiskey. In between, he was perfectly still and silent, listening to the night.

Across the fire sat his Yamaha four-wheeler, two large coolers strapped down to the back. The coolers, which were even older and more reliable than the ATV, were stuffed with grouse carcasses. He never intended to shoot anymore and could have gone home today, but why bother? So the wife could bitch at him for leaving dirty boots on the clean floor? Or telling him he had to bring his idiot kid to soccer practice? Not bloody likely. Blanchard preferred the cold and the quiet of the woods to that nonsense any day.

He was taking a risk, staying out. More chances for Fisheries and Wildlife to catch him. It was not, strictly speaking, grouse season, so all of his catch was very much illegal. It didn't worry Blanchard much. He was way out in the back of Area 8, probably even in Area 11. The warden didn't come out here much, not since Dick Jeddore, anyway. Jeddore had caught Blanchard a couple of times, and Blanchard had paid his fines without complaint. He figured if Dick could catch him, he'd earned his punishment. It was almost like a game between him and Dick, even if the warden didn't realize it. Dick was a good man. Too bad what happened to him. To be murdered by a crazy old woman right in front of his daughter, no one should go out like that. Blanchard shook his head and took a drink for old Dick Jeddore.

Something rustled in the underbrush to the right of the quad. It was probably a toad, a rabbit, maybe even a chipmunk up past its bedtime, but it didn't sound right. Blanchard knew the sound of every animal that walked in these woods at night, and that didn't sound like any of them. A snake? There weren't supposed to be snakes in Newfoundland, but stranger things had happened. Maybe some idiot brought it over from the mainland.

Blanchard crushed out his cigarette on a rock and quietly lifted his shotgun. He was as silent as the wind as he turned the weapon around and placed the butt against his shoulder. The critter in the brush was quiet for a moment, then rustled again a meter away. *What the hell are you?*

The hunter rose with quiet, practiced stealth. His footfalls barely made a crunch against the dry roots and grass. He took two steps toward the rustling, and the sound stopped. Blanchard paused and held his breath. He counted to thirty, sixty, and then the rustling came again, another meter farther away. Blanchard took a breath and took another couple of steps closer.

He didn't want to shoot whatever it was. At least not without knowing what it was first. Maybe it was someone's cat, though that seemed unlikely so far away from any community. The more he followed this train of thought, the more he realized he didn't really care what it was—cat, snake or garden gnome.

Slowly, carefully, Blanchard started to squeeze the trigger. Something flew out of the darkness at his face.

The gun went off, shooting uselessly into the darkness. Blanchard screamed and swatted at whatever was digging into its neck. He couldn't see it but felt flapping wings. It must have been some kind of bird. But what kind of bird latched onto someone's neck like that?

The pain was incredible. He grabbed at the creature with both hands but couldn't get a grip on it. He felt something sharp pierce his flesh and felt the hot spray of blood on his hands and chest. It must have hit an artery, and it was still digging toward his throat.

Blanchard screamed and flailed, all logical and rational thought leaving his body along with his blood, which was spraying across his ATV and his gun, lying useless on the ground. He had to get away, had to get the creature off of him. He stumbled and fell into the quad, knocking over the fuel can he had used to refill the vehicle when he parked a few hours ago. Blanchard was always prepared. He always kept the tank filled in case he had to make a quick retreat. But nothing could have prepared him for this.

He smelled the gas, but it was a far-away sensation. His vision was going dark, and his grasp on the thing on his neck grew weaker. He knew he was going to die. Greg Blanchard always swore he wanted to die in the woods, but now that it was happening, he was afraid. He wanted to hear his wife one last time. She would definitely bitch about the blood on his coat.

He stumbled and fell beside the fire. He felt an intense heat as the gas splattered on his pants legs ignited. Then the creature bit through his spinal cord, and he couldn't feel anything else.

Greg Blanchard saw a brilliant flash of blue-white light, and then nothing.

"Come on, Linda," said Angus. "It's a beautiful night."

"Pleasant weather is no reason for a young woman to give up her virtue," replied Linda. She laughed at her own joke; it was mostly a joke, but there was a good bit of truth behind it.

Linda Falstaff was seventeen years old, with top marks in school and a bright future. She did not intend to throw away her opportunities in the backseat of her boyfriend's Ford Edsel.

Angus was a nice boy and handsome, too. Tall, broad shoulders, a lopsided smile. He was the kind of man Linda could see herself marrying in a few years. In fact, she had explicitly told Angus they would have to get married before she would do any more with him than some kissing and heavy petting.

Usually, Angus was good with her rule about premarital relations, but he was acting exceptionally randy tonight. Maybe it was the thrill of finishing school or the strange beauty of the meteor shower, which Linda had to admit was pretty magical.

They were parked on the Lookout atop Micmac Head, overlooking the Bay, and every few moments, a colourful falling star would streak across the sky. Linda had never seen anything like it. With the brilliant full moon, the night was brighter than a Christmas tree, sparkling like a neon sign announcing Heaven was open for business.

Angus fell back into the driver's seat and groaned. "Yup, pretty stuff," he said absent-mindedly. His cheeks were flushed, and his hair was mussed, having gotten himself worked up for no good reason. Linda had told him nothing was going to happen. Why did he keep pushing her? Teenage boys were disgusting beasts sometimes.

"How do you know these falling stars aren't a sign from God, huh?" asked Angus. "How do you know they're not a message from Him telling you... telling us... to give in to our love for each other?"

Linda couldn't believe Angus sometimes. He was cute but dumber than a box of old boots. "You think God wants me to fool around with you? In your Ford Edsel?"

Angus pulled away from Linda as if her cardigan was on fire. "Don't you dare say a bad word about Eddy!"

"Who gives their car a boy's name, anyway?" asked Linda. "I mean, 'Edna' was *right there.*"

"I'll have you know I had Eddy blessed by Father Murphy!" Angus grumbled, settling back into his leather seat with a squeaking sound. "This automobile is touched by God!"

"Well, I guess that's the one thing getting touched by anyone here tonight," Linda replied, burrowing back as deeply into her seat as she could, her arms folded tightly across her chest. In the sky above Micmac Head, another shooting star streaked across the heavens. Linda liked to think it was God congratulating her on an excellent, witty remark.

The two teenagers sat in silence for a long time. A few more shooting stars lit up the sky like colourful, angry scars, and Linda focused on them instead of the insufferable moron in the seat beside her. Angus started squirming, and Linda was certain he would drive her home, but she realized he was awkwardly trying to see out the window at something above them.

"Something's wrong," he said.

"Yes, you're a creep with wandering hands."

"No, besides that. Why does the moon look like that?"

Linda looked up. Sure enough, the moon was a strange red, almost the colour of blood. She gasped, taken off guard for a moment. What did that mean? Was God actually angry at her for spurning Angus's advances? That was ridiculous. Then Linda remembered something Mr. Henry had said in class earlier that day. "It's a lunar eclipse," she said. "You must have been asleep in science class."

"No, look closely." Angus opened his door and stepped out of the Edsel. "Watch the shooting stars."

Confused, Linda opened the passenger door and followed, not taking her gaze off the moon. It was dreadfully upsetting to look at. Even though she knew it was caused by the refraction of the sun's light around the Earth, she still thought it made the moon look sick. Like it was dying.

The Micmac, and the Beothuk before them, called it the Blood Moon. It was an apt term for such a disturbing sight.

And then Linda saw it. One of the shooting stars streaked across the sky and curved abruptly toward the blood moon before vanishing. She gasped. Most of the shooting stars had some curve to them, but this one banked at a ninety-degree angle to change its course directly toward the centre of the moon.

A few seconds later, another shooting star, this one from the opposite side of the sky, turned completely around to aim toward the blood moon. Another followed suit, and then another, and another.

Within a minute, a dozen shooting stars had veered off toward the moon, all vanishing somewhere within its dull crimson glow.

"What does that mean?" asked Linda. Out of the corner of her eye, she saw Angus turn and open his mouth, but she immediately put up a hand to stop him. "No, it does not mean God is angry because I won't fool around with you."

"Hey, what are you kids doing up here?"

The voice came from behind them. The teens whirled and were blinded by the brilliant beam of a flashlight.

Angus cursed under his breath, and Linda wanted to sink into the dirt with shame. Technically, Micmac Head was part of the American Air Force Base. Kids snuck up here all the time to fool around, but getting caught was a big no-no. It wasn't like being caught by the local Mountie Constable, who would usually give you a little talking to, make a few rude comments about the length of the girl's skirt, and then send you on your way. Getting caught by the Yankee servicemen always led to your parents finding out because the soldiers were not keen on civilians sneaking onto their base. They would read you the riot act, then bring you home right up to your parents' door so they could read you the riot act, too. And then they would slap you around for being stupid after the Yanks left. Linda's heart sank. How could she have been so dense? To have let Angus talk her into coming up here, and for what? To *not* fool around with him? Girl, you need to have your head checked.

A radio crackled, and Linda realized that the man holding the flashlight was speaking into a walkie-talkie. She couldn't see his face. "Base, this is Airman First Class Wolfhard. Do you copy?" There was a distorted response, but Linda couldn't make it out. Then the soldier said, "I found a couple of kids up here at the Lookout again. Do you want me to..."

His voice trailed off, and Linda winced, waiting for him to start yelling at her. If she was lucky, he would shoot them, and she wouldn't have to face her parents. Or worse, Father Murphy, who her mother would inevitably drag her to before this was over.

"Holy shit..." said the voice, and dropped the flashlight.

Linda caught a glimpse of Angus, looking behind them, before he turned and bolted down the hill, away from the soldier, Linda, and even his beloved Ford Edsel. Linda could not fathom what in the world would have possessed Angus to run away from his stupid car, so she turned slowly, expecting the worst, like a bear, a pack of Indians, or a gang of Soviet spies with machine guns.

Linda looked up, her eyes full of awe and wonder.

Sobbing, she dropped to her knees, bowed her head, and began to pray.

The black sedan drove slowly past the front doors of St. Paul's High School for the third time in five minutes. After the first pass, Sergeant Marie-Ann Tanguay brimmed with anger. After the second, she was horrified and appalled by the audacity of these creeps. By the third time around the block, she was ready to get out of her car and shoot them on the spot.

Tanguay watched the scene from across the street, seated in an unmarked car. She was in her uniform, with a half-finished cup of cold coffee in her hand. The two guys in that car were the same two who had burst in on the Jeddores on Saturday night, and now here they were, scoping out the school Pius and Harper Jeddore attended.

Were they still looking for Pius? If so, why?

According to the names they gave at Doucette's Motel, where they were staying, they were Robert Stone and Randy Koch. A brief search revealed they were indeed American, but not much else. The CIA's Elevator Inspection office, which was, in fact, a real thing, had not returned her inquiries. Sunday had been rough, between looking for info on those clowns, dealing with a lost hunter that still hadn't been found, and fielding angry calls from her superiors about wasting the division's resources on wild goose chases like a couple of so-called "undercover American secret agents." Her boss, Inspector Williams, had chewed her out for that one last night.

Needless to say, Tanguay was not in a good mood.

She could see them staring at the kids on the front lawn as they cruised by. It was lunchtime, and dozens of students were outside, enjoying the warm spring day. The two creeps in the car were sizing them up like hunters picking out a moose. They were looking for something or someone, and Tanguay was sure it was not for good reasons. She could have stopped them right then for indecent behaviour, but they had stonewalled her both times she had approached them over the weekend, and she didn't want to scare them off now. She needed to know what they were after, but they weren't going to tell her, so she had to do this the hard way.

Tanguay was protective about kids at the best of times, despite, or probably because, she had no living offspring of her own. She was especially invested in Pius, Harper, and their friends after all they had gone through last year. She could've gotten into a lot of trouble for how she had handled that case and would have if the division hadn't covered it up for other reasons. Still, she would do it again if she had to, and she sure as *merde* was not going to let something happen to those kids because of a couple of arrogant American G-men.

Finally, after apparently not finding what they were looking for, the black car drove off toward downtown. Tanguay was about to follow them when a short, round kid on sparkly silver rollerblades appeared on the sidewalk in front of the school. The kid moved with all the grace and poise of a walrus strapped to a skateboard.

"Skidmark?" she asked out loud. She immediately felt bad for using the kid's dumb nickname. His real name was Brian Hawco. He had been there for a lot of the crazy stuff that went down last year and had come out of it much better than some of the others. Skidmark was surprisingly resilient, like a, well, like a crap stain that wouldn't come out of your underpants. Although, the rollerblades could be a sign he'd finally snapped.

Despite his oddness, the kid had a knack for knowing what was going on with his peers. If those creeps in the black sedan were up to something...

Tanguay grabbed her radio receiver. "Tanguay to dispatch, over."

"This is dispatch, over," Constable Cheryl Murphy's cheery voice from the dashboard speaker replied.

"Cheryl, that car I told you about earlier is heading down Harmon Highway toward downtown. Can you have someone keep an eye on them?"

Tanguay knew the constable would check her duty roster, but she replied quickly without missing a beat. "Constable Bennett is on Main Street. I'll have him be on the lookout."

"Perfect. Let me know what they're up to. I'll check back in a few. Over and out."

Tanguay replaced her receiver and pulled the unmarked car up to the school's front doors, alongside Skidmark and right below the looming, giant white crucifix on the side of the building. She shuddered, remembering her own grade school years with the nuns in Montreal, and wondered if the kids knew how good they had it these days. In her day, if someone had shown up with wheels on their feet and flapping like a dairy cow on a skating rink, they wouldn't have to worry about the other kids beating them up. The frigging nuns would have belted the kid themselves.

She rolled down the passenger side window and called out. "Skidma—Brian!"

Skidmark whirled and immediately fell over. He landed with a crunch on his hands and knees. Marie-Ann winced, but the kid quickly turned over and sat up on the sidewalk.

"Sergeant Tanguay!" He beamed, his round face glistening with sweat and adolescent acne. "To what do I owe this pleasure? I mean, I assume this is a pleasure, and you're not here to arrest me for some trumped-up charge that I was framed for. Whatever it is, I didn't do it. I mean, maybe I did, but you can't get me to admit to anything. Except for pulling my little sister's hair and taping over her *Goof Troop* VHS with *Nightmare on Elm Street*." He crawled over to the car and pulled himself up using the open window for support.

Kids were weird, but this one got odder every time she met him. "Aren't you afraid the other kids will give you a hard time for talking to a cop?"

"Sergeant Tanguay, please. You know I could not care less about what other people think of me. Plus, my reputation is so low already that talking to you could only bring it up. People might think I'm in trouble for stealing something, like a loaf of bread. No, how about a car? Oh, I know! A boat! Let's pretend I stole a boat from Port Hansen, and you're questioning me about it."

"Sure, sure." Tanguay tried hard not to roll her eyes. A dozen kids were watching their conversation, though Skidmark acted utterly oblivious to them. Let him tell them whatever they wanted; better that than they call him a narc. "Whatever you want. What's with the skates? Practicing for the hockey season?"

Skidmark scoffed and fell over again. He pulled himself back up onto the car. The palms of his hands and his forearms were covered in scabs and scratches. "Sergeant, you and I both know I would never demean myself for such a gross and ugly sport. Did you know they allow fighting and pushing people into plexiglass barricades in hockey? They think losing a tooth or breaking your nose is a badge of honour! It's barbaric! If people wanted to watch violence, they should televise Klingon *mok'bara* duels, something that requires honour and skill."

Tanguay nodded. She flashed back to watching the Canadiens' games with her dad. He was a tried-and-true Jean Béliveau fan, but she always preferred Yvan Cournoyer. "I am familiar with how hockey works, yes."

"The blades are for the school play. We're doing *Starlight Express*."

"You're skating *on stage*?" Tanguay asked, far more incredulously than she'd intended. She winced, but once again, Skidmark hadn't noticed.

"Oh, hell no. I'm the prop manager. They say I'm not a good enough skater to be in the show, though everyone knows I'm a better singer than most of the kids in there. I can sing an entire octave higher than Steve Goosney, who got the lead because he used to play hockey. It's all drama club politics. They would never let someone in junior high in the lead anyway. The director is a bitch. She doesn't like me and thinks that grade twelve deserves the role because it's his last chance before he graduates, even though he can't carry a note worth a shit, and his acting is more wooden than Pinocchio on prom night."

"So... why are you wearing the rollerblades, then?"

"Well, Andrew White already broke his ankle in rehearsal, and Mary Alexander blew out her knee. Those jumps and flips are no joke. If three more people get hurt, a spot will open up in the chorus, and I want to be ready to snatch it when it does."

Tabernouche, high school theatre was way rougher than hockey.

"Skidma—Brian, did you see a black sedan drive by here a few minutes ago? With two large, scary-looking men in it?"

"No, but I heard a couple of girls talking about them. They were going on about how they were cruising for underage girls and were total creeps. One of them said they saw the same car out by the swimming pool yesterday."

Salauds...

She had lost track of them for a few hours yesterday afternoon, and that's where they ended up, checking out youngsters in bathing suits? The idea of it made her skin crawl. She considered calling Bennett to arrest them now, but something told her there was more to it than that.

After all, they were, supposedly, American government agents. Newfoundland was a long way to go to pick up underage kids.

She had called her CO in St. John's to ask about these guys, and he had brushed her off. Her bosses kept her at arm's length after the incident last year. She figured they had been warned by someone high up in the government that Gale Harbour was best avoided and ignored as long as whatever happened there didn't get talked about in the world at large. On the one hand, she appreciated the freedom to do things her way. On the other hand, it would have been nice to have support when foreign agents from another friggin' country started poking their noses around her town.

It made her wonder if the higher-ups knew about the creeps and were either purposefully ignoring the situation or were directly connected to them.

"Thanks." She pulled a business card out of her vest pocket and handed it to Skidmark. "If you see those creeps again or hear about them messing with any other kids, you call me right away, okay? If I'm not at the detachment, tell them to page me immediately."

Skidmark saluted, surprisingly crisply. Then he hit the car so hard she was sure he must have left a dent. "Understood, Sergeant. I will be your eyes and ears. Don't worry. You can count on me. I'll be like an Imperial Probe Droid, hunting the galaxy for any sign of treasonous rebel scum—"

"Right. Good luck with your play, okay?"

As Tanguay pulled away, she radioed Constable Bennett to ask if the creeps had been up to anything. "Negative," came the reply. "They went into Nanny's Kitchen at the mall for dinner."

An idea struck her then. It wasn't a good idea, necessarily, but the fact that her CO gave her more than enough rope to hang herself opened up a few doors she wouldn't normally walk through. "Is Charlene Boulous working today?"

"Now, how would I know that?" asked Bennett.

"Because you stop to get a coffee at that crappy diner every time she's working, even though it's out of your way and it's the worst coffee in town."

There was a long pause on the radio. Bennett was married, but that didn't stop him from chatting up the blond-haired waitress at the greasy diner in the Gale Harbour plaza. Tanguay couldn't imagine what he saw in her; it certainly wasn't her shitty coffee or her sparkling conversation. It was likely the sweaters she wore that were two sizes too small.

Finally, Bennett sighed. "Yeah, she's working the dinner shift."

Good. That meant Creepo-One and Creepo-Two would be tied up there for a while. The one thing worse than the coffee at Nanny's Kitchen was the speed of Charlene Boulous' service.

"Ten-four. Can you stay in the area and keep an eye on them? Let me know when they leave."

"You got it, Sarge. You going to do something stupid?"

"Probably."

Tanguay was already pulling up in front of Doucette's Motel, a low-end flophouse on the north side of town, off Harmon Highway, several minutes drive from the plaza. It was owned by Keith Doucette's father, who owned several businesses in town. The rooms had private, somewhat secluded entrances, and the parking lot was off the main strip, so it was popular with people who wanted to do secret business in a town with more busybodies and gossips than street signs. Tanguay didn't think Bennett and Charlene had hooked up here yet, but it was not out of the realm of possibility.

She removed her bulletproof vest, badge, and any distinguishing features that identified her as a Royal Canadian Mounted Police officer. Since she couldn't remove her entire uniform, she grabbed a red-and-white windbreaker from her backseat and shrugged it on. It had the logo from the 1988 Calgary Olympics on the front and gravy stains on one arm from the last time she'd worn it, but it would do.

Before she was deployed to Gale Harbour, she had prided herself on doing things by the book. She excelled in training, shot up the ranks with glowing recommendations from her superiors, and filed the most detailed and accurate paperwork. But something about this town changed her. Perhaps it was the unkillable sea monster. Or the witch with a penchant for performing blood rituals. Or it was the kids who managed to get themselves wrapped up in the middle of all that ridiculousness. Or it was Dick Jeddore, the fisheries and wildlife officer. He had sacrificed himself to save his daughter and several others, including Tanguay herself, from the aforementioned sea monster. There was something about this town that made her think that promotions and paperwork were not the most important things in the world and that sometimes there was *l'enterrement de crapaud* out here for which no amount of procedure and policy could prepare you. Sometimes you had to do whatever it took to protect yourself, your loved ones, and the whole goddamn town from Psycho Hose Beasts from outer space.

So, without much thought on the matter, she took a deep breath, glanced around the parking lot one more time to make sure no one was watching, and then got out of her car quickly and broke into the motel room of Robert Stone and Randy Koch.

The locks on the Doucette Motel rooms were ridiculously easy to jimmy open, which she had learned after a spat of break-ins a few months back. She had strongly advised Cecil Doucette to replace all the locks on his doors. She had even demonstrated personally how to open them with a simple screwdriver, but the famed miser would never do it. She was glad now that he hadn't. She popped open the door and was inside in seconds, confident that no one saw her.

The inside of the room was as bland and ugly as any cheap motel room. The thick carpet and wood panelling hadn't been changed since the seventies, and the place smelled like fish. She doubted it was because the men had eaten halibut last night. Their clothes and suitcases were thrown haphazardly on the bed, much less neatly or carefully than most professional men she had seen travelling. That by itself wasn't odd; Stone and Koch could have been slobs, but the suitcases were particularly dishevelled as if someone had torn them apart looking for something.

Had someone else already broken in here?

Struck by a sudden dread, her hand went to the service revolver tucked inside her windbreaker, but a quick scan of the small motel room proved no one else was there. A slightly more thorough search found nothing incriminating, either. No guns, drugs, or illegal porn, which was the one thing she most dreaded finding. She was disappointed and angry at herself for taking such a risk and coming up empty-handed. What had she been thinking? What had she been hoping to find? Any real evidence would have been useless if she had discovered it like this.

She picked up a Manila folder full of a half-dozen sheets of computer paper, stamped at the top with an official-looking Canadian government seal. It was a typed report but heavily redacted. Most words were blacked out with a magic marker, but those sections she could read terrified her. She saw the dates around last year's "incident" and references to Hansen Air Force Base. She read the names of three of the kids: Niall O'Neil, Harper Jeddore, and Pius Jeddore. It also listed the Jeddores' address.

That explained how the creeps found the kids. But why did they have this report? And what the hell did they want?

A shadow passed the front window curtains, and Tanguay flattened herself to the wall. She bumped the small desk, and some papers and an envelope landed in the wastebasket with a bang. The shadow outside the room stopped. *Merde.* Had Stone and Koch come back to the room already? Why hadn't Bennett called her? She reached for her radio and froze, a ball of ice sinking into her stomach. She had left her radio in the car with her vest.

Cursing herself far worse than the nuns ever had, she held her breath and waited to see what the shadow would do. She could dive under the bed if they tried to unlock the door. It was risky, but she didn't have much choice. She tensed and prepared to jump, waiting for the tell-tale scraping of the key in the lock.

But then the shadow started moving again and disappeared from view.

Tabernac. That was too close. She had to get out of there but still had the presence of mind to pick up the papers and replace them on the desk. When she picked up the stack, a photograph fell out of the large manila envelope. She stiffened. It wasn't kiddie porn, and it was not something she would have expected.

Carefully, she picked up the photo. It was a cheap, glossy four-by-six, the kind you could get developed at the drugstore. Usually, these shots depicted kids' birthdays, dogs at the beach, or teenagers drinking Labatt's at a house party. This particular photograph wasn't that different. It showed a bunch of kids about Skidmark's age in a backyard, gathered close together and smiling for the camera. They were sitting atop an odd-looking, large, rusty metal cylinder. The yard, with its simple red-stained wood privacy fence and no other distinguishing features, could have been anywhere and looked like a dozen other yards she had seen in Gale Harbour.

At first, she had taken the cylinder for a fuel tank, but upon closer inspection, she noticed an American flag painted on it, as well as the emblem of the United States Air Force. Judging by the shape of it, it looked more like... a bomb? A very large bomb, for that matter. Was this thing somewhere in Gale Harbour? Was this what the creeps were looking for?

Where the hell was it? She didn't recognize the yard. She didn't recognize the kids. No, wait. There was one of them that she knew—the one in the Blue Jays World Series Championship cap.

It was Keith Doucette, the son of the guy who owned this very hotel. One of the kids who had been down in the tunnels with the sea witch monster.

<u>CHAPTER EIGHT</u>

Today
May 31, 12:20 pm

"Who were you talking to at lunch?" Pius asked Skidmark as he pulled his math book out of his locker. Their lockers were side by side, across from the cafeteria in the main corridor of St. Paul's High School.

Skidmark had recently experienced a growth spurt and was now a few centimetres taller than Pius, who hadn't grown since Grade One. Skidmark was also considerably taller because he was still wearing his rollerblades. He had to hold onto the lockers to keep himself upright.

"I have no idea what you're talking about."

"We saw you talking with someone in a car in front of the school," clarified Niall, who was at the locker on Skidmark's other side. He lowered his voice. "Was your mom bringing you new underwear?"

Within the social standing where he, Skidmark, and Pius lived, Niall knew that losing your underwear to a nasty prank or a particularly vicious wedgie was a serious occupational hazard. They commiserated about it often, like veterans sharing war stories.

"Oh, that. That was Sergeant Tanguay."

Niall slammed his locker, and his attention fixed on Skidmark. "Really? What did she want?" That was the second time their friendly neighbourhood Mountie had shown up in the last few days. Pius had told Niall about the Secret Service guys at his house and how Tanguay came to their rescue. They had barely seen the cop since last year, and with everything Niall and Harper had been through on the weekend, it was starting to bring up weird memories.

"Oh, nothing." Skidmark shrugged. "She wanted to question me about a boat I stole last week."

Pius adjusted his glasses. "Brian, while I know you and would not be surprised in the slightest if you actually stole a boat, I also know you didn't get a part in the school play because you're a terrible actor and liar."

Skidmark grinned, revealing chunks of chocolate stuck in his teeth from the Oh Henry bar he'd had for lunch. "You got me. That was a cover story for a super-secret spy mission she asked me to do for her."

Pius shook his head. "Again, I don't think that's true."

"It is true! Swear to God! She asked me to keep a lookout for a couple of creepy dudes in suits cruising around in a black car."

Niall and Pius looked at each other. Crap. Now, this was getting uncomfortable.

The awkward moment was interrupted when Chris Tobin, a high school hockey team defenceman, walked past them and yanked Pius' rat tail with one hand while shoving Skidmark into the lockers with the other. Chris was a brute in the eleventh grade, but Pius was so used to getting his hair pulled that he barely flinched and only yelped a little.

"Get a haircut, fag," Chris called over his shoulder from down the hall.

The other thugs walking with him cackled with laughter.

"Why *don't* you cut that thing off?" Niall asked Pius while helping Skidmark to his feet. Pius had started growing that long, thin string of hair in the third grade when all the boys were doing it. But unlike everyone else who had cut it by the fourth grade, Pius still had his, and it was now down to his butt, which served as a prime target for bullies.

"I wouldn't give jerks like Chris Tobin the satisfaction," said Pius in a surprising show of confidence and defiance for him. Usually, he folded under pressure like one of those deadly vinyl lawn chairs. Like the one that snapped closed and killed a kid in Keeping last summer, according to rumours.

"I totally agree," said Skidmark, patting Pius on the shoulder with a thick hand. He slipped on his skates and nearly took Pius down with him. "Neanderthals like Chris Tobin will always find some reason to pick on you, like your club foot or crossed eyes or ingrown nails or pimples on the back of your neck or that your father makes you sleep in the backyard in the rain if you disturb him while he's watching *Matlock*..."

"How many of those are from personal experience?" asked Niall.

Skidmark didn't answer or slow down. "...so why would you change something you like about yourself just because someone else, who is always going to find something not to like, doesn't like it? Anyway, I'm the one who should be asking *you* questions." Skidmark folded his thick, pasty arms and leaned against the lockers. "I heard you punched out Sally Alexander at The Hangar on Saturday."

Niall had been expecting this question all day. Though he had received a few strange looks, no one had flat-out asked him about the incident at the teen club. Pius had made a vague comment about it earlier in the day. Either Harper had told him the story herself, or—more likely—she had forbidden Pius from asking about it.

But since someone else had brought it up, Pius jumped on the opportunity. "Yeah, what exactly happened Saturday night? Harper came home with a bloody nose and a black eye, but she wouldn't tell me what happened."

Skidmark's mouth opened wide enough to insert a foot-long meatball sub. Sideways. "Did you punch Harper, too?"

Niall recoiled. "No, I didn't punch Harper!"

Skidmark chuckled at the absurdity of his own question. "Of course. She would have kicked your ass if you had."

"And I didn't punch Sally Alexander, either!"

"Really?" Skidmark asked. "All the kids in the drama club were talking about it. Aaron Wheeler and Jessica Skinner were there. They say they weren't on a date, but everyone knows that they make out behind the ball field at lunch, so if they were at the dance at the same time, you can bet they were sucking face in the corner every chance they got, like a couple of vacuum cleaners with the nozzles stuck together." He mimed the scene, mashing his hands together and making "clopping" sounds like smashed coconuts. "Anyway, Aaron and Jessica said Sally nailed Steve Goosney, who nearly got a concussion but unfortunately is still going to be in the show, and then Sally and Harper got into a scuffle, and then you beat the crap out of Sally."

"Were you standing up for Harper?" asked Pius. "That's ridiculous. She doesn't need you to stand up for her. She would have kicked your ass for that, too."

"He's covering for Harper for some reason," suggested Skidmark. "Is she on parole or something? Or trying to join a cult that forbids its members from physical violence? Or she's in Tae Kwon Do, and she's worried if they find out she got into a fight, her sensei will kick her out of class? I saw this old kung fu movie once where the guy learned this top-secret touch-of-death move and he was forbidden to use it, but he used it anyway to save his sister's life, but he was ashamed and refused to tell his master what he did, so they exiled him from the monastery..."

Pius was nodding along, his tiny eyes flickering with agreement behind his thick eyeglasses, utterly oblivious to everything Skidmark said after the first few words. "Yeah, that makes sense. You're covering for Harper, right? Because there's no way she would let you fight for her, and I know you would never hit a girl…"

"Well, I didn't exactly hit her…" Niall started to say when a shrill, commanding voice interrupted him from down the hall.

"Brian Hawco, why are you wearing one of my props?"

The voice, expertly projected, came from a small, thin woman dressed all in black except for a loose-knit lavender wool shawl. She wore tiny, tinted glasses on the end of her long nose, and her salt-and-pepper hair desperately tried to escape the sloppy bun she'd erected on the top of her head.

"Gotta go," said Skidmark, turning and flailing on his rollerblades with the grace of a hippo on a unicycle. He pushed off the lockers and rocketed down the hall in the opposite direction, sending kids diving for cover as he thundered past.

Mrs. Eleanor Walsh was the drama club teacher. She was a local woman who had studied two years at Memorial University of Newfoundland's theatre department and performed three summers at the Gale Harbour Theatre Festival in the 1980s. She thought her experience made her God's gift to all things dramatic.

"I was on my way back to the costume room, Mrs. Walsh!" Skidmark called without even looking back.

"Why are you even wearing them?" she demanded.

"Just testing them out, you know, making sure they're safe!" He rounded a corner and almost took out Craig Muise, who was coming out of the boy's washroom.

Mrs. Walsh hurried off after him.

"That woman scares me," said Pius.

The bell rang, and the crowds in the hallway dispersed. Pius and Niall followed a group of gossiping girls to their fourth-period math class. They were standing outside the door when Harper, dressed in an army surplus jacket, oversized jeans, and black boots, materialized in front of them to block their entry into the classroom.

"We need to talk," she said.

Niall had never heard a girl say those words before, and yet they still filled him with a staggering unease, a dread hardwired into the male brain over thousands of years.

"But I have math," said Pius, his mouth open wide enough to catch a significant number of flies.

"I'm not talking to you, barf breath. Niall, I need to show you something."

"But Niall has math, too."

"It's fine, Pius," said Niall. He had never skipped class before, but he had never had a girl ask him to skip class with promises of needing to 'show him something,' either. He could have been scheduled for life-saving brain surgery and would have skipped that, too. "Cover for me with Mr. Clark, will you?"

"Cover?" stammered Pius. "Cover how? What do I say?"

But Niall and Harper were already gone, leaving Pius standing by the classroom door, holding his books in his hands. Niall felt terrible for ditching class and, even worse, for leaving his best friend in that situation, but he found himself unable to make logical decisions when Harper was around.

He hadn't seen her since Saturday night. On Sunday, he tried calling a couple of times, but Pius' mom always said she was out for a walk. Now that he got a look at her, she had a nasty black eye, and when they ducked out through a side door into an alcove, he immediately reached for her face.

"Oh my god, are you okay?"

Harper flinched away. "Don't touch me!"

Niall withdrew his hand as if burned.

Harper looked embarrassed immediately, which was a strange look for her. This was the girl who had worn hot-pink, one-piece pyjamas to school last year on a bet and then punched the one boy who had dared to mock her for it.

"I'm sorry," she said. "But after Saturday night..."

"Right," said Niall, understanding but still hurt. "You don't want us to touch and put someone else in the hospital."

"Or worse. Sally Alexander is lucky to be alive."

"I didn't mean to! It was an accident!"

"Shhh," hissed Harper, glancing back through the door down the hallway. "Look, I know it was an accident, but never mind that. Look at this."

She handed him an old notebook. He flipped through it, but it didn't mean much to him until a couple of names caught his eye. "This is Theolina's journal! But this is not the book they showed us."

"I think it's their translation. I found it in the backseat of the car."

"You stole it?"

"I borrowed it. Look, it doesn't matter. What matters is what Theolina wrote."

"The weird stuff the goth kids were saying about the lunar eclipse?" Niall had thought about it a lot yesterday. What if what they were saying was true? What if there was danger? He didn't want to believe it. They had gone through all that last year. Surely kids in a small town in Newfoundland didn't encounter other-worldly entities more than once in their lifetimes. Then he started playing *StarFox* with his brother Nelson, and then they had supper with Nana Josephine and Uncle Archie. Niall had mostly forgotten about Anna and Keenan, until now.

"I think they were just weird witch groupies." He had to. If he accepted that they weren't and that what they said was true...

Harper shook her head. "I think they were right, Niall. I think this is Theolina's book, and all that stuff happened."

"How do you know?"

She held it open for Niall to see. Anna's writing was small and neat, almost too neat. Obsessive. "Look at those notes about an 'evil God from another world' that she and her sister tried to stop sixty years ago. It says her sister died trying to kill it, and then it was trapped at the bottom of the sea. Everything she told us about the Psycho Hose Beast is in here. She called it 'The Primordial One.'"

Niall read a few lines. It certainly sounded like the stuff they had experienced. There was even stuff about William Jeddore, Harper's grandfather, the man Theolina was arrested for trying to kill. She called him "blood of the blood," the same thing she had called Harper's father and Harper herself. Descendants of the first humans who had defeated the Primordial One.

"There's stuff in there no one should be able to know about," Niall whispered.

"No one except Theolina. And if this is right, then..."

"The stuff about the lunar eclipse is probably right, too. What does it say is supposed to happen?"

Harper flipped to the appropriate page. "Well, I'm not sure if Anna translated it right, but I think it says '*buteo apes*.'"

"Apes?" asked Niall. "Like monkeys?"

"Yup." Harper bobbed her head in agreement. "Butt Monkeys."

"Mister O'Neil and Miss Jeddore."

They jumped and turned as one to see a looming, towering figure silhouetted by the sun. Niall didn't need to see his features to know who it was—he could recognize that shape and voice anywhere.

"Shouldn't you two be in class?" boomed Mr. Bourgeois, the principal.

Mr. Bourgeois was a giant of a man, thin as a reed, and always dressed in a grey suit with a bow tie. He was as hairless as an egg, and his skin was equally white. He came from the old school of education and longed for the days when nuns could take a stick and beat a disobedient child black and blue.

"Sorry, Mr. Bourgeois..." Niall started but didn't even have time to get out an excuse. The principal snatched the notebook out of their hands.

"And what is this? More of your satanic dungeon games?" He flipped through the book, turning up his long, hooked nose at the scrawled notes. "This sinful filth has no place in our school. You know St. Paul's has a strict rule about dungeon games."

This was true. Nelson told Niall that it stemmed from the mid-eighties, when Mr. Bourgeois, then the vice principal, had watched the *Mazes & Monsters* movie.

"Don't have a cow, man," grumbled Harper. "It's just a game."

Mr. Bourgeois raised a hairless eyebrow. "Isn't this a magic spell?"

"Well, yes, technically it is," said Harper. "But this isn't actually part of the game..."

Shut up, Harper. He really, really wished she would stop talking before she got them in more trouble. Mr. Bourgeois had the sense of humour of a garden rake. A pious, self-righteous garden rake. If Niall concentrated hard enough, would he be able to communicate telepathically with Harper? He had to try. Anything was better than—

"Detention, both of you." Mr. Bourgeois snapped the book shut. "And I'm keeping this."

Oh, no, no.

"Sir, that book doesn't belong to us," said Niall. "We need to bring it back."

"You should have thought of that before bringing satanic writings into my school. Now, back to class. And I'll see you two at three o'clock."

"He's such a dillwad," Harper muttered under her breath as they trudged back through the doors and down the empty hallways toward math class. "I hope Butt Monkeys rip his eyes out."

"If we don't get that notebook back," Niall whispered, "that might be a distinct possibility."

<u>CHAPTER NINE</u>

Bad Boys
May 31, 2:55 pm

A high-fly ball soared across the outfield, a double, at least. But out of nowhere came a blur of long legs in red shorts, running down that fly ball like a pale Devon White and snatching it out of the air one-handed. Kids on both teams cheered.

"Ah, c'mon, man!" screamed the kid at the plate, who must have been at least sixteen. "It's practice. You don't have to catch me out every friggin' time!"

The kid in the red shorts shrugged and fired the ball toward the pitcher's mound like a rocket. "If you don't want me to catch it, you're going to have to hit it farther!"

Since Tanguay last saw him, Keith Doucette must have had a growth spurt, but she would recognize him anywhere. Not because he was missing an ear, which he was covering with his hair grown long and awkwardly combed to one side. Keith looked like one of those rotten kids who would end up in front of Tanguay or other RCMP officers like her far too often. He was tall, with that grin that said he was thinking about the next mean thing he would say or do. He also bore the wisp of a sad little adolescent moustache coming in on his top lip, which didn't help. Keith was fourteen or fifteen, and he already looked like a thug. Kids like him had teased her mercilessly in school, which ultimately led to her becoming a police officer. She didn't want to feel helpless and powerless anymore.

The fact that he was a skeet wasn't technically his fault. He had grown up with lousy parents and, worse, lousy parents with money. He was a close-minded jerk *and* an entitled brat, which made him insufferable at times. If Tanguay hadn't known Keith better, she would have written him off already.

But he had a good heart, and when everything went tits up last year, he stepped in and helped save the other kids—and her—more than once. From what she heard, he was abrasive, obnoxious, and still a bit of a bully, but he would grow out of it. Hopefully.

Seeing the sergeant standing by the right-field fence, Keith nodded toward her and yelled back to the rest of the players. "Sorry, boys, girlfriend's calling. Be right back." He hustled over to Tanguay with a broad grin on his face and to the sounds of cheers and whoops from his buddies.

"What's the problem, Officer?"

Tanguay rolled her eyes. "Quite an arm you got there, kid."

"What? Having a good throwing arm ain't a crime. Anyone can throw a brick through Arlene's store window. It don't prove nothing."

"What?" Shaking her head, she made a mental note to check on Arlene's, a discount department and souvenir store on Main Street, later. "That's not why I'm here. You weren't breaking windows again, were you?"

"I've never broke a window in my life, except my grandmother's when I hit a line drive through it. And she let me off easy. The old lady's pretty sweet on me."

Keith smiled his lopsided grin again, and Tanguay felt gross inside, knowing there were girls his age who found that attractive, even with the braces. She caught a whiff of something coming off him. Was it alcohol?

Brushing it off, for now, she produced her notebook. "Look, I'm not here *pour jaser*. I'm here to find out where this picture was taken."

From the notebook, she held out the photograph she'd found in the motel of Keith and a half-dozen other boys sitting on what appeared to be a bomb. Keith looked at it and nodded. "Oh, that's Darrell Jesso's place up in the Crossing. That was from his birthday party a few weeks ago."

Gale Harbour Crossing? She would never have thought to look out there. "And what exactly is it that you boys are sitting on?"

"That thing? That's an old oil drum his dad painted up to look like a bomb. Darrell's right into World War Two planes and stuff, so his dad made it as a joke."

"You sure about that?"

Keith looked at the picture again, and his jovial attitude faded from his face. As he leaned in closer, Tanguay was sure the kid smelled like beer. "I mean, I'm pretty sure. It looked authentic. You telling me that was a real bomb?"

His face went pale.

Tanguay shrugged. "I don't know. That's what I'm trying to figure out. Where exactly does Darrell Jesso live?"

"Down at the end of Spruce Road in the Crossing. Big red house, you can't miss it."

Tanguay was pretty sure she knew the place. "Thanks. I'll let you get back to your game."

She turned, about to walk away, but she couldn't let it go and looked back. "Keith, have you been drinking?"

Keith's look of fear and discomfort deepened for a second, but then hints of his smile crept back on his face. "What, is that a crime?"

She sighed. Yeah, this kid was heading down the wrong path. "You're underage, Keith. So, however you got it was a crime, whether you were stealing it or an adult gave it to you. Plus, it's the middle of the day, and you're at school. What the hell are you thinking?"

Apparently, he wasn't thinking because he didn't have an answer for her. "I was... I just..."

"Stay away from it, okay? Don't get yourself in trouble."

It wasn't a great warning. She should have a proper conversation about it and determine if it was regular teenage curiosity or if it was a genuine problem. But she didn't have time. There was a bomb out there somewhere, and some weird creeps were looking for it. She would have to talk to Keith's parents or baseball coach later. Right now, she needed to follow this Jesso lead.

She was walking away when Keith called out to her. "Should I tell the boys about the bomb?"

"I would prefer you didn't."

"Then what should I tell them you were asking about?"

"Tell them I had some questions about a stolen boat."

Keith's eyes lit up, and his smile returned. "Oh, that's wicked, yeah, thanks! I'll do that."

As he ran off back to his game, she shook her head. Kids were so dumb. She wished she didn't have such a soft spot for them, especially this batch of weirdos who were magnets for the strangest kinds of trouble.

***

Gale Harbour Crossing was another smaller community on St. Stephen's Bay, on the other side of a steep mountain called Micmac Head. The Head overlooked the matchstick factory, one of the town's main employers.

Micmac Head was also where many of last year's problems started. It was where Dick Jeddore drove his truck over the embankment, causing the injuries that indirectly led to his untimely death and to the disappearance of the three kids that turned the town upside down.

Every time she passed the freshly-repaired concrete barricade on the turn near the highest point of the Head, she thought about Dick. At first, she had found him irritating, too full of himself by half, but he had turned out to be a good man. He would have been a great cop, too. She found out after he died that he had been turned away from the Mounties back in the seventies when he applied. She couldn't find an official reason why he was rejected. He seemed like a perfect recruit, but she had an awful feeling in her gut: It was likely because of his Native heritage. She wished she had known that when he was still alive. She wasn't sure exactly what she would have done about it, but being a woman in the RCMP, she had faced her fair share of bigotry and discrimination. Could they have commiserated? Thinking about it like that felt trite. Perhaps she just wanted to talk to a kindred soul. She hadn't confided in anyone since her daughter Lynne had died.

After crossing the Head and descending the steep road on the opposite side, Tanguay reached the rocky shore on the outer edge of Gale Harbour Crossing. She passed the Western Health Nursing Home before turning into the town proper. It was a tiny town, the former site of a train crossing, built on the lowest part of a peninsula between Gale Harbour and the rest of the island of Newfoundland. Much of it was on swampland and sand bars, and the whole community would be underwater if the sea levels rose at all.

The town was so small she didn't need a street address, and Keith's directions were more than sufficient. Even if they hadn't been, she was sure she could have pulled over and asked anyone where the Jessos lived and gotten the correct answer. They could also tell her who owed who money. That was the way small towns worked.

Sure enough, she found the big red house in a wooded area at the end of Spruce Road. There was a large shed out back, and she recognized the tall fence in the backyard. A black Chevy and a red Ford pickup were in the gravel driveway, indicating the family was most likely home for supper. Of course, everyone hated it when the Mounties came knocking at their door, especially at supper time, but that's why they did it; that was when most people were home.

She parked her cruiser, strode to the front door, and knocked. A moment later, it opened, and a broad-faced middle-aged man with a neatly trimmed, salt-and-pepper moustache peered out. When he saw the uniform, his face turned bright red, and he yelled back into the house: "Jesus, Mary and Joseph, Darrell, what did you do now?"

"What the hell you talking about, old man?" came the reply from inside.

"Why is there a Mountie at my door?"

"Mister Jesso, Wayne Jesso, right? Your son isn't in any trouble. At least, I don't think he is. I'm Sergeant Tanguay, and if you don't mind, I have a couple of questions for you."

Jesso stepped quickly onto the concrete block front porch and closed the door behind him. "Is it about my brother Georgie? I always knew those salmon tags weren't right."

"What? No, it's not about your brother—"

"Is it about the minivan in the Foodland parking lot? I swear those tail lights were busted before I ran into it."

"Mister Jesso, please stop further incriminating yourself or any members of your family. I want to ask you about this." She held up the photograph.

Wayne Jesso squinted at it a moment, then shook his head. "Look, if all you want to talk about is underage drinking, what's the matter with boys having fun?"

"What? No, I don't..." She took a deep breath and squeezed her fist. "Look at what the boys are sitting on. Where did that thing come from?"

"Oh, that?" He shrugged. "My son's friends found that in one of the old tunnels under the base last winter. I helped them get it out a couple of months ago."

"And you didn't think it was a problem to remove a bomb from a military base?"

"Go on, the damn thing's forty years old. It's a dud. Besides, if it were going to blow up, it would have done so by now. We dropped the thing a half-dozen times trying to get it in the truck."

Osti d'innocent... "And you didn't have a problem with your kids and their friends playing on it, either, I suppose."

"Well, no, I told you, if dropping the thing off our winch wasn't going to set it off, a couple kids kicking soccer balls at it wasn't going to hurt it."

"Where is the bomb now, Mister Jesso?"

"Well, I got to thinking it might be worth something, you know? I figured I could bring it up to Hansen Field Day and see if any of the Yanks might be interested in it. I didn't want the kids beating it up before then, so I had to put it somewhere safe."

Hansen Field Day was an air show Gale Harbour put off every other summer to celebrate the town's history as a former US military base. American Air Force planes would fly in to put off aerial displays. At last year's show, working security was one of Tanguay's first assignments upon moving to Gale Harbour. She had helped a lost little girl find her parents. If only all her cases were so easy.

It was also at the air show that someone explained to Tanguay the story behind Gale Harbour's infamous "plane-on-a-stick"—the old F-102 Delta Dagger jet fighter that was mounted on a concrete pylon near the entrance to town. It wasn't a particularly interesting story, but it gave the town something else to put on its tourism brochure. The town's previous slogan, approved by the tourism council after expensive market research, was "Visit Scenic Gale Harbour—Might As Well!"

"Visit Gale Harbour—We Have a Plane on a Stick!" wasn't much better.

Tanguay wondered how successful Jesso would be in selling US military property back to the US military, but she didn't bring it up. She doubted he would get that far, anyway. "Where exactly did you put it?"

"In my shed, up at my cabin out in Robinsons. Figured it would be safe out there until I knew exactly what to do with it. That's where I keep all my Ski-Doos and ATVs, too, so I know it's locked up tighter than a nun's drawers."

She hoped to God it was. "Would you mind giving me directions to your cabin so I can go have a look myself and make sure it's secure?"

"Sure, sure," Jesso agreed, and Tanguay pulled out her notebook to take down the directions. As he finished, he added. "Funny thing, though. There were a couple of men here yesterday asking about it, too."

Tanguay's blood froze. "Two men? Who were they?"

"They said they were World War Two memorabilia collectors. Somehow, they had heard about the bomb and wanted to see it. Told them it wasn't available to show right now, and that I had it packed away but they were some eager. Something about them didn't feel right, so I told them to move along."

"Did they identify themselves?"

"Just said their names were Joe and Dave. They were dressed in black suits. Looked like those Secret Services guys from that JFK movie. Gave the wife the willies."

Strange. Why wouldn't they flash their credentials like they did to the Jeddores last week? Were they trying to keep a lower profile?

"Is the location of your cabin pretty common knowledge?"

"Sure, everyone knows everybody up that way."

"Thank you, Mister Jesso. If those two men come back again, you call me right away, okay?"

"Are they dangerous?"

"No," she lied. She had become pretty adept at lying after keeping her mouth shut about everything last year. "But I need to ask them some questions."

She left him with her number and headed back to her car. If they could find Jesso's cabin that easily, the bomb might already be gone. It was time to get in touch with her superiors, whether they wanted to hear from her or not. The Department of National Defence should probably be involved in this...

She was reaching for her radio in her car when it squawked to life. She jumped so hard she nearly banged her head on the roof.

"Constable Bennett to Sergeant Tanguay."

Constable Burt Bennett was the most senior RCMP officer stationed in Gale Harbour, but that didn't mean he was the best. He was a nice guy, but something about his voice irritated her every time he opened his mouth, usually because it was always full of donuts or cigarettes.

"Go for Tanguay."

"Sorry to bother you, Sergeant, but... uh... we have a situation."

INTERMÈDE

"Our father, who art in heaven…"

Linda could not bear to look upon its beautiful face. She was not worthy, a mere mortal, to look upon such glory and wonder. They had all been right: her mother, Father Murphy, her grandmother, Suzanne, the Sunday School teacher with three fingers on her left hand. God was watching out for her and had sent one of His angels to protect her.

"Thy Kingdom come…"

He had been protecting her, and she had done nothing but sin and disobey him. She had been up here with a boy she liked far too much. She was teasing him and dallying with him. What kind of harlot was she? She wanted to beg and plead for forgiveness but couldn't find the words. All that came to her were the words of the Lord's prayer. That, and the tears that were flowing down her cheeks.

"On Earth as it is in Heaven…"

She couldn't see its face. It was silhouetted by the blood moon. But it was large and majestic, hovering in the sky before her, with wings broader than a man was tall. Voices sang out. She wasn't sure if it was coming from the angel in front of her or other choirs in the Heavens above.

"Forgive us our trespasses…"

The singing became louder, more frantic. It was a sound not meant for mortals to hear. She was blessed with even this small taste of the divine. But why did the voice have an American accent?

"Jesus Christ, get down! What the hell is wrong with you?"

The gunshots were deafening, right above Linda's head. She screamed and dove face-first into the grass, covering her ears. Her cheek hit a rock, sending a sharp pain through her skull. She shook off the haze that had descended over her mind. What was going on? Where was she? What happened to Angus?

Why was the Yank shooting at the angel?

He kept firing until his handgun ran out of bullets, and then strong hands grabbed her arm and pulled her to her feet. "Come on! We have to get out of here!"

In a daze, she followed but did not know why. She wanted to ask why they would flee from an angel and why on Earth he would shoot at one, but she had trouble forming words.

Then a new sound came. A droning, buzzing sound pierced her ears and burrowed right into her brain. It made her whole skeleton vibrate. Her teeth hurt.

"What is that?" she screeched, trying to cover her ears in a vain attempt to block the sound.

The American didn't answer. He dragged her down the hill, away from the angel. The buzzing drone got louder and more maddening by the second.

CHAPTER TEN

Because the Night
May 31, 4:35 pm

Pius was sitting on the ground outside the school, with his science textbook on his lap, when Niall and Harper finally got out of detention.

"You waited for us?" Harper snorted. "You fart-knocker."

Pius sighed. He had been worried about them, but he wouldn't bring that up now. "I didn't want to walk home by myself."

"What are you afraid of?" Harper gestured to the beautiful spring sky and wooded area around the school. "Butterflies?"

"I saw Chris Tobin and some of the hockey team hanging out smoking in the parking lot after school." That part was true. "I didn't want to walk past them by myself." That part was also true. Sure, he was also concerned about his cousin and best friend, but he could be both, right?

"He's right, Harper," agreed Niall. "It's not safe to walk home by yourself with those jerks around."

"Fine, what odds. I hope you got lots of studying done because we need your help tonight."

Pius looked at them blankly. He didn't like it when Harper asked for things. "But it's a school night. And I'm supposed to be tutoring my dad for his trade school exam."

Niall helped Pius pick up his books. "I thought your dad didn't want you to help him study? Didn't he say it was emasculating to have his son help him with schoolwork?"

"No, what he said was, 'ain't no way I'm letting some smart-ass thirteen-year-old tell me how to do my job,'" Harper reminded them.

"That is closer, yes," Pius reluctantly agreed. "But it doesn't matter because I found a tutor for him."

Harper smiled. "Well, that's great! Then that means you're free to come with us."

"I still wanted to watch."

"There is no way Uncle Raymond is going to let you watch him get tutored."

"Well, no, I guess not…"

"So that means you're free to come with us!"

Pius didn't like the look on Harper's and Niall's faces. Those were the faces they used when they wanted him to do something he was going to regret.

***

Pius and Harper were in the middle of watching *Fresh Prince of Bel-Air* when someone knocked at the Jeddore's door and immediately let themselves in. Pius groaned, and Harper jumped to her feet. Raymond, dozing in his plaid armchair in front of the TV, didn't even stir.

"We gotta go," said Niall, stepping onto the shaggy brown carpet of their living room in his sock feet.

"But we're watching *Fresh Prince*," whined Pius.

"It's a rerun."

True. It wasn't even a new season rerun but an old episode he'd seen several times. He couldn't wait until the fall to find out what the family would do with a new baby in the house. "But my dad's tutor's going to be here any minute."

"And you said your dad didn't want you to be here when he was studying," Harper reminded him. She slapped him on the back, which hurt more than it should, and then she ran off to grab her coat.

"Well, how about we stay in my room and play Super Nintendo, then? I'm still trying to get through Sector Z in *StarFox*."

"Pius, you suck at *StarFox*. It's not going to happen," Niall reminded him. "We need you, buddy. Come on."

Pius groaned. "You still haven't told me where we're going!"

Niall shrugged.

"Which means it's going to be something I don't want to do!"

"If we don't tell you, at least you can claim plausible deniability later. Plus, you can rest easier knowing whatever trouble we get into won't be your fault."

Pius groaned again. "This is sounding worse and worse."

"Pius, hurry up and put your shoes on," Harper called from the front door.

They weren't going to let this go. They were going to keep pestering him until he agreed to come with them, and they knew he would give in eventually. He always did. Once, when they were ten, Niall had convinced Pius to pass a note for to Chad MacDonald, asking him how to beat the last guardian in *Zelda 2*. The teacher had caught Pius with the note, of course, and made him stand up and read it in front of the class.

And Harper had once forced him to eat a worm. Last week. She had claimed it was in the name of science, which is what ultimately caused him to give in. But Pius was pretty sure it was her way of getting back at him for eating the last of the Teddy Grahams cereal.

"Fine!" Pius threw up his hands. At least he didn't have to eat any invertebrates this time. He hoped. "Let me tell Dad we're leaving."

Grumbling, he stomped across the living room and gave his father a gentle shake. His dad stirred awake. "Hey, Dad, Harper, Niall, and I are going out for a bit, okay?"

Groggy, Raymond tried to look at his watch, but he couldn't seem to make his eyes focus. "What time is it? Where is your mother?"

"She has a night shift at the senior's home, remember? And your tutor is going to be here any minute. You should get up and splash some water on your face."

"Crap, that's tonight?" He rubbed his eyes with big, callused hands. His dad's hands always made Pius feel like a tiny baby. "Can't we do this some other time?"

The doorbell rang.

"That would be a no," said Harper as she turned and opened the door.

Standing on the porch was a small figure, not much taller than the kids. The hood of a grey jacket and a scarf obscured their face. The figure glanced nervously at the light over the front door. "Can I come in?" they asked. It was a woman's voice.

"Who the hell are you?" asked Harper, though she did stand aside and let the visitor in.

The woman quickly removed her head coverings to reveal unruly strawberry-blonde hair and a freckled face. "Sorry. It's getting dark, and the June bugs will be out soon."

Harper nodded in understanding. "I completely get it. Those little friggers are so gross. Hey, aren't you the lady we met last year? Jenny, right?"

"That's me!" Jenny smiled. "Jenny Oak. I work with your Uncle Raymond at Light & Power."

"Jenny?" said Raymond, approaching through the kitchen with Niall and Pius in tow. "What are you doing here?"

"Dad, Jenny's here to help you study for your exam," Pius explained. "Remember?"

Raymond swallowed hard. "I wasn't expecting... someone..."

"Young?" asked Jenny.

"Female?" asked Pius at the same time.

"Yes," answered Raymond, though it wasn't entirely clear to whom he was replying.

"Dad, Ms. Oak did all the exams and courses you're taking now. She knows her stuff. Plus, she's old like you, right?"

Niall, standing behind Pius, kicked him in the leg. Pius audibly yelped, but Jenny cut him off. "Actually, I'm twenty-five, but I did get top marks in all my fourth-year courses at Carleton University. And I was a peer tutor. I helped a ton of other students get through their programs."

"And she's doing her Master's Degree," Pius added, beaming.

His dad was growing increasingly uncomfortable, but Pius had no idea why. Pius would love to have a teacher like her.

Jenny blushed. "Well, I'm working at Light & Power now before I head back to Ottawa to finish my Master's, but yes, I am still paying the tuition fees." She awkwardly made a small fist pump. "Yay, student debt, right?"

Raymond coughed but didn't say anything.

"So, we should go," said Harper. "We'll let you two kids study."

Raymond snapped out of his daze as Pius pulled on his sneakers and prepared to leave. "Uh, right. Yeah, kids, be careful and don't be out too late. It's a school night." He turned to Jenny and grinned. "I should put on the kettle. Would you like a cup of tea?"

Harper ushered Pius and Niall out, and the screen door slammed shut behind them. She pulled her hat down tight over her head and her hood up over her ears.

"You know they don't really build nests in your hair, right?" asked Pius.

"Shut up, Pius."

"So that's Jenny?" asked Niall as they stepped down off the porch onto the front lawn. "She's kinda cute."

Harper glared at Niall so hard that Pius thought her eyeballs were going to blast laser beams through Niall's skull and spray his brains all over his mom's bleeding hearts bushes under the front window.

Weird. His best friend and his cousin were supposed to be dating, so Pius guessed it was inappropriate for Niall to be calling another girl cute in front of Harper. But Pius had never known Harper to be jealous. In fact, she was often the one to make jokes about other cute girls to make Niall squirm and feel uncomfortable. Was she upset because Jenny was much older?

Pius didn't understand women or dating, so he dropped it and returned his attention to more pressing matters. "Okay, now will you tell me where we're going?"

Harper grinned. "We're going to fight some monster demons from Uranus, duh."

CHAPTER ELEVEN

Them Bones
May 31, 6:50pm
Harmon Highway, North of Gale Harbour,
near Long Ice River

The truck was burned beyond recognition, but it was in better condition than its occupants. The two bodies inside the pickup truck were little more than piles of ash. Constable Bennett made retching sounds at the sight of them, and he had seen some pretty grotesque stuff last year. Tanguay felt a little sick herself.

"The truck was spotted by a skier earlier this evening," explained Bennett after he had regained his composure and wiped his thick moustache with the back of his uniform sleeve.

"A skier?" Marie-Ann asked. "In May?"

"Well, you know, one of those weirdos with the roller skis and the poles." Bennett made motions with his arms as if he were skiing. Or was he dancing? Marie-Ann suspected the man had never skied in his life. She supposed people did worse things than roller skiing, but it wasn't particularly safe on a dark road outside of town. There were no streetlights or buildings of any kind for several kilometres in either direction. The truck was in the ditch off the side of the road, partially obstructed by trees and brush. "Any ID?"

"The truck was rented in Halifax a week ago by a German tourist named Hans Meier. Meier and the truck came across on the ferry with another man, Klaus Fischer, last Wednesday, but no one saw them since they arrived in Port-aux-Basques."

Port-aux-Basques was the landing point of the ferry from Nova Scotia, about two hours from Gale Harbour. "That's random. Two Germans show up in Newfoundland and mysteriously explode?"

"Maybe they were listening to that European techno music and went off the road?" Now Bennett made different arm motions that Tanguay figured were supposed to be dancing, but it looked like he was trying to shake off a wet shirt that was sticking to his flabby arms.

"They didn't go off the road." She shook her head. "Not while they were alive."

"No, I know. There are no tire marks."

"And no scorch marks on the trees. The car was burned before it was dumped here."

"So, our Germans were burned, and then someone dumped their bodies here?" Bennett walked around the truck to the passenger side. He reached out and touched the door handle. "Why the hell would someone..."

"Bennett, don't touch—"

But the constable had already pulled the handle, and the door popped open. The body in the passenger seat flopped out onto the ground, the burned flesh ripping and tearing like the steaks that time someone burned and dropped the BBQ at the RCMP picnic. Coincidentally, it had been Bennett operating the grill that day, too.

"Don't touch anything until the lab guys get here!" She snapped and stomped around the truck. "*Tabernouche*, Bennett, you know better than to touch a crime scene before..." Her voice trailed off when her gaze landed on the deep-fried corpse dangling half out of the truck cab.

"Constable, what is that?"

"I believe it's an arm, boss. Though I could be wrong. Usually, it's attached to the rest of the body."

"No, I mean the markings on the bicep."

Bennett pinched his nose against the smell and leaned in for a closer look. "A tattoo? It's burned pretty bad, but it looks like a dog. A bulldog, maybe? And letters - U, S, M..."

"United States Marine Corp." Pieces were falling into place, but Marie-Ann didn't like the way they fit. A greasy rock sank into the depths of her stomach. She felt sick, but it wasn't from the stench or the sight of the smouldering corpses.

She turned on her heel and headed for her car.

"Where are you going?" Bennett asked.

"I need to go check something, and I need to talk to the inspector. When the crew gets here, tell them to contact B Division Headquarters. We need to get in touch with the CIA and tell them two of their Elevator Inspectors are dead in a ditch in backwoods Newfoundland."

CHAPTER TWELVE

Creep

May 31, 9:05 pm

They were crossing the parking lot of the Foodland supermarket shortly after dark, dodging some dick doing donuts in a Trans Am, when Pius asked for the hundredth time: "Where are we going?"

"To watch idiots get drunk and rev their engines in the parking lot, duh," replied Harper.

Pius knew Harper well enough to guess she was being sarcastic.

"Harper, we can stop messing with him," said Niall. "We're here now anyway."

Pius was horrified. He looked back and forth between his cousin and best friend, panic rising in his chest. "We're here? You mean we're really going to watch these Neanderthals hanging out in the parking lot?"

Niall cringed. "No, Pius, I meant Tim Hortons." He pointed to the glowing sign across the street. "That's where we're going."

"Why? You don't even like coffee. I saw you try to drink coffee once, and you spit it all over Craig Muise."

Harper guffawed. "Oh, and here I thought I was special."

Niall's cheeks flushed, but he did his best to soldier on. "We're here to see Anna and Keenan."

It took Pius a moment to register their names. "Those goth weirdos you met the other night? The ones who were following Theolina like groupies? Why are we here to see them?"

They exchanged a look Pius didn't quite understand. How were they getting so good at exchanging wordless communication? As far as he knew, they hadn't even kissed yet! He was Harper's cousin and Niall's best friend—he should be the one who understood them better.

"We think there's something about to happen in Gale Harbour," explained Niall. "Something bad. Like Psycho-Hose-Beast-levels of bad."

Pius fought down the fear trying to crush his windpipe. "How do you know?"

"Anna and Keenan have been studying Theolina's old journals," said Harper. "They think they found hints that butt monkeys are going to fly down from space and kill everyone."

"Why didn't you tell me? We need to… wait, flying butt monkeys?" After everything that happened last year, Pius was not going to discount the chance of a supernatural invader. However, butt monkeys sounded a bit far-fetched.

They crossed Main Street, entering the parking lot of Tim Hortons.

A crackling voice came from the drive-thru speaker a few metres away: "No sir, I can't take the filling out of the jelly donut. Do you just want a plain donut?"

Niall sighed. "It might be a bad translation, but either way. Something is happening. Look, I think that's their car. We'll explain everything—"

Suddenly, Harper screamed and bolted toward a green station wagon parked a few spaces away and jumped into the backseat.

Pius instinctively fell to the asphalt and covered his head with his hands. "Is it the butt monkeys?"

Niall pulled him back to his feet and pointed to the street lamp overhead and the cloud of black insect shadows buzzing around the fluorescent halo.

"June bugs?" Pius asked, hoping the dampness on his jeans was due to something he'd fallen on and not because he'd wet himself. "I can't believe the one thing in the world she's afraid of is June bugs!"

"Dude, you're one to talk." Niall brushed a cigarette butt off Pius' shoulder. "You're afraid of dryer lint."

"Dryer lint is highly combustible!" He couldn't believe Niall was so blasé about fire safety. "Did you know that over five hundred house fires are caused in Canada every year by improperly cleaned lint traps and dryer exhausts?"

Niall shook his head. "Get in the car, Pius."

Pius usually wouldn't hop into the car of strangers, but he didn't want to be left alone outside with those rednecks in the Foodland parking lot across the street, either. Grudgingly, he slid into the backseat when Niall opened the door, feeling like a criminal being shuffled into a police car by a cop.

A moment later, he found himself squeezed into the worn, threadbare seat between Harper and Niall. In the front seat, two strangers turned back to stare at him—a pale, large-chested woman wearing way too much make-up and a greasy-looking weirdo with a pock-marked nose and a top hat.

"You must be Pius?" asked the girl.

Pius wanted to jump out of the car. He did not do well in confined spaces. Or with strangers. Especially strangers wearing black lipstick who knew his name.

Harper squeezed his hand but said nothing. No mockery, no name-calling, just a subtle sign to show that she was there with him and he didn't need to be afraid. It was such a shocking display of concern and empathy from her that Pius was too stunned to be scared. At least momentarily.

"Yeah?" he replied.

"I'm Anna. This is my boyfriend, Keenan." The inside of her black lips was pink. It was so disconcerting. "I guess if Harper and Niall brought you back here, you guys must have believed us after all."

"We believe something is happening," Niall confirmed. "We saw too much last year to brush this all off."

"Tell us about the butt monkeys," demanded Harper.

Anna's face went blank. At a loss for words, she glanced at Keenan but found no help there, so she turned back to Harper. "What are you talking about?"

"The butt monkeys. I read it in your journal."

"So you did take my journal!" Anna's face lit up. She slapped her boyfriend on the arm hard enough that he winced. "I told you I didn't leave it in the McDonald's washroom!"

"I just suggested you might have left it there. You're the one who went in and threatened to cut the manager's throat for stealing it."

Please tell me they're kidding, thought Pius.

"Anyway..." said Anna as she slowly shifted her gaze back to them. "Let's look at the book and figure out what we're dealing with. Hopefully, with your help, we can piece together exactly what's supposed to happen on Friday."

Harper and Niall looked at each other nervously but wouldn't meet anyone else's gaze. Finally, Harper muttered, "We can't."

"We can't what?" asked Anna.

"We can't give you the book. We don't have it."

"Did you leave it at home or... "

"Our principal took it," Niall blurted out.

Anna's face went slack, and she became even paler. One of her grey eyes twitched. "We can get it back, right?"

Pius felt a burning sensation rising in his throat. "Is that why you guys were in detention? Of course, he's not going to give it back. Mr. Bourgeois never gives anything back! I saw him take a kid's photo album of baby pictures and throw it in the trash for reading during an assembly!"

"He still has my brother's Faith No More 'Real Thing' tape from like four years ago," added Niall.

Anna ran her hands through her jet-black hair. She was breathing hard. "This is bad."

"We still have the original journal," said Keenan. "Can't you translate it again?"

Anna gave him another glare that could have disintegrated a small animal. "You know it took me months to translate that book! Theolina's handwriting and grammar were atrocious. I could never... Where does Mr. Bourgeois live?"

"Why?" asked Niall. "What are you going to do?"

Anna rolled her eyes. "I don't need to go into details, but let's just say it involves pliers, his fingernails, and maybe a straight razor."

Harper nodded. "Sweet."

"No!" Pius couldn't believe they were talking like this. "This is not acceptable!"

"Then I'll break into the school and get it," said Keenan, as if it wasn't a big deal.

First, Harper lost this important book that didn't even belong to her, and now these random people they didn't know were talking about breaking into their school and torturing their principal?

"Let's go," said Harper.

Keenan shook his head. "I'll need to get a couple of things. It's easy, but I need the right tools. We can do it tomorrow night. Do you know where he might keep the book?"

"Probably in his office," said Harper. "There's a rumour there's a whole cabinet full of confiscated stuff in there."

"What's the layout of the offices? It would help to have a plan of the building or at least some good directions."

"I can go with you, but Pius knows the offices and teacher areas the best. He's on all the junior school councils and clubs. They're in there after school all the time. Can you draw us a map of the principal and secretary's office?"

"No!" Pius barked, unable to control his rage. "You can't break into the school!"

"Pius, we need the book. It may tell us how to deal with the butt monkeys."

"We don't know what's going to happen or even *if* anything is going to happen. I certainly don't think it's going to be 'butt monkeys'..."

"But it could be."

"I can't believe you, Harper. You know breaking in and stealing is wrong. And it's our school! We have to go back there the next day and every day for the next five years! What if we get caught?"

"It's not stealing," said Anna. "The book belongs to me. And I'm sure Keenan won't do that much damage."

Keenan shrugged and made a non-committal nod.

"No! This is crazy. Niall, you don't think this is a good idea, do you?"

Niall sighed. He was looking at his hands in his lap, unable to meet Pius' gaze. "Pius, what if they're right? I keep hoping this is all made up, but if it isn't, and there's another monster out there, people could die. A lot of people. Isn't it worth the risk?"

Pius couldn't believe it. First, his best friend and his cousin started spending all this time together without him. Then, they started getting into trouble, getting detention, and lying to him about what happened. Now, they were talking about committing actual crimes? And asking him to help them? He didn't even know them anymore!

"Let me out of the car!" He was on the verge of tears but didn't want to show it in front of strangers. Sure, Harper and Niall had seen him cry plenty of times, but no need for anyone else to have a low opinion of him. He tried first to get by on Harper's side, but she put up a hand and held him back easily. He went the other way to get out and had to physically climb over Niall, but at least Niall didn't try to stop him.

He stormed off into the night. They called after him, but he didn't look back. Harper said something about Pius being afraid of the dark, which was true, but he didn't care. He was getting the hell away from these people he didn't know anymore. He would figure out how to get home by following the streetlights. At least the June bugs buzzing overhead would keep Harper from following him.

***

A half-hour later, Pius made it home to find his mother screaming at his father on the lawn.

They lived on a quiet, wooded street called Townview, where nothing interesting or exciting happened. Tonight, Pius thought there must have been an accident or a fire to break their streak of uninterrupted boringness. When he saw his father in his underwear and his mother standing on the front porch throwing clothes at him, he ran toward them. Then he heard what she was saying, and he immediately slowed down.

"I can't believe you!" Her voice was hoarse. "In our bed, Ray. In our bed! I come home from work, and this is what I find?"

His mom was still dressed in her peach nurse scrubs. There was vomit on her pants. His dad wore white briefs, and his thick belly hung over his scrawny, hairy legs.

His dad was sobbing and pleading. "Samantha, honey, it didn't mean anything. It was an accident..."

"An accident?" She howled. "You fell into our bed naked with a teenager by accident?"

"Jenny's not a teenager, Samantha. She's twenty-five. And it didn't mean anything. We were studying, and it just happened. Can we please go inside and talk about this? The neighbours are watching!"

"I don't care about the Jesus neighbours! I care that you had another woman in our bed! Where are the kids? Did you kick them out so you could sleep with that little slut?"

"Samantha, please..."

"I'm so stupid. So stupid. I suspected you'd been fooling around for years, but I never said anything. I never dreamed I'd come home to find you in bed with another woman!"

"Aunt Samantha?"

The voice came from behind Pius. Pius had forgotten he was in the world for a moment. None of what he was watching was real. It couldn't be. It felt like he was watching *Melrose Place* or *90210*. It couldn't be his parents standing out on the lawn, his dad half-naked, yelling and screaming about the woman Pius had invited into their home.

Harper's voice had drawn him out of his daze. She and Niall stood behind him on the street. They must have followed him home from Tim Hortons.

Pius' mom and dad froze. A long moment of silence fell over the mad scene on the end of Townview Street. His dad shuffled uncomfortably.

His mom started to cry again. "Pius. Harper. Please come into the house."

"Pius, please let me explain..." said his dad.

Pius tried not to look at anybody. He couldn't imagine looking anyone in the face right now. "Niall, can I stay at your place tonight?"

"Yeah, yeah, of course."

Pius immediately turned and headed back down the street in the direction of Niall's house. Niall and Harper fell in behind him, but no one spoke. The only other sound was his mother sobbing on the front porch.

CHAPTER THIRTEEN

Mister Please
May 31, 8:10pm
Trans-Canada Highway, South of Gale Harbour

Sergeant Tanguay stopped at a gas station on the highway to use a pay phone to call her CO directly. This was a conversation she didn't want to have on the radio.

She pumped the phone full of quarters, dialled the RCMP headquarters in St. John's, and asked to speak to the inspector. When she told them who she was, the constable on the switchboard "tsked," and for a moment, Tanguay thought she wasn't going to put her through. Finally, after some muttering under her breath, the woman connected her, and the inspector's gruff voice came through loud and clear.

"Sergeant Tanguay, this had better be important."

"Inspector Williams, I found the bomb."

"Tanguay, stop talking crazy nonsense."

"No, sir, I found it!"

"You have visual confirmation that there's an atomic bomb in Gale Harbour?" The inspector's voice dripped with incredulity and disdain.

Marie-Ann gritted her teeth. "It's not right in front of me, no. I'm on my way to secure it now. But I've had multiple eye-witness confirmations, and I've seen photographs of it."

"So, it's like your monsters from last year?" Marie-Ann could hear the mocking condescension in his tone. "Lots of hearsay and no actual evidence?"

Marie-Ann bit her tongue to prevent herself from swearing at him. Williams knew everything that happened was true. It was *his* superiors who had told him not to discuss it. To destroy any evidence. Had he buried the truth so thoroughly that he'd forgotten himself? Or was he—more likely—condescending to her because she was the one female sergeant in the province? An anomaly and oddity that was amusing but not to be taken seriously.

"Sir, I will have the evidence in less than an hour. I need you to be ready because this could be dangerous. We need to contact Ottawa and National Defence and have them stand by—"

"Oh, like how I should contact the CIA and ask them about their Elevator Investigators?"

Dammit. Cheryl had already called him about that. "Inspector, I know it sounds crazy, but there's something fishy going on with those men. I think the bodies we found are the real CIA agents, and the suspects I've been following stole their names and files. I believe they're looking for the bomb."

Williams sighed, and Tanguay could feel his contempt through the phone line. "These mysterious villains killed two foreign secret agents looking for a bomb in backwater Newfoundland? A bomb that's been hidden under Gale Harbour for thirty years? Sergeant, I'm getting tired of your crazy theories and wild goose chases. You will drop this case immediately. Do you hear me? Or else there will be consequences."

"Yes, sir," Tanguay hissed through gritted teeth. She slammed the payphone receiver down on the hook, then picked it up and slammed it down harder. She let loose a string of French profanities that would have made her grandfather—a lumberjack who never set foot in a church for fear he would burst into flames—proud.

She stormed out of the phone booth, climbed back into her car, yanked the door, and rested her head on the steering wheel, breathing deeply and trying to keep her anger in check. Williams knew all about the weird shit that went down in Gale Harbour, but he was a gutless coward who towed the management line without question and was a misogynist bastard on top of it. She had met plenty of men exactly like him in her years on the force. Not every white-haired man in a position of authority was an asshole, but in her experience, an awful lot of them were.

She hesitated for a few moments longer before she peeled out of the gas station parking lot, back onto the wooded highway in the direction of Robinsons.

***

Tanguay arrived at Jesso's cabin half an hour later and parked on the dirt road leading up to the property. There was no lock on the gate, so she let herself in and continued up toward the cabin on foot. From a distance, the cabin looked uninteresting and secure. It was a small, single-story building with dark trim and a wide deck. It looked like a nice place to while away summer evenings, drinking with friends and neighbours. Behind the cabin was a large structure with double barn-style doors, and even from a hundred metres away, Tanguay could tell there was something wrong.

Fresh truck tire tracks marked the dirt driveway. She couldn't tell exactly how old, but it had rained yesterday morning, so they must have been made since then. Someone had driven straight up to the shed. She followed the tracks and saw that the vehicle—probably a cube van—had backed into the shed.

The large doors were still cracked open. The padlocks had been smashed and tossed carelessly into the mud.

This was an unfortunate turn of events. Who the hell had been in there? Were they still in there? If she suspected illegal entry, she could investigate, but what if it were those two thugs in black? She had no idea who they were or what they were capable of. And her CO had explicitly told her not to pursue this case. Still, if there was a nuclear bomb in there, she couldn't very well let those two—whoever they were—just walk out with it.

To hell with it. Neither the *salauds* nor Williams were as scary as an other-worldly monster from beneath the sea.

She approached the open door cautiously, keeping her hand near her sidearm. "This is the RCMP! Is there anyone inside? Identify yourself!"

There was silence for a moment and then a crash as something was knocked to the floor.

Someone or something was inside. Great. And they weren't answering her. She should call for backup, but if it turned out to be nothing and Williams found out what she was doing, she would be in it deep. So, there was nothing to do but check it out herself, like usual. She got herself into so many tight situations this way.

"This is the RCMP!" she called again. "I'm entering the building!"

With her back against one of the barn doors, she reached out and shoved the other one open. She hoped that if there were any trigger-happy idiots inside, they would shoot wildly and reveal their position. But no shots came. Taking a deep breath, she pulled a small flashlight off her belt and peered around the door into the dark, cavernous garage.

Nothing but snowmobiles and ATVs. She wasn't sure what Jesso did for a living, but he must have done well to own so many recreational vehicles. Perhaps some of them belonged to friends or relatives.

"Hello? Is there anyone here?"

Still no answer.

Tanguay stepped inside, and something didn't feel right to her. Not necessarily that there was a crazed shooter in the rafters with a rifle, but something. Still, she glanced up at the high ceiling. There were a few good places a sniper could be hiding, but she didn't spot any.

She moved slowly between the tightly parked vehicles. Truck tire marks on the dirt floor caught her eye, and footprints indicated someone had gotten out and loaded something into the truck. She had a pretty good idea what they had taken, though she didn't want to admit it.

There were a dozen high-quality vehicles in that shed, some of them worth over ten grand, easy. Not a single one of them was touched. The one thing she couldn't find was what she had come looking for. The one thing she desperately needed to find and prove existed. The one thing that was more valuable than everything in that building combined.

"*Tabernac!*" she wailed, slamming her fist onto the side of a black racing snowmobile.

Another noise banged behind her.

She whirled, drawing her gun in a smooth motion. Her flashlight beam fell on a three-legged red fox hiding under a four-wheel ATV next to a knocked-over gasoline can. It froze in terror before running past Tanguay and out the door.

This was getting worse by the minute. Not only was her proof gone, but the bomb was missing, too. There was an excellent chance Stone and Koch had it, but to what end? And Williams had explicitly told her not to investigate this, so she couldn't even go to him with her suspicions.

She searched the rest of the barn and the property but didn't find any further clues. Her mood was black, and she was still unsure what to do. She returned to her car and headed back toward Gale Harbour. Her one option was to go to Jesso and tell him his garage had been robbed. If he filed a police report, she could at least continue her investigation officially. Assuming Jesso was willing to report anything stolen in the first place.

She was less than fifteen minutes out of Robinsons when her radio crackled. She reached for it with a sigh. "Go for Tanguay."

It was Cheryl at dispatch. "Sergeant, Inspector Williams wants you to call him right away."

"I'm en route back to Gale Harbour. I should be at the detachment in about forty-five minutes."

"I don't think he can wait."

What the hell? Did he know what she'd been up to? Of course, she wasn't surprised he suspected she would go against orders, but there was no way he could have found out about her trip to Jesso's cabin yet. It must be about something she'd done previously. Tanguay wracked her brain for anything she may have done to piss off her boss. Honestly, there were a few.

A few minutes later, Tanguay pulled off at the same Irving gas station she stopped at on the way down and walked up to the same payphone. What the hell was so important? It was getting dark. The administration in St. John's should have been closed. Still, when she dialled, the operator picked up immediately and put her straight through to the inspector.

Williams picked up after one ring. "Tanguay." He spoke before she had even introduced herself.

"Yes, sir?" She didn't know what else to say. The inspector had her entirely off guard.

"Tomorrow morning, a pair of gentlemen will be arriving in Gale Harbour. One is an officer from the Royal Canadian Air Force representing the Department of National Defence, and the other is an American visiting from the CIA Elevator Inspection Division."

"What?"

"Please don't interrupt. The two other men in the area claiming to be from the CIA are imposters. They should be considered armed and extremely dangerous. The two visiting agents will have the suspects' complete files. They have full permission and authorization from DND, the RCMP, and the Prime Minister's office to track down these two suspects. You are to assist them in their investigation and give them access to all the detachment's resources."

This was the last thing Tanguay expected. What could have turned Inspector Williams around so quickly? An hour ago, he had torn her a new one about this case, and now she was supposed to follow along with these strangers?

"Sir, I don't understand, why did—"

"You have your orders, Sergeant. Be standing by tomorrow morning. They will contact you."

The inspector hung up.

Huh. His own higher-up must have chewed him out. Marie-Ann could tell by his curt, clipped way of speaking that he was angry. An older, whiter man must have given him new orders.

Whatever. Tanguay would take it. Even if it meant a Yank and an air cadet stepping all over her jurisdiction, at least they could, hopefully, finally get to the bottom of this case.

<u>CHAPTER FOURTEEN</u>

Trout
Tuesday, June 1, 9:55 am

"So, in short, if you have sex, you will get AIDS and die."

Mrs. Butt put down her chalk and brushed the white dust from her hands. She adjusted the glasses on the end of her crooked nose. Behind her on the blackboard were half a dozen crudely drawn depictions of reproductive organs and how-to-diagrams of vaguely human-shaped blobs having intercourse.

In the class in front of her, twenty-two students sat in deathly silence. Their eyes were glassy, their dreams crushed, their burgeoning adolescent libidos smashed under the heel of her sensible black flats.

You would think that Sex Ed taught by a woman named Mrs. Butt would be funny, but it was not. It absolutely was not.

"That was horrifying," hissed Craig Muise.

Sitting next to him, Harry, Mrs. Butt's unfortunately-named son, was trying to dig a hole under his desk to crawl into and die.

The bell rang, and Niall grabbed his books and bolted for the door along with his classmates. He wasn't sure about the rest of them, but he needed a shower after that... whatever that was.

"That was disturbing..." said Harper, falling into step with him.

"I don't think I'm going to sleep tonight." Niall's mind kept drifting back to the nightmare-inducing pictures of sexually transmitted diseases in the video Mrs. Butt had shown them.

"So, no nocturnal emissions tonight?" Harper teased, using the term Mrs. Butt had introduced to numerous sniggers.

Niall was too numb from the constant stream of oozing pustules to be embarrassed. "Nope. Not ever again. How can someone possibly make sex so un-sexy?"

"I was invited to Harry's birthday party next week," said Pius, walking beside them down the hall toward their lockers. "How am I supposed to look Mrs. Butt in the eye?"

"So, you're finally talking again?" Niall asked as they reached their lockers. Pius had slept at his house, but he hadn't said a word all night or over breakfast. They had decided to give him space while he processed the previous night's drama with his parents, and so far, he had taken all the space and more.

Harper had stayed over as well, on the couch in the downstairs rec room as far from Niall as physically possible. Niall'd had conflicted fantasies about her last night. Conflicted because they were still afraid to touch each other. All those thoughts were long gone out of his head, courtesy of Mrs. Butt.

"Sorry, I..." Pius stuck his head in his locker, and his voice trailed off.

Harper sighed. She leaned against the locker next to him. "I get it. Trust me. I know all about having messed-up relationships with your parents, but you'll need to talk to them eventually."

"I just... I can't right now..."

"We can't live at Niall's house," continued Harper. "Nelson is so gross. He clipped his toenails at the breakfast table this morning."

"That's better than when he wakes up screaming in the middle of the night," said Pius. "That guy must have some messed-up nightmares. Plus, sometimes Niall trims his nails at the ta—oof!"

Niall opened his own locker door and "accidentally" bumped Pius in the face. He didn't do it *that* hard. Despite his current confusing emotions, he didn't want to turn Harper off completely.

Pius peeked around the door and glared, then he noticed something behind Niall and disappeared back into the locker.

"What are you doing?"

"It's Mrs. Walsh," Pius hissed.

Niall turned and saw the hawk-nosed drama teacher approaching. Her head was held so high her beak was inches from touching the ceiling. Today, she was wearing a rainbow-coloured shawl.

"She freaks me out. Pretend I'm not here."

"Children," she said. The word was weighed down with more meaning than anyone had ever placed on it. It was at the same time irrationally chipper, condescending, irritated, and remorseful of so many choices she'd made in her own life. "Have you seen Brian Hawco?"

"Who, Skidmark?" asked Harper.

Mrs. Walsh shuddered. She was likely the one person in town who refused to use his nickname. Even the social worker who visited the family while his dad was undergoing substance abuse rehab called Brian "Skidmark."

"Yes, him. My Properties Master."

"I haven't seen him all day," admitted Niall. "Maybe he's out sick?"

"Mr. Kiebbler said he was in homeroom this morning, but no one has seen him since. He has a number of my properties and costumes that we need for rehearsal after school."

Odd. While it was not uncommon for Skidmark to fake being sick to get out of school (he once told the other kids he kept a bottle of ipecac under his bed to fake the stomach flu), he never missed a play rehearsal.

"If you see him, be sure to tell him I'm looking for him."

She was already turning around and walking away when Harper replied, "Why? You're not even a real teacher." Mrs. Walsh must not have heard her because that would have brought her ire upon them, real teacher or not.

Pius cringed. "Harper! You're going to get us in trouble!"

"From her? But she's not a real teacher!"

"She still frightens me."

Without warning, someone came up behind Pius and shoved him face-first into the lockers.

"What the hell?" Harper barked, whirling on the assailant.

A crowd of gathered kids "oh-ed" at the sight.

Pius went down hard. Niall immediately went to his knees next to him. His glasses were broken, and a trickle of blood dripped from a gash on the side of his cheek.

"Which one of you assholes ratted me out?" yelled Keith Doucette, dressed in an oversized Toronto Maple Leafs jersey and sweatpants. Spittle dripped from his braces.

Keith? It couldn't be. Perhaps a year ago, but current Keith wouldn't cheap-shot Pius like that. He was their friend now. Wasn't he?

"Pius?" Niall asked, trying to get him to his feet. "Are you okay?"

"I'm... I'm..." Pius was having trouble finding words, and his eyes were unfocused. How hard had he hit his head?

"You stupid dipwad, what do you think you're doing?" Harper yelled back, and Niall realized she was standing right up in Keith's face. Niall was going to end up with two of his friends smeared across the floor. He stood and stepped next to Harper.

Keith was fuming, and he looked like crap. His eyes were red, his face was flushed, and his greasy brown hair was all messed up, showing off the mutilated ear he usually kept hidden. And he smelled like... Uncle Herbert? The angry drunk who, whenever Niall's mom saw him coming, would lock the door and hide in the back of the house?

"Which one of you told on me?" Keith demanded again.

"What are you talking about?" Niall tried to maneuver himself between Keith and Harper. Keith had punched him once before when he stood up for her, so Niall certainly had reservations, but he also didn't want to see Harper claw Keith's eyes out.

"Someone told Principal Bourgeois that I was drinking at practice, and he told Coach Campbell, so Coach Campbell kicked me off all school teams!"

"You *have* been drinking," argued Harper. "You smell like the floor of the Black Bowler!"

The Black Bowler was a club down on Main Street, near Tim Hortons and Jerry's Video Shack. Niall had no idea how Harper knew what their floor smelled like, but he guessed it was an accurate comparison because Keith reeked.

"He kicked me off the softball team! My mom was coming to watch me play next week!"

Niall tried to be the voice of reason. "Look, Keith, I know you're mad, but I'm sure it wasn't Pius who ratted you out." What Niall wanted to say was anyone with two eyes and a working nose could have figured out you're drunk, but he bit his tongue. "Pius is terrified of you. He would never have done something to risk pissing you off."

"So you did it? Since you got a girlfriend now, you think you're all tough, and you don't need to be scared of me anymore?"

"Ah, screw off," said Harper. "That doesn't even make any sense!"

Niall *was* terrified of Keith and wondered if he could use the same trick he'd used against Sally Alexander at The Hangar. He would need Harper's blood, true, and he didn't want to hurt Keith since he was probably drunk and not acting like himself, but he also *really* didn't want Keith to hurt *him*, either.

Ultimately, Niall didn't need to decide because Pius launched himself off the floor and landed on Keith. He flailed with the most ridiculous and ineffective punches anyone had seen since The Brooklyn Brawler wrestled Razor Ramon on Maple Leaf Superstars a few months ago. Still, he caught Keith off guard, and they went down. Keith smashed his head against the lockers, and Pius ended up on top of him.

By now, the gathered crowd of kids had started to whoop and holler at the promised excitement of ringside seats, so Niall knew it would be mere moments before a teacher came to break it up. Before he even tried to pull the two of them apart, the booming and unmistakable voice of Principal Bourgeois came from down the hall.

"Mister Jeddore! Mister Doucette! What do you think you're doing?"

The gathered crowd fell silent.

Keith quickly crawled out from under Pius, shoving the much smaller kid away with one hand.

"Ah, crap," whispered Harper.

Mr. Bourgeois materialized beside them in a heartbeat. How that giant man moved so fast, Niall had no idea. Did he have magic powers, too? He grabbed Keith and Pius each with one hand and yanked them to their feet with frightening strength. He pulled on Pius so hard Niall was afraid he was going to break Pius' arm.

"Mister Jeddore, I expected better from you." His voice dripped with such disgust and disdain it made Niall's skin crawl. Still, he had to speak up for his best friend.

"Sir, Pius has some problems at home right now, I'm sure he didn't mean—"

The principal shot Niall such a look that it could have made small animals keel over, die, and shrivel up into mummified piles of fur and bone. Niall's words died in his throat.

"I don't care if someone murdered his father in front of him. You do not behave that way in school."

Several voices gasped at the principal's words. Niall couldn't believe the heartless son of a bitch would say something like that right in front of Harper. He had to know, right? He couldn't have said that by accident?

Niall looked at Harper. The mixture of shock, horror, anger, and sadness on her face was indescribable. He didn't know if she was about to burst into tears or attack Mr. Bourgeois herself.

"And Mister Doucette," continued the principal, oblivious to the pain he had caused. "You were in my office moments ago. I explained to you how thin the ice was beneath your feet. I guess you want to be expelled, do you?"

Keith sobered up immediately and started rambling. "No, sir, please. I made a mistake. I didn't mean to hurt anyone. You can't..."

"Too late, Mr. Doucette." He dragged the boys off down the hall toward his office.

Niall stood beside Harper as the crowd dispersed. He put his arm around her, and for the first time in days, she didn't push him away.

<u>**CHAPTER FIFTEEN**</u>

Cannonball

June 1, 3:30 pm

That day after school, Niall and Harper waited for Pius to get out of detention. He got out much earlier than they had the day before. Either his previous track record resulted in a lighter sentence, or, in Mr. Bourgeois' peculiar moral system, *Dungeons & Dragons* was a more serious offence than fighting in the school halls. Pius' eyes widened at the sight of them, but Niall reminded him that he had done the same for them. Behind his masking tape-repaired glasses, Pius looked ready to break down into tears.

Harper checked the Band-Aid over the gash on Pius' face, then patted him on the head. "Come on, one detention isn't going to ruin your chances of getting into university or anything."

They were walking home from the high school, crossing Harmon Highway on the North side of town, on their way to Niall's house, when Pius said, "Thank you guys for waiting for me. I can't believe anyone would care about me right now."

That sounded strange to Niall. Pius might have been afraid of everything, but he never suffered from low self-esteem. He had certain things he was good at, and he was proud of them.

"Pius, don't be hard on yourself. You think we're not going to like you because you punched out Keith? He deserves to be taken down a peg or two."

Pius was quiet for a long time. He had a strange look on his face that Niall couldn't quite read. As they walked down Ventnor Avenue, Pius finally said: "I can't believe I did that to Keith."

"I can't believe you got detention." Harper laughed. She tossed her long, black braid in the way that Niall loved. "You've never been in trouble before."

Pius shook his head. "I had to stay behind in fifth grade to fix Cindy Lamond's science project."

"No," said Niall. "Scott Legge got detention for breaking her project and had to stay after school to fix it. You volunteered to stay and help to make sure he put it back together properly."

"Scott had no idea how to fix an electromagnet! I didn't want Cindy to get a bad grade."

Harper snickered again. "You always had a crush on her."

Pius twisted his face in disgust. "Ew, no. I had an interest in science and preserving what is right and fair. Cindy had the best chance to beat me. I didn't want to win the science fair by default."

"You still won," Niall reminded him.

"Yes, but I felt better about it."

"And Cindy's been giving you goo-goo eyes ever since," added Harper.

They turned onto Niall's street and cut across the neighbour's lawn to get to his house. Old Mrs. White hated it when they did that, but telling thirteen-year-olds not to do something was the most surefire way to keep them doing it. To be fair, Pius didn't know she had told Niall to stop cutting across her yard. If he did, he would have been mortified.

The O'Neill family's Chevy was up on blocks in their driveway. Nana Josephine, dressed in grease-stained overalls with her grey-white hair pulled back from her face, was crawling out from under the vehicle. She smiled and waved as they approached but didn't turn away from her task.

"Your parents will be home soon!" she called out to the kids. "Don't eat anything to ruin your supper!"

Niall's mother had insisted Nana come live with them after last year's events; she didn't exactly trust to leave her at the senior's home anymore. Nana could have lived on her own after getting her memories back, but Niall didn't mind having her around. The whole family loved her, and not just because she did the housework and chores of three people. After her near-death experience last year, she had been invigorated with the energy of a woman a fraction of her age. That energy translated into love and support, as well as cooking, cleaning, sewing, replacing the shed's roof, and installing winter tires on the car.

"Isn't Nelson home?" asked Harper. "Why is your grandmother changing the oil on the car?"

"She doesn't trust him to do it. And she says the garage always rips us off."

They stepped onto Niall's porch and kicked off their sneakers. Nana Josephine's fluffy yellow cat, Joey Smallwood, came out to greet them. He curled around Niall's ankles, Harper patted him on the head, and then the cat hissed at Pius.

"Get away from me, you flea-bitten, walking allergen," Pius hissed back.

Harper shook her head and laughed. "That cat loves everybody. I don't understand why it doesn't like you."

"Because it knows I can't stand it! If it touches me, I'll break out in hives!"

They entered the kitchen, and Niall grabbed three plastic cups from the cupboard and handed around a bottle of Sunny Delight from the fridge.

Harper slammed back her drink and said, "So, when are you going to talk to your parents?"

She certainly knew how to kill the conversation in a room. Pius froze, with his cup of juice still at his lips. Bright orange fluid dribbled down his chin. He lowered his drink and wiped his face with the back of his hand. "I'm not going to."

"Pius, they're your parents. I know you're mad at them, but you can't ignore them forever."

"I don't want to talk about it." He turned as if he would walk away but then hesitated. He turned to go to Niall's room, then spun to head downstairs, and ultimately just stopped and stared at the wall.

Harper turned to Niall for support. "Help me out. Tell him he has to talk to his parents."

Niall wished she hadn't dragged him into this. He agreed with Harper, but at the same time, if he'd come home and found his parents half-naked and arguing on the front lawn, he'd be pretty upset, too.

"We should give him time—"

"How much time? We have no idea what's going on at his house. His parents are freaked out and upset. Yes, Uncle Raymond screwed up, and Aunt Samantha's angry, but I guarantee you they're worried about Pius and want to talk to him."

"No, they aren't," said Pius, softly.

"Oh, come off it. Get over yourself. They love you. They're mad at each other."

"They hate me." Pius started to cry.

Niall opened his mouth to speak, then closed it again. He didn't know what to say. What the hell was Pius talking about?

Oblivious, Harper pushed on. "Are you mental? Or just stupid? I know stuff is messed up right now, and it's going to suck for a while, but you need to talk to them. At least you *can* talk to them, Pius. Not all of us have parents we can yell at or forgive whenever we want to."

"It was my fault!" Pius blurted out, practically screaming in her face. Tears streamed down his cheeks. "I'm the one who brought Jenny Oak over! I was the one who badgered my dad until he agreed to go to school and get a tutor! If I hadn't done that, he wouldn't have slept with Jenny, and my mom wouldn't have kicked him out!"

Harper stepped back. Her big dark eyes were wide with shock. Niall felt like he had been kicked in the gut, too. Surely Pius couldn't believe that?

"You're kidding, right?" Harper asked, incredulous. "Pius, you're a smart guy, but that's the dumbest thing I've ever heard you say."

Pius, biting back a scream and flailing his hands in impotent rage, spun around and tried to storm off, but he nearly ran headlong into Nelson, who was coming around the corner from the dining room.

Nelson looked a lot like Niall, except taller, leaner, better-looking, and with fewer pimples. He had recently turned eighteen and was on the verge of graduating high school. He looked down at Pius, who was half his height. "Jesus, Pius, that sucks. Sorry, I didn't mean to listen in. I mean, I did, but I didn't mean to hear about something so personal."

"Get out, Nelson," Niall growled.

Nelson smirked. "Did he say it was Jenny Oak? Do you know she used to babysit us?"

Harper and Pius glared at him.

Niall jumped back. "What? No, she didn't. I don't know her!"

"Nah, you probably don't remember. I think I was about eight at the time, so you would have been three. Jeez, I wonder if she ever babysat you, Pius? Wouldn't that be messed up?"

Pius' red face turned green.

Niall felt his own anger rise. No one knew how to push buttons like an older brother. "Holy crap, Nelson, can you frig off? Please?"

Nelson laughed. "No, you're right. I'm sorry your dad's a lech. Still, Jenny was pretty cute, though. Is she still hot?"

Harper snatched the phone book off the counter and hurled it at Nelson's head.

He batted it away with ease—he was a pretty good goaltender—and laughed. "I'm off to work. Mom and Dad will be home soon, so stay out of trouble, okay?" He grabbed his car keys and slipped out; the screen door slammed behind him.

The second he was gone, the phone started ringing.

"What a massive dickweed," Harper hissed. "He's going to be pissed when he realizes the car is up on blocks."

Niall wanted to do something but didn't know what. "Pius, I'm sorry, don't listen to him."

The phone kept ringing.

Niall felt like he should hug him, but they didn't really do that...

Harper waved at him to get his attention. "Niall, answer the phone."

He grabbed the receiver off the kitchen counter, glad of the reprieve. "Hello?"

There was a weird whisper on the other end of the line.

"Hello?"

More mumbling.

"Who is this?"

Harper was talking quietly to Pius at the kitchen table. Niall tried to hear what they were saying and was half-paying attention to the phone call.

There was a muffled reply on the other end of the line that sounded like words, but he couldn't make it out.

"I'm sorry, I can't hear you... Skidmark, is that you? Do you have a towel over the phone receiver again?"

"No, I'm whispering."

It was definitely Skidmark. Niall recognized his nasally wheeze.

"I'm using the phone from the nightstand, and I'm hiding under a bed. I can't talk."

"Then why did you call me? Wait, no, why are you under a bed?"

"It's a long story."

Becoming more interested in the story on the phone, Niall turned his full attention to the call.

"I've never known you to shy away from long stories." Niall had once listened to Skidmark explain why he had chosen to play a fighter instead of a ranger in *D&D* for *four hours*. "And why weren't you in school today?"

"I told you, I'm hiding under a bed."

"The whole day?"

"No, for a while, I was in the closet, but it smelled like dirty boots in there. It reminded me too much of when my mom punished me for swearing by making me sleep with my dad's steel-toes boots beside my pillow. Look, can you call the cops?"

The cops? Now, Niall started to get worried. Pius and Harper must have noticed something was wrong because they turned their attention to him, too. "Brian, what are your parents doing to you? Should I call Child Services?"

"No, I'm hiding under a bed in Room Three at Doucette Motel. Sergeant Tanguay gave me a special secret mission to spy on a couple of crooks, and I may have taken things too far. And I lost her number, so I can't call her myself. I don't know the number for the police station."

"What?" There had to be more to the story, but with Skidmark it was always a lot of work to get all the details concisely. It was like trying to catch water in a bucket from a flailing fireman's hose. "What kind of crooks? Skidmark, what did you do?"

Pius and Harper stood, and Harper mouthed, "What's going on?"

Niall waved her off to focus on the call.

Skidmark still spoke quietly. "I don't know what they're doing. Kidnapping little kids and doing horrible things to them, I think. Maybe they're priests from Mount Cashel, and since they closed down the orphanage, they have to go cruising for their pickups now."

Harper and Pius were now leaning in, listening to the conversation. "What the hell is he talking about?"

"Oh, is Harper there? And Pius, too? Pius, have you read that *X-Men* comic I lent you? You better not have creased or bent the cover. It's the first appearance of Omega Red, and it's the direct-market edition. It's going to be worth a lot of money someday."

"Skidmark, forget the comic books." Niall's heart was racing. "What happened? Why are you hiding under a bed?"

"So the child molesters don't catch me, duh. I followed them to the motel and then used a screwdriver to pop open the lock to break in. Keith told me how to do it. Apparently, he breaks into vacant units so he can drink there. We should talk about Keith's drinking sometime. I think he has a problem."

Niall wanted to reach through the phone and throttle Skidmark's thick neck.

"But why are you under the bed?"

"Oh, because the crooks came back. I think one of them went out to get food. The other one is taking a shower."

"You're stuck in a room with a child molester?" Pius blurted out and covered his mouth in horror. Being pursued by a pervert was one of Pius' worst nightmares. After spiders, dogs, the goaltender from the Senior Hockey team, and a hundred other things. "Get out of there!"

"I can't. I mean I'm literally stuck under the bed. I think my rollerblades are caught on the bedsprings."

"Why are you wearing rollerblades?"

"I'm not *wearing* them. They're attached to my backpack."

"Then leave them there!"

"Are you kidding me? They're for the school play! Mrs. Walsh will kill me!"

There was a rustling and banging on the other end. Skidmark's voice became quieter and more frantic. "Oh, I think he's out of the shower. I have to..."

More rustling and banging. And then the line went dead.

"Skidmark? Brian?" Niall put down the receiver with trembling hands. "He's gone."

"Oh my god, the child molesters got him." Pius gasped and covered his mouth again.

"What do we do?"

"We go get the stupid space case." Harper was already heading for the door. "It's only a few minutes on our bikes."

"We can't barge in there!" countered Niall. "What if they *are* child molesters? Or rapists or murderers? What if they have guns?"

Harper waved her hand, fanning her fingers like a magician preparing to do sleight of hand. "Then you do the magic hand trick." She was out the door.

Niall growled in frustration. Hadn't they discussed that this wasn't a parlour trick he could do like a trained puppy? "I don't think we should use that as a basis for our plan! Pius, call the police station."

Pius turned pale as skim milk, which was impressive considering his complexion. He had gone through a lot of colours in the last twenty minutes. "You want me to talk to the cops?"

"Try and get through to Sergeant Tanguay. Skidmark said she put him up to it." Niall pulled on his sneakers in the porch.

"You want me to talk to the cops?" Pius asked again.

"You'd rather deal with the creepozoids?"

Niall walked out the door. He felt bad leaving Pius like that. Pius was afraid of everything, especially something like talking to the police. Not to mention all the crap he was dealing with that they had put on hold abruptly. But Skidmark might be in danger, so they were all going to have to suck it up and do stuff they didn't like. Like using magic powers he didn't understand, which might kill somebody. Or trying to keep up with Harper on a BMX.

By the time Niall got outside, Harper was already halfway down the street, pedalling like a bat out of hell, which was a dumb saying; bats couldn't pedal bikes. Cursing to himself, Niall hopped on his own bike and went after her, already dreading the stitches and muscle cramps that would be coming. They always did after he tried to keep up with Harper.

The American soldier threw Linda on the concrete floor of a bunker, and then he turned to close the steel door behind them. He sealed it shut by turning a large metal wheel.

Linda sobbed. Her pretty skirt was dirty and torn, and she was being manhandled by a Yankee. Her boyfriend Angus had fled, abandoning her at the first sight of trouble. And to top it all off, the soldier had actually tried to shoot and kill an angel.

It had been an angel, hadn't it? Or was she going crazy?

Her uncle Mortimer had been crazy. He lived in the woods by himself, living off chipmunks and fish and talking to himself for hours on end. Or maybe he was talking to the chipmunks. No one could get close enough to be sure. Local children would dare each other to sneak out to his cabin, and Mortimer would scare them away by exposing himself to them. Eventually, a couple of local men went out to Mortimer's cabin with shotguns, and no one ever heard from the old man again. No one seemed to care, either. The Mounties didn't even bother investigating what happened to him.

Something pounded on the outside of the metal door. It pattered against the steel like hailstones on the tin roof of her grandfather's shed. Except it sounded bigger than any hailstones she had ever seen.

"What is that?"

The American ignored her. He was young, not much older than her, and Linda could see the terror in his eyes under his helmet. He was breathing hard and fumbled with his radio. His hands were shaking so badly that he had trouble operating it.

"This is Airman Wolfhard!" he screamed, finally figuring out how it worked. "I need backup at the Micmac Head radio tower! Repeat, I need backup immediately!"

"Wolfhard, this is Base," came a crackled reply. "What the hell is going on up there? We've lost contact with the tower."

"There's something... there's a..." The American struggled to form words. "I don't know what it is! Send a squad up here now! Send a whole platoon! We're under attack from... something!"

"A patrol is on the way, Airman. Sit tight."

The American laughed bitterly. "Sit tight, my ass. They didn't see that... whatever that was. I'd like to see Colonel Franklin sit tight after staring down that... that... what the hell was that, anyway? Did you see it?"

It took Linda a moment to realize he was talking to her. She wiped her eyes and sniffed. "It was an angel."

Now, the American soldier laughed deeply from his belly. "An angel? Are you nuts? That was no angel. That was a monster, like Frankenstein or that robot from that *Forbidden Planet* movie we watched in the mess hall last week."

"It came down from Heaven on glowing wings. What else could it have been?"

The American reached into the front pocket of his uniform and pulled out a pack of cigarettes. His hands were shaking. "I don't know where that thing came from, sweetheart, but it wasn't heaven..." He stuck a smoke in his mouth and offered her the pack.

With trembling fingers, she took one. Her mother always said that proper ladies didn't smoke, but then Linda would see her light one up with her friends and cousins every time they went to bingo. Like a gentleman, the soldier reached down and lit Linda's cigarette first. She inhaled, and the smoke burned her lungs. She coughed, but she didn't care.

The soldier took a drag. "You Catholic?"

Linda nodded. "Yes."

"Makes sense. Only a Catholic would think that God sent an angel to punish you for something."

Linda was confused. Not that an angel would punish someone; ninety percent of the adults in her life told her she was going to Hell for something or another. No, she was confused as to why this particular angel was doing something to harm her?

"What are you getting on with? It didn't do anything to us..."

The soldier shook his head. "You were so busy praying you didn't see it raising that big fiery sword to chop you in half."

Linda choked, and it wasn't from the smoke this time. "You... I didn't, I mean..." She trailed off. She honestly hadn't seen anything.

"I don't know what it was. A sword, a flamethrower, damned if I know. But that's why I shot it. I thought it was going to kill you for sure."

"Then you... saved me?"

"Temporarily. The bullets didn't even seem to faze it. In basic training, I saw a guy shot by accident at point-blank range with a Colt pistol, and it took a piece out of him like this." The soldier held up thumbs and forefingers together, making a circle about the size of an apple. Linda felt her stomach turn at the thought of a man with a hole that size in his chest. "And he was wearing a bullet-proof vest. I shot that... whatever that was... eight times and only annoyed it."

"So, what did you see, then, Mister—?"

"Wolfhard. Airman First Class Erik Wolfhard. And I don't know what I saw. Body armour? Some kind of advanced secret high-tech Soviet weapon? For all I know, it was something out of those freaky sci-fi flicks we watch on rec night."

"Like... a moon man?" It sounded so stupid she could've laughed.

"Or a Martian or a Venusian. Who knows? There's a lot of strange stuff out there, doll, who knows what—"

Something heavy crashed into the metal door behind them. The concrete walls shook, and dust tumbled down on their heads.

Linda screamed. "What was that?" She covered her head.

Wolfhard was white as her grandmother's bleached sheets hung on the line to dry. "A bomb? I dunno..." He snatched up his radio again. "Base, this is Wolfhard. Are we under fire?"

The walkie-talkie crackled. "That's a negative, Airman. What are you talking about?"

"Something hit the bunker at Micmac Head—"

Another louder bang struck the door, and the tunnel shook again, harder this time.

"If we're not under attack, then what the hell was that?" Wolfhard screamed into the walkie-talkie.

"Do you hear that?" Linda hadn't noticed it before, but now that she was focused on the noises outside, she realized the incessant pounding outside the door had changed in pitch and tone. It was a faster, droning sound, like a motorized saw. "What is that?"

Wolfhard reloaded his pistol and stepped toward the door cautiously. He reached out and touched the metal, then immediately snatched his hand away. "Cripes, it's burning hot!"

Linda, convinced it definitely—probably—wasn't an angel, believed it could be a crazy Russian in a robot suit from outer space. "Is it trying to cut through?"

"I'm not sticking around to find out!" Wolfhard grabbed her by the hand and pulled her down the tunnel, deeper into the mountain.

CHAPTER SIXTEEN

My Name is Mud
June 1, 4:15 pm

Five minutes later, Niall and Harper dropped their bikes in the parking lot of Doucette's Motel on Harmon Highway. Niall was gasping for breath.

"We're too late," said Harper, her own breathing perfectly level.

Niall looked up to see multiple police cars outside the motel. "There's no way they got here before us. Pius just called them."

If he called them, Niall thought to himself.

"They must have been on the way already. But how did they know?"

Harper was looking around frantically for something. Niall tried to get enough oxygen to ask her what it was, but before he could form the words, she called out: "Sergeant Tanguay! Sergeant Tanguay!"

The sergeant, standing in front of an open motel unit door talking to the manager and two men in black jackets, looked in their direction. She held up a hand to tell Harper to be patient and wait a moment.

Harper tried to approach her anyway, but a tall cop with a creepy moustache blocked her way. "Sorry, kid, you can't go in there." He tried steering her away. "You hop back on your bike and get out of here."

Of course, Harper ignored him. "Sergeant Tanguay! Skidmark is in there! Is he okay?"

Visibly annoyed, Tanguay excused herself from the men she was talking to and approached the police barricade. "Harper. Yes, Skid—Brian is fine. He's a bit flustered, and he's blabbering a lot, but that's normal for him, right? How did you know he was in there?"

"He called us a few minutes ago," Niall replied between gasps. "He said you told him to spy on some bad guys."

The sergeant turned red, which Niall knew for her was more of a sign of irritation than embarrassment. "I did no such thing! What did he tell you—?"

She was interrupted by the approach of two men in black wind-breaker-style jackets and slacks. The older one, who had a thick grey beard and hair, wore a tie. They wore no identification, but even Niall could tell, from the way they stood and carried themselves, that they were soldiers or cops or something equally disciplined and authoritative. And also because Harper immediately bristled like a cat backed into a corner, which she always did in the face of authority.

"Sergeant, is something wrong?" asked the grey-haired man.

That was odd. He sounded American.

"No, these two are friends of the boy we found inside. Apparently, he called them and told them he was in trouble, so they came to check on him."

The old man looked them up and down. Even with sunglasses on, the gaze unnerved Niall. He looked at them like the T-1000 in *Terminator 2.*

Harper hissed beside him.

"Then they might know something," said the old man. "Captain Mason, we should ask these two a few questions."

The other, younger man with a military-style haircut nodded and withdrew a notebook.

Sergeant Tanguay looked oddly nervous. "I don't think these two know anything…"

Captain? American? It all came together. Could these two…?

Harper must have made the same connection at that exact moment and did not have any qualms about discretion or being respectful. "Are you two the same lamewads that harassed my cousin Pius and Uncle Raymond a few nights ago?"

Tanguay glared at Harper.

The two men looked from them to the sergeant and back to them again.

"So they don't know anything, do they?" said the older man. Suddenly, his cold, professional demeanour changed, and he smiled. It didn't look like a fake smile or anything. In fact, it was downright friendly.

He looked like a skinny, athletic Santa Claus. "No, that was not us, my dear, and you don't need to worry about those two men anymore. We'll take care of it. Now, you two run along and go play Cowboys and Indians, okay?"

"We're thirteen," said Niall.

"And this isn't 1955," added Harper.

A flash of annoyance crossed the old man's face, but it passed quickly, and his smile became warmer. "Well, in that case, go make out behind the high school and smoke drugs or whatever it is you kids do these days."

This time, Harper turned a bit red, and Niall was sure it wasn't because of the "smoking drugs" part. It was bizarre to see Harper embarrassed, and it was kinda cute.

"Uh, thanks." Niall tugged gently on the sleeve of Harper's plaid flannel shirt, pulling her away from the situation before she reacted. He wasn't afraid of touching her this time. Accidentally blasting someone with magic was nowhere near as bad as what Harper might do if she was embarrassed *and* told what to do by an authority figure she didn't respect.

As they walked away, Niall glanced back and noticed Tanguay and Captain Mason watching them. There was something about the two men that majorly weirded Niall out.

As they retrieved their bikes and headed for the road, Harper leaned over and whispered to him. "Follow me." And then she rode off.

Niall's heart and mind raced with the possibilities. What sort of crazy adventure was she leading him on now? Presumably, it was something that would get him in trouble or potentially injured. But maybe there was a chance it could be something good?

They rode a hundred metres down the road before Harper veered off into the bushes. For the briefest moment, Niall's hopes leapt. Was she going to take the weird old guy's advice and make out with him? In which case, the guy had jumped from the bottom to the top of Niall's list of Favourite People faster than anyone ever had in his life. Even faster than his brother Nelson when he had bought Niall a replacement copy of *Superman* #75 after their father had accidentally sat on and torn his original copy.

"What are you doing?" Niall followed her into the alder bushes alongside Harmon Highway.

"Trying to find a place we can hide and watch the motel." She stood on the tips of her steel toes and peered over the bushes. "I want to see what's going on and catch Skidmark when he comes out. Don't you want to ask him what he saw?"

His heart sank, and he sighed. He should have known. He considered asking Harper if she wanted to make out while they were waiting, but he shook the thought away. "They're probably going to call Skidmark's parents to come pick him up." And if Niall knew them, they would likely beat their son viciously for getting in trouble with the cops. "They'll take him straight home, and we won't be able to catch him here."

"Crap, I hate it when you're right. We should go to his place and wait for him there."

"You're not going anywhere," said a deep voice behind him, and a firm hand wrapped around Niall's mouth.

CHAPTER SEVENTEEN

Soul to Squeeze
June 1, 4:15 pm

A scream sounded from somewhere nearby, and Tanguay knew who it was instantly.

"Harper." She bolted off in the direction of the scream without hesitation.

She was aware that Colonel Wolfhard and Captain Mason were following her, but she didn't care. Tanguay felt a weird connection to all the kids involved in the incident last year, especially Harper. It probably was not a coincidence that Lynne would have been right around her age now.

Tanguay crashed through the bushes in time to see a black car peeling away from the shoulder of the road and speeding down Harmon Highway. That was them! The bastards from the hotel room. Did they have the kids?

She grabbed the radio from her shoulder. "Bennett, Brake. They took off down Harmon Highway, headed west. They might have the kids with them."

"On it," came the replay.

A few seconds later, police sirens wailed to life, and a few seconds after that, two police cars sped down the highway.

Wolfhard and Mason approached her, stepping through the trees the same way she'd come. They weren't rushing.

"I think they took the kids," said Tanguay, pacing back and forth. What the hell was she supposed to do? What was she supposed to tell their parents? That their kids got kidnapped... again?

"That is unfortunate," muttered Wolfhard.

Captain Mason seemed like an okay guy, and at least he was Canadian, but Wolfhard was an odd one. He weirded her out, worse than that creepy, old gynecologist who worked at the local clinic.

"Two of my men are after them," said Tanguay. "They can't get far. We'll catch them."

"For the sake of your officers, I hope they don't catch them, Sergeant." Wolfhard tore a leaf off a branch, held it up to his nose, and inhaled deeply. Then he ground it up in his palms and tossed it aside. "Those two are perilous men. Your officers would not survive an encounter with them. The two men I sent were ex-Marines, and you saw what became of them."

The two bodies Bennett had found on the side of the road. Tanguay had been right in her suspicions—the real Robert Stone and Randy Koch were CIA operatives, and the creepozoids had killed them a few days ago and stolen their identities. "You mean the two foreign agents you sent here illegally?"

Wolfhard chuckled, revealing yellowed, old-man teeth. "My dear woman, agents Koch and Stone were here on vacation. It was entirely by chance they got involved with this mess. Your government is well aware of the situation, but they asked me to come clean it up personally to avoid an international incident."

That story was bullshit, and they all knew it, but she couldn't tell them she'd broken into Koch and Stone's motel room and seen the documents. It made Tanguay's blood boil. Wolfhard and Mason showed up at the detachment that morning and started ordering everyone around. Then they didn't tell her anything and locked themselves in an office with *her* files for hours. When the call came in about the motel, they were out the door before she had even called her constables for backup.

"Who the hell are they? What are my constables and those kids getting into?"

"That is need-to-know information, Sergeant."

"If the lives of two minors and two constables are at stake, then I do need to know."

Wolfhard sighed. "Their names are Sarkis Garabet and Oleg Aminov. They are black-market arms dealers who made a king's ransom selling old Soviet weapons to Middle Eastern and African dictators. They provided an army's worth of munitions to Saddam Hussein before the Gulf War, and now they've been hired by one of Saddam's idiot sons to build a new stockpile to get back into his father's good graces."

"And they're here looking for a nuclear bomb? A nuke that the US government forgot for thirty years? Why the hell isn't there an entire battalion of soldiers looking for them?"

Wolfhard smiled. "It's more complicated than that. International incident, remember? Our governments want to keep this quiet."

Tanguay wanted to wring his wrinkly, old neck and ask him what the hell he was talking about, but Captain Mason interrupted her attempted manslaughter. "Sergeant Tanguay, Colonel Wolfhard, can you have a look at this?"

Wolfhard gave a cocky smirk that made her skin crawl. "I'm retired, Captain. You don't have to call me Colonel."

Marie-Ann resisted the urge to call Wolfhard out on his blatant lie. She knew many retired military officers who worked for the government, and they all loved it when people called them by their old ranks. She let her glare linger a moment on the "colonel" before walking over to the alder bush Mason was examining so intently.

"It's burned," Wolfhard announced before Tanguay even got close to it. Of course, he would want to be the first to notice it, especially before a woman.

"It's still warm," Tanguay added. "And is that blood?" She pointed to dark, wet spots on the ground near the bush.

"Looks like it." Mason got down on his knees and examined it more closely. He sniffed and wrinkled his nose as if he was smelling Constable Bennett after a lunch of baked beans. "Smells like burned hair and flesh."

"What the hell happened here?" Wolfhard asked. "First, two of my agents are burned to death outside of town, and now someone else catches fire not a hundred yards from where I'm standing? Who are those kids, Sergeant?"

"You wouldn't believe me if I told you."

"You would be surprised what I would believe."

"I *can't* tell you."

"Remember that your inspector ordered you to assist with this investigation in any way possible. We need to work together, Sergeant. I told you about Garabet and Aminov. Now, you need to tell me who those kids are."

She shook her head. "I will. But first, we have to make sure they're safe. They were kidnapped by a deranged... woman last year. The whole town thought they were dead. If someone took them again..."

"Or they didn't." Mason looked around, confused. "Where are their bikes?"

Of course! Harper and Niall had left the motel on bikes. If someone had taken them, their bikes would still be here, wouldn't they? Unless Garabet and Aminov took them, too. It was unlikely, but...

"We have to make sure they're safe."

"They could've gone home," Mason suggested.

"Do not call their parents," said Wolfhard. "Even if they're secure, we can't alert their parents. We can't let anyone else know about this investigation. I imagine they're already suspicious about the story you fabricated last year."

Tanguay froze. "How do you—?"

"Know about Theolina Benoit and the alien entity you encountered under the town last August? I know quite a lot, Sergeant. You need to learn to trust me."

"I don't trust anyone."

"Perfect. Then we will get along swimmingly."

CHAPTER EIGHTEEN

Low

June 1, 4:40pm

Pius sat at Niall's kitchen table, staring at the phone. Niall and Harper had left half an hour ago, and he hadn't heard anything from them. He'd gotten off the phone with the nice lady at the RCMP office twenty-five minutes ago. Her name was Constable Murphy, and she said that Sergeant Tanguay was out on an important assignment. Constable Murphy also had a son named Todd, who was Pius' age and went to the Amalgamated, non-denominational high school. He had top marks in his class, was on the honour roll, had perfect attendance, and loved math, science, and computers. He was currently into bugs and was talking about being an entomologist when he grew up. Although, Pius was pretty sure she didn't know the word "entomologist" because she'd said "bug scientist." She also had a niece who might like to meet a nice, smart boy like Pius.

Pius thanked Constable Murphy and hung up the phone with trembling, sweaty hands. Being afraid of space monsters was one thing. Even worrying about his friend was tolerable, but being threatened to meet and interact with other kids was the most terrifying thing he could imagine.

He stood and wondered what he should do. Alone in Niall's house, staring at the white plastic phone on the kitchen countertop, he was completely helpless. He didn't know where Niall and Harper were. They should have reached Doucette's Motel by now, but what did they find? Had Skidmark been neatly dissected by murderous creepozoids? His body parts carefully separated, catalogued, preserved, and stored in various Tupperware and Rubbermaid bins, like that serial killer Pius had seen on *Unsolved Mysteries*? (Which he had watched from the other room, with blankets over his head.) While he could respect the dedication to the scientific method, he also sympathized too much with the frog to do the dissection in science class.

Of course, it was also possible that Skidmark had made up the whole thing and was now hiding somewhere, laughing at them while Harper and Niall ran all over town looking for him. Skidmark had once convinced his parents that he was trapped in the floorboards under their shed for three whole days, using the creative application of a walkie-talkie. He'd gotten the idea from *The Simpsons*, but his parents were less than appreciative of the prank. Especially since he had been kidnapped by a homicidal lunatic a few months before.

Pius was freaking out, and thinking about serial killers and Skidmark's parents' penchant for child abuse was not helping. Should he call the police station again? Should he try to contact Niall's parents or some other parental figure? There was no way in hell he was calling his own parents. Should he call Mrs. Aucoin, the librarian? She was always nice to him, and librarians spent all day reading books, so she would have to know what to do.

He was about to grab his bike and ride out looking for Niall and Harper when the phone rang. It startled him so much that he nearly pooped himself. He may have peed a little. He snatched it up so quickly he dropped the receiver. It banged off the side of the counter and bounced up and down a few times until he could regain control of the slippery device.

"Ow!" The voice on the other end was annoyed. "What the heck are you doing?"

"Skidmark!" Pius whooped with excitement and relief, like on those rare occasions he beat Niall at *Mortal Kombat*. "Oh, thank God you're not dead."

There was a long pause on the line. "I don't think I'm dead. Hey, is Niall and Harper there with you?"

"No, they went looking for you thirty minutes ago. They didn't get to you? How did you get out?"

Another pause. Weird. Skidmark never left so much space in his conversations. Usually, he would have described everything he'd eaten today and the plots of at least three movies by now. "The cops showed up. I'm fine."

"You don't sound fine."

"So..." He trailed off.

There were muffled voices in the phone's earpiece. Were the lines crossed, or was Skidmark talking to someone?

"...so are Harper and Niall back?"

"No, I told you they went looking for you. I don't know where they are."

"Oh, okay. Well, if you hear from them, let me know, okay?"

"Wait, Brian, where are you?"

The line was already dead. Skidmark was acting strange, even for him. And who was he talking to? Was he not okay? Had the creepozoids gotten to him and forced him to make that call as their cover?

Pius wondered if he should go up to Doucette's Motel himself. Niall's parents would be home from work any minute, and Pius did not want to answer their questions. Like, what happened to Niall, or why are you still at our house? He also didn't want to be alone with Niall's parents when they asked him questions about his own parents. But did he want to avoid them enough to put himself within arm's reach of the creepozoids? Maybe not. But he still had to get out of this house.

He had to do *something*. He felt helpless. Left out. Skidmark was on secret missions for the police. Harper and Niall were off having their own adventures. There might be some kind of alien monkeys invading the town, and all Pius had accomplished was screwing up his parents—

Maybe there was something he could do. Something they'd asked him last night before his life completely fell apart. Anyway, if Niall and Harper were frigged off somewhere, it would have to be him.

Pius quickly went through a list of things he might need. Most of them were at his house. His mom should be leaving for work soon, and his father wouldn't likely be home, so he should be able to sneak in and get what he needed without running into anyone. He might also need to swing by the hardware store, but he had time.

He grabbed his schoolbag and carefully removed his books and binders to make room. His textbooks were all neatly wrapped in brown paper to protect them, and he had painstakingly written out a grading rubric on each one. Not for his grades, of course. He had 98% or higher in all his classes (that 97% on his religion midterm was a mistake, and he complained to Mrs. Butt about it ever since). No, the rubric was for the grades he gave his teachers based on the quality of their material, presentation style, evaluation standards, and desk-side manner. Pius put more work into his teachers' report cards than they put into his, yet few of them were ever appreciative of it.

Empty backpack in hand, he ducked out the door. Nana Josephine was raking up grass trimmings, listening to her Walkman. She had it turned up so high Pius could hear Randy Travis from across the yard.

Nana Josephine looked up and waved at Pius. "Where you off to, dear?"

"Just picking up some stuff for my friends," said Pius, waving back. He neglected to mention the illegality of what he was on his way to do. He hoped he would live to tell her the story someday.

<u>CHAPTER NINETEEN</u>

American Jesus
June 1, 5:00 pm

"We need to find those kids," Tanguay said to Colonel Wolfhard and Captain Mason.

Again, she added to herself.

They stood beside their vehicles outside Doucette's Motel. They had used the phone inside Koch and Stone's room to have Skidma—Brian call Niall O'Neil's house. Pius had been there alone, and he didn't know where Harper and Niall were. Brian was safely in the backseat of Sergeant Tanguay's car, where he couldn't do any more damage or get into any further trouble until his parents retrieved him.

"We need to find the asset," said Wolfhard.

"Koch and Stone, Garabet and Aminov, whatever their names are, probably have your 'asset,' so if we find the kids, we find them all."

Wolfhard shook his head. "If they have the asset, why are they still here?"

He had a point. They must still be looking for it. "How did they even find out the bomb was here?"

"The same way we did... from that picture."

Tanguay had guessed as much, but the part she didn't understand was how so many people had even become aware of a cheap drug-store photograph. "But how did you—"

Wolfhard waved a finger at her. What was she, a child? "Ah, I already told you who our mysterious villains are. Now it's your turn to reveal a secret to me."

Marie-Ann did not have patience for the Yank's weird games. They had to find the kids before it was too late. "What is this, Truth or Dare?"

Wolfhard removed his sunglasses, revealing blue-grey eyes surrounded by heavy wrinkles. "Oh, you are lucky it is not. I was Truth or Dare Champion '65 and '66 at West Point. No, this is a simple exchange of information. Now, who are those children?"

"Niall O'Neil and Harper Jeddore. Local kids. They were kidnapped last year by Theolina Kane—"

"I know the official story, Sergeant. I want to know the details that you redacted from the report."

"Those details are classified. They're a matter of national security—"

"Bullshit. You left them out to protect those kids. I need to know why. And this is a matter of *global* security. Why did the alien entity choose those kids?"

He knows. More than what he read in the report. He knows more than he's letting on, but she needed his help to find the kids.

"The creature—Theolina called it the 'Primordial One,' the kids called it the 'Psycho Hose Beast'—it took Harper because she was 'blood of the blood,' or something like that. Theolina had tried to kill her father and her grandfather, too. She thought she needed their blood to defeat the creature. She died before she could do whatever she planned to do."

Wolfhard stroked his beard while his blue-grey eyes locked upon her. He was considering her words carefully. "Then how did you defeat it?"

"The boy, Niall, his grandmother was... *ensorcelée* by Theolina's sister's ghost or something. I know it sounds crazy, but I saw it with my own eyes. Harper cut her hand, Niall touched Harper's blood, and then he destroyed the creature. At the same time, he took out a wall made of thirty-centimetre-thick steel."

Wolfhard's eyes sparkled. She had seen it before. In drug dealers and other addicts, when tantalized with the promise of their chosen vice. They couldn't hide it. It was the first honest emotion she had seen from Wolfhard. "The boy did that?"

"I don't think he knows how he did it. It was a fluke. I don't think he's done it again since."

"Of course, of course." Wolfhard's mind was working. Tanguay could see it on his face. He babbled, primarily to himself. "Latent psychokinetic abilities triggered by adrenaline. It may manifest more frequently through adolescence as hormonal changes in his body accelerate his genetic mutation. But the blood, that's new. It could be a psychological effect, a placebo, like a security blanket that puts him at ease and improves concentration. But what if something in her hemoglobin interacted with his genetic makeup? The possibilities are fascinating...."

Tanguay did not like where this was going, and the most pressing thing was the bomb that was still floating around town somewhere. A surefire way to distract an ass was for a woman to say something he could contradict. "What else do you know about the Russians, Colonel? How do we get to the nuke before they do?"

"One of them is Russian," he said dismissively. "Garabet is Libyan. And it's not a nuke."

Tanguay hesitated. She had taken the photo to the library and looked it up. "It's a Mark 6 eighty-kiloton nuclear bomb."

Wolfhard looked vaguely impressed. "Excellent investigation, Sergeant. But that's just the outer shell. Like we tell our children, it's what's inside that counts."

Inside?

"If it's not a nuke, then what is it?"

"It's difficult to explain. I believe it comes from the same world as the entity the youths so eloquently named... what was it, 'Psycho Hose Beast?'"

Tanguay gasped. No, it couldn't be. Not again. "Is it another one of those creatures?"

"Not exactly. And it should be inert and harmless, as far as I know. Garabet and Aminov have no idea what they're searching for. I cannot fathom they will know what to do with the asset if they find it."

"How do *you* know what it is?"

"How do you know about the 'Psycho Hose Beast,' Sergeant?"

"I was there."

"Exactly." His smug smile faded, and for the first time, she saw a hint of weakness. Maybe even fear. "So was I."

Linda and the American ran through a long concrete tunnel deep underground. They hurried down switchback metal stairs that made her feet hurt, but she dared not complain. The soldier let her keep up with him for now; she didn't want to upset him and risk getting left behind.

The tunnels were lit with electric lights every ten metres or so, giving barely enough light to see the concrete floors and walls. Every third or fourth light was out, leaving inky clouds of blackness between some of the pools of light. Those shadows frightened her. Any moment, the Martian Soviet angel could jump out of those shadows, and there was nowhere to escape from it.

She swore she could hear the buzzing from outside the bunker, but that could be her imagination running away with her. They were hundreds of metres from the door now. There was no way they could hear it.

Airman Wolfhard rounded a corner in front of her and crashed into something hard enough to almost knock him off his feet. His gun flew out of his hand and skittered across the floor.

Linda screamed. Oh my God, I'm going to be burned alive by a Commie Devil Robot. *Hail Mary, full of Grace...*

"Wolfhahd?" asked the monster.

Funny, Linda didn't expect the Soviet Moon Man to have a thick Boston accent.

"Why ah you running like that?"

"O'Brien?"

Wolfhard and Linda stepped around the corner to see that it was indeed a man, another young soldier with red hair and freckles.

"Thank God. Look, we need to get a full platoon with heavy weapons up on the Lookout right away!"

The red-haired soldier named O'Brien looked confused. He scratched at the peach stubble on his chin. "What ah you talking about, Wolfhahd? I already called off yah alahm. I caught yah tresspassah."

O'Brien pointed proudly at the dirty, trembling young man in a polo shirt and ripped slacks beside him.

"Angus?" asked Linda.

He looked terrible like he'd been run over by a truck. Or rolled all the way down Micmac Head. Served him right for running out on her.

Wolfhard grabbed O'Brien by the collar. "Jesus Christ, O'Brien, that's not what I called the alarm for! That's the girl's idiot boyfriend!"

Linda waved sheepishly. "Actually, I think we broke up."

"Linda?" Angus's brown eyes were wide and dejected. "I thought we had something special."

"Shut up, Angus."

"Do you have a banana radio?" Wolfhard demanded.

Stunned, O'Brien handed over his walkie-talkie. "Here you go, but you know they don't wohk down this fah."

Wolfhard growled in frustration. "Where's the nearest wire?"

"Phone box is about three hundred yahds that way." O'Brien thumbed over his shoulder. "What's got into you, Wolfhahd? What did you see out theh?"

Wolfhard didn't answer. He was already running down the tunnel in the direction O'Brien had indicated, once again dragging Linda behind him. They got a few paces before a loud, heavy crash echoed through the tunnel. The pair of them froze, listening. A few seconds later, the familiar, droning sound vibrated through the walls, making Linda's teeth vibrate.

"Run," Wolfhard hissed, and Linda did not need to be told twice. She bolted as fast as her Mary Jane's would allow, keeping pace with the American in his heavy combat boots. Angus passed them, arms and legs pumping like Bruce Kidd at the Commonwealth Games. He was always pretty good at track and field, plus he was a yellow-bellied coward.

O'Brien wasn't with them. He stood back to watch whatever was coming after them, shining his flashlight down the tunnel toward the stairs up to the Lookout. Linda never found out what happened to him, but she could make a pretty good guess based on the blood-curdling screams that echoed through the corridors.

Keith Doucette sat alone in the dark in his bedroom on the second floor of one of the larger houses in Gale Harbour. There was a Blue Jays game on his giant seventeen-inch screen in the corner—they were playing the Angels—but Keith wasn't paying attention. There were unopened copies of *Sonic the Hedgehog 2* and *Link's Awakening* on the floor, still in their shrink-wrapped packages. A stack of *Dungeons & Dragons* books was gathering dust on his desk; he hadn't touched them in months. The one thing in his room that ever got any attention were the cases of empty beer bottles under his bed—and he only bothered with them because he periodically had to rotate them out when his hiding space got too full. Not that it mattered. His dad never came into his room except to toss him some new games or a few bucks for pizza.

There were four freshly-emptied bottles of Black Horse beer at his feet. Keith didn't know the meaning of the word irony—he was failing English class—but if he did, he might find it amusing that he was drinking to forget that he'd gotten in trouble for drinking.

Of course, he could never forget. Not really. The beers gave him a buzz and numbed the edges, but they also strengthened and reinforced his self-loathing. He had shagged it all up. Again. He got himself kicked off the softball team. Despite numerous warnings—from friends and other players and even a friggin' cop—he kept showing up drunk to practice. As if he was *daring* Coach Campbell to kick him off the team.

Keith was the best player on the Junior boys' team, without a doubt. He usually scored at least half their runs every game and could be counted on to pitch five or six decent innings, too. He didn't think

Campbell would dare cut him, so he kept pushing it to see what he could get away with. And what did he do when he'd finally pushed the coach too far? Instead of admitting he screwed up and owning what he *knew* he was doing, he blamed it on someone else.

He felt awful for getting Pius in trouble. He didn't actually think Pius had ratted him out. He was pissed off and lashed out at the first person he saw. The same way he always did. The same way he always shagged everything up. And now his mom wasn't going to see him play ball.

She had officially moved out six months ago. She'd been gone most of the time for almost two years, but six months ago, right before Christmas, she finally decided she'd had enough of his dad and left and never came back. They weren't divorced or anything, but it was bad. They never got along. When she took off to go live with her friend Sharon in the town of Gander, halfway across the island, she asked Keith if he would come with her. Not wanting to leave his friends, his school, and his softball team, Keith had turned her down.

Now he had pissed away all those things, including his mom.

He had never been close to his dad, and they grew more distant after his mother left. His dad spent more and more time at his various businesses and almost no time at home. Tonight, he was stuck at the motel, apparently because the cops were poking around looking for somebody. That was hardly surprising. The cheap, dirty motel attracted all kinds of crooks and lowlifes, not to mention confused tourists who weren't smart enough to book a room at one of the nicer hotels. Poor suckers. Visiting Gale Harbour was bad enough. Having to stay at Doucette's Motel lowered your vacation from "sad" to "pathetic," with a free infestation of bedbugs.

The ball game on the TV reminded Keith of when he was little, and he would watch the Blue Jays games with his dad before everything got weird between his parents.

Once, Keith had asked his dad why mom left. His answer was something along the lines of "If she wants to go be an effing dyke, then to hell with her," and the topic never came up at the Doucette's dinner table again. Come to think of it, Keith couldn't remember the last time he'd sat down for a meal with his dad.

Something thumped against Keith's window, startling him to alertness. He'd been jumpy ever since his adventures in the tunnels last year. Ever since that crazy old woman had cut off his ear. He had nightmares a lot and slept with his baseball bat next to his bed.

He was reaching for the bat when another thump sounded. "Stupid June bugs," he muttered under his breath, relaxing slightly. Gross bastards. In the first grade, he had chased girls around the playground with dead June bugs, threatening to put them in their hair. He was always a charmer.

The room was spinning, his stomach twisting like that time his grandfather took him out on his boat. He should go to bed and sleep it off, but sleeping would bring nightmares, and he was already filled with anxiety. He needed fresh air and to relieve some stress. He pulled on a blue and white Tommy Hilfiger hoodie and grabbed his trusty, green, Easton aluminum bat from his bedside. The paint was chipped and dented from years of hitting pebbles and stones when baseballs weren't readily available. He'd gotten the Easton for his tenth birthday, his first "real" and expensive bat. It was big for him back then, but it now felt as comfortable and familiar in his hand as a Super Nintendo controller felt in Niall or Pius' hand.

Keith headed downstairs and for the front door but then stopped, went back to the bathroom for a whiz, and finally walked outside. He pulled his hood over his head and ears and yanked the drawstrings tight. He didn't want any of those little buggers to get in his hair.

The Doucettes had a big yard, but it was dimly lit. June bugs were attracted to bright lights, so he went across the street, where a pool of yellowish light from the lamppost illuminated the cracked asphalt below. The town was so bad at upkeeping the roads. At least a half-dozen kids wiped out on skateboards or bikes right at this same spot every summer, thanks to the broken and uneven pavement. It had nothing to do with Keith throwing rocks at them from across the street, of course.

He took a few swings to loosen up. Holding a bat was one of the few times he felt good anymore. Another time was when he was hurting someone or something, so this should work out perfectly.

A June bug buzzed in front of him, and Keith took a perfect home-run swing at it. The bug and bat collided with a gratifying little "ding," and Keith felt the vibration through the handgrip as the insect soared away into the darkness. It didn't have the impact or the distance of a pebble, but the slight "give" as the crunchy carapace collapsed in on itself was oddly satisfying.

Enough June bugs were buzzing around him that Keith barely needed to aim. He merely started swinging, relishing every little "ping" as the scarabs bounced off his Easton and hurtled into the night. He fell into a rhythm quickly, wading into the cloud of insects like his fourth-level dwarf fighter Snoop Doggius wading into a horde of goblins with his magic longsword.

Woosh.

Ding

Woosh.

Ding.

Woosh.

Ding.

Woosh.

THUD.

The bat collided with something solid.

Keith froze. Had he hit someone? It was dark, and he'd been swinging blindly. At first, judging by the size and weight, he thought he hit a softball. But softballs didn't *crunch*. Once, a few years ago, he and a couple of buddies had gone out on Halloween smashing jack-o-lanterns with bats and hockey sticks, leaving a trail of gourd guts and terrified children all over Gale Harbour. It had felt like that, like a small hollow pumpkin, because there was a hard outer casing, and it collapsed under the impact. But pumpkins didn't crunch like those cabins Mr. Dress-Up used to make out of popsicle sticks. Keith had stomped on a few of those, so he knew the brittle, snapping sound well. But popsicle stick cabins didn't make a wet, sloppy sound, either.

Cautiously, Keith examined his bat. Something was dripping off it, a dark fluid that, for a moment, he mistook for blood. Had he brained somebody? If he did, he might have killed them.

But there was nobody in sight.

He looked down at his feet. There was nothing but grass and rocks and...

Oh, God. No way...

CHAPTER TWENTY-ONE

Spy School Graduation Theme
June 1, 8:50 pm

Pius was sitting on the curb with his backpack on his lap in the Tim Hortons parking lot when Keenan and Anna pulled up in their battered, puke-coloured station wagon.

Keenan got out of the driver's side and automatically put his top hat onto his greasy black hair. "Pius, right? What happened to Niall and Harper?"

"How am I supposed to know? They do whatever they want these days. No one ever tells me anything." Apparently, he was still angry at them.

Keenan sighed and called back into the car. "Looks like the gig's off, Anna."

Anna hopped out of the other side of the car. Her cleavage was still threatening to burst out of her dress. Was that the same black and red dress she wore yesterday? Between the dirty clothes and the makeup and the greasy hair, these guys were kinda gross.

"What the hell?" she asked. "Where are Harper and Niall?"

"They may have been abducted by child molesters, I dunno."

"Are you serious?" they asked at the same time.

"Well, no, probably not. They're probably fine. But there is an outside chance."

"But they're not here." Anna hissed and dug her fingers into her hairline in frustration. She paced like an animal, quivering with anger. It frightened Pius. "We don't have time for this. The eclipse is in three days. We need to get that book back."

"You said you needed me to get into the school," said Pius. "I'm here."

The goths looked at each other. They appeared uncomfortable by the prospect, and Pius couldn't blame them. He didn't feel confident he could do anything right lately, either.

Anna whirled toward him. Her eyes darted about a moment longer before they focussed on Pius. "We need Harper and Niall to stop whatever happens."

"And they'll be back by Friday. Probably. Until then, you need to get into the school, and I'm your guy for that."

"Why the change of heart?" Keenan asked. "Last night, you were pretty clear you wanted no part of this."

Why *did* Pius change his mind? He'd been asking that himself all day. Ruining his parents' marriage had destroyed his self-worth, that's for sure. Was he acting out? Trying to lessen the impact of that terrible thing he'd done by doing something even worse? He had no idea. Psychology was such an imprecise and goofy science anyway, hardly better than Astrology.

"I just changed my mind. I figured I needed to be more proactive. And if we need the book to save the world, that's what we gotta do, right?"

"I like this kid," Keenan smirked. He gestured to the Band-Aid on Pius' cheek. "What happened there?"

"I got into a fight at school."

Keenan's eyebrows rose in some combination of surprise and admiration. "And what's in the bag?"

"Some things I might need."

Keenan reached into the back seat and pulled out a crowbar. "I've got everything I need right here."

Pius rolled his eyes. "Are you serious? I thought you knew how to break into places?"

"Well, I mean, you just smash the window and grab the stuff, right?" Keenan mimed hitting something with the crowbar. "You know, like a fistful of watches from a jewelry store or a wad of cash from a bank machine."

"Not that you have any first-hand experience in that, right?"

Anna snorted. "How else do you think we maintain this lavish lifestyle?" She gestured to their rusted station wagon with a month's worth of McDonald's wrappers in the back seat.

"Well, if you don't mind getting caught, I guess you can do it your way. But I have a future I don't want to ruin, so I'm going to do it my way."

Pius climbed into the backseat.

They exchanged a confused look. "Last night, I was sure he was going to narc on us," said Keenan. "What the hell happened?"

"Thirteen years old, getting into fights, doing dangerous or illegal things, and not caring if he gets caught?" Anna smirked. "He's gotta be pissed at his parents for something."

Keenan nodded. "I got my first tattoo at thirteen."

"Is that the terrible Cutting Crew one?"

"Shut up. They were awesome back then."

"Not." Anna grinned and slipped back into the passenger seat, bunching up her voluminous skirts as she did so. She looked back at Pius. "So, you sure you're up for this?"

"I just sat on a half-eaten McPizza," Pius moaned.

"Frig off, that was supposed to be my breakfast," Keenan grumbled as he hopped behind the wheel.

***

They pulled up in front of St. Paul's High School with the lights off. Pius directed them to park on the north side of the building close to the gymnasium, where their vehicle would be less conspicuous in an empty parking lot. The high school was on a street between Harmon Highway and a nice residential area, so there were bound to be a few people passing by, even at this hour.

Keenan put the car in park and turned off the engine. He hoisted his crowbar again. "Why don't we park around back and bust open a side door?"

Pius looked at him the same way he had looked at Niall when he said chlorine bleach was an acid. "You've never actually broken into anywhere before, have you?"

Keenan said nothing, but Anna sniggered.

Pius sighed. "The office is at the front of the school. If we go in the back, we have to walk through the entire building with the alarm going off the whole time."

"There's an alarm?" Keenan turned even paler than usual.

"Of course, there is. This isn't Gussy Shave's shack on the beach. They have important stuff locked up in there, like our permanent records!"

"And how are you going to get past the alarm?" asked Anna.

A broad grin spread across Pius' thin face. He loved knowing things that other people didn't. He unzipped his backpack and withdrew a pair of rubber gloves, which he carefully pulled on. "Leave that to me. Anna, you should stay here and have the car ready to go. Your ridiculous dress would get in the way." She looked put out, but Pius ignored it. "Keenan, come with me. Maybe you can do something useful. And put these on." He handed him another pair of rubber gloves.

Then Pius got out of the car and led Keenan around to the brightly-lit front doors of the building. A few June bugs buzzed around the glowing fluorescent lights above the entryway.

A car approached from down the road, and they quickly ducked around the corner, away from the light. They waited until the vehicle passed and was long gone before creeping back out again.

Until that moment, Pius had kept his anxiety firmly in check. He had thought about what he was about to do all afternoon, and through most of it, he had pictured it as a puzzle that had to be solved. How to get through the locked door. How to get past the alarm. How to get into the principal's office. These were all steps in a math problem. But now, in the moment, his heart rate increased, and he started to sweat profusely. His underwear was already damp.

No. He couldn't let his fear overtake him. He had to prove to himself that he wasn't useless. Niall and Harper had frigged off to God knows where, so he was the only one who could do this. He *could* do this. It was like taking a test, which he was good at; he always knew the answers.

He went straight to the door, knelt in front of the glass, and immediately pulled his first tool out of the bag—a small, metal glass cutter.

"Where did you get that?" Keenan asked, standing behind him and looking over his shoulder.

"Harper broke a window in our house last year with a soccer ball," explained Pius, already going to work on the glass with the small blade-like contraption. It wasn't as easy as it looked, but he had expected that, as he had practiced with an old piece of glass earlier. "My dad was too cheap to buy a new one, so he got a pane of glass from a friend at work and cut it to size himself."

While he spoke, he cut a small hole below the push-bar on the door handle, barely big enough to reach his arm through. Fortunately, he had scrawny arms. He carefully removed the glass and handed it to Keenan.

"Why not smash it if you're going to put a hole in it anyway?"

Pius had considered that. He would have liked to learn how to pick a lock and leave no sign of their entry at all, but he didn't have time. "When we're done, I'm going to epoxy it back in place and hope no one notices."

"You're going to glue it in? That would be pretty noticeable."

Pius gestured to the spider web of cracks in the window pane directly next to the door. "These doors and windows are always getting busted by people throwing bricks or nerds into them. That particular crack came from Steve Goosney when Chris Tobin slammed him into it two weeks ago."

"Christ, when I was in junior high, they just wedgied us."

Pius reached through the hole and pushed the bar above. The door popped open. A beeping started from the alarm box at the far end of the vestibule.

"Be right back." Pius hopped to his feet, ran to the alarm box, and punched in a six-digit code. He had sixty seconds and didn't need to rush, but beeping alarms made him jumpy. He didn't *really* think the whole place was going to be blown up by a bomb when the beeping stopped, but tell that to his amygdala.

The alarm went quiet immediately, and Pius returned to the door and let Keenan in. His heart still raced, but for now, it was more out of excitement than fear. Plus, he was pretty pleased by the shocked and impressed look on Keenan's face.

"How did you do that?"

"I usually get to school early and come in with the secretary. I've seen her punch in the code a bunch of times."

Keenan held up Pius' open backpack. Inside were the Javex and rubbing alcohol he'd packed earlier that day. "And what's with this? I thought we were planning to rob the school, not clean it."

"It's to clean up any fingerprints, of course. Grab a rag and wipe down anything you touch."

"We're already wearing gloves."

"I don't want to take any chances."

Keenan sighed but did as he was told, pulling a rag and the bottle of rubbing alcohol out of the bag. "Who knew nerd kids would be so good at being criminals?"

"How do you know I'm a nerd?"

Keenan shook his head. "Seriously?"

They went through the inner door, and now that they were inside the school proper, they were no longer at risk of being seen from the road. Even so, Pius reminded himself not to let down his guard. He needed to be on full alert to make sure there were no mistakes, not to mention it would be far too easy for his cautious nervousness to turn into nerve-wracking anxiety and hysterical panic. For him, it was a fine line.

The hallway inside the main doors was decorated with class pictures of former graduates, most of them with terrible haircuts from decades past. Pius hoped he would still be among them one day if this one misdeed didn't lead him down a path of burglary, vandalism, drug trafficking, prostitution, and, worst of all, being forced to drop out of school.

Across from the grad pictures was the door to the administrative offices. They slipped inside. Keenan carefully wiped down the doorknob behind them, and Pius was pleased to see his partner in crime showed the appropriate level of paranoia.

Pius was concerned that they couldn't see the front door from where they were, but there was nothing to do about that. They would have to be quick. He hurried behind the secretary's desk and opened the drawer where he found the spare set of keys for all of the offices—another feature he'd noticed by helping the secretary carry in her bags in the morning. He used the keys to open the principal's office, located in the corner of the administrative area beside the photocopier. Mr. Bourgeois was a strict supervisor when it came to the copier, closely monitoring anyone who used it to ensure they weren't wasting paper. Keenan followed dutifully behind him, wiping everything down.

Immediately inside Mr. Bourgeois' office was their goal: the tall, black filing cabinet where he kept confiscated contraband. The students at St. Paul's whispered about it—this secret trove of treasures pilfered unfairly for years from hard cases and model students alike. Some claimed there were decades of cool stuff buried in there, like Walkmans, comic books, and switchblades. Someone even claimed the principal had a gun in there, but Pius doubted that was true. While Mr. Bourgeois was known for snatching things from his students that he thought were inappropriate, there was no way he had been keeping it all in that single, four-drawer cabinet for years, let alone decades. Surely, he disposed of it or moved it somewhere else regularly, but since the book had been taken yesterday, it should still be in there.

Pius tried to find the filing cabinet key on the secretary's ring, but it was hard in the dark office. "Give me some light, will you? There's a flashlight in my bag."

Keenan pulled a small, cheap flashlight out of the backpack and clicked it on over Pius' shoulder. Pius found the key and unlocked the forbidden cabinet of mystery.

Pius pulled open the top drawer, and they peered inside. The older teen whistled, which made Pius jealous. He had never been able to do that himself.

"Look at this stuff." Keenan put the flashlight and the bottle of rubbing alcohol on top of the cabinet and started poking around. "There's so much candy in here... firecrackers... Playboy magazines..."

"Stop touching everything," Pius hissed. "Look for the journal!"

"Right, right." Keenan wiped the sweat from his forehead. He closed the top drawer and opened the middle one. There was a hardcover journal lying right on top.

A heartbeat later, they heard a crash of breaking glass outside the door.

Pius jumped and smashed into the filing cabinet. The bottle of alcohol fell over, and the flashlight rolled off and hit the floor hard. The light went out.

"What the hell was that?" Keenan said, the fear rising in his voice.

"We gotta get out of here." Pius' panic quickly rose to meet Keenan's. What the hell did he think he was doing? He wasn't a criminal. He didn't do stuff like break into schools. This was insane. What was he thinking? Was he trying to get back at his parents? Was he trying to punish himself? Why in God's name would he think this was a good idea?

The book. He had to get the book, or this was all for nothing.

"We have to get the journal," he breathed.

"Hold on, I have a lighter here somewhere...."

"No, wait—" But he was late.

Keenan flicked the lighter above the open drawer, igniting the alcohol vapours. The drawer below burst into flames.

"Shit!" Keenan screamed and dropped the lighter. "The book!" He tried to reach in for it, but the drawer was already engulfed in flames. He snatched his hand back and yelped in pain. "What do we do?"

Pius was no longer thinking. Rational thought was long gone. His fears of authority and getting caught, and getting into trouble in general, were ratcheted up tenfold by his even greater fear of being burned alive. The flames were already licking the ceiling, fueled by isopropyl alcohol and whatever other flammable goods were in the drawer.

"The firecrackers!"

A second later, they started to explode. The bangs of them bursting inside the filing cabinet sounded like gunshots.

Pius froze. The explosions reminded him of the gunshots last year inside the bunker. The screaming, the monster that nearly tore their faces off. What the hell had he been thinking?

"Move!" Keenan yelled.

Pius wasn't made for this sort of thing. He had fallen apart so completely last time that Keith had to carry him out on his back. What could have possibly possessed him to try to do this without Harper and Niall?

Something inside the filing cabinet exploded with such force that it blew one of the doors clean off, sending a steel square hurtling across the room directly at Pius' head. Pius, still paralyzed with fear, saw it coming but could do nothing. His failure was as inevitable as that chunk of metal slicing off his face.

The door never hit him. Keenan tackled Pius to the ground, and the metal square slammed into the wall above them. Keenan's frock coat was smouldering. In a daze, Pius dimly wondered why the cheap polyester hadn't gone up like the firecrackers in the cabinet.

"C'mon, get up!" Keenan shook him.

Pius was unhurt by the fall, but he was still having trouble making his legs work. Keenan dragged him to his feet and shielded him from the flames and the smoke as they stumbled out of the office.

They staggered out of the principal's office, through the admin office, and out the front door. Pius registered briefly that the door he had so carefully cut a hole into was now completely shattered, but he had no idea why. They continued on around the side of the building, with Keenan urging him along at every step. Pius gave up trying to hold back his tears.

Anna hopped out of the car as they approached. "What happened?"

Pius ignored her, leaving Keenan to explain their failure. He crawled into the backseat of the car. Sobbing and wiping snot from his face, he was surprised to find he wasn't alone in the car. Harper and Niall were there, staring at him, dumbfounded.

The sound of small explosions came through the side of the school; the principal's office was right on the other side of the brick wall behind them.

Pius couldn't get any words out. He had messed up so badly.

Harper's face was a mixture of horror and concern, with more than a bit of aggravation tossed in. "Pius? What the hell did you do?"

Niall didn't see who grabbed him, but he did see the man behind Harper.

He was tall and wide, with black buzz-cut hair and a square jaw with a large, pink scar. When Harper sensed the hands close to her, she didn't hesitate. She kicked backward, driving the heel of her Doc Martens into the thug's shin. He howled, and Harper dove out of his grasp, landing hard on her knees on the rocky ground. She rolled over, clutching her leg, revealing torn jeans and a scraped-up knee.

The hands holding him loosened. He tried to wriggle away and almost made it, but the man holding him caught him by the left arm. His fingers were like iron spikes digging into Niall's forearm. Niall reached with his right hand toward Harper. She lunged at him, fingers extended, with a smear of blood from her knee on her palm. The thug behind her grabbed her by the jacket, but not before their fingers touched. It was enough.

Power coursed through Niall's right arm, through his chest, and out his left hand. He didn't know what he did and wasn't even consciously trying to do anything. He just wanted the man to go away. Howling with pain, he released Niall's arm.

The other man let go of Harper. "Oleg, what happened?"

Harper screamed and kicked him in the face.

"Come on!" She grabbed Niall with her unbloodied hand and dragged him to their bikes.

Niall hopped on his, but his head was spinning. Every time he used magic like this, it weakened him. What had he done anyway? Did he smell burning hair?

They rode past the thugs' car, parked on the side of the road. Niall wished they could do something to disable it and prevent them from following, but the two men were already on their feet and coming after them. There was no time.

Harper peeled out onto Harmon Highway on her red BMX, narrowly avoiding a light blue Monte Carlo that blew its horn in response. Harper ignored it and pedalled off like a shot along the opposite shoulder of the road. Niall rode after her and, shockingly, kept up. Either her knee injury slowed her, or he was pumped up on superhuman levels of adrenaline.

They didn't go far, fortunately. A few hundred metres down the road, Harper peeled off into the parking lot of the Jehovah's Witness church. They rounded the corner behind the building a few seconds before the thug's big, black car roared past them on the highway.

"I think they missed us," said Harper.

"How long until they figure it out and come back looking for us?"

A moment later, a police car sped by with sirens blaring.

"I think they'll be busy for a while." Harper smiled, and Niall's heart raced. She had such pretty lips. Looking at her made him light-headed. Or maybe it was the magic.

He collapsed against the red brick wall of the church and slid down to the ground with a hard thump.

Harper knelt beside him. "Are you okay?"

"Yeah," he lied. "That always takes a lot out of me. What did I do, anyway?"

Harper's smile returned. "Oh, you're going to love this. You shot fire out of your hand."

"For real?"

"Burned off half that guy's face."

Niall's lunch threatened to come back up his throat. He hadn't meant to hurt him like that, never meant to hurt anyone.

"Hey, Dork-pie, they were about to kill us. A little fireball to the noggin is the least of what they deserve."

Despite his misgivings about hurting someone, even in self-defence, Niall had to admit it was kinda badass that he had shot flames from his fingers. "I cast a fireball?"

"Yeah, but don't get cocky about it. It's unattractive." Harper did something then that was more amazing than any fireball, more shocking than any horrors he'd experienced in the last year, more frightening than the monster they had destroyed under the Bay.

Without warning, Harper Jeddore leaned over and kissed him on the lips.

The universe exploded into a tiny singularity of light, focused on Niall's brain. Heat radiated from her mouth and down through his body, rejuvenating him and making him forget about all the hardships he'd endured.

She tasted like the strawberry-flavoured Fruit Roll-Up she ate at his house after school.

Harper pulled away and glanced aside. She was smiling, but there was a weird look in her eyes. Was she blushing? Was she embarrassed?

"Sorry, I don't know what came over me."

"Don't be sorry," Niall blurted out a little too desperately. "I mean, I liked it."

"Oh yeah? You're just saying that because it's your first time kissing a girl."

"There was..."

Harper held up her hand. "Your cousin when you're five doesn't count."

Right. Niall had forgotten he'd told her about that. Not one of his prouder moments. "I thought you were afraid to touch me."

"I was. I should be. Maybe I still am. I just... I guess the excitement got to me, is all."

"Do you... want to do it again?"

She laughed. "Shut up, Dork-pie." She kissed him again, more firmly this time, and Niall felt the world melt once more. He was painstakingly aware of the way his teeth felt, and he found himself wondering if he was doing it right. Should he open his mouth? Should he keep his eyes closed? They closed on their own; that was weird. He didn't remember closing them. What should he do with his hands?

And then she pulled away again, and Niall wished he hadn't been so self-conscious and had just enjoyed the moment.

Harper stood and cringed.

"What's wrong?" A million ideas of how he had screwed up their first kiss ran through his mind.

"I can't keep kneeling like that. My leg is killing me. I need to walk it off."

Niall glanced down at her leg, which was gouged open with bits of rock stuck in it. Blood was still trickling down her shin. If Niall had a wound like that, he would be crying for his mother.

He climbed back to his feet. "I'll walk with you." He had been exhausted a moment ago, but the kisses had energized him.

They walked across the parking lot one way, then back again. Neither of them spoke, but a million thoughts went through Niall's mind. Was he a good kisser? What could he do better? When would they do it the next time? Did Harper want to kiss him again? What was she thinking about right then?

"We need to stop getting into these death-defying situations together." Harper was still limping a bit, but she wasn't complaining.

"Hey, if it gets me more kisses, I'm all for it."

Harper elbowed him, but she laughed. "I didn't kiss you because we were in danger. I did it because I was curious about what it would be like. And if we get killed by those creepozoids, who knows if I would get another chance?"

"So, you kissed me because we were in danger."

"Shut up."

"Seriously, though, who were those guys?"

"The same ones Sergeant Tanguay has been looking for, the guys who harassed Pius and Uncle Raymond last week."

Niall suspected that, too, but that didn't explain who they were and what they were doing in Gale Harbour. "And what about those two men at the motel? They didn't look like Mounties."

Harper nodded. "Something is going on, and it could be connected to whatever is supposed to happen on Friday. We should talk to the sergeant."

"And tell her what, exactly? We don't know what's supposed to happen. All we know is that Theolina wrote a journal thirty years ago that said something bad *might* happen the night after tomorrow. And we don't even have the journal anymore."

"Fine. First, we'll get the book back, and then we'll let her know." Harper reached out and took Niall's hand in hers. Sparks exploded up his arm, through his spine, and into his brain. And not the kind that blew people up. This was a different kind of magic.

He wanted to squeal for joy and jump up and down and thank her for holding his hand, but he dared not say anything lest he draw attention to it and cause it to run away like a spooked rabbit. So, he held on limply, hoping his hand wasn't too sweaty and kept walking.

A moment later, Harper stopped short. "Crap, what if they go to our houses looking for us?"

"Those creepy guys?" He hadn't thought of that. Honestly, he hadn't thought of much of anything in the last few minutes except Harper's hand and lips. "You think they know where we live?"

"They knew where Pius lives, which means they know where I live. They could figure out your address, too."

Niall nodded. "And Pius is there alone."

"Well, your Nana is with him."

Niall considered that a moment. Nana Josephine was pretty formidable with a terse word or two, but he wasn't sure if that would work against those two goons. "We'd better go check on him. Are you okay to ride your bike?"

"Are you kidding me? I could outrace you with one leg." Harper darted off and grabbed her bike. She glanced back at Niall before racing off around the church and toward the road.

Niall followed with a growing sense of confusion. He was elated at his newfound physical relationship with Harper (mouth closed kissing and holding hands counted, shut up), but he was unable to shake the fact that they could've been abducted or murdered by thugs from the CIA's Elevator Inspection Division. That was what Pius said they claimed they were.

Pius! He could be in danger. Niall hopped on his bike and raced after Harper. His best friend was in trouble, a best friend who had difficulty keeping calm when the cashier gave him the wrong change. What would he do if the creeps showed up at the door again?

He couldn't catch Harper, of course, though he tried hard. He eventually caught up with her a few minutes later when she dropped her bike next to Old Mrs. White's garbage box and waved Niall down to do the same.

Harper crouched down and crept across the lawn to the white vinyl side of the house, where she peered around the corner.

"What's going on?" asked Niall. "Are the creeps here?"

"Shhh! No, it's your parents."

Niall couldn't understand why they were hiding from his parents. Was she embarrassed to be seen around them after she had deflowered their son? Was she afraid that they would know what the big, stupid grin on Niall's face meant?

His parents stopped to talk to Nana, who was finishing up her yard work. "No, the kids aren't here. Pius was the last one to leave a few minutes ago. He said he'd be gone awhile. I figured he was going home."

"I hope so," replied Niall's mom. "I spoke to Samantha earlier, and she was very upset that the kids wouldn't come home."

"They're thirteen," grumbled his dad. "We can tell them to go home."

"No!" Niall's mom was firm. "The kids need time to process what happened. They're upset. Samantha said she wouldn't push them, and I don't blame her. Besides, better they're safe here than running God-knows-where."

"Except, they're not here. We have no idea where they are."

"Oh, shut up, Johnny," chided Nana. "They're kids. They're out playing around. When Barbara and her brothers were their age, we didn't see them from sun-up until sundown."

"That's because they were out smoking cigarettes and gutting fish with their father."

"Go on with you. A few smokes would do them well. Might toughen up that Pius kid."

"Josephine, a lot of medical information has come out on tobacco in the last thirty years—"

"Leave them be." Niall's mom put her hand on his dad's arm. "We'll talk with them when they get home. I have to go start supper."

They went into the house, and Harper pulled Niall out of view. "We can't go in there."

"Why? Mom said that everything was okay."

"She said she wanted to talk to us. You know that will take hours, and she won't let us go out again. We have to go to the school tonight."

Niall didn't like the sound of that. He didn't like going out without telling his mom. Plus, if they didn't go home, he'd miss supper. It was meatballs and gravy night.

Harper must have been able to see the doubt on his face. "Look, I should go clean up my knee, and we also need to go check on Pius. If he did go home, he might be walking right into a trap from those creepozoids. If it makes you feel better, we can find a phone to call them and tell them we're going to Skidmark's to play games, okay?"

Niall was torn. He hated lying to his parents. It was something he did very rarely. Once, when he was ten, he had broken his dad's pen trying to build a rubber band slingshot and told his dad he didn't know what happened to it. He couldn't sleep for two days afterward.

Of course, the alternative was spending time alone with Harper and possibly more kissing.

Really, it wasn't a choice.

"I'm in."

They turned and headed back for their bikes.

When Harper bent down to pick up her BMX, she let out a scream.

CHAPTER TWENTY-THREE

Real World
Wednesday, June 2, 7:20 am

Marie-Ann didn't have time for this.

She stood in the burned lobby of St Paul's High School. The fire had pretty much destroyed the administrative offices and lobby, and there was smoke damage throughout the school. However, fortunately, the fire department had contained the blaze well enough that most of the building remained intact.

Firefighters were still picking through the rubble and making sure all the pockets of fire were out. A few teachers and staff stood in the parking lot, drifting about, except for a scruffy-looking old guy with a broom who must be the janitor. He had a determined look on his face like he was ready to take on the challenge.

The principal, a hawkish man named William Bourgeois, was talking to Fire Chief Hayward. Tanguay got a bad vibe from Bourgeois and completely understood why all the kids hated him. She was half-listening to their conversation, with her mind on the arms dealers running around their town looking for a secret weapon.

"...the fire seems to have started in a filing cabinet in your office," said Hayward, a cheerful old man with ruddy cheeks. "What did you keep in there?"

"Contraband," Bourgeois said disdainfully. He looked put out as if the dry cleaner had lost his favourite pair of trousers. "Inappropriate items confiscated from students."

"Anything flammable in there?"

"Certainly. Firecrackers, cans of spray paint, cigarettes and lighters—"

Hayward chuckled. "Well, I think we found your problem, Mr. Bourgeois. You shouldn't keep that stuff in your office, definitely not together. We have proper ways to dispose of stuff like that."

"Well, that's something I will consider in the future. When can we get the students back into the school?"

A few of the teachers within earshot turned to them with shocked looks on their faces.

Hayward couldn't stifle his guffaw. "We don't even got all the embers out yet, boy! And when the Ministry of Health gets a look at this, there's no way they'll let you open up."

Bourgeois sneered. Tanguay didn't think she had ever seen someone *actually* sneer before. Why was she stuck here with this idiot anyway?

She still hadn't even had time to look for the kids. Yesterday evening, she'd received a call that a patrol from Corner Brook had found the missing hunter. She was on her way to meet them when she'd gotten called about the school, which had tied her up the rest of the night.

There had been no sign of Oleg and Sarkis, either. Nor the bomb that wasn't a bomb. She was getting tired of Wolfhard's cagey answers and weird demands, which had continued well into the night, even while she was dealing with the fire. They had showed up at the detachment at one AM to go through her files again while Tanguay was here at the school. By the time she got back, they were gone, having left the office in a mess once again.

Fortunately, the fire had occurred in the middle of the night when the school was empty. Hayward said the flames had spread fast, so it would have been much worse if there'd been people around. Almost as bad as it would be if they didn't find the arms dealers and they got off the island with that "bomb" or whatever the hell it was...

"Hey, Sergeant, take a look at this?" Constable Brake's voice interrupted her train of thought. He had crept up behind her without making a sound. Bruce Brake always creeped her out like that. The pornstar moustache didn't help, either. "I found this in the principal's office next to the filing cabinet."

Wearing rubber gloves, he held up a blue and grey backpack, heavily scorched by the flames.

"So? It's a school bag. It's a school."

"Look at the name tag." Brake tilted his head toward a dangling plastic tag on the bottom of the bag, which had somehow avoided the worst of the flames.

Tanguay reached out and carefully turned it over with her pen. The tag read "Property of Pius Jeddore."

It had to be a coincidence. Pius went to St Paul's High School, after all. There could be a perfectly logical explanation of why his bag was in the principal's office. Pius was not the kind of kid to have his belongings confiscated by the principal. He could have been helping the staff after school and forgot it. Or someone might've found it and turned it in to the office. There were a dozen logical explanations for why it would be there.

Brake held the bag open. He poked around with his gloved hands. "There's some odd stuff in here that wasn't on my school supplies list when I was a kid. There's a glass cutting tool, wire cutters, duct tape, rope, a knife...."

Tabernac. What the hell was that kid getting into?

She sighed. "Did anyone else see this?"

Brake shook his head.

"Good. Bag it and label it all, but let me talk to the parents and the kid before we log it in, okay?"

"Ten-four, Sarge." Brake went back to his work. He probably would have thrown out the bag if she'd asked him. Tanguay wasn't sure if he was loyal to her or just crooked. She kinda hoped it was the latter. If he was that loyal, he might follow her too far down the dangerous path she was on.

Marie-Ann had stuck her neck out a lot for those kids since last year. They deserved it for everything they'd been through, but where did she draw the line? Blatant arson?

She would have to talk to the Jeddores. Find out what the hell was going on. Wolfhard and Mason were out in Robinsons, checking out Jesso's barn, and Tanguay had wanted to meet them as soon as they got back. But she had to get in front of the Pius thing before word got out. Wolfhard wouldn't like her talking to the parents, but screw him. If the kids were missing, their parents needed to know. And there were too many questions and mysteries floating around this damn town. She had to start getting answers fast so she could start making sense of something...

CHAPTER TWENTY-FOUR

No Rain
June 2, 8:15 am

Niall, Pius, and Harper sat around the kitchen table, each with an untouched bowl of Teddy Grahams cereal in front of them. They were dressed in their pyjamas and groggy from the late night. None of them spoke.

Niall's mom came into the room, smelling of drug store perfume that, as a younger child, Niall always associated with his mom going to work or out with his father. It was the smell of abandonment.

"So, you kids lucked out, huh?" she said as she crossed the kitchen, fixing her earrings. She grabbed her keys from the drawer by the fridge. "I heard they might have to cancel school for the rest of the year. What are you guys going to do? I could ask Nelson if he can get you a job, Niall."

Niall's stomach churned. The thought of stocking shelves with diapers, baby food, and feminine products at the drugstore with his brother was bad enough, but the real reason he was at war with himself was that it was *their* fault that the school had burned down in the first place. Niall felt a strange mixture of terror, guilt, and elation. It was not unlike how he felt about kissing Harper for the first time yesterday.

Did his mother know? Did the police know? Surely, someone was going to find out sooner than later about both the school and his dalliances with the Jeddore girl.

"I'm on my way to work, but you guys stay out of trouble, okay?" His mom smiled. Niall usually liked it when she smiled—it delighted him, and it usually meant they were having something good for dinner. But now, it made him feel guiltier. He wanted to blurt out that they were pyromaniac arsonists who deserved to go to prison, but he forced a feeble smile in return.

"Have a good day at work, Mom."

And then she was gone, and for the first time since last night, the three of them were alone together.

After he had returned to the car, Pius refused to tell anyone what happened. Keenan got in a few minutes later and gave them the gist of the story: that the journal with the secrets of Theolina's knowledge had been destroyed. Pius tried to get out and walk home, and it had taken Niall and Harper significant begging and pleading to get him back in the car, but Pius still wouldn't talk to them.

When they returned to Niall's house, Pius stomped off to the basement and locked himself in the bathroom. He wouldn't come out until Niall and Harper went to bed, and Niall still wasn't sure if he ever did or if he had slept in the bathtub. When Niall woke, Pius sat at the table, reading a *Spawn* comic and doing his utmost to ignore everyone else in the house.

Niall had gone through periods before when Pius wouldn't speak to him. Sometimes, if Pius got really scared, he would shut down into a near-vegetative state and not talk for hours. After he watched *Child's Play 3*, he had been useless for days. But this was different. It wasn't just fear— there was a certain restless unease and brooding indignation. Niall couldn't quite place it, not even with an entire thesaurus to help him out.

"So, now what?" Niall asked, finally breaking the tense silence.

"We wait for the butt monkeys to destroy the world?" replied Harper.

"I mean, do you want to go play Super Nintendo or watch TV..."

"You think this is a joke?" Pius blurted out.

Taken off guard, Niall didn't quite know what to say. "No, I mean we have a whole extra month of summer. We need to figure out what to do with our time. Should we start a new *D&D* campaign?"

"I burned down the frigging school!"

"The man on the radio said it wasn't the whole school," Harper clarified. "Only half of it."

Pius rocked back and forth on his chair with his hands under his legs. "I need to tell somebody. I should call Sergeant Tanguay and tell her it was me who did it."

"Mr. Bourgeois will kill you," said Harper. "I mean, he will literally chop you up into little pieces with a hatchet. Even if you survive, you'll be kicked out of St. Paul's. You'll have to go to the Amalgamated High School." She shuddered.

"I would be dead if Keenan hadn't pulled me out. And Mr. Bourgeois would have already caught me if it weren't for you guys." Pius wouldn't look up.

That part was true. Harper and Niall, having missed Pius at every step when they went looking for him the previous evening, arrived at the school right as a random passerby walked up to the front door, possibly alerted to the strange goings-on. Harper threw a rock through the window to distract the guy, and he ended up chasing Harper and Niall away.

Niall reached out and put his hand on Pius' shoulder. "Yeah, but we broke the window and startled you. It's partly our fault."

Pius shoved him away and snorted. "That's a nice sentiment, but all you did was break a window. I broke in, bypassed the alarm, and then set fire to the place. I deserve whatever punishment I get. I deserve to be chopped up into little pieces, fed to Joey Smallwood, and pooped out in his litter box."

"It was an accident," Niall reminded him. "And no one got hurt. What's the point of punishing yourself?"

"Because I *deserve* to be punished! Keenan should have let me burn! I should be put in jail where I can't mess up anything else!"

Harper shook her head. "You're talking foolishness."

"Am I? I broke up my parents' marriage, didn't I?"

"Pius, we've been over this—"

"And you guys can't even leave me alone," he screeched. "I'm useless by myself. I try to do one thing on my own, and I burn down the school! Why did you leave me alone?"

"What are you getting on with?"

Pius had tears in his eyes. "You guys keep leaving me alone! What were you doing last night that was so important that you couldn't be there to help me!"

Niall wanted to say they couldn't make it because they were making out, but he thought better of it. Of all the guys he knew, Pius would be the least impressed to hear about Niall's love conquests. Also, that wasn't the real reason they hadn't been there. He looked at Harper. "We need to show him the thing."

Pius looked up at him. A thin line of snot ran down from his nose. "Show me what?"

Harper nodded. "Sure, but you go get it. I'm not touching that thing."

Niall didn't want to touch it, either, but he certainly couldn't make Harper do it. Not because she was his girlfriend but because she would physically destroy him if he tried. He got up from the table, went out to the porch—he was too freaked out to keep it in the house—and retrieved an Adidas shoebox from under the BBQ on the patio. He had wrapped it in several layers of duct tape and was relieved to see that it hadn't been disturbed. On his way to the table with the box, he grabbed scissors from the junk drawer in the kitchen. Then he put the box on the table, and Harper immediately backed away.

"What's going on?" Pius asked, pushing his chair back and getting ready to bolt from the room.

"Just look." Niall cut the duct tape away carefully with the scissors. He removed the lid and laid it on the table next to the box.

Pius looked into the box and turned pale. He didn't scream, though, which Niall half-expected. He was doing better than Harper did the first time she saw it.

"Is that real?"

"Pretty sure," Niall replied.

Inside the shoebox was the largest June bug any of them had ever seen. It filled the box—a large, reddish-brown winged beetle the size of one of Nelson's size 10 sneakers. Usually, the June bugs around here got up to two or three centimetres long, which was big enough to be horrifying. This thing... whatever it was... was unimaginable, unfathomable terror.

"This can't be real." Pius picked up his cereal spoon and poked at the insect. "Is it dead?"

"It hasn't moved since yesterday, so I'm pretty sure it's dead."

"June bugs don't grow this big." Pius turned the box from side to side so he could look at it from every angle.

"Then what is it?" asked Niall. "Another kind of beetle?"

"I can't believe you're putting your face so close to it." Harper was on the other side of the room, with the dining table and the kitchen island between her and the giant, dead bug. "You are afraid of window blinds, but you look like you're about to suck face with a June bug the size of your head."

"This is amazing! Plus, most window blinds have dangerous levels of lead in them, not to mention the pull cords are a strangulation hazard."

"I told you he was into bugs," said Niall.

"Well, I don't know *that* much about them. I mean, I went through a phase in fourth grade where I used to read the *Guide to North American Insects.*"

"I remember that. You had to stop every couple of pages because you would see a picture of something that freaked you out."

Pius sighed. "I know. It took me all year to get through it. It was so embarrassing. Anyway, what we call June bugs are more accurately known as European Chafer scarabs or *Rhizotrogus majalis.* But they shouldn't get this big. The largest bug in the world is the titan beetle, which grows to about fifteen or sixteen centimetres. This thing is even bigger than that."

Harper rolled her eyes. "Oh yeah, you're totally not that into bugs."

Harper was teasing him, but Niall was glad to see some energy and enthusiasm in Pius again. He'd been so off lately, so different.

"I'm not," Pius insisted. "I'm not up to date on the newest research or studies."

"Maybe it was exposed to toxic waste or something?" asked Harper. "And it mutated?"

Now, it was Pius' turn to roll his eyes. "That only happens in the movies."

Harper snorted. "Need I remind you that last year, an undead sea witch from the bottom of the ocean almost killed us?"

"Good point. This could be a baby dragon, for all I know."

"So, what do we do with it?" asked Niall.

Pius scratched his chin and adjusted his glasses. "Well, actually, I might know someone we can ask about it."

At that moment, Niall's brother Nelson shuffled into the kitchen. He was shirtless, dressed in boxer shorts, and his hair was a tangled mess on top of his head. Judging from the red creases on his bare, peach-fuzzed chest, he had just rolled out of bed.

They froze. The box with the June bug in it was open and on full display. Niall's brain raced. Should he try to close it and risk drawing more attention to it? Nelson didn't seem to be paying attention to the bug anyway. Did it even matter if he saw it? They had no idea if it was magical or alien or a toxic-waste-radiated mutant, but Niall had gotten so used to hiding these things from his family that he felt like he should conceal everything.

Nelson looked like crap, as he did most mornings.

"More bad dreams?" Niall asked.

"Shut up, nerd." Nelson walked past them without so much as a sideways glance. He went straight to the fridge, farted a couple of times, and retrieved a two-litre carton of milk. He turned and headed back toward his room, taking the milk with him. He said nothing else and disappeared around the corner.

Niall breathed a sigh of relief, and the others relaxed.

"That's one ugly-ass bug," Nelson called from down the hall right before his door slammed closed.

CHAPTER TWENTY-FIVE

Two Princes
June 2, 8:00am

"No one home," Sarkis Garabet reported in Russian, returning to the kitchen from one of the bedrooms.

Oleg Aminov gestured to a cloud of flies buzzing around the overflowing garbage can and the layer of dust on all the surfaces. "No, you think so?"

"Cannot be too careful." Garabet was always careful. In his line of business, it was what kept you alive.

It was being careful that allowed Garabet to slip out of London quietly during the chaotic aftermath of the Pan Am bombing over Ireland in 1988. He hadn't planted the bomb himself, but he had been one of the key players who got it into Heathrow Airport. Being naturally light-skinned for a Libyan, he had certain advantages travelling in other countries. After the political fallout, Libya disavowed itself of Garabet and wiped all records of his involvement with their military, but Gaddafi had given him a good recommendation to the Soviets.

Against his best instincts, they had not been careful in choosing this abandoned shack on a treacherous road on the shore of this cursed island as a hideout. Garabet and Aminov had been desperate. This mission to secure an old American bomb was supposed to be easy. Both the Canadians and the Yankees were not supposed to know the bomb was here, and the damn thing was more an antique than anything else. Saddam Hussein's son Uday, out of his father's good graces again for some reason or another, wanted the Mark-6 as an olive branch for his old man, but the local authorities had proven to be far too much trouble, not to mention the feds showing up out of the blue...

As if reading Garabet's mind, Aminov grumbled, "I'm beginning to think this job was not worth the trouble." The Russian was laying out his weapons and ammo on the kitchen counter, taking stock of what they had left. It wasn't much. They had been forced to leave the motel in a hurry.

Garabet began to go through the kitchen cupboards. Mostly, he was doing it out of habit to familiarize himself with his surroundings; partly, he was looking for something to eat. "I think you are beginning to lose your nerve."

Even Aminov, who had the sense of humour of a turnip, had to chuckle at this. The two men had known each other for several years, and Garabet usually prided himself on making his dour-faced partner crack a smile, but this time it was Animove who teased his partner. "You are the one who jumps at shadows and nearly shot a cat when it startled you last week. I am just sick and tired of this stupid island."

Garabet had to agree with that. They had been in worse places, but none so unusual.

The Soviet Union fell shortly after he'd started working with Moscow, so Garabet and a young, eager KGB agent named Oleg Aminov had gone into business for themselves, using Soviet arms depots as their warehouse. From his time with Gaddafi, Garabet knew plenty of African dictators and guerilla groups who were more than happy to buy the surplus Soviet weapons. There were so many guns and bombs lying around that it was laughably easy. The new arms dealers sold AK-47s by weight; it was simpler than counting them.

"You remember the time we got double-crossed by that African warlord who left us in the jungle to die?" Aminov mused as he cleaned his handgun.

"Of course. I had to carry your sorry ass out after you got malaria."

"You misremember, comrade. It was I who had to carry you."

In truth, they had both contracted malaria and had to help each other out. Neither would have survived alone. They both knew this; it was just friendly teasing. Perhaps they had been doing this for too long. They were starting to sound like an old married couple.

Garabet opened another cupboard and found a couple of tin cans. Both were missing their labels. It could be cans of beans, or it could be motor oil. Dinner was going to be interesting tonight.

Something rustled in the garbage can behind him. Garabet whirled and drew his sidearm.

"You jumping at shadows again, Sarkis?"

"There's something in the garbage."

"You're as nervous as an old woman. It's probably just a mouse. Or maybe another cat? You got a phobia of cats now?"

The garbage can fell over, and even Aminov jumped, scrambling for his gun. Garabet didn't fire, but it was a close thing. His years of military training—which told him to shoot first and survive—were in conflict with his obsessive caution.

The latter won out in this case, and he held his shot. A chipmunk skittered out of the garbage can and bolted across the kitchen floor.

Aminov guffawed and nearly fell out of his chair. Garabet lowered his weapon and shook his head, but he had to laugh at himself, too. Perhaps they really had been doing this for too long. His nerves were shot, and this job was turning out to be a bust. They still didn't know where the bomb was, the Canadians and the Americans were on their ass, and he had just nearly shit himself at a goddamn chipmunk. He was too old for this. Maybe it was time to hang it up and retire to a quiet Mediterranean island. He's saved up enough money.

Sarkis Garabet shook his head, opened another cupboard, and briefly heard the buzzing of insect wings. There was a brilliant flash of light, and he smelled the distinct odour of burning flesh. Aminov screamed, but Garabet didn't know why. His vision suddenly blurred; something leapt out of the cupboard at his face, and Garabet fell to the floor.

CHAPTER TWENTY-SIX

Never Said
June 2, 9:05 am

"You just missed them," said Niall's grandmother, Josephine Whillet. She was standing at the door in her bright yellow tracksuit and a flour-covered apron. A large tabby cat curled around her legs. "They were on their way over to a friend's house when I got back from my run."

Marie-Ann Tanguay breathed a sigh of relief. She'd been meaning to check on them since last night before she was called away by the Corner Brook detachment. Apparently, the missing hunter had burned himself to death when he tried to light a fire to keep himself warm. Unfortunately, he had used gas from his ATV to start the fire, which he'd spilled all over himself, trying to siphon out of the tank. She went straight from that to the fire at the school.

"Are they in trouble, Officer?"

"Oh, no, not at all," Tanguay lied. "I wanted to ask them about some kids stealing a boat. Thought they might know someone who was involved."

"So, it has nothing to do with what happened at the school?"

Marie-Ann tried to keep her face passive. Did the old woman know something? Josephine was a cagey one, even if she no longer had the ghost of a witch living inside her. "Why? What do you know about the school?"

The old woman shrugged. "Seems a bit odd for a Mountie to be showing up at my door looking for kids the night after their school burns down, don't it? Bit of a coincidence? Especially when those kids were running around all hours of the night doing God knows what."

The cat at Josephine's heels hissed at Marie-Ann. Josephine nudged it back into the house with the toe of her slipper. "Go on with you, Joey Smallwood. Go piss under Nelson's bed."

The cat grumbled and stalked off, and Tanguay wondered if it was actually going to listen. "The kids were running around all hours of the night? With all the trouble they got into last year, I thought their parents would keep them on shorter leashes."

"Well, Pius' parents are going through some sort of row. Samantha caught Raymond fooling around on her and kicked him out. Pius and Harper have been staying here the last couple of days. The kids have been taking it hard, especially Pius, so my daughter, Barbara, has been giving them a lot of leeway. I don't think it's a good idea personally, but you know what kids are like."

Tanguay wasn't sure if Josephine was talking about her daughter or her grandkids, but if Pius was having family problems, it might explain his erratic behaviour. Breaking into the school and setting fires might be pushing it a little too far, but...

"Do you know which friend they went to see?"

"I told you, nobody tells me nothing. They could be out there smoking the dope for all I know."

"Thank you, Mrs. Whillet. Appreciate your time."

Josephine didn't seem to be one for beating around the bush. "So, did the kids set fire to the school or what?"

"We're still investigating the cause of the fire, Mrs. Whillet. We'll be in touch if we have any more questions."

Tanguay turned and started back toward her car. She wondered if Josephine was the type of woman who would immediately call up a half-dozen of her friends to tell them that a Mountie had shown up at her door, but she doubted it. Josephine may have forgotten most of last year's adventure details, but she knew some of it, and as best Tanguay could tell, the old woman hadn't told the story to a soul.

Tanguay nearly bumped into Keith Doucette, who was coming up the garden walk toward the O'Neil's house.

There had been a significant change in Keith since she'd seen him a few days ago. Back on the softball field, he had been smiling and acting like his own crap didn't stink. Now he looked dishevelled; his clothes were dirty, his eyes were bloodshot, and he had a nasty shiner. He stank, and not from alcohol, but from that unmistakable funk of adolescent boys. Keith was usually such a well-put-together and groomed kid, so the change in him was jarring. He was also carrying something wet and lumpy in a plastic bag from Foodland.

"Sergeant Tanguay?" He fumbled his words. She was used to people being nervous around her in uniform, but never Keith. "Is something wrong?"

"No, not at all." She looked Keith up and down. He looked like garbage. "Are you okay, Keith?"

"Me? Yeah, I'm wicked." He laughed awkwardly, proving that he was not, in fact, wicked. "I was worried Pius and Niall got themselves kidnapped again or something."

"No, they're fine. They went over to another friend's house. I don't guess you know where they went?"

"Skidmark's place?" Keith suggested. "If I knew where they were, I wouldn't have come by to look for them, would I? Anyway, gotta run. Places to be, kids to pick on, all that. See ya later, copper!"

Tanguay called after him as he started to walk away. "What's in the bag, your lunch?"

Keith froze and turned a grey colour. He glanced at the bag before turning back to her and forcing a smile, but he still looked ready to throw up. "No, just something interesting I found, thought the boys would like to check it out. See ya!"

Probably some dead animal he scraped off the side of the road. Kids were so weird. And gross. Still, she had a soft spot for those weirdos. She felt personally responsible for every one of them, and it often got her in trouble, like right now when she was chasing them all over town while she had far more pressing matters to attend to.

Her radio crackled as she headed to her car. She pressed the button on the receiver. "Go for Tanguay."

"Sergeant, Colonel Wolfhard is back. They've spotted the suspects."

"I'm on my way."

CHAPTER TWENTY-SEVEN

Loser

June 2, 9:30 am

The door creaked open a few centimetres, revealing a pair of muddy green eyes that appeared to be pointing in two different directions.

"Whaddya w-want?" asked a high-pitched voice that sounded like it was coming straight through the speaker's nose.

Niall looked at Pius, cocking his head as if to ask, "Are you sure this is the right place?"

Harper muttered something about a "Gollum-looking space case."

Pius shrugged.

Niall sighed and turned back toward the door. The Murphys lived in a modest green-coloured house on Woodward Avenue, not far from Niall's home. Niall had never heard of Todd Murphy until Pius brought up his name an hour ago, so he had no idea if the odd-looking creature crouched inside the porch was the one they were looking for.

"Are you Todd Murphy?" Niall asked.

"Who w-wants to know?

"I'm Niall. This is Harper and Pius. You don't know us, we go to St. Paul's High School. Your mom told us you would be home. Can we come in?"

"I don't open the d-door to strangers."

"The door is literally open right now."

The door slammed shut, and Niall groaned.

Pius and Harper shook their heads at him; such was the problem when your girlfriend and your best friend knew each other so well.

"Smooth move, Ex-Lax." Harper elbowed Niall aside and pounded on the door herself. "Hey, Todd. We have a weird bug here for you to look at."

There was the slightest pause before the door creaked open again. "What k-kind of bug?"

"We have no idea. That's why we brought it to the expert."

Todd sighed and opened the door the rest of the way, revealing a tall but severely hunched teen with mish-mashed eyes. They appeared to be pointing in opposite directions—was it even possible to have two lazy eyes?

"You came to the r-right place." Todd grinned. Unlike the rest of his body, his teeth were shockingly straight. "How d-do you know my m-mom?"

"We, uh, get in trouble with the cops a lot," said Niall, which was not precisely accurate but not exactly a lie, either. Beside him, Pius shifted awkwardly. Technically, Pius wasn't in trouble with the cops for burning down the school, but he was still touchy about it.

Todd's mom was Cheryl Murphy, the local RCMP dispatcher. She was a nice lady who offered Niall, Pius, and Keith tea and Purity Cream Biscuits when they met her at the detachment last summer. "Well, not a lot," said Pius. "But I happened to talk to her yesterday, and she mentioned she had a son who wanted to be an entomologist..."

"W-wait a minute." Todd leaned over to look at Pius more closely. Niall was struck with the image of an ape examining a small toy. "I know you. You w-were at the regional science fair last year. You extracted DNA s-strands from a s-strawberry. You came in s-second place."

"Yeah, I thought I recognized you, too. You wrote a BattleTech video game in QBasic. You came in first place."

"It only t-took me a weekend to w-write it. The judges always love c-computer programs."

"Yeah, Pius hated you for that," said Harper.

"Harper, we need his help," Niall whispered. Obviously, not quietly enough because Todd glared at him.

"N-no one ever w-wants my help unless their computer's broken."

"This one is different." Pius held up the shoe box. "Is there somewhere we can look at this? Privately?"

"Come into m-my office."

They took off their shoes, and Todd led them through a tidy but dingy-looking kitchen with faded wallpaper, peeling linoleum, and those weird yellow appliances that probably started out as off-white or beige.

The place reeked of cigarette smoke, and from the living room, the TV played daytime talk shows, but it couldn't drown out the loud snoring. Todd didn't acknowledge any of it or even say a word but led them down a set of narrow steps into a damp, cold basement that smelled like mould.

Past an oil furnace and a washer and dryer, Todd opened the door to a small but crowded room. Three of the walls were unpainted chipboard, and the fourth was bare pink insulation, but the many shelves, desks, and tables in the room were a nerd's treasure trove. In one corner, a computer monitor glowed, showing lines and lines of nonsensical text. Programming code? Opposite the computer was a TV-VCR combo and racks of VHS tapes. The shelves on the walls were sagging, stuffed with books on Biology, Physics, bugs (there were many books about bugs), and dozens of *Star Trek* and *Star Wars* novels. The table was covered with disassembled machines and computer parts. There was a black scorch mark in one corner where someone had obviously left a soldering iron on it at some point.

Harper wrinkled her nose and whispered to Niall. "Oh my God, it smells like an entire boy's locker room worth of gym socks died in here."

Niall thought some of the stuff in here was pretty cool, but the smell was indeed horrific. Body odour mixed with sour milk, old cigarette smoke, and mould. Niall could taste it, and it made his skin feel greasy.

"So, what's the b-big secret?" Todd asked.

Pius carefully placed the box on the table. Todd didn't offer to move any of his stuff, so Pius gingerly shoved the electronics aside before removing the lid.

Todd stared at the box, and his jaw fell slack. Then he turned his head and stared with his other eye. "This is f-fake, right?"

"I don't think so. Do you know what it is?"

"It looks l-like a European Chafer, but it can't be...." Todd poked the bug in the box and squealed.

Harper cringed.

Niall had once seen his brother hit a stray cat with a golf club, and the screech it made wasn't as disturbing as the sound of delight that came out of Todd.

"It's f-frigging *real*?"

Pius, Harper, and Niall nodded.

"This is unb-believable. Where d-did you find it?"

"Near my house, on Civil Street," explained Niall. "We found it lying dead on the grass."

"I can't, I d-don't..." Todd had more trouble than usual forming words, which was saying something. He snatched a battered book off the shelf and flipped through its dog-eared pages until he found what he was looking for. He shoved the tome in their faces. The pages he pointed at featured a detailed black-and-white drawing of a familiar bug. "That's a European Chafer, a c-common June bug. It's s-supposed to be a few centimetres long."

Harper shoved the book away, recoiling in disgust.

"How could it get so big?" asked Pius. "Is it a natural mutation, or is it genetically altered?"

"No one really g-grows giant bugs in labs, stupid," Todd scoffed.

Harper tensed beside Niall. No one was allowed to call Pius names except her.

"That's just something in m-movies."

"So, you're saying it's an alien, then?" demanded Harper.

Todd cackled. Actually cackled. Niall had never heard anyone make that sound outside of cartoon witches and Halloween decorations.

"How d-dumb are you people?"

"Actually," said Pius, his gaze a million kilometres away. "Maybe that's exactly what it is."

"This is a j-joke, right? You c-came here to mess with me? Who put you up to it? W-was it Keith Doucette? That guy's an asshole."

"Yes, he is," Pius agreed. "How do you know him?"

"L-look, I'll show you it's not an 'alien.' It's probably fake anyway." Todd opened a drawer in his desk and pulled out a yellow boxcutter. He turned the little, rattly knob to reveal a rusted blade. He held it over the giant bug. "May I?"

Niall, Pius, and Harper looked at each other. They shrugged.

"Be our guest," said Niall.

Todd began cutting into the bug with surprising care. Its carapace crunched and cracked under the blade.

Harper gagged.

Todd's pimply, nonplussed face changed as he cut into the scarab. First, surprise flickered across his face, and then excitement. Niall imagined that was how he looked when he opened the new CD Walkman he got for his birthday, except that his eyes pointed in the same direction.

Suddenly, Todd's expression changed to one of shock and disgust. "What the hell is that?"

Niall and Pius quickly approached the box. The giant bug had been split open, and from the look and smell of the guts inside, it certainly seemed to be real. Niall had never seen the inside of a bug, certainly not at this scale. Still, even he was pretty sure that the insides didn't look right, possibly because of the fluorescent green liquid pouring from its thorax and pooling in the bottom of the box.

"That is... not normal, right?" asked Pius.

"It looks like the gunk inside of a glow stick," added Niall.

"The insides look organic, but it d-doesn't look like any insect I've ever seen. Maybe it's because it's so b-big, but none of the structures and organs are in the right p-place. And I have no idea what that stuff is." Todd looked up at Harper. "W-why did you say this was an alien?"

"Oh, poor, poor, Todd." Harper smiled and winked. "Your world is about to get a hell of a lot weirder than this smelly basement."

Airman Wolfhard picked up the receiver and flicked the control button incessantly. He screamed for the dispatcher again and again.

He, Angus, and Linda huddled in the flickering pool of a single yellow lightbulb above the call box. It was the lone light in the long dark tunnel, which appeared to stretch forever in both directions, like a tiny desert island in the middle of the sea. Angus was curled up on the cold concrete floor, with his knees pulled up against his chest. He was breathing hard, but Linda wasn't sure if it was from exertion or terror.

When she was younger, Linda had watched her father fall off the roof while he was shingling the house. He survived, praise the Lord, but had knocked himself silly, and for a few minutes, Linda didn't know if he was dead or alive. The panic she felt that day, that lung-crushing terror that squeezed her chest and prevented her from catching her breath, must be what Angus was going through right now.

They had lost sight of whatever was chasing them. They couldn't hear it, either. They may have shaken it off their trail in the maze of tunnels beneath the base, but Linda didn't think so. She suspected it was still busy eating poor O'Brien.

"Dispatcher," came a tiny voice from the radio receiver. Linda could hear the voice from where she stood.

"Thank God!" howled Wolfhard. "Dispatcher, this is Airman First Class Eric Wolfhard. We have a situation in Tunnel Twelve!"

"Airman O'Brien said that your intruder had been apprehended."

"No, it's not an idiot kid! There's a creature or thing inside the base! I need a full platoon with heavy weapons!"

"Airman Wolfhard, we did have reports of another possible unauthorized individual who crossed onto the base near Gate 13. Please return to the garrison for further briefing."

Wolfhard shook the receiver in frustration. "We can't find our way back. There are no lights in the south tunnels! And this is not some 'unauthorized individual.' This is a dangerous weapon and a serious security threat. We need an escort team immediately! Do you copy? Hello? Dispatch!"

Linda's heart sank into her Mary Janes even before Wolfhard dropped the receiver.

"The line went dead."

"Are they sending anybody?" Linda asked, but she feared she knew the answer.

"I don't know. I don't think he believed me. I don't even know what to call the thing!"

"How do we get out of here?"

Wolfhard shook his head. "I don't know how to get to the garrison from here, but there's gotta be a hatch to the surface around here somewhere."

"What are all these tunnels, anyway? Do they go all over town?"

"Most of it, yeah. They're emergency tunnels in case of nuclear assault from the Commies." Wolfhard paced back and forth in their tiny circle of illumination. "It started as access tunnels for the stand-by fighter pilots, but a few years ago, they expanded the network to house the entire garrison, if necessary. Thousands of people could live under here for weeks."

"If there wasn't a fire-breathing angel chasing them." Linda smiled weakly.

"Someone's coming," said Angus, squinting at the darkness.

"Who is it?" Wolfhard levelled his pistol in the direction Angus was looking.

It took Linda's vision a moment to pick it out in the darkness, but yes, she could make out a humanoid figure moving through the shadows toward them. She didn't think it was the monster, but it didn't look like a soldier, either.

Wolfhard's hands shook, and the gun along with them. "Identify yourself, or I swear to God I'll blow your brains out!"

"Stand down, soldier," came a woman's voice from the darkness. She had a weird accent but also a steady, unmistakable aura of command.

Linda wasn't sure how someone could sound so confident with a gun pointed at them. She would have collapsed into a blathering ball.

"Who the hell are you?" demanded Wolfhard as the woman emerged from the darkness.

She was olive-skinned, with long, greasy black hair dangling over her face. She looked gaunt and thin, dressed in what appeared to be green hospital scrubs. Despite looking like a water-logged sea witch that had crawled out of the Bay, Linda sensed an incredible presence and certainty from the woman. She had never felt anything like it. She wanted to throw herself in front of this woman and do whatever she said.

The woman walked up to Wolfhard without fear and put her hand on his, lowering his gun. "I'm here to help. Come with me, and I'll try to keep you alive."

CHAPTER TWENTY-EIGHT

Can You Forgive Her?
June 2, 10:10 am

Brian "Skidmark" Hawco rolled down his driveway on sparkly, silver rollerblades, trying to stop before he hit the lip of the curb and fell over. So far today, he had attempted this feat forty-seven times. The outcome of his effort was precisely zero instances of stopping on his own accord, two bruised and scraped knees, a wicked gash running from his palm to his elbow on his left forearm from where he fell on broken glass, and smears of glittery silver paint all over the freshly-paved black asphalt of the driveway. As he lay on his back on the grass, tasting blood from his split lip, he contemplated who was going to be angrier with him: Mrs. Walsh, for scuffing all the paint off the skates, or his dad, for putting that silver paint all over the driveway. Probably his dad. He could repaint the skates, and it was looking like the school play wasn't going to happen anyway, but that paint was not coming off the asphalt as easily as it did the cheap plastic skates. His dad was going to be pissed when he got home.

"What the hell are you doing?" asked a familiar voice from somewhere near his head. Brian couldn't see who was approaching with the sun in his eyes, but he knew that voice anywhere. Somewhere deep in his tired, bruised bones, the flight-or-scream instinct of all bullied kids kicked in, and he immediately rolled over onto his knees and tried to crawl away across the lawn toward his house. The grass stung his scraped, bloody knees.

"Ow. Ow. Ow." He muttered through his awkward belly crawl each time his knees went down.

"Whaddya at, buddy?" Keith Doucette stood behind him.

"Don't call me 'buddy!'" Brian replied, not looking back. "You have reverted to your prior villainous ways, and you forfeit the right to speak to me with genial terms!"

"What are you gettin' on with?"

Brian stopped and rolled onto his butt to address Keith. His hands and knees were too sore to keep going anyway. "You went back to your old dickwad self. I heard what you did to Pius the other day."

Keith ran his fingers through his lopsided bowl cut. He grimaced and sighed, looking genuinely uncomfortable. And dirty. Was he having regrets for his regression back to Neanderthal tendencies? Why did he look like he crawled through a culvert on his way over here? And why the hell was he carrying a plastic grocery bag full of wet meat?

"Look, that was a mistake." Keith shook his head. "It was an accident. I didn't mean to do it."

"You were drunk," said Brian. "Sloshed. Wasted. Buzzed. Half-cut."

"Yeah, maybe."

"But you chose to get drunk. Ergo, you were at fault. You made a series of choices that led to your behaviour, and whether or not the outcome is what you planned or expected, the choices you made directly influenced the results of your actions."

"Geez, Skidmark, knock it off. You sound like the goddamn guidance counsellor."

Brian nodded. "Mr. Isaac? Yeah, he talks like that a lot. My parents make me go to him because they say I have behavioural issues and ADD, but I can't take anything he says seriously because his own life is falling apart. Did you know his wife beats him with a stapler? I heard she's a hard drinker, but I think it's because Mr. Isaac is such a dipwad. I know I usually want to hit him with a stapler myself after our sessions."

Keith groaned and threw up his hands, exasperated, but Brian couldn't imagine why. "Oh, me nerves, Skidmark, I'm looking for Pius and Niall to apologize. Have you seen them?"

"Not since yesterday. Pius was staying at Niall's house. He was there alone when I called him looking for Niall. Niall wasn't there. He and Harper got kidnapped by child molesters."

Keith's jaw dropped. "What?"

"Well, I don't think they were *actually* child molesters. That's what we were calling them, but from the information I overheard from Sergeant Tanguay and those secret agent guys, I think they're some kind of international spies or war criminals or something. It definitely sounded like they were more likely to kill Niall and Harper rather than diddle them or something. I mean, I was hiding under their bed for hours, and no one tried to diddle me."

"What in God's name are you talking about? What happened to Niall and Harper?"

Brian thought he had explained the situation pretty succinctly. Still, he was about to go over it again when an old, rusty, vomit-coloured station wagon pulled up in front of the house. Two people dressed in cool outfits got out. One was a tall, greasy-looking guy with a top hat and a velvet coat. The other was a girl in a corset with the second-largest boobs Brian had ever seen in real life, after his mom.

"Are you Brian Hawco?" the girl asked, and Brian was immediately smitten. She knew his name? He didn't care if that was creepy. He was going to marry her.

"Who the hell are you supposed to be?" Keith asked, being completely rude to the woman who would one day be the mother of Brian's children. The guy had no manners at all.

"We've been looking all over town for Niall O'Neil and Harper and Pius Jeddore," said the guy in the top hat, coming around the car to stand next to the girl. Brian disliked him immediately, despite his fabulous taste in clothes. "When we couldn't find them, we started with the next person on the list."

"The *list*?" Keith asked, his voice dripping with disdain. "What are you guys, assassins or something?"

The girl looked Keith up and down carefully, and a burning sensation crept up Brian's throat. Was that... jealousy? Brian had felt that once before when the kid next door had gotten the Ninja Turtles Party Wagon and all four Turtles for his birthday a couple of years ago. It hurt extra hard because, for Brian's birthday a few days later, his parents had only given him a set of ProStars collectible glasses from the gas station. It had two Bo Jackson's instead of a Michael Jordan.

"Are you Keith Doucette?" asked the girl.

"So what if I am?"

She looked back at the guy in the hat, and Brian's rage bounced from Keith to the sad Slash wannabe. What was happening to him? Had he suddenly hit puberty? Had his hormones suddenly kicked in like the warp engines on the Enterprise?

"Keenan, we found them both!"

"Look, who the hell are you, and how do you know who we are?" Keith was starting to get angry, and Brian was beginning to get worried. What if he scared them away?

The girl clapped her hands together and giggled. It was either cute or crazy; Brian couldn't decide which. "I'm Anna, and this is Keenan. This is going to sound nuts, but we know you were kidnapped by Theolina Kane last year, and you saw the Primordial One, the thing you guys called the Psycho Hose Beast."

Keith didn't say anything. He looked too shocked. They weren't supposed to talk about these things in public. No one outside their group was supposed to know about this stuff.

Brian hadn't said anything for several minutes. He suspected this was the longest he had ever gone in his life without opening his mouth. What the heck had happened to his voice?

"We think there's another monster coming to Gale Harbour, and we've been working with Niall, Harper, and Pius to figure out what it is and how to stop it. I need to find them because I think we figured out the 'what it is' part, at least."

Keith gestured vaguely at the world around him. Was he pointing at Brian's white clapboard house? His street? The whole town? Brian wasn't sure; he couldn't pull his gaze away from Anna's cleavage. "Yeah, we'd all like to find them, but apparently, they've been kidnapped by child diddlers!"

"What are you talking about?" asked Anna, but Keenan spoke over her.

"What's in the bag?"

Keith froze. "This bag?"

"Yes, the gooey, sloppy thing you're lugging around in that plastic bag."

Brian hadn't looked at it closely, but the goo in the bag wasn't red like bloody meat. It was green.

"It was flying around outside my house last night. I smashed it with a baseball bat."

Keenan put up his hands as if to tell Keith to stay away. "Very carefully put it down on the pavement and back away."

"It's already dead. I told you I smashed it."

"Put it down," Keenan growled.

Shocked, Keith did as he was told and backed away to stand on the grass beside Brian.

Keenan approached the bag carefully and nudged it with the toe of his boot. "This is what we were trying to warn you guys about. Anna figured out more of the translation last night."

Green, glowing slime ran out of the bag onto the driveway.

"What is it?" Keith asked.

Keenan pulled a pack of matches out of his velvet coat and lit one. He took a few steps back to stand beside Keith, and then he flicked the lit match at the bag.

A blue light flashed so brightly that Brian was afraid he was blinded. It took several moments for his vision to clear. The heat was incredible, like that time Chris Tobin had threatened to throw him face-first into a bonfire down at the beach.

When the spots finally faded, Brian saw a pillar of black smoke rising over the house. A small but still bright blue flame burned where the bag had been, and the asphalt around it had melted into a black puddle.

"What the hell was that?"

Keenan grinned. "I think Harper called it a 'butt monkey.'"

Brian stared at the flame, watching the tar and asphalt run down the driveway into the street, Anna momentarily forgotten.

"My dad's going to kill me."

CHAPTER TWENTY-NINE

I'm Gonna Be (500 Miles)
June 2, 10:40am
Cape-de-Cape Peninsula, West of Gale Harbour

Wolfhard and Mason had tracked Garabet and Aminov to a small shack overlooking St. Stephen's Bay on the Cape-de-Cape peninsula. It was in one of those tiny communities Tanguay could never remember the name of: Boat Cove or Lower Boat Cove or Gerald's Ear or one of those. She'd been the RCMP Commanding Officer here for over a year now, and she could never keep them straight. Each village only had a population of a hundred people or so, so she wasn't sure why each of them needed their own name.

The small house was topped with a sagging roof missing several shingles, and the once-white clapboard siding was cracked and greying. It was located a ways off the main road in a large, open field of wild grass that hadn't been mowed yet this year. When Tanguay arrived, Wolfhard's black 4x4 and another RCMP cruiser were already parked in the field. Constable Bennett was leaning against the side of his car, chatting with Captain Mason, and Wolfhard was staring at the shack like a hawk. Although Tanguay couldn't see his eyes, she wouldn't have been surprised to find that he wasn't blinking.

"Sergeant," Bennett called out as she approached. "Beautiful day, isn't it?"

"What's the story, Burt?"

"We got a tip about an hour ago that two men matching our Ruskies' descriptions went into that old house early this morning. A neighbour called it in because no one has lived in that place for years."

Neighbour? Tanguay scanned the area. There was a sheer rock face on one side of the shack and dense trees on the other. The only other house visible was on the other side of the road, several hundred meters up a hill.

Bennett must have noticed her confusion. "Yes, well, she 'noticed' it in her binoculars. You know what people around here are like."

She did. Everyone watched through their front windows to see what everyone else was doing. Most of the time, they were just pretending not to see each other hiding behind the curtains in their living rooms.

"We spotted movement in the house when we arrived, so we think the suspects are still inside."

"Then why are we out here?"

Bennett cleared his throat and pointed at the soldiers. "They said those guys have heavy weapons, explosives, laser scopes, ninja stars—"

"We did not say that!" Mason interjected.

"It was implied. Anyway, I'm not going in there without backup."

"Those are dangerous men, Sergeant." Wolfhard still hadn't moved his gaze from the house. Tanguay was surprised he even knew she was there. "Unfortunately, Officer Bennett here informed us you don't have a SWAT team."

"We've got a shotgun back at the office," Bennett offered.

"The only other person on duty is Constable Brake, and he's occupied out in Long Ice River. I called for backup from Corner Brook, but they're an hour out. Sorry, Colonel, we're not a New York City police precinct with an entire army at our disposal."

"How do you people operate under these conditions?"

Tanguay sighed and straightened her bullet-proof vest. She checked her sidearm and headed for the house. "Bennett, cover me."

"Sarge, shouldn't we wait for the backup? The suspects aren't going anywhere...."

Wolfhard had a sinister sparkle in his wild old eyes. "No, I like how she operates. Captain Mason, if you would join the sergeant and myself." Walking around the vehicles, Wolfhard popped the trunk of his 4x4 and handed Mason an automatic shotgun. Wolfhard, himself, took a comically large rifle with a scope.

Bennett whistled, impressed. "You guys have a friggin' armoury in there! Is that a Barrett M82? *Dee-cent.*"

Marie-Ann forced herself not to roll her eyes and make a comment about how Wolfhard was overcompensating for something. She didn't want to risk offending him when he was so eagerly offering to back her up.

There was no way in hell he was hitting anything with that rifle, of course, but maybe the mere sight of it would make the bad guys crap their pants.

"You know, if we approach that shack, we're sitting ducks in the field." Tanguay pointed toward the house. Though the grass was tall, they would have to crawl on their bellies to stay covered. If either of the creeps were sitting in the window of the house with a rifle like Wolfhard's, someone's brains would get splattered all over Cape-de-Cape.

Wolfhard, reaching into his seemingly endless Tickle Trunk of weapons, pulled out a metal canister with a handle and a pull ring. He offered it to Captain Mason. "Think you can get it through their window?"

Mason scoffed. "Tear gas? From fifty metres? Not likely."

"I thought you played college football?"

"I was a wide receiver. I can't throw like that!"

Bennett whistled and held out his hand. "Give it to me."

Three sets of dubious eyes turned to the portly constable. He removed his hat and rotated his throwing arm like a relief pitcher warming up. "I didn't play no fancy college sports, but I can pick off a Labatt Blue can with a rock from thirty metres. When Constable Brake and I were out camping in the gravel pit behind Porter's Brook last May Two-Four, and the wind was just right, I put out the tail light of his pickup truck with a rock from about forty metres. Of course, I was aiming for the beer bottle on the tailgate, but that window's a lot bigger than a long neck. I'm pretty sure I can hit it."

Wolfhard leaned into Mason. "What's 'May Two-Four?'"

"May Twenty-Fourth weekend. Like Memorial Day in the States."

Wolfhard nodded and looked at Tanguay with a raised eyebrow, for once actually deferring to her. She almost laughed. *This* was the thing he decided to ask her opinion on?

She shrugged. *What odds?* as they said around here.

"Give it to him."

Bennett pulled the ring from the canister. He took a couple of steps back, ran a couple of steps forward, and lobbed the tear gas grenade like Joe Carter throwing a fly ball in from right field. He bent over, gasping for breath, and the canister soared through the air in a high arc. Tanguay thought for sure it was going to fall short. There was no conceivable way Burt Bennett—the guy who had to take sick leave a few months ago when he hurt his back picking up a box of donuts he dropped coming out of Tim Hortons—was going to put a metal canister through a window at fifty metres.

Then the glass shattered, and Tanguay smiled despite herself.

"Well, damn," said Mason. "That was a nice throw."

"Owes me a beer!" Bennett whooped in triumph, though it wasn't clear who he was talking to.

Smoke billowed from the old house, and Tanguay gestured for them to move in. Mason took point, followed closely by Tanguay, and then Wolfhard took up the rear with his giant sniper rifle.

"Why isn't anyone coming out?" Tanguay asked, mostly thinking out loud.

"Gas masks?" offered Mason. "Or they're unconscious or dead?"

"They're not the types to do themselves in if that's what you're suggesting," replied Wolfhard.

They reached the house's front porch, but there was still no sign of the occupants. Could Bennett's info have been wrong? Maybe they weren't here at all? If someone was inside, wouldn't they have taken a shot at them by now?

"This is the Royal Canadian Mounted Police!" called Tanguay. "Come out with your hands up!"

"You're going to feel really stupid if there's a harmless old lady in there with her cats," said Wolfhard. "She's in there trying to knit a doily."

Tanguay couldn't tell if he was trying to be funny, but she wanted to slap him anyway. Not to mention, in her experience, harmless-looking old ladies were sometimes anything but.

They circled the house, checking for other exits. There was another door on the far side, where the unkempt lawn grew right to the back step. The grass was crushed and broken, revealing a rough trail where someone had apparently crawled out the open door and straight into the grass.

"*Merde*," Tanguay hissed.

Mason crouched down and went to follow the trail through the grass.

Wolfhard peered inside. "Not sure how the laws work around here, Sergeant, but if you need probable cause to enter a premises, I suspect the dead body lying on the floor is a pretty good excuse."

Tanguay and Wolfhard entered, stepping into the abandoned kitchen. Dusty dishes and trash lined the counters. Stained white linen covered the table. On the floor, propped up against a yellowing refrigerator, was the body of one of the men Tanguay had been following for the last week. It was the taller one, the one she had spoken to at the Jeddore's house on the weekend. He was still dressed in the same black pants and white shirt, though his jacket was gone. There was a gaping wound in the centre of his chest. Tanguay could see the yellow fridge door through the hole.

Wolfhard leaned in close. "It's Garabet. He's been dead for hours."

They scanned the rest of the house quickly. It wasn't large, and they found no sign of Aminov. There were clues that someone had been here recently—cigarette butts, food wrappers, empty bullet casings—but whoever left them was long gone. They returned to the kitchen to examine Sarkis Garabet more closely.

"What did that to him?" Tanguay asked.

It didn't look like a bullet wound. And for a hole big enough to put her fist through, there was nowhere near as much blood as she would have expected.

"The wound is cauterized," said Wolfhard. "Whatever it was burned right through him."

Tanguay shook her head. "I've never seen anything like it."

Wolfhard stepped back. There was a strange look on his face. He was paler than usual, and there was an uncertainty that Marie-Ann was not used to seeing in him. "I have. A long time ago."

More of Wolfhard's cryptic bullshit. But now that he mentioned it...

True, Tanguay hadn't seen anything quite like Garabet, but there had been a strange rash of fires around town lately. The high school, and that hunter who had been burned alive...

"So, you've seen that before, huh?" said Tanguay. "In that case, Colonel, when we get back to town, I need you to examine a body for me."

The corner of Wolfhard's lip raised ever so slightly. "You have an interesting way of asking a fellow out on a date, Sergeant."

Mason appeared in the doorway. "I followed the trail down to the beach. I lost it on the rocks, but I suspect whoever it was has been gone for hours." He looked at the body on the floor. "Is that Garabet?"

Wolfhard nodded. "Which means Constable Bennett didn't notice Oleg Aminov slipping away."

Tanguay had already come to the same realization herself. She was going to kill Burt, not only for screwing this up and letting a dangerous criminal get away, but also for making them look like fools in front of the Yankee. She reached for her radio, but it crackled to life before she touched it, startling her. She quickly composed herself and pushed the talk button.

"Go for Tanguay."

"Sarge, this is Brake. There's a fire in town, and we need you there right away."

Another one? It wasn't even Guy Fawkes' night. Maybe she was onto something. "Can't you and Chief Hayward handle it?" She looked down at Garabet's body. "I'm kinda busy here."

"It's Constable Murphy's house."

<u>**CHAPTER THIRTY**</u>

Livin' On The Edge
June 2, 10:15am

"What the hell is this?" Harper asked, with her head tipped to one side, trying to make sense of it. "And why is it all in Japanese?"

"It's oddly fascinating," agreed Niall. "I have no idea what's going on, but I can't take my eyes away."

"It's making me feel weird things I've never felt before," added Pius.

"It's c-called 'anime,'" Todd explained again. "It's a Japanese cartoon."

The trio was watching one of Todd's bootleg tapes on his small TV that sat on the desk in the corner of his room. He called it his "room," as if it was his bedroom, but there was no bed to be seen. Did Todd sleep? Niall wouldn't have been surprised to find out he was a troll who didn't need to sleep.

"Why are there so many tentacles?" asked Harper. "And why doesn't she have any clothes on?"

"That's how they make cartoons in Japan."

"Oh wait, now I see what's going on." Harper cringed. "This is so disgusting."

"Where do you get this stuff?" Niall asked, entirely out of morbid curiosity, of course, and not because he wanted to get some of his own.

"The comic shop in c-Corner B-brook. It's on the top shelf behind the counter."

The comic shop in Corner Brook, a larger town about an hour away from Gale Harbour, was where they got more interesting comics and most of their *Dungeons & Dragons* books.

"I thought that was porn?" said Harper.

"It's *not* porn!" Todd snapped.

Touchy subject. If he had to go out on a limb, Niall would guess Todd had argued about it with his parents.

"Do they show this stuff on Saturday Mornings in Japan?" asked Pius, staring intently at the screen. Niall didn't blame him. He was trying to keep discreet due to their current company, but if Harper hadn't been there, Niall would have had his face plastered to the screen with Pius.

"Can we get back to the bug, please?" Harper tore her gaze away from the screen and shook her head as if she were trying to knock the memories out of her skull. Her black braid flopped adorably.

The bug was still lying in the shoebox on the table, not entirely forgotten, but certainly not the current centre of attention. Todd said he was going to look something up about the bug "online," but he had to wait for his sister to get off the phone for some reason. They had turned the weird, sexy Japanese cartoons on while they were waiting.

Todd took a broom handle from beside the door and used it to pound on an overhead metal duct that ran across the ceiling. The wood hitting aluminum made a loud clanging sound that echoed through the house. "Sheila!" Todd screamed at the ceiling. "You off the phone yet?"

"Yes, I'm off the phone!" came the muffled reply through the floor. "Stop banging on the goddamn pipes!"

Todd smacked the duct again. "Why didn't you tell me you were off the phone?"

"Shag off, Todd!"

A new voice joined into the argument, coming from somewhere else in the house. A deeper, scratchy voice, one that was hoarse from smoking several packs of cigarettes a day for who knows how long. "Jesus, Mary and Joseph, the two of you better knock off that racket, or I swear to God, I'll give you something to cry about!"

"Sorry, Dad!" Todd and his sister called out at the same time.

Pius and Niall shied away into the corner of Todd's room, embarrassed by overhearing this family conflict. Pius, especially, looked ready to crawl under the table and slit his wrists with one of the rusty screwdrivers lying on the stained carpet.

Harper was unfazed; in fact, she was downright beaming, seemingly amused by the scene. "I wonder if they always talk to each other through the floor and walls like that?" she asked no one in particular. "Did you notice that Todd loses his stutter when he's talking to his family? Or maybe it's just when he's yelling...."

Niall realized, like a punch to the gut, that the reason Harper was fascinated by the Murphy family's dynamics was because she had none of her own. Sure, Raymond and Samantha treated her well, and they were close to her, but it would never be the same as what she had with the father she lost or the mother that she never knew. Even the Murphys' dysfunctional communication was more than she had. Niall felt sick.

And then a weird, mechanical-style screeching and scratching startled him.

Harper flinched.

Todd and Pius were crouched over Todd's computer, where the noise came from.

Harper leaned in close to Niall. "Is it supposed to be making that high-pitched screaming sound?"

"It sounds like a fax machine." His mother had one at her office. "I think it's the modem?"

"What's a modem?" Harper whispered.

"That is a U.S. Robotics Sp-Sportster 9600 baud modem," said Todd. "Duh. I want to get a new fourteen-point-four kilobits one, but my parents won't get it because they p-paid eight hundred bucks for the other modem only last year."

Eight hundred bucks? He couldn't imagine asking his parents for anything that cost that much, let alone asking for it twice.

"That is so cool!" Pius beamed. "What do you do online?"

"Actually, I spend m-most of my time on a BBS run by a guy in Kentucky. We ch-chat about our favourite episodes of *Star Trek*, and I laugh at him when he tries to say that Captain Picard is b-better than Captain Kirk."

"Oh yeah," Pius agreed. "*Next Generation* is cool, but Kirk will always be the best captain."

"I like Picard," Harper chimed in. "I think bald men are sexy."

Pius and Todd suddenly looked uncomfortable, probably due to a cute girl using the "s" word in their vicinity. Niall wondered if he should find out if she was joking before he shaved his head.

"Who is this guy?" asked Pius.

"He's a retired astronaut and jet fighter pilot." Todd gushed like Niall's aunt Darlene when she talked about Jesus. "He fought in Vietnam and got a Purple Heart."

"Wait a minute," said Harper. "Have you ever met him?"

"No, of course not. I t-told you he lives in Kentucky."

"Then how do you know any of that stuff is true?"

"Of c-course it's true. Why would he lie?"

"Who do you tell him you are?"

Todd didn't answer, merely turned his face back to the screen. "Oh, good, he's online. I c-can ask him now."

White text against black scrolled by on the screen. Someone had drawn a dragon out of lines and dots. Todd went through a few menus until he started typing, apparently talking to someone named "GoldLeader1."

"Is that him?" Pius pointed at the names on the screen.

Todd nodded.

"And you're 'PrissStingray?' What's that?"

"It's from B-Bubblegum Crisis. She's a r-robot hunter."

"She?" Harper asked. "Does he think you're a girl?"

Todd muttered under his breath but didn't answer.

"What are you doing?" Niall asked. "I thought we were trying to figure out more about this bug?"

"I am. B-but you mentioned it was extraterrestrial in origin, so I thought I would ask Gold Leader about it."

"I don't think he's really an astronaut," Harper whispered to Niall.

Pius, wholly fascinated by the computer, was giddily reading over Todd's shoulder. "This is so cool! I can't believe you're talking to someone thousands of kilometres away!"

"I mean, he could use the phone," muttered Harper. "If he's paying long-distance anyway, it would be faster and cost just as much to talk to the guy. But then I guess you can't pretend you're a girl on the phone...."

Niall tried to shush Harper. On the off-chance Todd's friend knew what they were talking about, they didn't want to piss him off.

"He's not dismissing you outright," Pius noted. "That's a good sign, right?"

"He's asking all kinds of questions about its chemical c-composition. How am I s-supposed to know that? It's not like I h-have hydrochloric acid lying around that I could use to d-dissolve its exoskeleton."

"Of course, you don't," said Harper.

"I mean, I d-did, until my parents made me get rid of it after the incident with Sheila's hamster."

"He suggests burning it," said Niall, reading over Todd's shoulder and trying not to breathe in his devastating body odour. "We can learn a lot by how it oxidizes."

"Simple enough." Todd rolled his battered office chair away from the computer, opened a drawer in one of the desks, and withdrew a long, thin barbeque lighter. "C-can you scrape a bit of that goo out of the box, and we'll see what happens?"

"On it." Pius leapt into action. He was in his element now, doing science experiments, and Niall was happy to see his friend so eager and excited about something. The last couple of days had been so rough since the incident with his parents. Pius fished around through piles of garbage and junk on the table and removed a thin, flat piece of metal, like the blade from a utility knife. He used it to poke around the box and withdrew a large gob of the fluorescent green slime.

"Too much?"

Todd shrugged. "I'm sure it's fine. Put it on the table."

Pius put it on the table beside the box, and Todd clicked the trigger on the plastic lighter. A small orange flame flicked from the end. "He w-wants to know how fast it burns and what colour the flame is."

"I hope it doesn't give off any toxic fumes," said Pius.

Todd touched the flame to the goo.

The next few seconds were a blur. A blinding glow burst from the tip of the lighter. At first, Niall thought the lighter had exploded, but the green goo flashed into a searing flame so intense that the force had thrown Pius and Todd away from the cluttered table. Niall rushed to Pius, lying on the floor. The side of his face was red and blistered. Niall smelled burning hair.

Pius moaned.

"Niall, the box!" Harper screamed.

Niall looked up. The dancing blue flame on the table had spread to the Adidas box, which was full of that highly flammable, explosive green slime.

He had a fraction of a second to react. The fire was between them and the door, and there was no way they could get past it. There was nothing within reach to smother or put out the fire. He was about to reach for the box, try to knock it off the table onto the floor to buy them a few seconds, when Harper grabbed his hand. He turned, and she pressed her mouth against his. Niall's mind went blank, and his fear melted away. Was she kissing him goodbye? Was this how it was going to end? Why did he taste blood?

"Save us, Niall," Harper whispered against his lips.

Save them? How? He had destroyed monsters and burned creeps with his power. How was he supposed to save them?

Suddenly, Niall's mind flashed back to a year ago. Falling, in Dick Jeddore's truck, hanging over the embankment at Micmac Head. The world spun around them; the truck bounced down the cliff, coming to a rest in a mangled heap in the trees below, but the three of them had walked away without a scratch.

He had never consciously tried to make the magic have a specific effect or take a particular shape. He didn't know how to do it now. He just wanted to protect his friends and himself. Instead of pushing, like he usually did offensively, he tried to draw the others to him, draw them into his protective 'circle.' With his eyes closed, he could see a shimmering aura surrounding him, keeping the fire at bay.

Despite the heat of the flames, Niall's entire body suddenly felt cold.

Harper, pressed against him, was safe. Pius, just out of reach, was a bit more difficult. He had to concentrate hard to extend the bubble. It wasn't like trying to solve a complex math problem—his head actually hurt, as if he was trying to change the shape of his brain in order to change the shape of the aura. Through the smoke, Niall thought he saw the fire withdraw and curve around his friend. Todd was a lot farther away. Niall couldn't reach him. He wondered if he moved closer if the circle would move with him, but before he had a chance to act, the flames flashed impossibly bright.

Niall didn't remember anything after that.

CHAPTER THIRTY-ONE

Daughter
June 2, 8:35pm

Tanguay thanked the nurse and followed her directions down the hallway toward the room. As she passed through those familiar halls with beige brick walls and ugly off-white linoleum floors, she had an uncomfortable sense of déjà vu. She was flooded with memories of last year and hunting a vicious monster through these same halls in the dark. Everything looked so clean and sterile now—the incident had resulted in the hospital getting its first renovation in twenty years. If she looked hard enough, would she be able to find traces of blood or bullet holes in the walls?

She had rushed to Cheryl's house as soon as she could get away from Cape-de-Cape, but by the time she'd arrived, the Murphy family had been taken to the hospital. The house was a total write-off—the second major fire in town in less than twenty-four hours. And what do you know? Pius, along with Harper and Niall, had been at the site of this one, too.

Tanguay wasn't aware that Harper's friends even knew Cheryl's kids because they went to different schools, and mixing Catholics and Protestants was like mixing, well, Catholics and Protestants. The kids probably didn't care, but they had grown up with years of their parents telling them something was wrong with the other, so the two groups didn't tend to mingle much.

Were Pius and the other kids setting these fires? What was the connection? She had stopped by the hospital later in the day to check on Cheryl and ask the kids some questions. Cheryl's son had been in surgery, and Niall hadn't woken up yet. She didn't get a chance to talk to Pius and Harper before she got called away by Wolfhard and Mason again on a tip that Aminov had been spotted. That tip had been a dead end, and then she got tied up with the coroner about Garabet's body... she had been running in circles all day and gotten nowhere.

She found the trio in Niall's room. Niall lay in the hospital bed, and Harper and Pius were sitting squished together in a chair off to the side. Pius had bandages on the side of his face and a black eye. Niall's mother, Barbara, was seated beside her son, holding his hand. A heart monitor above the bed showed a steady heart rate and oxygen levels, and the kid looked peaceful as if he was sleeping. His mother, however, was a wreck. Her hair was frazzled, and her make-up was streaked from tears. The poor woman. After everything last year, now she had to deal with this?

She looked up at Marie-Ann and wiped tears from her eyes. "Sergeant Tanguay?"

"I wanted to check in to see if the kids are alright."

"They're fine, thank you," said Barbara, but she did not appear to believe what she was saying. "I don't know... I don't know why these things keep happening to them."

There were a few reasons, but Tanguay couldn't blurt them out. "It's not your fault, Mrs. O'Neil. They're good kids. They know the right things to do. And they're also very lucky."

Tanguay looked in the kids' direction, and Pius wouldn't meet her gaze. There was definitely something going on there. Harper, though, spoke up immediately.

"We pulled Niall out and helped Todd's sister Sheila drag their dad out. He breathed in a lot of smoke, and he was in rough shape. And Todd got burned pretty bad."

She was going to check on Cheryl next, but he had to find out what was going on with the kids first. How were they connected to this?

"What happened?" she asked.

"It was a bug..." The voice came from the bed.

Barbara shot up and leaned over her son. "Niall?"

Niall opened his eyes. His voice was weak, and his gaze unfocussed, but he was coherent. "I'm so thirsty. Can I have some water?"

Barbara slapped the call button beside the bed repeatedly. "Niall, are you okay? Does anything hurt?"

Pius and Harper joined on the other side.

"I'm fine. I just feel a little weak. And hungry. Why am I so hungry?"

"You've been out all day," said Harper. "We were getting worried about you."

Harper wasn't looking at Niall like a friend. There was a different kind of sparkle in her eye. Tanguay always knew that Niall had a crush on Harper, but was she starting to reciprocate it?

"You said something about a bug?" Barbara asked. "What are you talking about?"

"It was a bug that started the fire."

Barbara looked at Harper and Pius. "At the house, you told the firefighters Todd started it with a science experiment."

"Well, yes, of course," Harper said quickly. "It was a bug in his experiment that started it. You know, like a mistake. It was a computer virus."

Pius groaned. "Bugs are not computer viruses."

"Whatever. I don't know. I'm not a nerd. You and Todd were going on about sixty-nine-hundred bods and tentacle girls, and I don't even know why I hang out with you guys sometimes."

Barbara and Tanguay looked at each other in confusion, unable to grasp the strange language of these kids. Tanguay knew they were lying, but before she could follow up, a nurse and doctor burst into the room to check on Niall. They started poking and prodding him, elbowing Tanguay away from the bed.

"I have to check on Constable Murphy and her family," she said as she backed out the door. She still needed to talk to the kids, but it would have to wait a bit longer. "If we have any other questions, we'll be in touch. I hope you're all feeling better."

Tanguay was barely three steps down the hall when Harper caught her.

"It *was* a bug."

"What kind of bug?"

"A giant June bug. Like this big."

That was impossible. But coming from these kids, she was inclined to believe it. "It set the house on fire?"

"No, Todd and Pius tried to burn the bug to see what would happen, and it exploded. I've never seen anything like it. It burned with a blue flame, and it was so hot."

Tanguay noted that Harper had a fading black eye, but she didn't look anywhere near as bad as Cheryl's family.

"Why weren't you guys hurt?"

"Todd was burned pretty bad. But the rest of us... I didn't know how to get Niall my blood quickly, so I bit my lip and kissed him. He used his powers to protect us. It must have taken a lot out of him because he passed out right after. He didn't wake up until now."

"Where did you find this bug?"

"In the yard next to Niall's house. There's something else, Sergeant. We think it's an alien."

Tabernac. "And why would you think that?"

"We met some people recently who found Theolina's journal. There were notes detailing an alien invasion that she helped stop in Gale Harbour in June 1964. But it also said that they were going to come back this year. We think this bug might be part of their invasion fleet or something."

"When?"

"When what?

"When is the invasion supposed to happen?"

"Friday."

Aliens. It was a testament to how messed up the last year had been that she was seriously contemplating that Harper's claim might be true.

But there was one other thing that didn't add up. "Harper, did Pius have anything to do with the high school catching fire last night?"

The girl froze. Her dark eyes darted back and forth as if searching for an exit. Or an excuse.

"Harper!"

A woman rushed down the hall toward them. She was dressed in nurse's scrubs and lugging a large purse over her shoulder. It was Samantha Jeddore, Pius' mom and Harper's aunt. Before Harper could even open her mouth, Samantha threw her arms around her and squeezed her so hard Tanguay imagined Harper's head would pop off.

"Oh, thank God, Harper, are you okay? Where's Pius?"

"I'm fine, Aunt Samantha." Harper struggled to disentangle herself. She looked like a puppy being choked by an octopus. "Pius is inside with Niall."

Samantha grabbed her by the hand and dragged her toward the hospital room, but then she looked back at Tanguay and smiled. "God bless you, Sergeant Tanguay, bless you. I don't know what this town would do without you!"

Harper looked at her imploringly as Samantha dragged her into the room. Tanguay wasn't sure if she was begging for help with her aunt's clutches or with the aliens.

The door slammed closed. So there were aliens, and Pius Jeddore set fire to the school for some reason. Tanguay had work to do, but first, she had to check in on Cheryl and her son. She headed toward intensive care.

In her head, she played, again and again, one of the last things Captain Mason said to her before she left Cape-de-Cape a few hours ago.

"Wolfhard knows more than he's telling. I'm being kept in the dark, same as you, but DND wants me to follow him around and ply him for information. And I did figure out something. The colonel was here before. In Gale Harbour, years ago. He served on the base. No one will talk to me, but you should ask around. Find out how Linda Falstaff died."

That was all Mason had said. The colonel returned from the bathroom or wherever hideous creatures like him deposited organic waste, and Tanguay didn't have a chance to ask any more questions. But now it was coming together. If it connected with what Harper just told her...

Tanguay stood outside Todd Murphy's room.

Cheryl's sobbing voice carried from inside.

Tanguay took a deep breath and opened the door. She didn't particularly want to do this, but it was her duty. Cheryl was part of her team, part of her community. It was her job to take care of her.

How she was supposed to take care of the rest of Gale Harbour, she had no idea.

CHAPTER THIRTY-TWO

Are You Gonna Go My Way
June 2, 9:50pm

"So, you guys knew the old witch?" Keith asked from the backseat of the station wagon. He was leaning forward, with his head shockingly close to Anna. Brian was beside him, pressed as far back into the worn upholstery as possible. He was afraid that if he got too close to the goddess, he would burst into a fiery ball, like Icarus flying too close to the sun. Or like the bag of shit they lit on fire in his driveway.

"No, we didn't know her, personally," said Keenan from the driver's seat. "You could say we're fans."

They were driving across town on a mission to prepare for the impending alien invasion. Brian thought he should probably focus more on that, but he was having trouble focusing on anything except Anna.

"I was working at the library at Memorial University in St. John's," Anna explained. "I found her journals in an old storage bin in the basement. Keenan and I had already heard about what happened with you guys last year, and once we put everything together...."

They had already stopped at Keith's house for a few things. His parents had a huge place. Brian had asked Keith if he had any snacks, and he returned with several bags of Hostess chips and a half-dozen cans of Pineapple Crush. Brian would have fallen in love with Keith if he hadn't already promised his heart to Anna.

"You figured out that aliens are dropping out of the sky over Gale Harbour," said Keith. "Because of course they are."

"Fall from the sky, phase-in from another dimension, it's hard to put a fine point on it." Anna took one of the bags of chips and opened it with what appeared to be a switchblade. "The notebook describes them as 'surfing in,' like on the tide, but the human understanding of extraterrestrial life is admittedly pretty flimsy."

She was so smart. Brian always dreamed of smart girls. Sure, it wasn't the *first* characteristic on his list of what he was looking for in a mate, but it was up there. His number one crush, up to a few hours ago, was Deanna Troi, and Counsellor Troi was brilliant as well as beautiful.

Keith, who for some reason did not believe every word that came out of the goddess's mouth, wasn't buying it. "If they're aliens, then why do they look like June bugs?"

Keenan shrugged. "They copied the shape of something they found here? Or maybe June bugs could've evolved from them. It seems like these creatures have been coming to Earth for a long time."

"And what are they supposed to do? Mind control or something?"

"No, the butt monkeys are like scouts, the harbingers of something else."

Anna snorted. "I wish you would stop calling them that. You're going to make it stick. Why couldn't we have come up with something cooler, like 'Death Bugs,' or 'Flame Stirges' or something."

"Hey, I didn't name them. Harper came up with it."

"*Buteo apes* means 'swarm of buzzard bees,'" groaned Anna. "It does not mean 'Butt Ape.'"

Keenan smirked at her. "Yeah, but it's funnier."

Brian's stomach clenched. The sight of that greasy, pasty jerk smiling at Anna made him want to throw up. And he was on his second can of Pineapple Crush. If he spewed now, it would be neon yellow.

"No, I agree, it's pretty good." Keith's head bobbed in agreement. "But what's this thing the bugs are hard binging for?"

"That part we don't know. Theolina's journal led up to the day she went to face the invader. We don't have any notes from her about what happened after."

"Did she survive?"

Keenan and Anna looked at each other. "Didn't you meet her? Didn't she cut off your ear?"

Keith glowered. "Hey, I'm not stunned, but with the weird stuff we run into, I think asking if it's dead or alive is a valid question."

The car came to a stop. Why was it stopping? Where were they going? It took Brian a moment to remember that they had been on their way to Pius' house. He had even given them directions. Brian hoped they had been the right ones. He may have directed them to Mary Brown's Fried Chicken, for all he knew.

Keenan craned to look out the window with that big stupid hat on his head. "This is the place, right?"

"Yup." Keith was looking out at the small, yellow house surrounded by thick trees.

"The lights are all out. You think they're asleep?"

Keith opened the door. "I'll go around back and knock on Pius' window."

"Do it subtly," Anna suggested. "If you scare him, he won't piss in the bed, will he?"

Keith guffawed. "You do know Pius, don't you?"

The car door slammed, and Keith disappeared into the dark trees beside the house, leaving Brian alone with the strangers. Getting himself stuck in a car alone with a pair of weirdos he didn't know, one of whom was wearing what appeared to be a thrift-store Halloween costume of Slash from Guns & Roses, may not have been a good idea.

"So, Brian," said Keenan, turning around in his seat to face him. "It is Brian, right? You don't talk much, do you?"

Brian wrinkled his nose. He had been called many things in his life, but quiet was not one of them. "Most people call me Skidmark. A derogatory nickname resulting from an unfortunate peer-bullying incident in Grade One. I haven't been able to shake it, so I embraced it. I use it everywhere now. It's even on my report card, but I'm not sure if it was meant as a mean joke from the administration. My French teacher hates me. She's held it against me ever since I pushed her down the stairs in the Grade Seven hallway."

"You pushed her down the *stairs*?" Keenan's eyes grew wide.

Was he wearing eyeliner?

"It was an accident. She asked me if I'd seen *Dirty Dancing*, so I assumed that meant she wanted to re-enact the famous star lift between Patrick Swayze and Jennifer Grey, but I guess that's not what she meant because when I grabbed her hips, she freaked out and fell backward down two flights of stairs. She hasn't been back to school since, but she did give me a 'D' on my midterm report card, which was total bullshit because it wasn't my fault she failed her saving throw."

It felt good to talk again. It helped keep his mind off Anna. However, talking about *Dirty Dancing* made Brian feel like he wanted to do the lift with Anna. He wasn't sure if he could pick her up, but putting his hands on her hips was an exciting prospect, way more exciting than putting his hands on Mrs. Boisvert's hips, which were all bony. Brian broke into a sweat at the thought of it. The next time he put his hands on a woman, he hoped there would be less screaming and fewer paramedics involved.

Brian didn't notice the multiple phases of horror that went over the older teens' faces, but he did perk up when Keenan asked, "Did you say 'saving throw'? Do you play *D&D*?"

"Yeah, I play with Pius, Niall, and Harper sometimes. Keith used to play, too. He played this mean fighter with a plus-two long sword he called Weenslice, and he would always use it to castrate his enemies after he defeated them. He hasn't played with us in a while because hockey season started and he had to practice for that, and then when hockey was over, he started playing softball, but there was this one time he tried to castrate this elf assassin they defeated, but then I tricked him, and it was actually a female elf assassin, and Keith was all shocked, so the assassin stabbed him in the wiener. Do you guys play *D&D*? What kind of characters do you play?"

Keenan grinned. "I haven't played *D&D* in a long time, but Anna and I do play this new game called *Vampire: The Masquerade*."

"Vampire? Do you play as vampires?"

"Yup. It's cool; they have different clans, and every clan has different powers and backgrounds."

Brian was about to interrupt and ask how they could maintain any game balance or create interesting level design with the insane power imbalance of letting the players play as vampires when Keith came running toward the car. Harper came behind him, barefoot and dressed in a long plaid shirt, carrying a rifle.

"I went to the wrong window!" Keith yelled at the car. Then, over his shoulder, "Harper! Harper, it's me, Keith Doucette!"

"I know." Harper calmly raised the rifle to fire.

Keenan leaned out the window. "Harper, what are you doing? Don't shoot him!"

"I wasn't going to shoot him. Not badly, anyway. I was just going to scare him. Do you know what he did to Pius at school a couple of days ago?"

"What *I* did to Pius?" Keith was crouching behind the car. He poked his head over the hood to yell back at her. His braces glittered in the light of the street lamp. "He beat the shit out of me!"

"You jumped him from behind, dickweed! He trusted you! You were supposed to be his friend!"

"Look, I know it was a crappy thing to do! I'm sorry! Will you let me apologize to him?"

"Will you let me shoot you in the knee? Pius is going through a tough time, and I think this will make him feel better."

Brian, realizing it would all come down to him and his silver-tongued eloquence to diffuse the situation, rolled out of the station wagon. "Harper! Keith! We've all got stuff going on. Keith has a drinking problem, Pius' parents are rowing because his dad is screwing around on his mom—don't look at me like that, everyone knew about it but Pius—and my parents are going to beat me with an orange in a sock when I go home because I burned a giant hole the size of a hula hoop in the driveway again."

"Wait, you did what?" Harper interrupted. "What do you mean, 'again?'"

Brian didn't slow down. He gestured toward the station wagon. "Not to mention that these poor vampire dorks are living in their car, and they're barely out of high school, so I assume their parents are either drug addicts or abusive or Jehovah's Witnesses or all of the above because driving around in an old station wagon looking for aliens does not seem to indicate a stable home environment. The only one of us who isn't from a screwed-up family is Niall, and he's a self-righteous prick about it."

Harper lowered the rifle. "No, he isn't. And his grandmother was possessed by an undead witch, in case you forgot."

"Yeah, but she got better. *Pfft*. It's not like Pius' folks are going to magically get back together because the sex-crazed incubus possessing his dad is just going to leave."

Keith, poking his head up from behind the hood of the car, called out to Brian. "Skidmark, what in God's name are you getting on with?"

"I have two reasons for my current diatribe. First, I wanted Harper to stop pointing the rifle at you so we could have a sensible conversation. This isn't the Old West. Or Gale Harbour Crossing. Second, I needed to distract her so she wouldn't notice the grapefruit-sized June bug flying around her head."

Harper screamed and dropped to the lawn. The gun went off with a loud bang, which caused Keenan to scream as well. He obviously wasn't used to firearm discharges.

Anna didn't flinch.

"See?" said Brian. "That's what I was trying to avoid."

"What the hell did you think was going to happen?" spat Keith. "You know she hates June bugs!"

"She didn't shoot *you*, did she?"

Harper scrambled to her feet, darted to the car, and jumped in through the open door behind Brian. She slammed it closed and locked it.

"Um, Harper?" Brian asked.

Harper, her face pressed against the window, pointed behind him. "Skidmark, look out!"

Brian turned and ducked right as the June bug buzzed past his head. His butt hit the asphalt hard, knocking the wind out of him and dazing him for a second. The giant bug scraped across the roof of the station wagon, leaving a trail of blue sparks as it did. The people inside the car were screaming, and Keith pulled open the back passenger door. Brian figured the four of them were going to take off and leave him to deal with the June bugs from Mars on his own, so he resigned himself to the fate of having his face chewed off by its giant mandibles, but then Keith leapt over the hood of the car, with his trusty aluminum baseball bat in hand.

Keith stood over Brian protectively, scanning the darkness for the buzzing monster. The people inside the car were pointing and screaming in every direction, trying to direct him, but that only confused him. When the bug did come soaring into view, Keith wound up with a home run swing and succeeded in smashing the back window of the car.

"Shit, sorry! My bad!"

"Are you drunk?" Harper squealed through the shattered window.

"No, I'm not... well, maybe a little. The little frigger's fast!"

The bug came back again. This time, Keith lined it up perfectly. He connected with a thunderous *crack*, and the creature exploded in a ball of fluorescent goo.

"Wicked." Keith smiled. "You can go back to Uranus, you little bugger!"

Brian, carefully raising his hands from over his head, peered upward. Keith towered over him triumphantly, with his bat in hand and glowing goo running down the length of it. He extended his hand toward Brian but stopped and retracted it. His face twisted in horror.

"Uh, crap..." Keith moaned.

Brian sighed. "It's on me, isn't it?" He reached up and touched the side of his face. It came away sticky and covered with glowing green slime. Now that he was aware of it, he could feel it running down the back of his neck into his sweatshirt, soaking through his clothes, even running down the side of his cheek. He tasted something spicy and metallic.

"Oh my god, it's in my mouth."

The next few moments were a blur. Brian did things he was not proud of, like leaping to his feet, tearing off all his clothes, and dancing naked around Pius' front lawn, screaming like his little sister when he put the rubber snake in her Barbie dollhouse. Harper shoved him toward the front door, yelling about getting him inside to clean him up. In a daze, he pushed past Pius and his confused-looking mom in a housecoat. He may even have rubbed his naked junk against her in the process, but he was too concerned about alien parasites growing in his stomach to worry about that now.

They were all so distracted that no one noticed the cloud of fist-sized bugs flying around the lamppost above the house. They ran inside so quickly that none of them saw one of the bugs shoot a beam of blue fire at the light, burning a hole through it instantly and sending a shower of glass and metal raining down to the street below.

CHAPTER THIRTY-THREE

Freeze Don't Move
Thursday, June 3, 1:00am

Tanguay took a deep breath of fresh air after leaving the hospital. She'd been in there, talking to Cheryl for hours. Todd was going to live, but it was too early to say how extensive or permanent the damage would be. The poor woman was a wreck, and Marie-Ann had long ago run out of comforting things to say. Her child was hurt, she was scared and confused, and there was little Tanguay could do but sit with her and hold her hand while she cried.

Sometimes, it was part of a Mountie's duty to inform loved ones about an accident or death, and it was by far the worst part of the job. Usually, she didn't have to sit around while the family member digested that, but when the next of kin was one of her team, it was hard for her to slip away. She stayed as long as she could, though, until Cheryl's sister came in to relieve her.

It wasn't just Cheryl that was bothering her. Sir Wilfred Grenfell Hospital was the site of some of the worst encounters with the monster last year. People had died here, and there were nights Tanguay woke screaming from nightmares of blood-splattered walls. She should have accepted the Division's offer of a therapist. Still, there was never time for that sort of thing, even when there wasn't an alien invasion imminent. Marie-Ann and her small team covered all of St. Stephen's Bay and the Cape-de-Cape Peninsula, some forty small communities over a few hundred kilometres of coastline. There was no time for a therapist; there was hardly time for a day off. Tanguay couldn't remember the last time she'd had more than a single day off at a time. It was undoubtedly before last year's horrors.

But now, tonight, she needed to sleep, even if it meant a nightmare or two. She needed at least a few hours before she had to deal with Wolfhard and his missing bomb again. She had an idea about that, something that had been stewing in her head ever since Mason had slipped her the info about Linda Falstaff.

She was approaching her cruiser when her radio cracked to life, and Constable Brake spoke. "Sarge, I've spotted someone who matches your description of Oleg Aminov. I'm following him out to the Strip now."

The Strip was what the locals called the old airfield, over which now ran a road out of town towards the matchstick factory. "*Merde*, Brake, are you sure?" Tanguay's heart started to race. If she could catch Aminov without Wolfhard's help, if they could find out where the bomb was, if they could stop everything before it started...

"Pretty sure. Plus, when he saw me, he took off running. He's guilty of something."

"Do not let him get away, Brake! I'm only a few minutes away."

The drive from Sir Wilfred Grenfell Hospital to the Strip usually took about four minutes; Tanguay did it in one. Sirens on, she blew through every stop sign and one of the town's three traffic lights. She almost took out an elderly man walking his dog on Omaha Drive and hoped he would forgive her.

She blew past Gale Harbour's infamous "plane-on-a-stick". She followed Brake's flashing lights to building Number 8, one of the several large abandoned hangars that stood as decaying reminders of the US's presence here. Some of them had been converted to warehouses and storage facilities, but this particular building, with its peeling red paint and smashed windows, was empty as far as Tanguay knew.

She pulled up beside Brake's cruiser, which in turn was parked beside an unmarked brown sedan. She was already talking before she jumped out of her car. "Is he inside?"

"Yup," replied the rat-face Brake, rubbing the edge of his slick, black moustache like a cartoon villain.

"We're sure this time?"

"I did a quick perimeter check." Brake spat on the ground. "There's one other way out, and the door is padlocked from the outside. He's not going anywhere."

"Unless this building has an entrance to the underground tunnels." Tanguay had no idea if there was one here or not. It was impossible to keep track of all the secret passages.

Brake shrugged. "Let's hope he doesn't know about that. What's the plan, Sarge?"

"We should call for additional back-up." She ran through various scenarios through her head, but her gaze never left the rusted metal door in front of them.

"We should, but Burt's not on call. Anyone else would have to come from Corner Brook or Port-aux-Basques. Could take'em an hour to get here."

"If Aminov finds the tunnels, he'll be long gone."

Brake nodded like a rat chewing a mouthful of cheese. "Probably. Don't suppose we'd call Colonel Sanders and G.I. Canuck for help?"

"Not on your life."

"Didn't think so."

There was a long pause. Brake chewed on a fingernail, bit it off, and scrutinized it before flicking it away. Finally, he said, "So, do you want to kick down the door, or will I?"

Tanguay smiled. "Cover me."

Marie-Ann liked Constable Brake. Sure, he was a bit skeevy, but he listened to orders, and she trusted him to watch her back. She would never willingly go into a situation like this with Bennett, who would have shot her by accident himself.

"This is the RCMP. Come out with your hands up!" She kicked open the door, which came open quite easily (she probably should have checked to make sure it swung inward) and entered the dimly lit warehouse with her sidearm pointed in front of her. She took three steps, staying close to the wall for cover, scanning the darkness. The room was cavernous and virtually empty, besides debris and garbage scattered across the floor.

Brake came in behind her, and then a gunshot boomed. Brake howled in pain. Without hesitation, Tanguay whirled in the direction from where the shot had come. She saw movement on the top of a ladder, five metres above the floor, and fired. Another scream of pain, and something fell to the ground with a heavy thud.

"Bruce, you okay?" Tanguay didn't take her gaze off the place where the shadow hit the floor. She would go to Brake if she had to but would rather not lose Aminov if she could help it.

"I'm okay. He just winged me," Brake groaned from the floor.

"Winged you?" Marie-Ann breathed a sigh of relief. "Who are you, John Wayne? No one says 'he winged me' anymore."

"Jumping Joseph Murphy, the bullet grazed my side, and I'm bleeding profusely, but I don't think he hit anything vital. Is that what you want me to say?"

"Good, put pressure on it and keep talking. I'll be right back."

She stepped carefully through water-logged cardboard and smashed bottles, following the sounds of moans. Something moved ahead and kept her gun trained on the form.

"He's still alive!"

"Well, shoot him and then call me an ambulance!" Brake yelled back.

"Oleg Aminov? You're under arrest for the suspected murder of Robert Stone and Randy Koch and probably a whole lot of other stuff I don't even know about."

"Go to hell," moaned Aminov.

Tanguay recognized the buzz-cut hair. The right side of his face was red and blistered as if burned, but that wound was a couple of days old. A pool of blood slowly widened under his body, and his left leg was twisted at a horrific angle, but Tanguay couldn't see his right hand or his gun.

"Put your hands above your head!"

Where the hell was his gun?

Aminov shifted slightly, apparently trying to get up, but he cried out and fell back, face-down on the floor.

"I said put your hands above your head!"

"Stupid woman... stupid town. We never found it... I hate this god-forsaken island."

"I said put your hands above your head!" She should have moved to restrain him, but she hadn't located a weapon and had no way of knowing if he was seriously hurt or playing possum.

"This is for Sarkis!"

Aminov whirled, and Tanguay saw a glint of metal in his hand. Once again, she didn't hesitate. She pulled the trigger, there was another roar of gunfire, and Oleg Aminov slumped to the floor, unmoving. The shiny, silver semi-automatic handgun in his right hand fell from his fingers.

Merde. Tabernac. Son of a bitch! Tanguay ran through another dozen curses in her head. She kicked the gun away from Aminov's hand and quickly checked the body. The last gasps of breath were leaving his lips. She leaned down close to his seared face. Was the injury caused by whatever killed his partner? Or had Niall burned him? "Where is the bomb? What killed Sarkis Garabet?"

Blood gurgled from Aminov's mouth. "Stupid... island..." He whispered. "Stupid... bugs..."

And then he was gone.

Bugs. Just like Harper had said. What the hell was going on?

"Sergeant?" called Brake. "Is the Ruskie dead?"

"Yeah."

"Gee, that's nice. Now, come help me before my gallbladder leaks out through the hole in my side."

CHAPTER THIRTY-FOUR

Will You Remember Me
June 3, 7:30 am

Marie-Ann met up with Josephine Whillet during the old woman's daily morning power walk. When she pulled up alongside her, Josephine was strutting down Queen Street in a bright yellow tracksuit, her elbows pumping like pistons. Garth Brooks was blaring out of headphones so loudly Tanguay could hear it over the noise of her engine.

The old woman did a double-take before realizing there was a police car alongside her, and then she finally stopped and took off her headphones. Tanguay rolled down the passenger window, and Josephine leaned in.

"Is there a problem, Officer? Was I going too fast?"

Tanguay smirked despite herself. She was soft on this whole goofy family. What happened to the hard-ass bitch that first showed up in Gale Harbour? "I saw you when I was driving by, and I wanted to ask you a question." That was a lie. Tanguay knew this was Josephine's regular route for her morning walk, and she wanted to catch her away from the kids. "How's Niall?"

"He should be fine. Barbara's still at the hospital with him. What about the Murphy boy?"

"Not so good." Tanguay felt terrible for Cheryl, especially since she wasn't there as soon as it happened. Not that she could do anything. "He received serious burns to a large portion of his body."

Josephine shook her head. "What a sin. And he was such a... well, I can't say handsome, as I've seen the boy, and he was homely as a shovel full of cow pucky, but he's pretty smart, isn't he?"

"Very. Top of his class, science fair winner, that sort of thing. Doctors say it's too early to tell exactly how bad the long-term effects will be."

"Was that all you wanted, Sergeant?"

"Actually, there was another question. You've lived in Gale Harbour for a while, right?"

She nodded. "We moved here in 1951. My husband Alphonsus got a job on the base, doing maintenance, cleaning, that sort of thing. Why?"

"Do you remember someone named Linda Falstaff? She was a bit younger than you but older than your kids."

Josephine's brow immediately furrowed. So, she did know. Tanguay had counted on it.

After Captain Mason's mysterious tip the day before, Tanguay had done some digging but had turned up little about Linda Falstaff. She was born in Gale Harbour, went to St. Paul's High School, and died on June 25, 1964, at sixteen years old. Everything she found said the girl had died on Hansen Air Force Base due to an accident. But what the hell was a civilian doing on the base? And why wasn't there any investigation or report on exactly *how* she died? Tanguay had her suspicions, of course, suspicions that turned her stomach, but she needed to talk to someone who had lived during that time. Someone whose husband worked on the base might have heard gossip or rumours that could lead Tanguay to what she needed.

"I remember Linda," said Josephine with a great sigh. "What a sin that was. She was so young. I knew her father. He was a tailor down at the shop on Main Street. Nice fellow, had these red cheeks like big apples. He had a huge laugh that could fill a room, but he didn't laugh much after Linda died."

"Do you know how Linda died?"

"I don't. Not really. I heard rumours, of course, about how the American boys did something to her. But I don't know. Only one person knows what happened to poor Linda Falstaff..."

Marie-Ann nodded. Looked like she wouldn't get any new information after all.

"...Angus Shave."

Tanguay's head shot up. Did she hear that correctly? "Angus Shave? *Gussy* Shave? The crazy old hermit who lives in a shack on the beach down at Port Hansen?"

"The one and only. He was there that night. He and Linda were dating. Some people thought he might have had something to do with her death, but I can't imagine it. He was a sweetheart, and he loved that girl. Almost as much as his car."

Nothing in any of the records Tanguay had searched mentioned Gussy Shave. Not in the newspaper clip she'd found, not in the shockingly brief police report.

Gussy Shave was a nuisance, yelling at kids on the beach and throwing rocks at them if they got too close to his shack, but he was mostly harmless. "I guess he wasn't a reliable witness for the police to question?"

"Because he's nuttier than a cat with a cheese grater tied to his tail? He wasn't always like that. He was sharp as a tack back then. He used to come by and talk to my husband about cars, and the boy was good with tools and engines."

"What happened to him?"

"The Americans questioned him, but as far as I know, the Mounties never did. He was never right in the head after that night. Might be he did have something to do with Linda's death, or he saw something that cracked him up. He never was the same, poor thing."

"Thank you, Mrs. Whillet, that was very helpful."

How she was going to talk to Shave, she didn't know. The weirdo hated cops, probably due to the last several Mountie Sergeants in Gale Harbour trying to run him off "his land."

"Why are you looking at Linda Falstaff anyway? Opening up some old cases, are we?"

"Something like that."

Without warning, Josephine opened the passenger door and climbed into the car.

"Mrs. Whillet, what are you doing?"

"With all the questions you've been asking me lately, I figure I must be on the payroll now."

"Mrs. Whillet—"

"And I don't know what Linda Falstaff and Gussy Shave have to do with my grandson and his friends, but I'm not so old and senile I can't put two and two together."

Tanguay tried to keep her face neutral. "I have no idea what you're talking about."

Josephine scoffed. "I don't know exactly what happened down in those tunnels last year, but I know it was something strange. And I've got a hunch something like that is happening again."

"Mrs. Whillet, I don't want to get you involved—"

"But my grandson is involved, isn't he? I can tell by the look on your face that he is, so that means I'm in this, too."

This was why Tanguay never played poker.

"Besides, Angus Shave won't talk to you. He might talk to me, though. I used to give him lemonade and tea biscuits while he puttered around the cars with Fonze. If you must know, I think he was sweet on me."

Tanguay sighed. She could certainly use help talking to Shave. And Josephine was involved in this, whether she remembered or not. "Okay, fine. Just... you're not going to get into as much trouble as your grandson, are you?"

Josephine didn't seem to be listening to her. She was absorbed in the buttons on the dashboard. "How do you turn on the sirens?"

CHAPTER THIRTY-FIVE

Ordinary World
June 3, 8:10 am

Pius awoke to a fousty smell assaulting his nostrils. He opened his eyes to find Keith Doucette's filthy sweat socks in front of his face.

Why was Keith in his bed?

Pius sprang into a sitting position, and the memories came flooding back to him. Keith, Skidmark, and the older Townie kids had shown up at their house in the middle of the night. There was screaming and arguing on the lawn, and then a naked Skidmark was being shoved in through the front door, and Pius' mom hosed him off in the bathtub. They told his mom that Skidmark had fallen into a ditch and gotten some kind of weird chemical on himself, and the kids from St. John's gave him a ride to Pius' house because he lived the closest, but they told Pius the truth later. Keith had killed one of the giant June bugs right in the front yard and gotten the creature's guts all over Skidmark.

Skidmark, dressed in Pius' dad's old sweatpants and a Light & Power T-shirt (Pius' clothes would never have fit the rotund boy), was asleep on the floor. His mom was happy to let Skidmark and Keith stay over, anything to keep Pius home.

Pius and his mom hadn't spoken much since she picked up him and Harper at the hospital the day before. They each waited for the other to say something first, but for the life of him, Pius couldn't figure out what he was supposed to say. He wanted to apologize for bringing Jenny into their house and destroying his parents' marriage, but an apology felt so trite, and so he said nothing.

Unable to take the smell of Keith's feet any longer, Pius disentangled himself and crawled out of bed. Keith was lying on top of the covers, still fully dressed and clutching his baseball bat to his chest. He'd sworn he would stay up all night and keep a lookout, but that obviously didn't happen. Keith also said he wasn't going to pick on or beat up Pius anymore, either. He wasn't good at keeping promises.

Feeling bummed but unable to stay in the room with Keith's feet or Skidmark's farting any longer, Pius stepped out of his room and smelled the delicious aroma of his mom's cooking wafting from the kitchen. He walked out to find her busy at the stove and Harper sitting at the table reading The Western Bulletin newspaper.

"Good morning, sweetheart," his mom chirped. "Bacon and pancakes for you and your friends?"

Pius grunted in agreement and slipped into the seat beside Harper.

"I hope Ski—Brian's okay," said his mom. "He and Keith looked pretty rough last night."

"Well, that's what happens when you roll around in toxic waste," said Harper, not lifting her face from the newspaper. "And Keith was probably drunk."

His mom sighed. "I would be concerned with you hanging around with bad influences, but I know Keith is having a hard time at home. I heard his parents are..." She stopped herself again. "Well, I heard they're having problems at home. I hope that black eye didn't come from someone in his family."

"It didn't," said Harper. "Pius punched him."

Pius wanted to crawl under the table and die. He wondered if he could find any more of that bug juice in the yard to roll around in.

"Pius?" His mom had a weird tone in her voice. It wasn't as mad or condemning as he was expecting. "Is that true?"

"It's okay. Keith hit him first. Where do you think Pius' black eye came from?"

His mom stared at him, but he wouldn't look up. He couldn't do it.

"I just... I thought it happened during the fire." She put her pancake flipper down, then held onto the counter for a moment to steady herself. "Well, Pius, I can't say I approve of fighting, but it's certainly nice to see you standing up for yourself."

She turned her attention back to breakfast, and he was glad for a brief moment of quiet respite. Of course, it didn't last long.

"Did Skidmark ever say anything about what happened at the hotel the other day?" Harper whispered, her face still buried in the newspaper. "What were those guys looking for?"

"Apparently, he didn't actually see or hear anything. He said they only spoke Russian, and they definitely didn't say anything about butt monkeys. How he would know that if they only spoke Russian, I have no—"

Harper interrupted Pius with a swift elbow to the ribs. Pius was sure she cracked a few.

"Ow, what?"

Harper slid the newspaper in front of him and tapped a small article on the bottom of the front page. Pius glanced at it and froze. Icy fingers crawled over his head, down his spine, and burrowed into the pit of his stomach.

Total Lunar Eclipse Tonight, read the headline.

"Tonight?" hissed Pius, trying to whisper but failing at it. "It's supposed to be Friday!"

"It is happening on Friday, dipwad. The article says it will be at its most visible at three a.m."

Pius couldn't believe how stupid he was. Why didn't he check the time of the eclipse? That means they had barely twenty hours left until... what? They still didn't know what the 'invasion' was supposed to look like. If the bugs were the harbingers of something else, what exactly was that "something else" going to be?

Gussy Shave lived in a small shack on the beach of St. Stephen's Bay, down behind the primary school and the Catholic church. The kids from the school would sometimes play pranks on the old hermit, such as throwing rocks at his tar-paper-walled shack or setting his boots on fire. Kids have been little bastards since the beginning of time.

Marie-Ann was worried that Josephine would have trouble navigating the steep, rocky bank down to the shack, but she needn't have been. The old woman picked gracefully over the rocks like a silver-haired, yellow-track-suited goat. Marie-Ann wasn't sure if her agility came down to good genes, exercise, or a preternatural side effect of her body housing the spirit of a witch for decades. Honestly, Tanguay would consider letting a demon possess her, too, if it left her so fit when she was Josephine's age.

A damp, cool wind blew in off the Bay. The smell of saltwater wrinkled Tanguay's nose, and she watched, fascinated, as Josephine stopped and breathed in the sea salt spray. Tanguay never quite got Newfies' connection with the sea. She had grown up in Quebec, outside of Montreal. The closest thing she had known to the ocean was the St. Lawrence River, which was so choked with industrial waste that you could walk on it. It might dissolve your boots, though.

"Let me go first," said Josephine as they approached. "If he sees you coming, he might run off."

"Or shoot me."

"No, he wouldn't do that. I don't think."

Tanguay wasn't so sure. Back when she was stationed in New Brunswick, there had been a few incidents where mild-mannered loners had rapidly turned into the violent, homicidal kind at the drop of a hat. Especially when uniformed cops came knocking. A hint of authority and *les pauvres fous* would become convinced they were about to be persecuted for their crimes, whether real or imaginary. Tanguay felt for the poor people who couldn't get help and whose lives went down that path, but that didn't mean she wanted to get blasted in the chest with a .22. She wondered if bringing a civilian here was a good idea, but it was too late. Josephine was already knocking on the door.

"Wazzit?" came a grumbled response from within the shack. It sounded far away as if the small, dilapidated building made of weathered lumber and stretched tar paper wasn't barely three metres across.

"Gussy Shave?" Josephine asked. "Angus? I'm not sure if you remember me. It's Mrs. Whillet. Alphonsus Whillet's wife."

There came smashing and crashing noises inside the shack, and the door was wrenched open with such fury that Tanguay's hand instinctively went to her sidearm. A tall, rail-thin man appeared from the darkness inside the hovel. His scraggy, greasy grey hair was receding from his sun-scorched and peeling scalp. His face was mostly obscured by a thick, unruly beard stained with years' worth of nicotine, mouthwash, and either blood or Campbell's tomato soup. He was dressed in a ratty, thick winter coat even though it was June. The man reeked of rotten fish, urine, and untold decades of body odour. Tanguay had once been present when they'd opened up a cabin where a pair of bodies had been rotting for an entire summer. She couldn't tell you which one smelled worse.

"Phonse Whillet's wife? Gone wit'chu."

Josephine nodded. How was she standing so close to him? Did she not have a sense of smell? "It's me, Angus. Been a long time."

"House ol'man? Amiss goan round visiting ease cars."

"He passed away a few years ago."

"Sorry tear dat. Yeast'll gotat Chev Impala?"

"No, Angus, the transmission fell out of that when Frank Moores was still Premier."

"Peashit dating, wa? Showat brings yowta Angus's place? Sorry dint cleanup. Looking fernew usband? You wantsa get murried, wa?"

Tanguay was glad she had brought Josephine. She was going to need the old woman to translate everything Shave said. She didn't think most of it was English or French.

"No, Angus, but the sergeant and I wanted to ask you something."

Gussy Shave noticed Tanguay for the first time. He appeared panicked and looked in every direction for an avenue of escape. To the water, up the bank to the road, straight up into the sky, even under his boot—no option seemed out of the realm of possibility. He cursed and swore the whole while. "JumpingsChristMotherFriggerHolyShit-DuckBalls! Wider bring der mounties 'ere? Eye diane steal no boat. I fawking swears!"

"You're not in any trouble, Mr. Shave," Tanguay said cautiously.

That I know of.

"We want to ask if you know Linda Falstaff."

Gussy Shave froze. His weird twitching and tics stopped, and for the briefest moment, his bloodshot eyes held a small measure of lucidity. And fear.

"I knows Linda," he said, and then he shook his head. "I knowed her. She died a long time ago."

"We know," said Josephine. "Can you tell us how she died?"

Gussy Shave nodded. And then he told them.

"Who the hell are you?"

The filthy woman rolled her eyes and tapped her foot impatiently as if Wolfhard's question was the most foolish thing she'd ever heard. Linda thought it was pretty reasonable under the circumstances.

"My name is Theolina Benoit. Happy?"

"Not even remotely," grumbled Wolfhard.

"She did technically answer the question," said Angus.

"Fine. Who the hell are you, how did you get in here, and what are you doing?"

"Do you want to get away from the monster or play twenty questions? I know you Yankee soldiers aren't too bright. Can you walk and talk at the same time?"

The woman turned and walked fearlessly into the darkness, back the way she came. The rest of them hesitated. How could she see where she was going?

"You coming?" she called from the blackness.

"We can't see anything!" Linda yelled back.

"Godforsaken children, afraid of the dark now. Here." A ball of light appeared above Theolina's hand, illuminating her face with a sickly green glow. It could be a torch, but it gave off weird green and purple sparks. What was she burning?

"Now, keep up."

Linda looked at Wolfhard, who shrugged. "She's heading in the right direction. Better than waiting here." He and Linda hurried down the tunnel to catch up with Theolina and her light. They didn't wait for Angus, who was forced to jog to keep up.

"I've been looking for that thing for years," she explained as they walked. "It's the physical form of an immaterial entity from another dimension. It's a carapace the creature can travel in, like a hermit crab in a conch shell."

"Are you quoting Jules Verne?" asked Wolfhard.

Linda didn't know who that was, but Wolfhard looked as confused as she felt.

"Jesus, no, that man was a hack. Look, it's like a living suit of armour. It calls to monsters from space, and they can come down to wear it.

"Where did it come from?"

"I found records that miners dug it up near here fifty years ago, but it was missing ever since then. And it's much older than that. It came to Earth over three billion years ago."

Linda gasped. Three *billion*. She couldn't imagine a number that big, plus it didn't sit in line with other things she'd been taught. "Was that before or after God created man and woman?"

Theolina stopped so abruptly that Wolfhard almost bumped into her. She turned slowly, with a strange look of shock, confusion, and anger on her face. It made her ugly and terrifying in the weird, flickering green light. Then she cackled horribly, like a witch from a children's story.

"Oh, girl, you're sweet but stupid."

Insulted, Linda considered not following when Theolina started walking again, but since the other option was to stay in the dark by herself, she fell into step.

Wolfhard leaned in close to her and winked. "Don't worry. She's a heathen. She's going to hell."

"I heard that!" The scary woman snapped. "And yes. I am."

They weren't sure if she was talking about being a heathen or going to hell. Linda decided she meant both.

The group came to a ladder leading up a narrow tunnel to a round metal hatch a few metres above their heads. "Where does this go?" asked Wolfhard. "I lost track of where we are under the base."

"Does it matter?"

Wolfhard nodded. "Good point." He holstered his pistol and started to climb, hand-over-hand, up the ladder. Linda was scared for him, being in that tiny tunnel, travelling blindly into the unknown. But they were right. The monster, whatever it was, was down here. The only option was to get out.

Wolfhard was at the top of the ladder, reaching for the hatch, when a rumble shook the tunnel and sent dust and rubble tumbling down from the ceiling. Linda released a small scream but stopped herself quickly, embarrassed. She would have felt worse, except Angus screeched even louder than she did.

"What was that?" Angus clutched Linda like a child clinging to his mother. Linda might have found a strong man holding her to be comforting, except Angus wasn't either of those things. And he stank horribly. Had he peed himself? "We don't get earthquakes around here."

"No, we don't," grumbled Theolina. "I don't think the carapace is in the tunnels anymore."

Wolfhard opened the hatch above their heads to reveal sounds of screaming, explosions, and gunfire. She had seen a war film with Gregory Peck a while back, and it sounded like someone was playing it up above, except it was a lot louder than the cinema in Gale Harbour.

"Son of a bitch," Wolfhard growled and disappeared out of the hatch.

"Go on, girl," Theolina pushed Linda toward the ladder. "Get up there."

"Isn't it safer down here?"

"Maybe. Maybe not. Depends on if the carapace left any of its little buzzards down here." The woman began to climb, taking her light with her and leaving Angus and Linda down in the dark by themselves.

"Let them go," said Angus. "I saw that thing, and it will tear them apart."

"And what happens if all of them die? What happens to us?" Linda couldn't see him in the dark, but she could hear and feel Angus looking around frantically.

"I guess we live down here now."

Linda could think of quite a few things she would rather do than live in a dark cave with Angus Shave for the rest of her life. She wasn't sure if being ripped to shreds by a giant bug from Venus was one of them, but it was close. She grabbed the ladder and began to climb; fortunately, it was too dark below for Angus to look up her skirt.

She poked her head up out of the hole and gasped. Warehouses she didn't recognize surrounded them, but the smell of seawater told her they were near the port. A few metres away from her nose, hovering in the sky like a giant bird, was the beast from another world. Before, she had thought the fiery wings and the flaming sword looked like a sign of God's divine power. Now, it looked like a devil out of her nightmares.

In the floodlights of the port, she saw that the monster had black, shiny skin and looked oddly insect-like. It hovered around like a bug, too, and tiny, buzzing motes of light circled it like flies on a pile of cow manure. Some of them blinked away and vanished every few moments but were quickly replaced by more. Were those the buzzards Theolina mentioned? Was that what caused the awful sounds they heard droning in the tunnels?

"Fire in the hole!" someone screamed, and Linda heard a whistling sound as something flew over her head. A blinding flash of light filled her field of vision, and she was hit with a wave of hot air like being slapped in the face with a burning iron. She slipped off the ladder, and the hatch slammed shut above her head.

Linda fell into darkness.

CHAPTER THIRTY-SEVEN

5 Days in May
June 3, 9:20 am

When they returned home from the hospital that morning, Niall's dad made him a late breakfast of bacon, eggs, and burnt toast. His mom, at Dad's insistence, went to sleep. She had refused to leave Niall's side and had been awake at the hospital most of the night. Niall wished his mom had made him breakfast before she went to bed, though. Somehow, his dad's eggs always came out runny and overcooked at the same time.

Having choked down his meal, Niall was now seated on the armchair in the living room, half-heartedly flipping through RA Salvatore's novel *Sojourn* while his dad read a Reader's Digest.

"Aren't you supposed to be at work?"

"Your mom asked me to stay home with you." He adjusted his thick glasses but did not look up from his book. It was odd to see his dad home on a weekday. He was usually exacting about work.

"I'm fine," Niall grumbled. "I'm thirteen. I can take care of myself."

"I know that. But your mother insisted. And one does not argue with Barbara Whillet."

Niall's dad said that a lot. "One does not argue with Barbara Whillet," which was, of course, her maiden name. If you asked him about it, he would insist in his dry, humourless deadpan that it was a joke, but Niall knew it wasn't. His dad always deferred to his mom on everything. Niall didn't think he was afraid of her necessarily; he just didn't want to fight or argue. Honestly, Niall couldn't remember his dad ever arguing with anyone. Whatever the reason, it seemed to work because his parents never fought.

"Did you hear about Pius' parents?" Niall asked out of the blue, surprising even himself. His dad was so shocked he actually lowered his Reader's Digest. Of course, his dad knew; Pius and Harper had been staying in their house all week. He was shocked because he and Niall rarely had serious conversations about anything.

"Yes, I did. How is Pius handling it?"

"Not good. I don't think he's spoken to his parents all week."

"He's angry. He'll come around."

"He blames himself for it because he brought Jenny over to be his dad's tutor."

Now, Niall's dad put his book down on the coffee table and sat up. "It is not Pius' fault. His father is a grown man and makes his own bad decisions. And Ray Jeddore has made a lot of bad decisions."

"I know. I think Pius is the only one who didn't know about it. We saw his parents fighting the night Sam—Mrs. Jeddore kicked him out. Why don't you and mom ever fight?"

"Because I don't make bad decisions like Ray Jeddore." This was the longest conversation Niall had ever had with his father, and he was feeling uncomfortable, but his dad pressed on. "Ray is a good guy, but he's human, and he makes mistakes. Whether he and Samantha can work it out is between them and has nothing to do with Pius. I'm sure they love him very much, just like your mother, and I love you."

"You guys aren't in any trouble, are you?"

His dad chuckled. "No, son."

"Okay, good. Because all my friends have weird stuff going on in their family lives. Mine seems boring by comparison."

"Don't knock boring. And besides, in our family, *you're* the one who keeps causing trouble."

Niall supposed that was true. His parents were pretty boring—his dad worked for the matchstick factory, and his mom was a secretary at the college—and neither had much in the way of interests outside of work. Despite being a jerk, even Nelson coasted through life without making a scene or causing any trouble.

Come to think of it, Niall couldn't think of anything his father liked to do outside of work. He had a weekly poker night with his friends—or was it hockey? Maybe it was just hockey in the winter. People didn't play hockey in the summer, right? And he did occasionally go fishing and stuff like that, but so did everyone else in Gale Harbour. It wasn't like a hobby or anything. What the hell did his father do for fun?

Niall briefly thought about asking him, but this conversation had gone on long enough, and he was getting weirded out from talking to his dad for so long. His father must have been getting uncomfortable with it, too, because neither of them spoke for a long time.

Finally, blessedly, there came a knock at the door. Niall nearly jumped out of his socks, then ran to the porch to open it.

Pius and Harper stood on the step outside.

"We need to go," Harper said without further explanation.

There was an urgency in her voice that Niall rarely heard. If Harper was worried about something, it must be bad. Sure, Pius looked scared, too, but he was always scared of something.

"I'm supposed to be resting," said Niall, and his father must have heard him from the other room.

"You're fine!" He called out. "The doctor said there's nothing wrong with you. Your mother is overly worried. You go out and have fun with your friends."

"This is not going to be fun," Pius muttered under his breath.

"Thanks, Dad!" Niall knew his dad wanted him gone so he could have a nap on the couch in peace, but he wasn't going to argue. Niall wasn't going to wait for his dad to change his mind, so he grabbed his sneakers and headed straight out the door.

"What the heck is going on?" Niall asked as they crossed the front lawn to where Keith Doucette and Skidmark were waiting for them by the telephone pole. "Why are they here?"

"It's bad," said Harper. "The lunar eclipse? It's happening tonight."

"Tonight?" Niall ran that through his brain. It couldn't be tonight. It was supposed to be Friday, the Fourth of June. That was tomorrow. How long had he been unconscious in the hospital? Then it smacked him in the face like a cross-check from Marty McSorley. "Tonight. After midnight."

Harper smiled and squeezed his hand. "That's why I like you. Sharp as a crayon."

They stood in Niall's front yard, hardly an imposing group. "So, the five of us are supposed to do what, exactly? Stop an alien invasion?"

"Well, there's seven of us, including Anna and Keenan," Pius reminded him. "We're supposed to meet them at Zig-Zag Pizza to make a plan."

"A plan for what?"

"To stop an alien invasion, duh." Harper winked.

She acted shockingly chipper about all this. Did she forget that they nearly burned several people alive yesterday? "Aren't you terrified of June bugs? Did we confirm the aliens are June bugs?"

"Yup, big ugly butt monkeys." Keith nodded his head. "One of them exploded all over Skidmark last night."

Niall noticed for the first time that Skidmark was wearing poorly-fitting sweatpants and a T-shirt—well, more poorly fitting than usual. He also had a weird discoloration on half of his face, like a sunburn.

"It exploded because Keith smashed it with a bat right over my head," Skidmark explained. "And I only found myself in that awkward situation because Harper tried to shoot Keith, which he may have deserved, but if she had killed him, then we'd be short his batting expertise, which may come in handy against the butt monkeys. He was batting over four hundred on the school softball team before the coach cut him for drinking. Still, you already knew that, but if he hadn't gotten cut, then he wouldn't have been out swinging his bat in a depressed haze that led him to discover the butt monkeys are indeed weak against aluminum bats, which we can hopefully use to our advantage."

Niall wanted to ask about the Harper-almost-shooting-Keith-part, but he couldn't get a word in once Skidmark started rolling.

"We also learned that the butt monkey goo, if not exposed to open flame, causes mild skin irritation, or maybe I'm allergic to it. Then again, it might have inserted some sort of parasite inside me that will grow and hatch at a later date, but we haven't reached its incubation period yet, so I can't say. All I know is that Pius' mom saw my wiener, which Pius told me to tell you was entirely an accident because he thought you might be jealous for some reason, but I told him that you were with Harper now, so why would you be jealous. Plus, Pius' mom is like twenty-five years older than you. If she breaks up with his dad, I guess she is technically available, but I would never date one of my friends' moms. I would date Anna, though, and probably will, once I figure out a way to break up her and Keenan. I don't know him that well, so I don't feel so bad about that, though. So, are you ready to head to Zig-Zag yet? I could really go for a donair."

***

Twenty minutes later, after a short walk during which Niall clarified all the details of Skidmark's story, the group found themselves at a crowded table in the corner of Zig-Zag. Zig-Zag's was a popular local pizza parlour on Main Street, directly across from another popular pizza place that was part of an Atlantic Canadian chain. It was not uncommon to find similar or even identical businesses right next to each other in Gale Harbour. If one person had a good idea, someone else would immediately come along to copy it.

Zig-Zag's had been around since the days of the Air Force base, and Niall was reasonably confident the place hadn't been painted or cleaned since then. There was a layer of slime, composed of equal parts grease and cigarette smoke residue, coating every surface. Sitting between Pius and Harper on one side of the booth, Niall tried hard not to touch anything. Despite being in the "non-smoking" section, everything reeked of cigarettes, likely due to the thirty years of smoke absorbed into the upholstery, carpet, and ceiling tiles.

"So, we're supposed to stop an alien invasion?" Niall asked again while they waited for their subs, pizza, and donairs. "The seven of us?"

"Eight, if you count my Easton." Keith smiled a metallic grin.

Harper rolled her eyes so hard that Niall wondered if she made herself dizzy.

"Great, so our numbers keep going up anyway." Niall sighed.

"It's bugs," Anna reminded them. "I've pieced together as much as I can from Theolina's notes, and I'm pretty sure it's just a swarm of big bugs."

"Explosive bugs," Pius clarified.

"What about the hard binging part?" asked Keith.

"Excuse me?" Anna looked confused.

"You told me the bugs were hard bingers for something else."

Dawning rose in Anna's big, sparkling grey eyes. "Harbingers, right. Well, that's what our secret weapon is for." She winked at Niall and Harper.

Anna didn't seem to notice, or at least acknowledge, that Skidmark was constantly leering at her chest. Niall and Harper took turns kicking him under the table. "Whatever it is, if Theolina dealt with them all by herself, then I'm sure the two of you can handle it. Especially with the rest of us to help you."

"Yeah, but Theolina was a witch," Niall reminded her. "An actual witch who had magic powers."

"Yes, and so do you," said Keenan. "We saw you use your powers to throw that girl across the room at The Hangar last week. And you used them to save you and your friends yesterday."

"Didn't help Todd or his family." Niall wondered how they were doing. Last he heard, they were hurt pretty bad.

"You can't save everyone." Anna reached out to take his hand. "But if we stop these creatures, we can save a lot of people."

"You're asking a lot of me. I can't even make these powers work reliably most of the time. I have no control over it."

"You're not doing it alone." Keith patted his bat, sitting next to him in the booth. "That's what me and Easton's for."

"That's what *all* of us are for," corrected Keenan. "We're doing this together. You're our ace in the hole, but we all have a part to play."

Pius looked a little green. He wasn't as excited about this as some of the others. "I think we should involve the actual authorities in this. We're a bunch of kids. We should call the cops, or the military, or something."

"I agree we should get in touch with Sergeant Tanguay," said Harper. "But do you think we have the time to convince anyone that there are actual aliens on their way to Gale Harbour in a few hours? Our only evidence has either exploded or gone down the drain at Pius' house."

"There might be some in my belly." Skidmark rubbed his navel. "Which reminds me, where is my donair?"

Harper snorted. "If you're offering to be dissected in the name of science, go for it. But I still don't think we have time for it before tonight."

"That's why we need to do it ourselves. We need to be ready for nightfall." Keenan produced a notebook from his velvet frock coat, full of scrawled lists and diagrams. "Keith, while I think you and your bat are effective, we need more weapons."

"Harper has a gun," said Skidmark. "As long as she promises not to shoot any of us with it."

Anna shook her head. "A gun's no good against those things. They're too small and fast. Haven't you ever hunted June bugs before? Regular ones, I mean. We need things like bats and tennis rackets. Maybe nets."

"Bug spray?" suggested Harper.

"A flamethrower!" said Keith.

"No flames," Keenan reminded him. "We don't want to blow half the town to kingdom come."

"I'm calling Sergeant Tanguay." Pius squeezed out of the booth and headed for the blue payphone by the front door.

The others leaned in to discuss their plans and strategies, and the food was brought to the table. The waitress looked at them sideways until Skidmark explained they were talking about a game and asked her if she might be interested in joining them because they always needed extra players, and it was a great way to build your problem-solving and math skills. She disappeared quickly and didn't come back, tip be damned.

Niall slouched back in his seat, half-listening to the animated discussion. He still thought it sounded crazy. They were seven kids talking about saving their town from an alien invasion, and they were relying on him to use strange powers he didn't understand to be at the forefront of the battle. Powers that only worked when he touched Harper's blood.

That was the other thing that bothered him. Should he be paying for Harper's lunch? This boyfriend/girlfriend thing was new to him, and he wasn't sure what the protocol was. He didn't have a job or a lot of money, so he would go broke pretty fast if he paid for her every time they went out somewhere. Nana's birthday money would only go so far.

At one point, Harper got up to go to the washroom, and Keenan slid around to slip in next to Niall. He leaned in close. "You look bummed, and I don't think it's because we're making ridiculous plans to fight aliens."

The greasy young man in a top hat was perceptive. "Yeah. It's girl stuff."

Keenan might have some advice on that front. He and Anna seemed pretty happy, and Niall had no one else to ask. None of his friends had girlfriends, and Nelson had even worse luck with dating than he did. As he was reminded earlier that day, talking to his dad was more painful than getting teeth pulled, so that option was out. Niall figured this was the best chance he was going to get.

"How long have you and Anna been together?"

"A couple of years. Anna ran away from home when she was in her last year of high school. Her parents were into some bad stuff, and she didn't want to be a part of it. I met her because she was crashing at a mutual friend's house. She was a mess back then. She was into drugs and was doing whatever she had to to survive. I probably should've stayed clear of her, but I couldn't help it." Keenan chuckled. "I fell for her, and we helped each other out. I kept her clean and even managed to get her to finish Grade Twelve and made sure she got a job."

Niall suddenly felt a great kinship with Keenan. Harper wasn't in quite as bad a place as Anna, but they both had fallen for complicated girls. He was also surprised at Keenan's selflessness. "How did she help you?"

Keenan winked. "We've all got our issues. That's a story for another time. But what's bugging you?"

Niall wasn't sure where to start, but Harper returned to the table then.

Keenan stood. "We'll talk later," he whispered before sitting back down by Anna. He put his arm around Anna and gave her a kiss on the cheek, and she smiled and squeezed his hand.

Harper plopped onto the seat next to Niall. "Move over, Dork-pie."

Niall reached over and took her hand under the table. He half-expected her to pull away, but she squeezed his fingers and kept her hand there. It was still a bit wet from where she'd washed her hands. Harper smiled at him nonchalantly before yelling at Skidmark for picking his nose. Niall was content for a moment, but he looked forward to his chat with Keenan later. And he still wasn't sure if he was supposed to pay for Harper's lunch.

CHAPTER THIRTY-EIGHT

Courage (For Hugh McLennan)
June 3, 12:00pm

"You were there."

Colonel Wolfhard hesitated a moment before bringing his spoonful of soup to his lips. A dribble of red tomato ran down into his silver beard. He swallowed, wiped his chin with a paper napkin, and placed his spoon down on the laminate table before sitting back and responding. "Excuse me, Sergeant?"

Tanguay stood over Wolfhard and Captain Mason's table at Nanny's Kitchen. A few metres away, crowds of people strolled through the Gale Harbour Shopping Centre, blissfully ignorant of what was coming for their town. Inside the diner, a half-dozen other lunch patrons pretended not to be listening to their conversation, but Tanguay knew every one of them was dropping eaves like a drunk roofer and would be spreading news around town before her afternoon coffee break. She didn't care anymore.

"You were there. On Hansen Air Force Base in 1964. Right here in Gale Harbour."

Wolfhard picked up his Styrofoam coffee cup. "Anyone could check my service records." He took a sip from his cup. "Christ, this coffee is terrible."

"Give it a chance. It grows on you," Constable Bennett called from the next table, where he was sitting, flirting with Charlene Boulous.

Marie-Ann wasn't getting distracted, though Bennett was supposed to be on duty right now and not dallying with the incompetent waitress. She'd call him out for that later. "You were here the night Linda Falstaff died."

Wolfhard smiled an unnerving grin. "I was wondering how long that would take you to figure out." He took another sip and grimaced.

Then he called over his shoulder: "I think your insides would need to be made of Saskatchewan seal-skin leather to drink this, Constable."

Then to the Sergeant: "How did you do it?"

"Angus Shave." It had taken a while to translate his barely coherent gibberish, but it made sense in the end.

Wolfhard looked surprised. "He's still alive? He was made of tougher stuff than I imagined."

"We should talk about this somewhere more private," suggested Mason.

Marie-Ann ignored him. Sure, his job had been to keep an eye on Wolfhard and keep things quiet, which Tanguay could appreciate, but she was tired of sneaking around. "You're still alive, aren't you? How did you make it out of there?"

Wolfhard clutched the Styrofoam cup with his hands and stared at a dirty spot on the wall where the paisley-patterned wallpaper was peeling. "I was fortunate. And it took me many years of therapy to get past it."

That was more honest and vulnerable than Tanguay had expected.

"So, you figured out what happened back in '64. Did you also figure out that it's all about to happen again?"

"How do we stop it?"

Wolfhard settled back into the booth. "We need to find the asset. It's the key to all this. But since you killed Aminov, we have no idea where it is."

"He didn't know where it was!"

"And you believed him?"

"Yes, I believe him."

She did believe him, didn't she? Why did this asshole make her second-guess herself all the time? Tanguay had always been good at reading people until she met Wolfhard. But if Aminov and Garabet didn't take the bomb, then who the hell took it out of Jesso's shed?

"*Je suis niaiseux,*" Marie-Ann breathed. The answer was obvious.

Wolfhard took another sip of the coffee. "It does grow on you. Like foot fungus. Are you having a 'Eureka' moment, Sergeant?"

CHAPTER THIRTY-NINE

I Feel You
June 3, 1:15pm
Gale Harbour Crossing

Some young kids were playing in the road when Tanguay, Wolfhard, and Mason pulled up in Tanguay's cruiser in front of the big red house at the end of Spruce Road in Gale Harbour Crossing. The kids backed up half a step out of the way but didn't run. They stared at the police car with a mixture of fascination and apprehension. It promised far more exciting entertainment than a rerun of *Eek! The Cat*.

"Go home, kids," said Marie-Ann as she got out of the car. "Don't play in the road."

The children scattered and fled, but she was confident they had only gone looking for hiding places a bit farther away. They needed gossip to report to their parents before they went home.

"I still say we should have taken my car," grumbled Wolfhard. "I have far more artillery in my trunk."

"We don't need guns," replied Tanguay.

"You sure about that?"

"From now on, we're doing this my way. The way we do things in Gale Harbour."

Wolfhard raised an eyebrow. "Like when you shot Aminov?"

"He wasn't from around here." Tanguay pounded on the front door of the red house.

A woman's voice called back from inside. "Who is it?"

"This is the RCMP. We're here to talk to Wayne Jesso."

Silence.

Wolfhard fidgeted impatiently. "Why would you announce who you were?"

There was a bang from around the other side of the house as the back door slammed open. Tanguay smiled at the old colonel. "That's why. Captain Mason, if you would go that way?"

"On it." He bolted across the front garden around the right side of the house, showing off the skills he must have employed as a wide receiver.

Tanguay went left, circling the house to get a clear view of Jesso running across the back lawn toward the large shed. "Freeze!"

Jesso immediately halted, hands in the air.

"Don't shoot," he whimpered, turning around slowly. "I'm not armed, I don't...wait, you don't even have your gun drawn?"

"Nope," she said, and Mason tackled Jesso to the lawn.

"Son of a... you can't do that!" Jesso struggled under the much stronger man. "This is police brutality!"

"Sorry, Captain Mason's not a cop. Now get up and open your shed, Jesso."

Jesso stopped struggling. His beady, bloodshot eyes widened. "I don't have to do that."

"I could get a warrant, yes, but I'm really not in the mood to wait, and since what's in your shed may be attracting an alien invasion tomorrow, we're on a bit of a schedule here."

"An alien... ow, get your elbow off my neck, you arse! What the hell are you talking about?"

"Open the goddamn shed and find out."

Mason eased up on Jesso, and the surly man pushed him off. Struggling to his feet, breathing hard, the pot-bellied, salt-and-pepper-haired man looked at the three armed and unhappy-looking people standing on his lawn. He seemed to briefly consider making a run for it but decided the better of it. Finally, he brushed off his jeans, shrugged, and fished a set of keys out of his pocket. He flung them at Tanguay, and she caught them handily.

"Open it yourself, bitch."

"Thank you for your cooperation, Mr. Jesso. Captain Mason, please keep an eye on him. Wolfhard, if he makes a break for it, shoot him."

"Happily," replied Wolfhard with a sick smile. Tanguay wasn't sure if he was kidding, and she could tell by the blanched look on Jesso's face that he wasn't sure, either.

Tanguay headed for the shed door, flipped through the bottle opener keyring until she found the appropriate key, and unlocked the padlock. "Breaking into your storehouse and moving the bomb was dumb. It cost us several precious days, and how did you possibly think you could get away with it? What did you possibly think you were going to do with an atomic..." She opened the door and trailed off. "*Chalice de tabernac....*"

The bomb was torn to pieces. The metal casing was split open, and metal shards were embedded into the walls, ceiling, and floor of the small wooden building. Well, in three walls. The fourth wall, the one opposite the door on the other side of the yard, was mostly gone. Something had smashed through it, leaving splintered studs and shredded vinyl siding. The fence behind the shed was also knocked over, revealing a small copse of trees beyond.

Whatever had blown out the wall had come from the inside.

Tanguay whirled on Jesso, but she could see from the slack-jawed look on his face that he had no idea what happened. The look on Wolfhard's face, however, spoke volumes.

CHAPTER FORTY

Oh Carolina
June 3, 8:45 pm

"That's an interesting selection of movies you have there, Eleanor." Jerry rattled through the wall of VHS tapes behind the counter, quickly sliding out the hard plastic cases and replacing them with the empty cardboard boxes from the shelf. "*Glengarry Glen Ross, Scent of a Woman, Wuthering Heights...*"

Eleanor Walsh looked down her hawk-like nose at the burly man in a Deep Purple T-shirt behind the counter. She had the general shape and personality of a sickle on top of a broom handle. "I am a scholar of the arts. I enjoy powerful, dramatic films."

"*...Beethoven, The Mighty Ducks, 3 Ninjas.*"

Mrs. Walsh cleared her throat and scoffed. "Yes, well, I am also a high school drama teacher, so I need to be familiar with the fare in which my students are interested. Besides, I might find inspiration for a future show."

"I thought the school burned down?"

"The children are so disappointed that our production of *Starlight Express* was cancelled, but the show must go on! To make up for it, I'm thinking about turning one of these popular films into a show over the summer."

Jerry held up one of the movie cases. "You're going to do a show about *3 Ninjas*? You know this is stupid, right?"

Eleanor sighed. "No, probably the *Ducks* one. All the kids had to learn to skate for *Starlight Express*, but none of them can sing a note to save their lives. It works out better this way."

"Kids are the frigging worst."

"Children are the future, Mr. Jerry. We need to teach them to be open to the arts and culture, to be able to think creatively and critically." Eleanor kept telling herself that, hoping one day she might believe it. It sounded good on grant applications, anyway.

Jerry did not seem to share her delusions. "They're in here all the time, taking too long to pick out their stuff, getting sticky fingerprints on everything. They never bring back their tapes on time, and they hardly ever rewind them. There's this one kid, he's in here every Friday night, he won't stop yapping about *Star Trek* or *Star Wars* or whatever other nerd crap he's into."

Eleanor shuddered. "Yes, I know the kind. The dreck that passes for art these days is abhorrent."

"He's got some stupid name, too. The other kids call him Treadmark or something...."

Now Eleanor shuddered so hard her glasses vibrated right off the tip of her nose and fell, dangling around her neck on their gold chain. "*Skidmark*. Brian Hawco. Yes, he's a pupil of mine. He is... challenging." She didn't think it was right to badmouth a child in front of a stranger, even if he was a maddening little pox mark on the ass of humanity.

"He's a weird little perv, that's what he is. You should see some of the movies he picks up."

"Please, Mr. Jerry, I am his teacher. It'd be best if I don't hear about anything that I would need to report to his parents."

Jerry shrugged and finished ringing her up. He handed her a bulging plastic bag full of video cassettes. "That's a lot of movies, lady. No plans for the weekend?"

"Yes, well, there's no school tomorrow, and Mr. Walsh and myself like to curl up on the chesterfield and watch a few films." Which was a bald-faced lie. Mr. Walsh, if he came home from the club at all, would fart, burp, and pass out in the chair across from her. If she was lucky. Still, there was no need to air her dirty marital affairs in front of strangers.

Jerry winked and grinned, revealing a mouth full of yellow teeth under his scraggly moustache. "I bet you don't get to see the end of many movies, am I right?"

Now Eleanor not only shuddered, but she threw up in her mouth a little as well. Why was the round, hairy man so obnoxious and revolting? Did she exude vibes of "please talk to me, I would love to hear from unwashed, gross proprietors of celluloid filth?" Mr. Jerry reminded her of a director she'd met during her very brief dalliance with adult films back in the early eighties, which was not a compliment.

Too embarrassed and disgusted to form a witty response or even to open her mouth without the risk of throwing up on the counter, Eleanor merely glared at Mr. Jerry, grabbed her shopping bag, and stormed down the steps and out the front door.

She stepped out onto Main Street and opened her mouth to take a breath of fresh air. A June bug immediately flew into the back of her throat. She gagged and coughed, spitting the foul insect on the sidewalk. Now on the verge of actually retching, she dropped her bag and staggered backward against Video Shack's large display window. Behind the glass hung posters for *Hoffa* and *A River Runs Through It*, as well as a sign advertising two-for-one Tuesday rentals. She fell to her knees, fumbling through her bag for a bottle of Diet Pepsi to rinse the taste of the repulsive creature from her tongue. She was so focused on the insect she'd spit out that she was utterly oblivious to the much larger bug now buzzing up to her from behind. It landed on the back of her head, latching firmly onto her tight hair bun. She instinctively tried to brush it away and discovered something large, hard, and scaly resting on the back of her skull.

She screamed and turned to see the swarm of fist-sized June bugs flying around in the glow of the street light in front of Video Shack.

"Protective headwear," said Niall, holding up his clipboard.

Keith smacked himself on the side of his hockey helmet. "Check."

Niall checked something off on the clipboard with a pencil. "Protective gloves."

Everyone raised their hands, all wearing some manner of protective gear. Keenan had on heavy work gloves. Keith wore his hockey gloves. Skidmark wore a set of oven mitts with a floral print.

"Weapons?"

"Check and double-check." Keith took a couple of practice swings with his aluminum bat and nearly took off Skidmark's head.

"Can I change mine?" Pius held up a metre-long wooden ruler. "I don't think this is going to be an effective weapon."

Harper, beneath her glossy black snowmobile helmet, shook her head. "We all had a chance to pick weapons hours ago. If you're not happy with it, you should have taken something else."

"You picked when I was in the bathroom! The metre-stick is all that was left."

"You could have taken the garden hose," Keith reminded him.

"For some reason, I don't think that will be any better." Pius' shoulders slumped. "I should call Sergeant Tanguay again."

"Constable Murphy is not working," said Harper. "And the new dispatcher won't put you through to the Sergeant."

The group stood beside Keenan's car parked behind White's Hardware on Main Street, which shared a parking lot with Foodland supermarket. They'd spent the rest of the afternoon scrounging and borrowing the mishmash gear they were now wearing, and they stopped at the hardware store before it closed to get the last items they needed.

"You do realize this is insane, right?" Niall put the clipboard under his arm so he could pull on his heavy welder's mitts. "We're planning to go fight an alien invasion with sports equipment and Ski-Doo helmets we stole from Skidmark's dad's shed."

"Between this and the driveway, he's definitely going to murder me." Skidmark lifted the visor of his yellow helmet. Then he sat down to put on his sparkly, silver rollerblades. "Pius, can I come live with you after all this is over? I'm low maintenance. I can live on Fruit Roll-Ups and chicken nuggets if I have to, and I just need an hour of TV time a week to watch new episodes of The Next Generation. I can be flexible on the time if you give me access to the VCR. In fact, I'm great at programming VCRs. I can make sure the whole household doesn't miss any of their favourite shows, and then I'll edit out the commercials afterward."

"Shut up, Skidmark," said Harper. "Pius doesn't even know if he lives at his house anymore."

"Is that 'cause your dad is banging your babysitter?" Skidmark stood, flailed violently on the inline skates, and crashed into Keenan's car, adding a new dent to the front bumper.

"She's not my babysitter," roared Pius. "She was Niall's babysitter! And how does everyone know this?"

Skidmark pulled himself up to a standing position. "Your mom was yelling about it pretty loud. It's all over town now. I assume Mrs. Downey, who lives in the green house on the corner of your street, heard about it. She's a big blabber-mouth and gossip. That's how I heard about Keith's drinking problem and that Sally Alexander takes estrogen pills for some reason. I don't know why, but that's what Mrs. Downey told me when I was walking by her house, and her dog peed on my foot. I wouldn't worry about your dad, Pius. Lots of couples have worse stuff happen, and they stay together, and even if they get divorced, your mom's hot, so I'm sure she'll find another man."

"Will you shut the hell up!?" Pius smashed his metre-stick over Skidmark's yellow snowmobile helmet, snapping it in half. "See? I told you this was a stupid weapon!"

Keith shook his head. "You've gotta work on your anger issues, dude."

Skidmark fell again, and Keenan helped him up, probably hoping to keep him from scratching the car even more. Keenan wore only plastic goggles, forgoing other headwear so he didn't have to lose his top hat. "Why are you wearing those stupid skates?"

"They increase my land speed fourfold," Skidmark explained. Everyone glared at him, and he shrugged. "Okay, one-and-a-half fold. As long as I don't fall down."

Anna sighed. "I've never seen him stay up."

Skidmark blushed. Niall didn't think he'd ever seen that before. Brain Hawco had no shame. He once had his sweatpants stolen by Chris Tobin and the hockey team, and he went back to finish math class in his underwear. Oddly enough, that wasn't the occasion that had earned him his nickname.

As three people tried to keep Skidmark on his feet, a scream split the night from somewhere nearby.

"Probably just some dick doing donuts again in the Foodland parking lot," muttered Harper.

"No, it came from across the street," said Keith.

He and Keenan ran around the corner of the hardware store to get a better look, and Niall followed. Across the street, right in front of Jerry's Video Shack, a woman was flailing on the sidewalk, covered with the butt monkey June bugs.

"Christ, that's the drama teacher from school, Missus What's-her-name!" Keith pointed his bat.

"She's not a real teacher!" Harper called from behind them.

"Mrs. Walsh," Skidmark bellowed. He took two steps on his rollerblades and fell on his face.

Keenan looked at Niall and Keith and hefted his shovel. "I guess the plan starts now. Come on!"

Keith took off after the Townie. The two of them raced across the street and nearly got smoked by a passing taxicab. Niall was a few steps behind them, with the tennis racket in his hand, feeling inadequate. What the hell were they doing?

A passerby in a windbreaker stopped and tried to help Mrs. Walsh, but when the middle-aged man realized what was crawling on her, he screamed and staggered backward. Keith reached the scene first. He brushed several bugs off the drama teacher's back and proceeded to smash them with his bat on the concrete, spraying the sidewalk with glowing, green goo. Another one swooped down, and Keenan batted it out of the sky with his shovel, sending a spray of fluorescent slime across Jerry's front window.

Niall reached the others and swung with his racket. The bugs hit with the force and weight of a tennis ball and went hurtling into the night. They didn't explode like when they got smacked with a shovel or a baseball bat, but they did make a satisfying little whump. Niall swatted two, four, eight bugs, quickly losing count. All three of them were swinging wildly, but there were butt monkeys everywhere. Niall looked up to see a heavy cloud of them swirling around the streetlight above his head, and his heart jumped to his throat.

They had planned to drive around town and smash any bugs they found. He had no idea they'd find so many at the first freaking streetlamp.

"Guys, we need more help!" he screamed, but the others were already darting across the parking lot, sticks and clubs bobbing up and down as they ran. Even with everyone, though, there was no way they could handle this many, could they? If he and Harper worked together, could they make a spell that could stop them? He didn't know any anti-monkey spells, or any anti-bug spells, for that matter.

That's when the butt-monkeys started shooting laser beams at Mrs. Walsh.

Niall didn't see the first one. He heard the weird zapping sound and smelled the burning stench of ozone. A flash of blue fire came with the second one, and a black patch of scorched concrete appeared where it touched the ground next to Mrs. Walsh. She was still trying to get to her feet, swatting at the monsters and trying to crawl away, but the bugs were everywhere. Niall looked up and saw a trio of June bugs glowing a bright aquamarine colour, apparently charging up for more blasts. There was nothing he could do to stop them. They were too high for him to reach with his racket, and he didn't have any of Harper's blood to use his powers. He was going to have to watch the butt monkeys disintegrate Mrs. Walsh on the sidewalk on Main Street, real teacher or not.

And then there was a yellow and silver blur, and something heavy flashed by and scooped Mrs. Walsh off the street a split second before a volley of blue energy beams burned a small crater in the ground right where she had been a moment before.

Skidmark and Mrs. Walsh crashed through the front window of Jerry's Video Shack in a shower of glass and movie posters.

Keenan nodded in admiration. "Damn, I guess he stayed up after all."

They kept swinging, and the others joined in, but there were too many bugs. Skidmark had saved Mrs. Walsh, but it was only a matter of time before the butt monkeys started shooting lasers at someone else, and they didn't have enough Starlight Express rollerblades to save everyone.

Someone yanked off Niall's glove, and a hot, sticky hand slipped into his. He looked into the black facemask of a Ski-Doo helmet and gasped with fright.

"Let's kill these buttmunches," said Harper.

Niall racked his brain. What could he do against so many? He could make a shield to protect them like he did at the Murphys' house, but that wouldn't get rid of the bugs, and it wouldn't stop them from hurting anyone else. He couldn't telekinetically slap them like he did with Sally Alexander. "Maybe I could burn them up—"

"No!" screamed Pius. "You can't burn them! They'll explode! With this many of them, they'll take out the whole block!"

Duh. Of course. But then, how could he make them go away? What was the spell he'd used on the Psycho Hose Beast? He'd wished her to go away. He willed her to go away. He thought about driving the bugs away, far away, then reached out and pushed...

Niall saw a blinding light, and then there was nothing.

CHAPTER FORTY-TWO

Runaway Train
June 3, 9:25 pm

Niall slipped in and out of consciousness.

There was swirling chaos around him. People were screaming, but he couldn't hear them. Something was falling from the sky. Was it snow? Ash? It was coming down heavy, like embers from a dirty fire.

There was a fire, but he hadn't caused it. He didn't burn the bugs; he was sure of that. But something had still caught fire. Flames licked from the top of a telephone pole across the street, threatening to catch the hardware store next door.

He closed his eyes.

When he opened them again, Anna was kneeling on the ground. She was crying and screaming, and her make-up was running down her face in black streaks. She kept putting her head down on something on the sidewalk, a long, dark figure that wasn't moving. A crushed top hat lay nearby. A crowd of people gathered around her.

He closed his eyes again.

When he opened them next, he was in a cold, empty place, surrounded by the deepest, most endless darkness he ever thought possible. Something streaked by his head, a flash of blue-green light hurtling toward a tiny blue sphere a million kilometres away in the darkness.

Another flash went by, then another, and another. Soon, the flashes filled his entire field of vision, all these streaks of light converging on a single point. Niall realized he was moving too, being pulled toward... something. Something on that blue sphere. But what was it? It was so powerful it was reaching out to the other side of the universe, but he couldn't tell what it was. He tried to see it, to reach out with all of his mind and strength. But when he grasped at it, all he found was his own body.

Suddenly, his eyes opened again.

Sergeant Tanguay knelt over him. He was still lying on the sidewalk outside of Video Shack. "Niall? Niall, can you hear me?" she asked in her funny Quebec accent.

"The butt monkeys…" It was the first thing out of his mouth. "Did I get them?"

Tanguay's face twisted in confusion and disgust. "What?"

"The bugs, he means the bugs." It was Harper's voice. She knelt next to the sergeant. She'd taken the helmet off, and her hair was sweaty and sticking up in all directions. It was cute. "Yes, you got them, Niall, you got all of them."

"All of them that are here, anyway," Tanguay muttered.

Niall heard the crackle of a radio, and a voice came out of her shoulder:

"Uh, Sarge, this is Bennett. I have a report of someone who said they hit a bird or something, and it exploded the front end of their car. I'm looking at the damage, and it looks like a friggin' bomb went off in his engine."

Another crackle, another voice.

"Sarge, Sarge! There's another swarm of those things on Queen Street! They set the Smoke Shoppe on fire!"

"Tabernac," Tanguay hissed under her breath.

Two men stood next to the sergeant that Niall recognized from somewhere. A tall man with broad shoulders and a white-haired man with a stern face. They were the men from Doucette's Motel.

"It's worse than last time," said the white-haired man. "The creatures are agitated, looking for it. It's going to keep getting worse until they find it."

"What happens when they find it?" asked the other man.

The white-haired man's jaw clenched. "Then it really gets bad."

Red lights were flashing all around. Ambulances, fire trucks. Niall didn't know there was more than one of either in town. He was still lying on the sidewalk and didn't have the strength to sit up and count them.

"Is everyone okay?" Niall asked.

"Skidmark got cut up pretty bad when he went through the window, but he saved Mrs. Walsh," Harper explained.

A vision flashed through Niall's mind. Anna, kneeling over something. "Keenan. What happened to Keenan?"

Harper and the sergeant looked uncomfortable. Neither of them spoke for a long moment. Finally, Tanguay said, "He's fine, Niall, he—"

"Tell him the truth," Harper cut in. She took a deep breath. "When you zapped the butt monkeys, a lot of other stuff got smashed, too. Windows, cars, an electrical transformer. Shrapnel and stuff were flying everywhere. Keenan got hit in the head...."

Niall's stomach clenched. No. He was trying to kill the bugs. It wasn't supposed to hurt anyone. "Is he...?"

Harper's lips tightened to a thin line. "If he had been wearing a helmet like he was supposed to and not that stupid hat...."

"He's... dead?"

Harper was still for a moment. She nodded.

Niall's vision blurred. He'd killed somebody. He killed Keenan. He had been so terrified when he accidentally hit Sally Alexander, but this time, he'd really done it. A million and one thoughts raced through his head at once. Barely remembered Sunday school lessons and church sermons. Thou Shalt Not Kill. Video games where you mowed down soldiers with laser guns. Laughing with Pius, Harper, and Skidmark when he rolled a critical hit in D&D and chopped the innkeeper's head off.

What were his parents going to say? What was Nana going to say?

"Niall, it was an accident." Tanguay's voice cracked.

Was she... crying?

"This place is crazy here. Monsters and debris are flying everywhere. We don't know what happened. It wasn't your fault."

"You saved a lot of people." Harper squeezed Niall's hand, and he felt the sticky, half-dried blood on it. He pulled away.

"Niall, I'm going to call your parents to come to get you, okay? You're going to be okay." Tanguay stood, and the white-haired man stepped directly in front of her.

"Sergeant, we have to go. We have to find the carapace before those things tear the entire town apart."

Carapace? What was he talking about?

"I know, let me just—"

"We need the kids. They're the only ones who can stop this."

Niall saw a strange look pass over Sergeant Tanguay's face. He had never seen it before, at least not on her. He had seen fear, anger, rage, and confusion, but not this. The way her eyes pinched, and her lips tightened as if she was having trouble speaking. The look in her eyes reflected a deep, deep regret—for what she had done and what she was about to do.

"I know," said Tanguay through gritted teeth. She turned away, unable to look at any of them.

"It's okay," said Niall, pulling himself up to a sitting position.

Everyone turned to look at him.

"I think I know where it is. The thing you're looking for."

"Niall, you don't have to do this." Tanguay's voice quivered.

"Yes, I do."

Linda awoke in incredible pain, laying on her back, staring at a starry sky.

She had fallen into a hole, so how did she get outside? There were men around her that she didn't recognize, and her first thought was to make certain her skirt wasn't riding up. She tried to reach down, but everything hurt too much to move.

"Where am I?" she asked, to no one in particular. "What happened to me?"

"You're okay, little lady. Take it easy," said a man next to her. Like Wolfhard, he wore green army fatigues, but he was older, carried a black doctor's bag, and had a stethoscope around his neck. "You had a nasty fall."

"Where's Eric?" She asked.

"Who?"

"Airman Wolfhard." She wouldn't be playing soccer anytime soon, she guessed. Even her hair hurt.

The doctor called out for Wolfhard, and with great difficulty, Linda raised her head to look around. She was lying on a stretcher near the dock by the warehouses she'd seen earlier. There was controlled chaos all around her as soldiers ran back and forth and officers barked orders. Angus and Theolina stood off to one side. Angus looked terrified and tried to make himself look as small as possible, but the dishevelled woman was yelling at the soldiers and telling them off something fierce. Linda couldn't hear her words, but they made the soldiers blush.

And then she saw it. The monster, the moon man, the fallen angel. It was sprawled on the dock, unmoving and still. If she didn't know better, she might have thought it was just a pile of rocks. Had they killed it? Whatever that rocket was that flew overhead, had it done its job?

Wolfhard appeared, and judging by the broad smile on his face, that's precisely what happened. "We got that bastard." He stopped mid-fist-pump and looked sheepish. "Sorry, pardon my language."

"It's okay," said Linda. "I think the situation calls for it. That thing was a bastard."

"The brass are on their way down now to see it for themselves." He was bouncing around, excited like a boy on Christmas morning. Linda hadn't seen him like this before, and it reminded her that he wasn't much older than her or Angus. She smiled despite her aches. "This is the damnedest thing. The eggheads down in New Mexico are going to flip their spectacles when they get a load of this."

"I want to see it," said Linda, surprising herself.

"I think you should take it easy, miss," said the doctor. "At least until I finish examining you."

"Let her go, Doc," said Wolfhard, offering her his arm. "She encountered that thing up close in the tunnels and survived. She's a tough doll."

Linda didn't correct him. She had never let Angus call her that, but now that she thought about it, he was a bit of a bummer. She didn't know what she ever saw in Angus. She didn't know what it was she saw in Eric, either, but she was definitely seeing—and feeling—something.

Eric helped her to her feet. They walked her toward the dock, where the large pile of black rocks lay under floodlights. She still ached, but everything seemed to be working—nothing broken, at least. Being next to the young soldier, with his arm around her, made her feel much better for some reason. He smelled good, like her father after a hard day's work, but different, too. She certainly didn't feel this when she smelled her father, that was for sure.

As they approached the creature, they were stopped by other soldiers with "MP" stamped on their helmets. They were keeping everyone a safe distance from the black rocky remains. Linda couldn't get a great look at it, but she didn't need to. She knew what it looked like and that it would haunt her nightmares for the rest of her life.

The giant, glowing bugs were still buzzing around the remains, like huge fireflies over a pile of cow manure, but no one paid them much attention.

A sudden gust of wind and a deafening sound came from beyond, and everyone's heads turned toward a helicopter flying in low above the dock. Linda held up a hand to shield her eyes from the bright lights on the aircraft.

"It's the big wigs from the base!" said Eric. "They love to make an entrance. I want to be the first there to give them my report. Wait here."

To Linda's shock, before he ran off, he leaned over and kissed her on the cheek. She blushed. Why was he being so forward? Was he caught up in the adrenaline and excitement?

She was caught up in all of it, too, she supposed. A few hours ago, she thought she was going to die. Now she was safe and alive and was excited about some of the new possibilities life was presenting.

Out of the corner of her eye, Linda saw the pile of rocks move.

Time seemed to slow around her. People were screaming, but no warnings could be heard over the roar of the helicopter, which was now right above their heads. Eric, in particular, had his back to the dock, watching the helicopter land, and didn't see or hear the cries from his fellows. Linda saw Theolina, her eyes wild and black hair flowing as she shoved through the crowd, trying to reach them. The monster rose back up to its feet, and the fiery sword came to life in its hand again, slicing three men in half in a heartbeat. The monster moved toward the helicopter, toward Eric.

Linda ran. It was a few dozen steps, and she crossed them faster than she ever had in gym class or on the soccer pitch. But she wasn't fast enough. Eric turned as the monster lowered the flaming sword. It was going to cut him in two, and there was nothing she could do to stop it.

In a split second, she made a choice and changed her direction slightly. She shifted her weight and slammed into Eric with her shoulder. She shoved him away, and he fell to the ground, out of the way of the burning sword.

She didn't feel the blade slice through her head.

CHAPTER FORTY-THREE

The River
June 3, 11:15pm

Mason drove the black 4x4 across town toward the Strip. Old army base buildings flew past them, long ago converted to apartments, offices, and the movie theatre. Above them, stars streaked across the sky in the same direction they were travelling.

"So, what exactly do you expect us to do?" Harper asked from the backseat, next to Niall, who was sandwiched between her and Sergeant Tanguay.

The white-haired colonel tried to turn toward them. He struggled with his seatbelt a moment, unbuckled it, and then faced them. "I was here, on this base, thirty years ago, the last time there was a lunar eclipse during the Areitid meteor storm. The storm brought alien creatures down to Earth that were looking for an other-worldly vessel."

"The carapace?" Niall asked, trying to follow along.

He nodded. Flashes of light in the sky above illuminated his face. "Exactly. It resembles the shell of a large insect, like a carapace." He mimed weird hand gestures with clawed fingers, like someone playing "Itsy Bitsy Spider" with an infant. "We didn't know what it was at first. A girl I met that night, Linda, thought it was an angel that came down from Heaven." His voice and gaze drifted off for a moment. "We think it came to our planet millions of years ago, but it was lost until recently. Every time the meteor shower passes Earth, the aliens look for it, but 1964 was the first time they found it."

"But it didn't destroy the world then," said Harper. "Obviously."

"No. Theolina Kane defeated it. Our best weapons couldn't hurt it, but she stopped the thing dead in its tracks with a wave of her hand. We took the carcass and were supposed to bring it back to the States when we pulled out in '66, but something went wrong. It was left behind and lost here for thirty years."

"I still don't know what's worse," grumbled Tanguay. "That you lost a nuclear bomb or an alien creature."

Niall pressed his head against the window. Theolina stopped it with a spell. What spell? He didn't even know if what he did were "spells." Last year, Theolina and her sister had told him that the words and the gestures didn't matter, that it was the "intention" of the magic that made it work. But his powers never completely did what he intended. He didn't know how to control them. Was that the problem? That his intention wasn't focussed and precise enough? He wished there was someone to ask.

Outside the car, more and more streaks of blue-white light lanced across the sky.

"Is that the aliens?" Niall asked. "The June bug things?"

"Butt monkeys," Harper corrected.

The colonel grunted. "They've found the carapace."

The streaks of light converged on a point a few hundred metres ahead of them on the Strip. They curved downward and collided, flashing briefly before vanishing. Mason slowed the car as they approached.

"What are you doing?" the colonel demanded.

"I don't want to run headlong into it, do you?" snapped Mason.

A soft glow started to form a nimbus around the point where the streaks were disappearing. It grew brighter with every butt monkey that added its power, and soon the glow took shape. It was humanoid, but it must have been three metres tall or more. What appeared to be wings of glowing blue energy grew from its back, and it rose into the air.

Niall could see how Linda had mistaken it for an angel. It looked beautiful and terrifying at the same time, like a girl when you approached her to ask for a dance. As it rose into the sky, Niall couldn't fathom what someone who had never seen a sci-fi movie or read a comic book would have thought of this thing. How long had it been on Earth? What would ancient societies have thought of this thing?

They would have called it a god.

"Target sighted. You have clearance to engage. Repeat; you are clear to engage."

Captain Mason was talking into a hand radio he'd produced from somewhere. Niall was so engrossed by the monster that he hadn't seen where it came from. He was about to ask what was going on, but before he could open his mouth, the colonel was already yelling at him. "What the hell are you doing?"

Mason didn't answer. He threw the car in reverse and slammed on the gas, rocketing them backward. Niall smacked his face on the back of the colonel's seat.

"You're attacking it?" Tanguay asked, holding Harper back with one hand so Harper at least hadn't banged her head. "Why didn't you tell us before?"

"Because your weapons can't hurt it!" The colonel was so angry he was spitting. "This is a mistake!"

"That's why I didn't say anything. Thirty years ago, your weapons didn't work, Colonel Sanders, but we're in a different world now. Those are CRV-7 rockets with tungsten anti-tank flechettes. They can punch through thirty centimetres of Soviet T-72 tank armour. Your 'carapace' isn't getting back up."

Niall stared through the front windshield as new streaks of light appeared in the sky, hurtling toward the fiery creature. These were different, though; they were reddish-orange, came from a higher angle, and moved at a slower but still substantial speed.

"You all may want to close your eyes," said Mason and slammed on the brakes.

Niall averted his gaze in time, but the detonation from the missiles hitting the carapace sent a shockwave that struck the car with such force that it was pushed back across the asphalt. The front windshield exploded in a spiderweb of cracks, showering the interior cabin with glass and debris. Sitting in the back seat, Niall, Harper, and Tanguay were mostly shielded, but Wolfhard flew forward, face-first into the windshield.

Niall's ears were still ringing when they staggered out of the car a moment later. There was smoke everywhere, and Niall fumbled through it, feeling like that time he went on the roller coaster at the amusement park. Pius had refused to go on it, and Niall wished he had stayed with him; Niall had ended up throwing up his overpriced carnival hotdog a few minutes later.

"Bennett? Forrest?" Tanguay was yelling into her radio. "Is anyone available? We need backup and medical on the Strip!"

Mason was also yelling into his radio, but he ran toward the pillar of smoke and flame a few hundred metres away, and Niall couldn't hear what he was saying.

Colonel Wolfhard fell out of the passenger seat. "My eyes... I can't see..."

Niall looked at him and did throw up a bit this time, at least in his mouth. The old man's face was a bloody mess.

Tanguay knelt over the old soldier. "There's glass everywhere. Don't move, old man. There's help on the way."

"What... what is Mason doing?" Wolfhard breathed.

Niall turned away. He couldn't look at him.

Harper, standing beside Niall, couldn't seem to pull her gaze away.

"The hell if I know..." Tanguay mumbled but trailed off. "Wait, I hear helicopters."

Niall looked up, glad to have anything to look at besides the shredded mess of ground meat and spaghetti sauce that used to be the colonel's face. "Yes, there's a bunch of them. Coming in over the Bay."

"He called in the Royal Canadian Air Force," breathed Tanguay.

"That's a good thing, right?" asked Harper. "The military is way better equipped to handle this than we are."

"No," growled the colonel. "I've watched my government screw up things like this for years. They will try to capture it, and people will die. They will try to dissect it, and more people will die. They will try to weaponize it, and even more people will die unless it attracts more of its kind from wherever the hell it comes from. Then everyone will die."

The colonel didn't sound crazy, though everything he was saying was insane. He spoke about this like all of it had happened before, and though his warnings were urgent, they were perfectly coherent. All that stuff about aliens and Area 51 and government conspiracies, none of it was real, right?

Niall felt like such an idiot. Of course, it was all real. He'd been living it for the last year.

"It needs to be destroyed," Wolfhard groaned. "It's too dangerous, too unpredictable. There are things mere humans are not meant to meddle with."

Tanguay nodded and squeezed the colonel's hand. "I'm going to talk to Mason. I'll try to talk some sense into him." She looked up at Harper and Niall. "Kids, you stay with him, okay? Help should be on the way soon."

She ran off toward the fire, leaving Niall and Harper with the old man whose head looked like he had dove face-first into a cheese grater. They glanced at each other uncomfortably.

"Uh, Mr. Wolfhard," said Harper. "I took first aid, but I don't know what to do about... this." She gestured vaguely where his nose and eyes used to be.

His hand shot up, and he grabbed Niall by his jacket. Niall was so startled he almost leapt out of his Reeboks. "Kids, don't worry about me. You have to help the sergeant."

"We're just kids..." Harper reminded him. "There's a whole army on the way to help."

"You're the only ones who can stop it. You destroyed the Primordial One."

Niall was taken aback. "How do you know about that?"

"I knew Theolina. And I know you fought the monster last year." Frantically, the colonel flailed until he grabbed Niall's hand. He pressed his fingers into Niall's palm. "Here. Its weak spot is right here, where the fire beam comes out. It's how Theolina defeated it last time."

Niall looked at his hand, still stained with Harper's blood. He looked at Harper, at the frantic, terrified look on her round face, but there was certainty in her eyes. She was nodding along to Wolfhard's words.

He looked at the colonel's shredded features. Is that what Keenan looked like, too?

"I can't do this," he breathed. "You're telling me I have to do these things, but I'm afraid."

"Niall." Harper reached for him, and he backed away. "Niall, we have to stop it."

"Harper, I killed Keenan tonight."

"That was an accident."

"How many more people could we kill trying to fight that thing?"

"How many people will get killed if we don't? We have to do this together."

"It's not together, Harper. You might hand me the bullet, but I pull the trigger. And I can't control where it goes."

"This is not about you," Harper snapped. "It's us! We are both a part of this! You can't risk everyone else's life because you're a coward."

Why was she talking like this? Why was she being mean? Couldn't she tell that he was terrified?

"Not everyone is as fearless as you, Harper."

"Niall O'Neil, I am scared shitless right now, but we have to do this."

"What if I die?" Niall was crying. He tried to get the words out, but he nearly choked on them. "What if you die?"

"My father gave his life to save mine," she reminded him. "I should do the same for someone else."

"No, you should do everything you can to save yourself, so his sacrifice wasn't a waste."

She grimaced and clenched her fists. For a second, he thought Harper was going to take a swing at him, but she took a deep breath and steadied herself. "My life won't be a waste. You can choose what you want to do with yours."

She whirled and stomped off in the direction Tanguay left. Niall called after her, but she didn't respond or look back. He looked down at Wolfhard one more time and saw that he was still, maybe not even breathing. Niall quickly tore his gaze away. Choking back tears, he followed Harper.

CHAPTER FORTY-FOUR

Strangers When We Meet
June 3, 11:10pm

Pius and Keith sat on the curb across the street from Jerry's Video Shack in the glare of the bright lights of a street lamp. A few June bugs buzzed around the light, but this time they were regular-sized, run-of-the-mill horror scarabs.

Niall and Harper were gone with the cops, Skidmark was being loaded into an ambulance, and Keenan was being zipped into a body bag. It had been one hell of a night. It had been one hell of a week.

The adrenaline gone, Pius was now racked with guilt and fear. His knees were up against his chest, and he hugged them, rocking back and forth slowly. What the hell had he been thinking, running headlong into a cloud of alien insects? He had made a lot of boner decisions in the last week.

"Look, I'm sorry again about the other day at school."

It took Pius a moment to realize it was Keith talking. Not because he was apologizing but because he sounded genuinely contrite and sincere.

"It's okay," said Pius, unsure of what else to say. He was bullied and picked on so much that he honestly hadn't been that surprised. "It's been a rough week."

"No, I messed up. I was a right arse, and I deserved the shiner you gave me. I've been having some problems at home. It's not an excuse. It's just... I'm not dealing with it well. That's all."

Keith's honesty and openness surprised Pius. The last time he'd heard him like this was last year, coincidently also right after he'd nearly died at the hands of otherworldly forces. "Yeah, we've all got stuff going on at home, don't we?"

"I'm sorry about that, too. It sucks when your parents split up. It's easy to blame yourself for it, man, but it's not your fault. They're adults with a whole lifetime of crap between them from before you were born. You might be the one good thing that came out of their messy, complicated relationship."

Pius stopped staring at the horror show of emergency vehicles and turned his full attention to Keith. Braces-faced, lopsided haircut, mean jerkhole Keith. Had Keith Doucette just said something profound? And what the hell was going on in his house? Pius had no idea his parents were split up, though some of the rumours he'd heard and some of the comments Keith had made now made a whole new world of sense.

"Pius!"

He looked up, and through the chaos and the crowd, Pius saw his parents pushing through the mass of gathered onlookers on Main Street, heading toward him. He started to stand, and his mom nearly bowled him over, but she caught him so tightly in her arms there was no way he was going anywhere.

"Oh my God, Pius, we were so worried. Are you okay?"

"Yeah, Mom, I'm fine. A little banged up, but I got lucky." She was all over him, checking his face, poking and prodding him, looking for injuries.

"I kept an eye on him for you, Mrs. Jeddore," said Keith, smiling.

"What happened?" asked his dad.

"I don't know," replied Pius. They hadn't come up with an "official" story yet, so he tried to keep it vague. "There was fire and an explosion."

"I don't know what the hell is going on with this town." His dad gestured to the burned electrical pole right outside the video store. "I'm going to find out who worked on that transformer."

"You guys came together," said Pius, unable to hide his shock and excitement. "I hadn't seen you together since...well, since..."

"Of course, we came for you, Pius," said his mom. "You are the most important thing in the world to us."

"I'm sorry," Pius blurted. He'd wanted to say this to them all week, and when everything was hitting the fan a few hours ago, he wasn't sure if he would get the chance. "This was my fault. I shouldn't have brought Jenny to the house."

His mother pushed him out to arm's length so quickly that Pius wondered if he got whiplash. Through vision clouded with tears, he saw the most deadly-serious looks on his parents' faces, the most serious they'd looked since they sat him down to have the talk about Santa Claus.

"Don't you dare apologize for that, Pius William Jeddore."

"You did absolutely nothing wrong, you understand?" insisted his dad. "Don't you ever think that."

"No matter what happens between your father and me, none of it was your fault. None of it. We love you more than anything in the world."

They hugged him again, and for a brief moment, everything was all right. He forgot about monsters, affairs, lies, and school fires (he would have to tell them about that one) and felt like a kid again, safe in his parents' arms.

The feeling lasted but a moment. When they eased up their hug, Pius once again saw the flashing lights, the scared people, and the destruction that had been wrought on their town.

Finally, his mom asked, "Where's Harper?"

"She's fine," Pius lied. It bothered him how easy that came these days, so he tempered it. "I mean, I think she is. She and Niall are with Sergeant Tanguay."

"Where the hell are they?" asked his dad. "I saw some cops over here. Let's go ask them."

His parents led him away. His mom gripped his hand as she pulled him through the crowded, debris-strewn street, and he liked it. Feeling like a kid again, he trusted his parents to take care of everything, and he didn't try to fight it.

He glanced back once to where Keith stood, now alone on the sidewalk outside the hardware store. No one came to check on him. No one came to get him. Keith turned and started to walk down Main Street by himself. Pius wanted to call out to him, but then his mom yanked him around a parked car, and Pius lost sight of him in the crowd.

CHAPTER FORTY-FIVE

Round Here
Friday, June 4, 12:05am

"I can't believe it's still in one piece." Mason stared at the creature in awe, walking around the crater in the asphalt.

Helicopters circled overhead. A few started to come in for a landing. Ignoring them, Tanguay marched straight up to Mason and grabbed him by the shoulder.

"Why the hell didn't you tell us you were doing this?"

"I couldn't let the Americans know what we had planned." He barely looked at her. Instead, he waved at one of the helicopters as it touched down. "This is a Canadian issue on Canadian soil. We didn't want the Americans swooping in to steal the asset."

He sounded so blasé about it. Marie-Ann wanted to tear his throat out. "Then why didn't you come for it a week ago? Why wait until now? How many people died while you were jerking us all over town?"

"We didn't know where it was. And even if we did, we wanted a clear shot at it to minimize casualties." He gestured to the crater. "We couldn't have asked for a better shot than this."

"You may have killed Wolfhard!"

This time, he shrugged. "Minimal casualties. Lieutenant Bamber!"

Mason wandered off to talk to a soldier climbing out of one of the helicopters, completely dismissing her. Enraged, she turned and almost ran headlong into Harper and Niall.

"What are you two doing here?"

"The colonel told us that we needed to destroy the thing. Holy Crap, is that it?" Harper looked over the side of the blasted road into the crater where the 'carapace' lay unmoving.

Tanguay realized she hadn't looked at it closely herself. It had a mostly human shape, with two arms and legs and a vague-head-like knob on the top. It appeared to be made from black stone or metal, but it had an organic texture, like the shell of a beetle. It had no visible joints or seams that she could see, and despite lying completely still, it appeared otherwise unscathed by being blasted with missiles that would have disintegrated a tank.

"You have to get out of here. It's not safe." Tanguay shuffled the kids away from the hole while Mason barked orders behind her.

"Get those cables in here and start tying that thing down. I want to be airborne in five minutes, people!" He stopped and turned back toward Tanguay. "And take the kids. Just in case."

"You are not going to lay a hand on either of these children." Tanguay maneuvered herself between Mason and the kids, painfully aware of the vulnerable position she was in, surrounded by armed strangers.

He couldn't be serious, could he? The military wasn't going to grab two kids off the street of their hometown. And for what?

"I've seen their handiwork all over town," Mason said flatly. "They're almost as dangerous as the alien in that hole. They have to be secured."

"You have got to be kidding me!" This asshole thought he could just walk in and take Niall and Harper? Tanguay had worked too hard, for too long, to protect these children. "They're kids, not weapons!"

Mason stepped forward and stared directly into her face. His eyes were black and deadly serious. "For national safety and security, I am taking those children into custody."

"Over my dead body."

"You were given orders to cooperate, Sergeant Tanguay. Don't stop cooperating now." He turned his back on her and started to walk away.

"You can't do this!"

Harper screamed. Someone had grabbed her and was trying to pull her away. Marie-Ann's anger turned to sheer terror, and she stepped after Mason. She grabbed him by the shoulder. "You can't do this!"

Mason whirled, and a gunshot exploded.

Marie-Ann fell to the pavement, but she didn't know why at first. Then she felt a burning, horrible pain in her abdomen. She hadn't felt anything like this since childbirth, but this honestly might be worse. She reached down, and her hands came away slick with blood.

Now, both kids were screaming and crying. Some of the soldiers looked shocked, even horrified, but none of them moved toward her. They stood silent, holding Harper and Niall back.

"She tried to pull a gun on me!" Mason yelled to no one in particular. "You all saw her! It was self-defence! Now get those kids in the chopper, and let's get this thing out of here."

Tanguay reached helplessly toward Harper and Niall, but she couldn't move. Couldn't do anything. She lay on the ground, sobbing and helpless, just like last time.

CHAPTER FORTY-SIX

Refuse / Resist
June 4, 2:50am
Somewhere over St. Stephen's Bay

Niall had never flown in a helicopter before. He thought he would be excited, or at least afraid, but he felt numb. Sure, he was afraid, but afraid of where they were going, not of the helicopter itself. Everything would be easier if they crashed into the Bay instead of reaching whatever horror awaited at the end of this helicopter ride.

But even the fear of never seeing his friends and family again or being dissected in a lab like poor Alf (he still hated how that show ended) could not overcome the crushing numbness that was overtaking him. He shot Sergeant Tanguay, the woman who had protected them and fought for them, the only one who knew the truth about everything. Captain Mason had shot her like an animal. He couldn't believe it.

He didn't want to believe it.

Two people died tonight directly because of Niall. First, Keenan, because of his careless actions, and now the sergeant, because she had tried to protect him. His brain couldn't process it. It was like when he looked at his brother's Calculus book, and none of it had made sense.

Nothing made sense anymore.

He was sitting in the back of a large military helicopter, flying over St. Stephen's Bay, heading God-knows-where. There was a soldier with an assault rifle sitting next to him, and a few metres away, sitting opposite them, were Captain Mason and Harper.

He couldn't even be happy about being here with Harper. Normally, he would be excited to be close to her, or at least, if they were in trouble, they would be in trouble together. But they were in this mess because Harper had insisted they follow Sergeant Tanguay, and the sergeant had been shot because of it.

Usually, Niall thought Harper could do no wrong. Now, he couldn't look at her. It wasn't because he blamed her exactly. He was more upset because he was *ashamed* of blaming her.

Though he couldn't see it, Niall knew the monster was directly beneath them, bound and carried by steel cables beneath the helicopter. He could feel it, like an immeasurable weight pulling down on the aircraft and his soul. He didn't like that he could feel it. Something about it felt dirty. Oily. Like grime smeared on the edges of his brain.

Lost in his misery, Niall didn't notice at first that Harper was trying to get his attention. She was barely moving her head, but he saw it when her gaze darted back and forth between him and something behind his head.

As nonchalantly as possible, which Niall assumed was obvious because he was terrible at being subtle, he turned his head and looked out the small window behind him. Beneath them stretched the black ocean, and the small town of St. Stephens glowed distantly on the other side of the Bay. Above him, the moon, which hung low and bloated in the sky, was turning blood-red.

The eclipse. It was happening.

The soldier nudged Niall, and he turned and sat back in his seat. "Sorry. Trying to see where we are," he said weakly and glanced up at the window behind Harper, with a view of the Gale Harbour side of the Bay. He couldn't see much at first until a falling star blazed across the sky above the town.

Then he saw another one.

And another one.

The Chinook helicopter rocked suddenly.

"What the hell?" Mason jumped to his feet and headed toward the cockpit. "Are we under fire?"

Niall couldn't hear the pilot's response over the roar of the helicopter engines, but he could guess. Leaning forward as far as he could in his restraint harness, he looked toward the cockpit window. Thousands of streaks of light filled the sky before them, all coalescing on their location. The streaks looked like those they saw chasing the monster on the Strip, except now there were ten times as many.

And then Niall felt the monster move beneath them.

He didn't really feel it. There was no way he could feel it over the vibration of the helicopter, but something in the back of his head told him the monster was stirring, and that those glowing insects were filling up the empty shell hanging beneath them. Powering it. The vague, empty fear and dread from a moment ago was replaced with overwhelming, desperate terror.

Niall yelled at the soldier next to him. "We have to drop the monster! Now! It's waking up!"

"Settle down, kid," the soldier grumbled. He didn't look much older than Nelson. He also shifted uncomfortably, his complexion green, but he set his jaw and gritted his teeth. "It's fine."

Niall grasped at his buckles. Harper did the same. "No, we have to get rid of it!" The soldier continued to ignore him, so Niall turned his attention to the cockpit. "Mason! Captain Mason! It's waking up!"

The captain either didn't hear him or didn't care because no response came. The helicopter was surrounded by streaks of light on all sides now as if they were travelling through hyperspace on the Enterprise. Wait, the Enterprise travelled at Warp Speed; hyperspace was the Millennium Falcon. He was so freaked out he was mixing up his sci-fi universes.

Niall felt a surge of energy beneath him, and he knew it was too late. A few seconds later, the helicopter trembled violently. Alarms blared, and red lights flashed in the cockpit.

The side of the helicopter disappeared in a scream of metal, and a giant, glossy black monster tried to climb inside.

June bugs swirled around the beast. Some of them vanished in a flash of light as they were drawn inside the carapace. The frequent flashes gave the beast a strange glow, creating eerie dancing lights across the glossy surface of its shell. Captain Mason stepped back into the cargo hold, blasting uselessly at the monster with his handgun. The creature reached up with a giant, pincer-like hand and waved at the captain—a beam of searing flame shot from its palm, like a lightsaber or flaming katana. A second later, Mason's head and arms fell to the floor with a thud. Another second after that, the rest of his body followed.

The energy sword disappeared for a moment, and the young soldier beside Niall jumped to his feet. He stumbled as the helicopter rocked, causing him to drop his assault rifle.

"The hand!" Harper shouted. She pointed frantically at the creature, still strapped into her seat. "The hand!" She reached back to the wall behind her head, felt around for a moment until she found a sharp piece of metal, and then scraped the back of her fist against it. She grimaced in pain but did not hesitate for a second. Niall wished he had her willpower.

He unbuckled his harness. As he was about to leap toward Harper, the energy sword flashed to life again, illuminating the cargo hold in a flickering glow. Distracted, Niall turned to the monster at the exact moment the helicopter pitched again. He was thrown off his feet and hurtled toward the creature right as it swung the blade.

Niall slid across the floor, and the fire beam flashed past his face, centimetres from his nose. It was so hot it scorched his skin, and he smelled his own hair burning. The beam connected with the young soldier, slicing him in two.

Niall's tumble across the helicopter ended abruptly when he collided head-first with something. A shock went through his skull and down his spine, and he lost all feeling in his limbs. Stars burst in his vision—or maybe that was glowing butt monkeys swirling around his head.

Niall fought against unconsciousness, but he was losing the battle. He couldn't feel the helicopter moving anymore. He turned his head. The creature was still trying to climb inside, and the flame blade flickered out of existence. For a split second, he saw the hole in the palm of the creature's "hand" and remembered that it was important for some reason. He couldn't piece together why, though, couldn't recall why he was fighting. Why he wanted to. Everything he did was wrong, and everyone died in the end...

Something heavy crashed into Niall, knocking the wind out of him but shaking his mind alert. It was Harper, who had unbuckled and thrown herself across the hold of the helicopter. She screamed at Niall, but he couldn't understand what she was saying. Everything was just noise.

The creature's massive black pincer appendage scrabbled closer and closer to where their heads lay on the floor.

Harper took his hand. He thought she was holding it lovingly to say goodbye. After everything that happened, they were going to die here together. He hoped she would kiss him one last time. He would have preferred a long and healthy life, but there were worse ways to go.

Instead, she lifted his hand above their heads. Her blood ran over the back of her wrist, down Niall's hand and arm. She thrust his hand into the middle of the creature's pincer and shrieked into his ear, "Fry it! Damn it, fry the goddamned thing!"

So he did.

CHAPTER FORTY-SEVEN

Heart-Shaped Box
Friday, June 18, 1:00pm

Niall sat on his bed, leaning back against a pile of pillows and blankets, staring at the title screen for *Mario Paint* on his small colour TV in the corner of the room. The game had been waiting for him to press "start" for hours, but the controller was discarded somewhere on the floor. Joey Smallwood was curled up asleep at his side. Occasionally, Niall reached over to pat him, and the cat would purr for a moment, then get up and move away when he got tired of the attention.

The Cure's "Disintegration" played on repeat on his RCA CD player. Niall had a book balanced on the door of the CD player to keep it closed. He'd broken the latch two days after he got it for Christmas last year.

At some point, the door opened, and Pius and Skidmark walked into his room. Niall had no idea how long they were standing there, but he didn't acknowledge their presence until Skidmark knocked the book off the CD player, and Robert Smith's wailing came to an abrupt halt.

"God, it smells awful in here," said Skidmark. "Do you sit around all day sweating and farting?"

"What do you guys want?" Niall asked, his voice hoarse. He couldn't remember the last time he'd spoken out loud.

Skidmark's face and arms were covered in scabbed wounds and Band-Aids. It had taken dozens of stitches to close all his lacerations. Still, he'd fared better than a lot of people did the night of the "freak electrical storm" that blew up power transformers all over town. It also caused an "old forgotten fuel tank" under the airstrip to explode. It was fortunate the military was in the area on "training maneuvers" and could step in and help with the clean-up so quickly.

"We're on our way to the hospital to visit Todd," said Pius. "He looks like a mummy with all the bandages, and he smells gross, but his parents got him this new game called *Magic the Gathering* to keep him busy while he's in the hospital. It's pretty cool."

"I've already bought myself three decks." Skidmark beamed, holding up a long, narrow, white cardboard box.

"Weren't you guys at the hospital yesterday?" Niall asked.

"Yeah, but Skidmark insists on going back until he makes a deck that can beat Todd."

"I got a Shivan Dragon in my last pack." Skidmark nodded, bouncing like a junkie. "I think I'm going to get him this time!"

Pius shrugged. "I feel bad for Todd, being stuck in there by himself. He's a cool guy."

That was Pius. Besides a few burns, he had come out of the recent ordeal better than most of them. Even his parents were getting along better. Niall's parents, on the other hand, were not doing so well, not since his mom blamed his dad for letting Niall leave the house while he was supposed to be home recovering. But Pius was fine. After his brief period of adolescent rebellion, he was back to worrying more about everyone else than himself. Except for being hit by a runaway bread truck. He was still terrified of that one and wouldn't leave the house on days the grocery store received deliveries.

Pius came by every day to check on Niall, though Niall kept telling him he didn't want to hang out or do anything.

"Did you see Sergeant Tanguay?" asked Niall. She had slipped into a coma for a few days after she got shot, but last he heard, she had come out of it.

"Oh yeah, we even spoke to her." Pius sat on the foot of the bed. Skidmark sat on the floor and started playing *Mario Paint*. "She seems coherent and everything. She asked about you and how you were doing. She kept telling us she was fine, but I heard her talking to the doctor. He said it didn't look good. The bullet shattered her pelvis and came close to her spine. They don't know if she'll walk again."

Niall lowered his head and cursed. That was on his hands, too. Anna had gone home to St. John's with Keenan's body last week for his funeral. Todd looked like Jason Vorhees without his hockey mask. Colonel Wolfhard had been flown out to Corner Brook for surgery, but last Niall heard, he would never regain his vision. And now the sergeant, though she survived, would never walk again.

And all of it was his fault.

"Harper's been asking about you, too," said Pius. "She wants to talk to you."

"I don't want to talk to her."

Pius sighed and adjusted his glasses. "I'm not sure how to tell you this, then. She's outside the door."

Niall jumped to a sitting position on the bed. Joey Smallwood screeched and leaped off the bed.

Pius cringed away.

"She's here?"

"Right outside, yup." Pius didn't take his gaze off the cat lest it came too close.

"Assuming she didn't run off when she caught a whiff of your BO," called Skidmark from the floor.

Niall shook his head. He did not want to talk to her. He didn't want to look at her. There was something he needed to do, but he didn't want to do it. "Why did you bring her here?"

Pius shrugged. "She asked me to. You're my best friend, but she's my cousin. Plus, she threatened to kick my ass if I didn't bring her."

Pius stood. "We'll leave you to talk. Come on, Skidmark."

"Wait, wait, listen!" He held up his grey controller triumphantly and pressed a button. Flowers and mushrooms bopped across the screen as ungodly, tinny music blared from the small TV. "Isn't it awesome?"

"What is it?"

Skidmark's face fell. "'Smoke on the Water,' duh!"

"Get out of my room."

Pius shuffled Skidmark out, who looked insulted that no one recognized his song. Niall was sure he would get over it as soon as he bumped into the next shiny thing that caught his attention. Or ate some Pop-Tarts.

Suddenly, Niall realized he was alone in his room with Harper, and he wished he had cleaned and taken a shower. Now that he thought about it, it really did stink in here.

"Hey," she said. She wore jeans and an Alice in Chains T-shirt with a plaid flannel shirt tied around her waist. Her hair was pinned up but not neatly. It spilled from a haphazard braid in every direction.

Niall sighed. She was beautiful.

"Hey," he responded, wishing he could think of something cooler to say.

"I called a few times, but you didn't call me back."

"I'm sorry, I... I didn't feel like talking to anyone."

She nodded and sat on the bed, right where Pius had sat earlier. "I get it. Sometimes, I don't want to talk to anyone, either."

They sat quietly for a long time, staring off into space. Niall focussed on a battered paperback copy of *Jurassic Park* lying on the floor. It was a great book, and he looked forward to the movie. It should be coming to the Hansen Theatre soon. He should ask Harper...

He stopped himself.

"So, are we going to talk or what?" she asked.

"Harper, a lot of people got hurt."

"I know. And I've told you a hundred times it wasn't your fault."

"Thank you. Maybe one day I'll believe it. But right now, I can't. Because if I think about it as an accident, that it wasn't my fault, that means I might make those mistakes again, and more people will get hurt."

"Niall..."

"No, let me finish. I have to take responsibility for it. I have to accept that I did it, and I have to make changes to make sure it doesn't happen again. I don't want anyone else to get hurt because of me. So that means I have to make sure I don't ever use these powers again."

"What are you saying?"

"I'm saying we can't see each other anymore."

Harper bit her lip. She tried to refrain from showing emotion, but she looked hurt. Betrayed. "So, you're breaking up with me?"

"It's not that I don't like you. I care about you a lot. But what if we did what we did and more people got killed? What if *you* got killed?"

"If we did it saving the world, I don't care."

"I care. And the only way I can be sure that I don't hurt anyone else is to make sure that we are never close to each other ever again."

Harper stood. "The creature is gone, you know. They've been dredging the Bay for two weeks and can't find anything."

"Good. Then, no one needs our powers anymore."

"That means we don't have to use them. There's nothing to be afraid of."

"Please. Harper, I don't want to do this, but I have to."

"Fine." She exhaled. "Goodbye, Dork-pie."

"Goodbye, Harper."

The door closed, leaving Niall alone. He put his head on his pillow and started to cry.

Alien Nation
Somewhere under the North Atlantic

Beneath the waves, it waited.

It had waited for thousands upon thousands of years. What were a few more cycles around the solar primary?

Once, eons ago, a great civilization of avian creatures spread across this tiny blue and green rock. These beings were of no small intellect and built sprawling, towering cities and discovered science and magic far beyond the imagination of the gibbering apes that now feigned dominion over this world. It had watched them, learned from them, and fed off them until it grew bored and exterminated them. They were obliterated down to an egg, and it gorged upon their feathered corpses until nothing was left but a memory.

Once the bird people were extinct, it waited hundreds of millions of cycles until the next interesting life form clawed its way up the evolutionary chain. It was used to waiting.

The worst part was that it needed to feed. It was so hungry. The last battle with the imperious apes left it completely drained. There was so little sustenance this deep. Nothing but microbes, idiot fish, and bigger idiot fish that fed on its small dumb cousins. It would take a long time to build strength on such pitiful fare. Usually, it was so patient, waiting for eons between the fall and rise of civilizations, but recent... experiences caused its patience to wear thin. A flash of weakness, of vulnerability, of mortality, the likes of which it had not known since the dawn of time, triggered new sensations in the Primordial One. Not fear, but apprehension. Uncertainty. Unease. It did not want to wait to deal with this new problem.

Then, quite unexpectedly, a revelation.

Something entered the water, far away but close enough that it could still sense it even with its dimmed faculties. Something it had not felt in a long time, something it had long thought lost.

The vessel. The vessel that had transported it from the homeworld all those billions of cycles ago. It was still intact? And it had been activated recently, likely by other-worldly forces trying to bring it back.

The vessel could bring it anywhere it wanted to go. It was a portal to an infinite number of planes. If it could get to the vessel, it could finally be rid of this irrelevant planet for good. It could go home.

But first, it would wipe out every living thing on the face of the earth.

About the Author
C.D. Gallant-King is a writer, tabletop gamer, pro-wrestling aficionado, father and husband. He was born and raised in a town that looks suspiciously like Gale Harbour, and currently resides in Ottawa, Ontario, Canada. Find out more at www.cdgallantking.ca

The Gale Harbour Series
Psycho Hose Beast From Outer Space
Revenge of the Space-Surfing Butt Monkeys
Dirtbag Satan Worshippers From Down By the Bay

Other Books by C.D. Gallant-King
Ten Thousand Days
Hell Comes to Hogtown

<u>**CHAPTER ONE**</u>

Burn
Wednesday, October 19, 1994
Gale Harbour, Province of Newfoundland
8:15 pm

There is a scene in the 1994 film *The Crow* where Brandon Lee, his character struggling with returning to life, full of broken memories of his and his wife's brutal murders, smashes a mirror and then paints his face like a sad Pierrot clown. Moody music by The Cure plays throughout. It's supposed to be a stirring scene to show the character's disorientation, barely controlled rage, and propensity for completely unnecessary theatrics. Since seeing the movie, fourteen-year-old Niall O'Neil had tried to recreate the drama of that scene many times but only succeeded in making a fool of himself.

First, his older brother, Nelson, had walked in on him, and once he stopped laughing, he demanded to know why Niall was painting himself up like a depressed Krusty the Clown. His brother also suggested, sniggering at his own wit, that Niall ask their mom for makeup tips.

Next, there was the time that Niall couldn't find his CD, *The Crow (Official Movie Soundtrack)*, which was essential to setting the mood, so he put on a Cure CD instead. Midway through applying his makeup, Lovecats came on. Niall recalled his friend Skidmark dressing up like Mr. Mistoffelees for drama club, and laughing, he poked the Revlon #7 eye pencil he was using in his eye, spoiling the gothic mood he was going for and necessitating the use of an eye patch for several days.

Most recently, he'd punched his bedroom mirror a little too hard and accidentally broke it for real. *That* resulted in a trip to the emergency room, four stitches on his hand and no end of weird looks and rude comments from other ER patients. Niall had gone into the hospital with his makeup half-finished and streaked from his tears. He looked like someone had beat up a mime. The doctor, who had provided Niall's eye patch several weeks earlier, was mercifully silent.

The truth was Niall was trying to find a way to express his misery, but he was screwing it up.

Sixteen months ago, Niall killed someone using preternatural powers he inherited from his grandmother while she was possessed by the soul of a dead witch. No longer possessed, Nana's magic didn't work anymore. Niall's powers, which he barely understood, only worked when he was in physical contact with the blood of his ex-girlfriend, Harper Jeddore. Apparently, she was the "blood of the Blood", the last surviving descendant of Kluskap, an ancient mystical warrior, and Niall could use her hemoglobin to do things like create fire, protect himself and his friends from injury, and banish otherworldly entities. It all sounded ridiculous, so he tried not to think about it.

To ensure that he never hurt anyone with his magic again, he broke up with Harper and hadn't spoken to her in over a year. He had regretted it every day since.

Heartbroken but unburdened by a healthy level of self-consciousness, Niall contemplated joining the drama club so they could show him how to do his makeup correctly. The lady at the cosmetics counter at the drugstore where Nelson worked was another possible alternative. Of course, if he did that and Nelson found out, he would make his life hell, and not in a cool cinematic way. He couldn't talk to his mom about it. He found he had a lot of trouble talking to his parents. His dad blamed it on him becoming a "surly teenager." Niall felt it was more likely due to all the secrets he was hiding and being unsure of what he could talk about. Killing monsters and burning down half the town really ruined the ability to have regular dinner table conversations.

So, with no other options, Niall was left to figure out how to apply eyeliner alone. At least tonight, it would be quiet, with no interruptions. His brother was at work, his mom and Nana Josephine were playing cards at the seniors' lounge, and his dad was gone to do whatever his dad did on Wednesdays. Poker? Hockey? Niall didn't care as long as it left him some time by himself. Usually, he used his alone time to watch vaguely inappropriate anime like *Dirty Pair* and *Ranma*

½. Tonight, he would listen to Nine Inch Nails and decide which shade of eyeshadow suited him best: Obsidian Beauty or Midnight Enigma?

Another drawback of killing Keenan was that he was the only guy Niall had ever met who wore makeup. He would have been the perfect person to ask for tips.

With his meagre supply of Halloween makeup laid out atop his dresser beside his Oxy wipes and an old bottle of his dad's Ralph Lauren Polo cologne, Niall stared at himself in the mirror. He was wearing his favourite plain black t-shirt, his blond hair was wet and spikey from gobs of Dippity-Doo gel, and he could clearly see in his mind's eye what he wanted his face to look like. He picked up an eyeliner pencil and set to work turning his vision into reality while the dulcet tones of Trent Reznor wailed in the background.

About fifteen minutes into his routine, Niall heard screams outside the house.

With reflexes honed by years of paranoia from fighting creatures from another world, Niall leapt into action. He raced out of his room and down the hall, snatching up the baseball bat he kept in the porch closet for such situations. The bat had been a gift from Keith Doucette last Christmas. Keith gave them all aluminum baseball bats—both as a memento of surviving an alien invasion and a handy weapon in case of the next one. Niall kept quietly placing it back by the front door every time his mom found it and yelled about the kids leaving their crap everywhere. She always blamed Nelson. No one imagined Niall doing anything sports related.

The bat served its purpose tonight as Niall raced outside to find a blond girl being savaged by a large black dog. He didn't recognize the girl or the animal. Aggressive strays weren't uncommon in Gale Harbour, but he never heard of anyone being attacked by one.

Two years ago, Niall would have frozen in panic at the sight of a werewolf-sized canine mauling a human being. Hell, he probably wouldn't have come out of his room. But after everything he'd been through, all the sacrifices they'd made to protect this town from freaking aliens, there was no goddamn way he was going to let a poor girl get taken out by a stupid dog on his watch.

Without hesitation, Niall rushed into the fracas and swung the bat at the dog's rib cage with all his might. He felt a sickening crunch, and the animal howled a horrible, guttural screech of pain. It leapt away, then backed up, limping.

In the light of a streetlamp with some distance between them, Niall got a good look at the animal. Though it was large, at least as tall as Niall's waist, it was thin and bony. Its matted black fur was falling out in clumps, and its eyes appeared to be bleeding. He realized with an unpleasant shock to his guts that the beast was probably rabid, and he started to second-guess his eagerness to jump into this particular situation.

Fortunately, the dog must have been badly hurt because it turned and limped away into the darkness. Niall watched it go and almost pitied it. He should probably call the dog catcher. That animal was definitely not right.

Something heavy slammed into Niall, and he nearly swung the bat again before realizing it was the girl he'd just saved. She threw her arms around him like a drowning swimmer grabbing onto a rope.

"Oh my God," she breathed, her face buried into his shoulder. Her shampoo smelled like oranges and berries. "Thank you so much. The dog came out of nowhere, and I panicked."

"You're okay now." Niall awkwardly patted her on the back. He wasn't used to close physical contact with any female that wasn't his mom or Harper. "I think I scared it off. What about you? Are you okay?"

The girl pulled away, and Niall looked at her for the first time. She was cute and couldn't be more different from Harper in every possible way. Where Harper was dark of complexion, she was pale and freckled with strawberry-blond hair. Harper was tall and wiry, while this girl was short and curvy. Where Harper was always dressed in baggy jeans and army surplus jackets, this girl wore a tight pink top and a colourful puffer vest.

Niall suspected that whoever she was, she probably wouldn't appreciate being compared in such detail to his ex-girlfriend, but honestly, Niall had no other frame of reference.

"I think so," she said. She looked down at her arm. Her pink sweater was torn, and blood was soaking through the material. "Ah crap, maybe I'm not okay. Am I going to need a tetanus shot?"

She was surprisingly level-headed for someone who had just been mauled by a wild dog. "No, that's for stepping on a rusty nail. You will probably need a rabies shot, though." Niall was well acquainted with different types of shots and vaccines after being kidnapped and held in a filthy underground bunker two summers ago. He didn't bother telling her that she would need *several* rabies shots. No sense in upsetting her further.

"Oh, that's just great. I hate needles."

"It's no worse than getting bitten by a dog, and you seem to be taking that pretty well."

"The dog came at me so fast. I still don't know what happened."

"You're probably in shock." Again, he had first-hand experience. "We should get you home. Do you live around here?"

"Just down on St. Anne Street. And I think you may be right. I'm starting to feel light-headed."

"It's okay, I'll walk you home. Do you need to lean on me?"

"Thank you. I'm Stacey, by the way."

"Niall."

They started to walk, with Niall holding her forearm to keep it elevated. That was good; he would focus on her physical injuries, so he didn't have to think about the fact that he was *holding a girl's hand*.

"I haven't seen you around," said Stacey. "Have you lived here long?"

"Just my whole life." He didn't add that he had spent most of that life in the house playing video games and watching movies, which explained why she'd probably never seen him. "I don't think I've seen you around either. You must go to the Amalgamated. I would remember meeting you."

The Amalgamated High School was for everyone who wasn't Catholic and was the bitter rival of St. Paul's, which Niall and his friends attended. It was only Christian to teach Catholics and Protestants to hate each other from a young age. "And why would you remember me, huh?" she asked him.

Niall almost said, "Because you're cute," but stopped himself. Was that appropriate? Were they flirting now? Unsure of the social rules in this situation, he said instead, "I would have remembered the dog bite on your arm."

Stacey laughed. It was an easy, girly laugh. Harper didn't laugh so easily; when she did, it was more of a chortle. Like she was laughing at you. Which she often was. "I don't usually go around with dog bites on my arm, silly."

"Oh, well, that's good then. Probably for the best." It was good to keep her talking and distracted. Niall noticed that blood was still soaking through her sleeve, so he squeezed her arm a little harder.

"I usually wear them on my face, like right about here. It goes better with my earrings that way."

Niall was embarrassed that it took him a moment to realize she was kidding. "Oh, right. Yeah, the blood would go well with them, wouldn't it? Would look nice with your eyes, too."

Stacey laughed again, and Niall joined in with her, uncomfortably. He was so far beyond everyday conversations with the opposite sex that there was no way to know if it was going well or not. Maybe he should ask her.

Instead, she asked him an awkward question first.

"Niall, not to judge or anything, but are you wearing black lipstick and eyeliner?"

Niall almost threw her on the asphalt and ran back home. He completely forgot about the makeup. What the hell was he supposed to do now? How did he explain that he was testing out being goth because he was depressed about accidentally killing somebody and dumping his girlfriend?

"Oh... I... I just..." Niall said eloquently.

"Hey, you just saved me from a rabid dog. You could be wearing a clown nose and fishnet stockings for all I care."

"I was just... experimenting..."

"I told you, don't worry about it. I think it actually looks kinda good on you. But if you want some pointers, I can show you how to keep your eyeliner from getting so smudgy. And your lipstick must be the cheap Halloween kind. It's all chunky and flaking. I can hook you up with some good stuff."

As they walked along Woodward Avenue toward St. Anne Street, Niall noticed his heart felt the lightest it had in a long time. Somehow, this cute, funny girl dropped out of the sky right into his front yard, and she came with makeup tips? How was it possible that she could be so perfect? They continued to laugh and talk the rest of the way to her house, and Niall registered that for the first time in a year, he had gone twenty minutes without thinking about Harper or about Keenan's dead face being zipped into a body bag.

It wasn't until hours later, when he was lying in bed replaying that evening's events in his mind, that he realized why the dog looked so strange while it was walking away. It had a freakish, hairless tail, like a rat's, over a metre long. It dragged on the ground behind the creature as it slunk off and disappeared into the darkness.